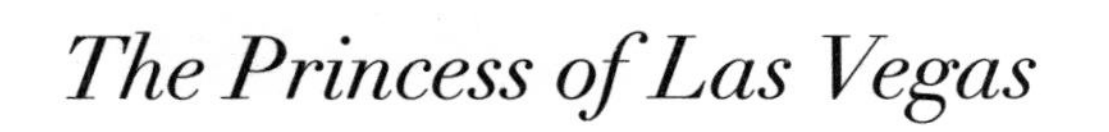

The Princess of Las Vegas

Also by Chris Bohjalian

NOVELS

The Lioness
Hour of the Witch
The Red Lotus
The Flight Attendant
The Sleepwalker
The Guest Room
Close Your Eyes, Hold Hands
The Light in the Ruins
The Sandcastle Girls
The Night Strangers
Secrets of Eden
Skeletons at the Feast
The Double Bind
Before You Know Kindness
The Buffalo Soldier
Trans-Sister Radio
The Law of Similars
Midwives
Water Witches
Past the Bleachers
Hangman
A Killing in the Real World

ESSAY COLLECTIONS

Idyll Banter

STAGE PLAYS

The Club
Midwives
Wingspan (originally produced as *Grounded*)

The Princess of Las Vegas

A NOVEL

Chris Bohjalian

Doubleday
New York

 Published in the United States by Doubleday,
a division of Penguin Random House LLC, New York, and distributed in
Canada by Penguin Random House Canada Limited, Toronto.

www.doubleday.com

Jacket art by Tom Hallman
Jacket photograph © Alexei Vladimir/Arcangel
Jacket design by John Fontana
Book design by Maria Carella

Library of Congress Cataloging-in-Publication Data
Names: Bohjalian, Chris, 1962– author.
Title: The princess of Las Vegas : a novel / Chris Bohjalian.
Description: First edition. | New York : Doubleday, [2024].
Identifiers: LCCN 2022052867 | ISBN 9780385547581 (hardcover) |
ISBN 9780593315002 (paperback) | ISBN 9780385547611 (ebook)
Subjects: LCGFT: Novels.
Classification: LCC PS3552.O495 P75 2024 |
DDC 813.54—dc23/eng/20221201
LC record available at https://lccn.loc.gov/2022052867

MANUFACTURED IN THE UNITED STATES OF AMERICA

1 3 5 7 9 10 8 6 4 2

First Edition

For Rose Mary Muench,
my second mom

For Victoria and Grace,
my inspirations

The mere fact of Vegas, its necessity, was an indictment of our normal lives.

If we needed this place—to transform into a high roller or a sexy swinger, to be someone else, a winner for once—then certainly the world beyond the desert was a small and mealy place indeed.

—Colson Whitehead, *The Noble Hustle*

Being a princess isn't all that it's cracked up to be.

—Diana Spencer, Princess of Wales . . . for a time

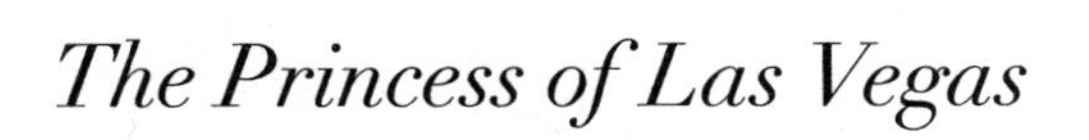
The Princess of Las Vegas

Prologue

The sun was setting as they drove west from the strip, and the two men in the car were squinting behind their sunglasses. Eventually, there was but a fleeting gold band on the horizon, and Richie Morley, who was behind the wheel of the Jag, observed how the vista never grew old—it was one more reason why he lived here—and then he took off his shades and tossed them into the caddy in the wide vehicle's door. Behind the car, the first garish lights from the casinos great and small were making their nocturnal birth, a twinkling aureole that indiscriminately beckoned the damaged and the dreamers alike.

Morley never suspected this was a hit until the passenger beside him pulled the gun. The guy told him to slow down and keep both hands on the wheel. Morley watched from the corners of his eyes as the fellow reached into the glove compartment and retrieved the handgun Morley kept there. Richie himself had never killed a man. Once, he'd had a guy on his knees, and he'd stood behind him and pressed his own Beretta into the fellow's nuchal ridge—the concave space where the occipital knob meets the spine, a bit of anatomy Morley had looked up out of curiosity when he'd gotten home—but he hadn't killed him. He wasn't a killer.

He wondered now how he would talk his way out of this, and the wheels were turning. He'd say whatever he had to say to see the sun rise tomorrow, and deal then with whatever compromises he'd made or whatever he'd given away.

When they reached the sightseeing pull-off on the two-lane

road, he started haggling. Suggested he could talk to his brother about selling his shares in the casino, the Buckingham Palace. Said he didn't know how important the casino was to them, and now that he understood, he was happy to make a deal, and he knew his brother, Artie, would be, too. But that ship had sailed. Next, he offered his crypto seed phrase, but the fellow beside him said, "Your password? What makes you think we don't already have it?"

So, finally, he begged, pleading, while wishing to God he had a wife or kids that he could use as leverage. *Please, you gotta spare me: I got two kids.* But he didn't have children. All he had was a brother, and he supposed someone else right now was taking him out, too.

"Richie," the guy told Morley, "no one is going to kill you because you won't sell the casino."

The hit man had selected a pull-off that was paved so he wouldn't leave footprints when he exited the Jag.

"Then why?" Richie asked, his voice quavering.

"Because you're a fucking FBI informant. Because, Richie, you're a rat."

And there he ended it, putting a bullet into Richie Morley's temple at point-blank range. He used Morley's own gun he'd taken from the glove compartment. Then he put on plastic gloves, unbuckled Morley's seat belt, and wiped off the parts of the car he'd touched while riding beside him. He swabbed off the handles inside and outside the vehicle, as if he were working at a high-end carwash and the detailing mattered. He put Morley's gun half in the dead man's hand.

But he didn't touch the great Rorschach of blood on the headrest or adjust Morley's skull, which had whipsawed unexpectedly and come to rest against the window. He sent the text—empty air, no words—that signaled it was done and to send the car to retrieve him. In the distance, he heard coyotes howling.

Then he stood by the side of the road and waited, watching

the constellations appear in the darkening sky, hoping no other drivers would stop, curious about the Jaguar in the pull-off and whether the driver needed assistance, until after he was gone. None did.

He was back in Las Vegas thirty-five minutes later, and he ordered a steak and wedge salad at the casino that the Morley brothers, one dead, one alive, still owned, and was brought a chunk of iceberg lettuce drowning in blue cheese dressing and topped with fried onion rings from a can. The salad was, he thought to himself, an indication of just what an absolute trash heap the Buckingham Palace had become. If they didn't have that crazy woman re-creating Lady Di in their showroom? They'd have nothing, nothing at all.

Part One

I've seen grown-ups go bitchcakes. Full-on toddler tantrums, screaming and yelling and throwing shit. It's scary. It's embarrassing. Who does that when they're not, like, three years old?

CHAPTER ONE

Crissy

Luck.

It transcends the craps tables and the slots. It's the fulcrum around which all stories spin: The chap who misses the plane that augers into a mountain because—and it seemed like bad luck at the time—his taxi had a flat on the way to the airport. The aspiring actor with a West End or Broadway belt who shares her chairlift with a casting director one chilly afternoon at a ski resort. The fellow who has what should be the stroke that kills him, but the blood vessel in the deep recesses of his brain happens to burst in a hospital lobby—he's leaving when it ruptures, he's on his way to the parking garage—because his mother has just died three floors above him, and so the fact that he is in the O.R. in minutes means that he lives and has a full recovery. Had the tsunami of blood swamped his gray matter ten minutes later, after he had retrieved his vehicle and started back to the hotel where he had been ensconced the previous three days, waiting for his mother to expire, he would have perished in traffic. He might even have taken someone with him to the other side, blacking out and slamming his car into some *unlucky* pedestrian in a crosswalk.

Las Vegas is a city built on luck. None of us, even when we are breathing our last, understand fully the role that chance will have played in our lives, the ways that what we supposed was good luck prevented us from experiencing better luck, or the ways that a small misfortune saved us from a far worse one.

The truth is, I laugh when someone says about a book, *Oh,*

that's an unreliable narrator. Aren't all narrators unreliable? Who in bloody hell remembers anything, much less what people said at a casino at two or three in the morning? The whole idea of a first-person novel makes my head spin. And a memoir? Someone trying to share with you their childhood and regaling you with things their parents said when they were eight years old? That's barmy.

Because memory is fungible and we lack the omniscience to understand what role chance has played in our lives.

So, let's begin with this: this story isn't about my childhood. I don't want to talk about my childhood.

And I won't.

Instead I'm going to tell you what happened in Las Vegas, and I'm going to tell you everything as best I can, but my best is hampered by the fact this all occurred when I was doing two shows a night, channeling a dead princess, sleeping until lunchtime, popping a bit too much Adderall and Valium (yes, both), and periodically—like that princess—purging over a jet-black toilet. (Fine, I flirt with an eating disorder, just like that princess, which my therapist says is one of the reasons why I do what I do for a living. I wonder what, pray tell, was her first clue?) It was the late summer of 2022, though late summer means less in Las Vegas than it does in much of the world. Charles was about to become king and Camilla the queen, though if you'd asked me that August whether I thought I'd need to rewrite moments in my show in September because Elizabeth would go the way of all flesh—even a monarch subject to no earthly authority bends her knee to God—I would have said no. The woman, it seemed to some (probably to Charles), was going to outlive us all.

Ukraine had no plans to surrender, though Kharkiv and Mariupol were rubble. As was the ruble. The word *oligarch* had, with cause, morphed from a straight line about yachts and statuesque hookers to a shorthand for corruption and moral turpitude. The pandemic was endemic. We lived with it the way we lived with the flu, except some nights I would peer into my audience and see more masks than on others. But this was Las Vegas, and so the vaccinated and the unvaccinated mingled and gambled and tried to live in a bubble in which the possible end of the world, triggered either by a virus or a madman in the Kremlin, could be ignored for a couple of hours. A night. A weekend.

Cryptocurrency was exploding from the preferred tool of libertarians and renegades, Bitcoin bros and niche investors, raw meat eaters and dark web madmen, into the next big thing in, it seemed, every blockbuster television commercial and streaming TV series. The bubble had not yet burst, in other words. But the crypto exchange FTX was soon to go belly-up, and Sam Bankman-Fried would be arrested in the Bahamas soon after that.

I had, by then, stopped sleeping with the senator. Some families grew closer in the pandemic, and others, like John Aldred's, fell apart, people falling away like petals from a dying rose. But the senator and his wife never publicly separated and had, in fact, reconciled about the time they were getting their first booster shots, and I supposed that no one other than the two of us, his key Vegas staffers, his driver, and a few people at the casino—such as the two brothers who owned the place—knew that we had been an item for not quite half a year. (So, I suppose, a lot of people knew. But Las Vegas is a world known both for ostentation and discretion.)

This story is, at its core, a tale of two sisters. The sisters are from Vermont, not an especially diabolical little world, which may explain their naivete. Our naivete. But maybe not. You could argue that grown-ups in their thirties should know better, but how many adults, in the end, only make what we like to call good choices?

And while it is the Vermonters in the story who were the ones who grew up in a land that some months was a world of frigid, impenetrable sand dunes of snow and cold that could turn exposed skin the color of cornflowers, it was everyone else, it seemed, who had ice in their veins.

Do I make this sound like a fairy tale? It's not. I was never a real princess.

Yes, I can be glib. I'm sorry. It's just that it's so much easier to be glib than sad. If I ever succumbed to history and sadness, I fear the tears would be an alluvion.

And, I know, I am among the lucky ones.

* * *

My name is Crissy Dowling. That is my official moniker for SAG and Equity—the unions—and what you will find on my credit cards. I could have grown into Christina, my given name. Or I could have been Chris.

But, instead, I became Diana. Not with my friends and family. But with the Nevada paparazzi and sometimes with my creepier hookups. (And given that I work and *live* in a casino, the epic creepiness of some of my hookups is unparalleled. Moreover, you have to have certain proclivities to hit on dead royalty, so a lot of the men who are drawn to me fully expect that if I talk dirty in bed—which I usually don't, because two shows a night is my max—I'll sound like Emma Corrin or Kristen Stewart or Elizabeth Debicki. But, yes, I do let men call me Diana when, forgive me, we're having a proper good shag.) I am also, on occasion, Diana with my agent, Terrance Pelletier. Terrance was a friend from college who was the Svengali who first pulled the strings and created the Las Vegas "legend" that is Diana.

Please hear the sarcasm in my voice when I use the word *legend*. Certainly, there is nothing legendary about the off-the-strip casino in which I perform.

But it was Terrance who saw that I had more than a passing resemblance to Diana Frances Spencer—aka Diana, Princess of Wales, first wife to Charles, the heir apparent to the British throne when they wed—and suggested it would be a shame to waste such windfall genetics. I left my old agent and signed with him. We were six years out of college, and I had a rather nice career going: lots of two- and three-line guest appearances on *NCIS* and *Law and Order,* and a steady stream of two- and three-month gigs at two- and three-hundred-seat houses off Broadway. I think I was the Emily Webb that John Mulaney loved in *Our Town,* but I've never met John, so this could be rubbish. For the record, I know I was the Sister Mary Leo in a *Nunsense* revival that inspired a deliciously filthy Nikki Glaser joke about nuns and bondage and a ballerina's toe shoes. Terrance and I reconnected at a party in the East Village. The Diana show grew from downtown party act to performance art to road show to Vegas nightclub eccentricity. It was Terrance who convinced the UK-themed Buckingham Palace Casino that a Diana tribute show was just the ticket. They tried me out at a ten p.m. slot, following an eight p.m. comic who'd been there longer than I'd been alive, and my show—forgive this boast—became one of the off-the-strip must-see eccentricities if you were of a certain age. Soon I replaced the comedian, who, it turned out, was a bit of a groper and needed to go. When everything began to unravel in the late summer and early fall of 2022, my little cabaret had been running five nights a week, two shows a night, at the casino's theater for seven years—minus, of course, the Year That Satan Spawned (2020) or the weeks when I was on vacation or when my sister and I were burying our mum or the Tuesday night after the Route 91 Harvest Music Festival massacre. But I even went onstage the night I am going to tell you about when I was hoping like hell not to get arrested and trying like hell not to get killed.

A few years ago, East Coast friends tried to persuade me to return to New York when they were casting the Diana musical on Broadway. I was tempted. But I think after being Diana in my cabaret for so long, I would have been crushed if I flew east to audition and they went with another actor who looked less like her, sounded less like her, and simply knew her less. I knew Diana as well as anyone who didn't actually know her, if that makes sense, and I think quite possibly better than many people who did. And, very likely, the Broadway producers would have wanted someone who grew up in Britain, even if I had made the effort—which they did. They went with a very talented Brit, and that's fine.

The fact is, I liked my life in Las Vegas. I liked my world at the Buckingham Palace, even if it was the antithesis of an actual palace.

And with my hair dyed and properly styled, I am Diana. My British accent is impeccable. When Naomi Watts, Emma Corrin, and Kristen Stewart wanted to resurrect Diana's unique way of speaking, they all used the same dialect coach. I had no such luxury, and learned to replicate her distinct pastiche of privilege and—likely cultivated—lower-brow cockney. (The trick is to swallow the final *t* periodically.) Meanwhile, when I am singing, I am reminiscent of Petula Clark, the 1960s British pop star known best for "Downtown." Onstage, I walk a standup tightrope between heartbreak and hilarity. It's rather like watching Madame Tussauds's wax figure come to life, the princess one moment regaling her audience with what it was like to wear a wedding gown with a train that seemed to stretch miles, and then sharing with them the despair when it became clear that the Prince of Wales was always going to love Camilla Parker Bowles more than me.

Or her.

Some days even I got confused. Or nights.

My Vegas Diana talks openly of her bulimia, and no one in the audience suspects I am speaking of my own firsthand struggles: they simply savor the soul-piercing sadness of it all. But not for long, because then I reel them back in with a joke about the first time Diana heard her father-in-law call the queen of England by his pet name for her: "Cabbage." *Cabbage* is a very funny word to my audience demographic. Most of the people who come to my show are between the ages of fifty and embalmed.

I have now spent years joking and singing about all things Diana except, of course, the car crash. I never go there. Too ghastly. It's the elephant in the room that is kept behind the curtain but still makes everything work. Bulimia is fine—though, in truth, it is less fine now than it had been when the tribute cabaret first opened. Now, the show begins with a voice reminiscent of Queen Elizabeth telling the audience that some content might be disturbing, before reminding them to silence their cell phones before the princess arrives. But the audience never hears the words *Paris, tunnel,* or *Dodi Fayed.*

Never.

It isn't simply that discussing her actual death is a bit of a buzzkill; it would place me—Diana—in some strange, untenable purgatory. Am I speaking to my audience from beyond the grave, or am I but an impersonator? The former would be ridiculous, and the latter would take a wrecking ball to the theater's fourth wall. I know most of the better sort of tribute entertainers in Vegas—even such also-rans as Blond Elvis and Tighty-Whitey Conway Twitty—and one of the things we who perform in homage to the dead (and to pay the rent) agree upon is this: if you're bringing someone back to life for that person's biggest fans, it's bad for business to kill that soul in the third act.

* * *

I was a year younger than Princess Diana had been when she died when it became clear—to use what I've come to call Palace Speak—we had a situation. Having a situation is rather like when the Roomba vacuums over the dog shit on the carpet, but we royals don't say *shit.* We don't, in fact, shit, period. Nor do the corgis. That's a fact, too.

The twenty-fifth anniversary of Diana's death, August 31, was two weeks away, and given what I had experienced past years on that date and the reality that the cabaret had grown even more popular, I was confident that soon I would be awash in bouquets and the theater would look like the largest florist in Las Vegas. A few years ago, when I saw where this was going—the avalanche of cards and letters on the anniversary of the car crash—I started stashing the memorabilia and trinkets in my dressing-room closet, and created an Etsy shop, Diana's Castle, to resell it. The gist of the cards fans gave me was simple: thank you. Thank you for bringing Diana back to life. Or they were letters addressed directly to Diana by people who either loved her or loved what she represented: an amalgam of decency among the indecent, humanity among the inhumane, vulnerability among the invulnerable, and—yes—unrequited love. I gave the money I made to a very particular teen shelter.

So, it was August 17. That morning, when I'd looked at myself in a mirror bordered by a filigree of faux-gold flecks, I thought I looked thirty years older. I didn't, not really, and I figured I could do this for at least another fifteen years, thank you, Botox. The cabaret was in the Buckingham Palace's 150-seat venue, and my show had grown from forty-five to sixty minutes and the band from a single piano player to a trio, two of whom sang backup on "Downtown" and "Don't Sleep in the Subway." The biggest change, however, was the revelation that was Nigel Ferguson, a waiter at the casino's Irish pub whom I had spotted one night a year or so earlier while I was drinking alone at the bar. It was the day the senator had told me that he and his wife were going to try again and our dalliance—for me it was more, for him it was (alas) only that—was over. I had wished him well, done my two shows, and gone for a drink. Nothing maudlin about it.

Nigel was taking a young couple's order and slouching rather like the Prince of Wales, and his ears had the prince's Dumbo-in-launch-mode mien. He was in his midthirties. When he started to share the order with the bartender, his accent was Scottish, and so I studied him carefully.

"Can you sing?" I asked.

"A bit," he said, smiling sheepishly, his head bowed rather like Charles. Then softly he crooned, "I love a lassie, a bonnie, bonnie lassie," while the bartender made a martini and a gin and tonic. He could sing more than a bit. That was clear. And most of my audience couldn't tell the difference between Scottish, Welsh, and Irish accents. Hell, he could have spoken like an East End boy, and a lot of the crowd would have thought it was the King's English. Yes, the Buckingham Palace casino had a British theme—it always felt to me sort of like the Excalibur meets Hogwarts, except much lower rent and a lot more secondhand smoke—but like every Vegas casino, the theme was mostly an architectural facade. Oh, our "fantasy" burlesque show was "The Six Sexy Wives of Henry VIII" (thank God that king had only had six wives, because we couldn't have afforded a seventh stripper or fit one on that stage), and we had an ice-cream parlor called "William's Milk-Shakespeare." We had darts in our "pubs." But every casino has the same slot machines, sportsbooks, gaming tables, and concourses with restaurants and shops. Some (not us) also have grand auditoriums for the likes of Lady Gaga and smaller showrooms for the likes of me. The same discreet corridors or sections of the parking lots where a john could meet up with his or her escort. Some casinos were nicer and more elaborate than others, but it all came down to the same reality: you had to ensnare the souls from Kingman, Arizona, or Stamford, Connecticut, who were willing to drop eighty bucks in eight minutes playing video poker.

Terrance, who had relocated to L.A. years ago as he'd taken on other clients and his stable had grown, didn't love the idea when I called him to tell him about Nigel, but it was my show and he came around. The cabaret was still *Diana, Candle in the Darkness*—we'd never been able to secure the rights to *Diana, Candle in the Wind*—but now Diana had company onstage periodically, other than her band. Nigel was especially moving toward the end of the reimagined show, when he was made up to look older, his hair thinned and powered white, and spoke to his ex-wife (ageless at thirty-six) about the ways he had wronged her and the things he wished he could do differently.

So, the situation—the news that greeted me like a cold shower that August 17 . . .

I was at the casino's swimming pool, bordered from the parking lot by a fake castle wall and fake brick turrets, lying back in my private cabana. (Terrance is a very good agent. In all fairness, there'd been a time when I'd had my booze comped, but when we did my last contract, the casino thought a cabana would cost them less money, and cabanas at the hotel begin at a hundred dollars a day—a fraction of what a cabana costs at a place like the Bellagio, but still a testimony to how much I once drank.) The cabanas look a bit like the tents from the *Game of Thrones* TV series, except they're smaller, and it's frowned upon when people fornicate inside them. I was sipping tonic water while flipping pages in the biography I was reading about Edward VIII and Wallis Simpson—I am always looking for new material for the show, and Diana's post-Charles exile from the royal family was reminiscent of that pair's—when Nigel texted me that he was going to pop over. It was early afternoon, so I'd been up a solid two hours, one of which I'd spent here, the corner of the pool I viewed as my spot. You can see why I was in no hurry to return to a one-bedroom in Queens and resume my quest to be the next Patti LuPone or Kelli O'Hara, even if now I had to pay for my own buzz. The poolside music that day was the Studio 54 track: a lot of Bee Gees and Earth, Wind & Fire, but not so loud that it interfered with the guests' ability to chat and flirt, or exacerbated the pain behind the eyes of those who were hungover. Sometimes I'd hear an extra-loud splash as someone cannonballed into the pool, but mostly I heard the low burble of conversation, the occasional raucous laugh, and Barry Gibb. The world there smelled, as it did always, of coconut sunscreen.

When Nigel arrived, he sat in the cabana's other chaise, his feet on the coralline deck that surrounded the water, his knees at ninety-degree angles and his hands on his thighs. He took off his sunglasses. I kept mine on.

"You know, if you bent over, you'd be in the crash position," I told him.

"And if I didn't move and breathed through my nose into my abdomen, you might think I was going to meditate."

"I'd never think that about you."

"I have some news."

I waited.

"Richie Morley killed himself."

Instantly I was roused from my cabana torpor. "Richie's dead?"

"Yes. His body was discovered by a pair of do-gooders out near Red Rocks. He drove his Jag to some vista pull-off and shot himself in the head. A couple of campers were driving by and pulled over to see if someone in the car needed help. But, by then, Richie was way beyond needing help."

The Morleys were among the local faces of the Buckingham Palace—or what people in the know or who had never heard of British Petroleum called the "BP." (Full disclosure: BP was also a shorthand, in some of the tonier Vegas circles, for "Bullshit Property.") I was a local face, too, of course, a sort of low-rent equivalent to the way Siegfried & Roy were associated for years with the Mirage. Still, most of my contact had been with Artie, Richie's brother and the sibling who'd made the final decision to hire me, though even that was limited. Richie was the property's chief financial officer, Artie was the general manager. But even a casino with the same number of floors as tourist guide stars (three, which was generous and, I like to believe, as high as it was because of a certain tribute performer) had layers of bureaucracy between the GM and the "talent." Nevertheless, I was stunned—and there was suicide aplenty in my family and suicide aplenty in Vegas. The city was an actual destination for people who wanted to kill themselves. Moreover, when it's not only someone you know but also your employer who decides to call it a day, you are left with the realities of grief *and* the sense that your job security might not be all that you supposed it was. I worked at a second-rate casino, and now the second-rate CFO and brother of the second-rate GM was dead.

"Do we know why?" I asked.

He shook his head. "Maybe Artie knows. But if Richie left a note, it wasn't on the news."

"That's where you heard it? The news?"

"Yes."

When the Morleys had bought the place, apparently their initial plan had been to turn it into an upscale, boutique casino. They hired the likes of me. But then, I suppose, they discovered there was no need to turn it around: you could make a mint catering to the world's castoffs. Why not bask in its tawdriness and exploit the downtrodden? Our gaming floor mostly torpedoed locals, tourists on a budget, and out-of-town gamblers who had reached the end of the line and had no business losing the little money they had to a roulette wheel. I brought in a higher-end (and older) clientele, though I'm not sure people who came to the BP to see my show from the Bellagio or the Four Seasons spent much time in the poker rooms or blackjack tables. They certainly weren't eating at our restaurants.

"I'm in shock," I murmured.

"When was the last time you saw him?"

"Maybe a month ago." I pointed at the snack bar across the pool. "He was over there at a table. In a meeting of some sort. We waved. That was it."

"You worried?"

He felt the same anxiety I did. Las Vegas was filled with gig performers without gigs. The BP may have been the sort of place where the room service came on chipped plates and the wallpaper in the corridor corners was peeling and stained from decades-old water damage, but Nigel and I still had a residency there. We each had a hotel suite, and if the suites were not luxurious, they were airy and bright and came with kitchenettes with coffeemakers and microwave ovens. Most performers would have killed for what we had.

"A little," I admitted.

I heard someone approaching and felt the shade change ever

so slightly. A young waitress was standing at the entrance to the cabana, and Nigel ordered us each a Bloody Mary. I didn't know her, so she must have been new. But she knew me, introduced herself as Lily, and said it was an honor to meet me. I said it was an honor to meet her, though I wasn't sure why either of us should have been honored to meet one another: we were both casino drones who helped people pass the time when they were tired of losing money or had simply run out of money to lose. When the young woman had retreated, Nigel said, "I should have ordered some food. Want something? The avocado toast, maybe?"

"No, thank you. You know I don't eat much this time of day. Besides, I want to be sure the Bloody Mary can do its magic and take my mind off poor Richie."

He reached into the kangaroo pocket of a sleeveless hoodie—he had cut off the sleeves because he liked kangaroo pockets and, I suppose, his arms, but this was Las Vegas and sleeves on a sweatshirt in August was just asking for heatstroke—and pulled out an orange vial. "Valium?"

"I already have five milligrams in me. No, wait. Seven and a half."

"Go for twelve and a half."

"We have two shows tonight. I should be at least a wee bit sober."

He smiled. "I love it when you use the word *wee*."

"God. Maybe I need a day off."

"Maybe. Wouldn't it be heaven to sit inside a cabana at the swimming pool all day long, nursing a Bloody Mary?"

I flipped him the bird good-naturedly, but I did see his point. "Okay," I said. "A night off."

"My favorite memory of Richie was the first time he saw the show after you invited me in. He and Artie and Eddie Cantone came backstage with a bottle of champagne, and Richie said the real Diana deserved a prince like me. It was so kind of him." Eddie was the entertainment director at the casino, but we were small and so he did much more; entertainment director was but one of his hats.

"I remember," I said. "Of course, the champagne wasn't exactly a Krug Vintage Brut."

"No. But it was the thought that counted. And it was made from grapes and it did have bubbles. I know Richie didn't have any kids and he wasn't married. Did he have anyone in his life?"

"I don't think so. He had a girlfriend for a while. But they broke up a year ago."

"So, there's no one he left behind—other than Artie."

"I guess."

"Will it be a big funeral?"

"What do you mean by big?"

"Hundreds?"

I contemplated the number of BP employees who would be there. I tried to decide whether Richie was a fixture in Vegas or if he was on the periphery, one of the many with his fingers pressed against the outside glass windows of the properties that mattered. "Maybe a hundred," I decided. "And that includes you and me. I don't think he and Artie came from a big family or that he had lots of close friends."

He seemed to take this in. I couldn't decide from his face whether the fact that Richie had died alone made his demise more or less sad, but I had the sense that Nigel was relieved there wasn't a grieving widow or girlfriend.

"Do we go on tonight? Is there a show?" he asked.

"The show always goes on. Unless Artie or Eddie tells us otherwise."

"Understood. You'll be okay?"

"Yes."

"I'm sorry, Crissy. You knew him a lot better than I did."

"Thank you. But let's face it: I didn't know him well."

There were bottles of sunblock and moisturizer standing like toy soldiers on the table beside my chaise. He adjusted them as if he were a little boy. "In other news," he said, "your sister called."

"Checking on me?"

"Right."

My sister, Betsy, and Nigel had met twice: a postshow drink one night and brunch the next day, when she flew west from Vermont to see the show after Prince Charles had been added. It was when our mother was still alive. I leaned back on the chaise and closed my eyes. "I'm sorry. She called me, too. I should have called her back. I just didn't get around to it."

"I told her you're fine."

"Well, I was before the news about Richie. I think I still am. Mostly."

Betsy was my younger sister, but somehow, as adults, we'd swapped roles and she viewed herself as the older sibling who needed to look out for me. I was eighteen months her senior, but our resemblance had always been uncanny. Schoolteachers had often confused us, though I was a grade ahead of her. Strangers, when they saw us, supposed we were twins.

"Ever since your mum died," he started to say, but I cut him off. A reflex.

"Since she killed our mum," I corrected him, *she* being my sister.

Nigel and I had been onstage together barely a month when—wait for it—my sister killed our mother. It was an accident. But she still had blood on her hands, a spot that would never out—though, it seemed, it was my hell that was left murky.

"Our mum didn't just die," I went on. "That is a far too passive construction. I detest it when people go passive."

"You'll ring her back?" He didn't mean to shame me, but still I felt shamed.

"Yes. Of course."

Our mother rarely bought us matching outfits, but other people did. Every Christmas, the two of us were deluged with overalls and jumpers and dresses that made it clear to even the most oblivious onlooker that while we weren't twins, we were close in age, and the resemblance was eerie. Nevertheless, in elementary school, our lives started to separate. It was just the two of us, and I started kindergarten first, which I suppose felt deeply unfair to her. Still, we never shared a bedroom. We never tried to create a special sisters' language or fool people into believing one was the other. We had different friends as we grew up, despite the reality that our schools always were small, because other than the remarkable glimpse we gave the world of the numinous—two people who looked as much alike as two acorns—in most ways, we were profoundly different. I could sing. I could dance. I could act. But I could not have kicked a kickball eleven feet if you put a gun to my head. Betsy, on the other hand, was a beast at kickball, gymnastics, and on the ski slopes. She was ferocious, athletic, and the consummate risk-taker. (Arguably, she belonged in Las Vegas, not me.) She could sing too, but performing wasn't something that interested her: she preferred athletics to the high school stage, and dropped out of dance class when she was in eighth grade and I was in ninth. A part of me had been relieved, because I sensed my kid sister had talent that dwarfed mine, but the decent part of my heart wondered at the waste of aptitude. Still, I was happier knowing that now she had her world and I had mine.

She had also been a nightmare of a teen. Her endless litany of regrettable, ill-advised, and occasionally calamitous choices had made our poor mother's life embarrassing some days and terrifying on others. She got to know the local police awfully well, and one state trooper must have had our mother's number on speed dial.

In all fairness, she rallied in college and turned her life around. By the time we were in our midtwenties, despite the inherent, diminutive nature of the name *Betsy,* she carried herself more like a marine than a social worker who helped teens in trouble. Or, maybe, carrying herself like a marine was how she was able to do what she did, since teens in trouble can be awfully—again, to use a Windsor Castle colloquialism—pikey.

Or, to use the Las Vegas vernacular, happy to cut your balls off. Not literally. At least not in Burlington, Vermont, where she worked, but you see my point. If teens don't respect you when you're their social worker, you're in trouble. So, it made sense that she moved like she was an alumna of Parris Island. Meanwhile, I moved as if I were holding flower bouquets that adoring throngs had just given me as I emerged from one of the royal Bentleys or Aston Martins to greet the people.

True, our mother's death had diminished her. The guilt had diminished her. I saw that when I flew east after the accident. Growing up, her mistakes were Olympian compared to mine, and they had been since our stepfather had died when we were in elementary school. (We never knew our father. He'd died when I was a toddler and Betsy was an infant, when a milk tanker hit a patch of ice on a two-lane road and plowed into his Plymouth Colt, slamming it into a massive shagbark and collapsing it like a beer can.) But if I wanted to cling to whatever remnants of sanity I still had, I needed to release her. We'd never been the sorts of sisters who spoke or texted all the time, and now the less contact we had, the better. It would have been a failed charade if we had tried to feign closeness.

"Families are complicated," Nigel was saying.

"I know," I said. "Don't fret. I'll call her back."

Lily returned with our drinks, and Nigel ordered his avocado toast. He tried to order a plate for me, too, and while the casino's avocado toast was rather scrummy—Diana might have used that slang pre-Charles, but after wedding the prince she would have been more likely to refer to the BP's avocado toast as brilliant—eating it here in the cabana might have precluded me from giving it back. So, I told Lily that Nigel was chivalrous, but a Bloody Mary would suffice for my breakfast today. Or brunch.

"Betsy sounded like she has news," he said. "That was the vibe I got."

From outside the cabana I heard an Earth, Wind & Fire

track I liked a good deal. It would be followed by a KC and the Sunshine Band song I loathed and then another Bee Gees hit. Sometimes it worried me that I knew the playlist so well.

"For what it's worth," he went on, "I have issues with my siblings, too."

Not like mine, I thought, but I didn't verbalize it. Not like mine.

I was in one place when I was ten, and they wouldn't let us on the Wi-Fi, even for homework, unless they were watching. Insane, right? It was extra crazy because they never wanted to help us with homework or let us on the computer. (Not that I ever needed anyone's help with homework, especially from the pair getting paid by the state that year to "raise" me.) So, I took the mom's phone when she was taking a nap and downloaded an app that cracks passwords. I got the password for the home Wi-Fi—it was super easy—then deleted the app from her phone. But, from then on, I was able to get online when they left me alone and even do some homework. I gave the password to one of the other kids they had at the time, because he was eight and cool enough to keep a secret.

CHAPTER TWO

Betsy

She was burned out, the woes of the world and her own laments as a Dowling too much with her. They were inside her, lurking like free radicals waiting to blossom into tumors as solid as golf balls. That, she would tell herself later, would explain a lot of it: she was impelled by the amplified grief—harmonies of pain sung by teens—that had been her job for a decade. She'd seen one too many kids who were cutting or popping oxies like M&M's, she'd counseled one too many girls who'd been abused by their uncles or one too many boys with learning disabilities that no one diagnosed until the child (and these were children to her) dropped out of high school, got kicked from his home, and wound up on the street. She'd seen one too many trans kids vilified by their families or bullied on playgrounds. They all took a little piece of her heart.

Some people imagined that Vermont was an oasis where teens lived on ice cream and skiing, and the state was awash in dairy farms and sugarhouses. For the grown-ups, there was an endless array of microbreweries and craft distilleries. But, Betsy knew, the state was more complicated than that. Vermont did many things well, but like every state it had always had its share of children who were deserted and teens who imploded and families that fell apart.

She knew—or thought she knew—what had been happening years earlier in her own family's Victorian.

She got sick during the pandemic in 2020, prior to the rollout of the vaccines, and she supposed that was a factor, too, a part of the demonology explaining why she did what she did. She wasn't hospitalized, but she couldn't get out of bed for two weeks in the fall of that year. She could always breathe, but the fever and the weakness and the chills were terrifying, and she was all alone. At the time, she was between boyfriends. Crissy was in Las Vegas, and there was no way in hell that Betsy was going to let her mother near her and risk her health. She didn't even have a cat or a dog, which exacerbated the loneliness and the bleak places where her feverish mind would stagger, but was probably a blessing since she had no idea how she would have walked a dog, or scooped a cat's litter box. She wouldn't regain her sense of smell until the summer of 2021. (First aroma? Fried dough with maple syrup. She was at a county fair, and son of a bitch, there it was. She was in heaven.)

All of the therapists at the counseling service got sick in 2020. Including Betsy, there were six of them who worked with teens or teens and their families, and five more who worked at the shelter in Burlington, and there wasn't enough hand sanitizer (or masks) on the planet to keep them all from, eventually, coming down with the virus. They did a lot of the counseling via Zoom, but a shelter for homeless teens is going to be a hot spot. Fortunately, they weren't all sick at the same time.

And so when she got involved with an older man whose own family was unraveling and he threw her a lifeline—a way out—she grabbed it. Yes, she was working with his son. Yes, she was working with the whole family. But the marriage wasn't salvageable. Staying together wasn't going to save their son. And while sometimes in her mind those sentences sounded like a justification on her part for sleeping with the father—a euphemism, because at the beginning there had been no sleeping—she would take a breath and reassure herself that they weren't. That was just the way it was.

She was attracted to Frankie Limback in part because he was nothing like her image of an investment banker, an impression, she had to admit, generated wholly by what she saw in the movies and on TV, and the father of one of her friends from college. He wasn't clad in Italian suits and red power ties, and his accent oozed the Long Island suburb where he'd grown up. But he traveled a lot, and the places were toasty (Grand Cayman) or chilly (Moscow, prior to Putin's invasion of Ukraine) or storied (Cambodia, including Angkor Wat). And she appreciated how much he loved his children and was broken by his son's persistent struggles. She was awed by his life experience. She was seduced by his kindness.

And she began to understand with intuitive precision that he was her ticket out of Vermont. Oh, she knew nothing about running a hedge fund (Frankie's old business) or cryptocurrency (his new one), but even if the ethereal machinations of invisible money were beyond her ken, she had concluded now that she had to get out of social work. She was thirty-four, and she felt the funnel of life's opportunities starting to narrow. She was desperate. She was done.

And she was grieving. Not mourning. Grieving.

The difference was not semantics. After her mother's death, she knew firsthand that those two words were not synonymous.

* * *

Betsy's first exposure to cryptocurrency was at the counseling service, and it had nothing to do with Frankie Limback. It was in that period when much of the nation thought—the first time—that it was in the tail end of the pandemic: people were getting vaccinated, and the Delta variant hadn't created the first of what everyone feared would be seemingly endless Greek-lettered waves. Betsy had just met with a sixteen-year-old client, and the teen's older brother was picking her up after their session. Her brother was twenty-three and had moved back home in March 2020, his senior year of college, and stayed after his virtual graduation. While the siblings and Betsy were making small talk in the counseling center's parking lot, he joked about the new car he had bought, thanks to Futurium.

"What's Futurium?" Betsy asked.

He laughed. "You're kidding, right?"

She shook her head.

"It's a cryptocurrency. I was living at home and had, like, zip expenses, and so I took my pandemic stimulus checks and bought some. When I showed my parents how much money I'd made, they loaned me some cash and I bought some more. They bought some, too."

She'd seen the ads for the new currencies and the exchanges everywhere. The likes of LeBron James and Larry David had starred in them. She scrolled past articles about NFTs on her phone.

"What kind of car did you buy?" Betsy asked. She was expecting a used Hyundai. Maybe, if the wheels were new, a Chevy Spark.

He pointed at a red Audi sedan parked against the small lot's metal fence. "The S3. I didn't get the carbon atlas inlays in the seats or the nineteen-inch wheels, so we brought it in for under fifty Gs."

"New . . ."

"Oh, yeah."

She had been driving the same Subaru for six years. It had nearly 127,000 miles. He started telling her about the Bang & Olufsen 3D sound system in his car and the vehicle's virtual cockpit, but it was all a blur. His sister rolled her eyes at the alpha swag name-dropping and put her elbow around her brother's neck, collaring him good-naturedly.

Betsy had never expected to get rich as a social worker, but among the ways she changed during the pandemic was the realization that when she had been a mess in high school, she had been on to something: life is short, and there is no one steering the big blue gumball on which she lived. Since college, she had been trying to make the world a better place, and for some families and a few kids, she had. But now, post-pandemic, she was in her midthirties and living in the sort of apartment that parents rented for their kids when they were in college: part of the second floor of a Victorian at the edge of the University of Vermont campus.

There had to be more. She'd spent her adult life trying to save others. Maybe it was time to try and save herself.

When she started falling for Frankie, she tried to understand this new currency. While she found the machinations of crypto byzantine, she thought the nomenclature was precisely the sort of techno teen-speak she had mastered from years around adolescents: apes and bags and DAOs and FUDs and moons and normies and rug pulls and (her favorite) WAGMI, as in "We're all gonna make it." How could you not like that optimism? Oh, there were some terms that caused her eyes to glaze, such as "proof of stake," but all of them were signposts to a different future.

A life that wasn't hers and that sure as hell wasn't Crissy's, because Betsy most assuredly did not envy the specifics of her sister's Nevada biosphere. There was something dark and sad about living in a second-rate casino, a mutable world that wobbled between the faux ostentatious and the very, very bleak. And unlike the vast majority of Vegas performers, Crissy was living large. She wasn't living the life of Barry Manilow or Celine Dion, but her existence was one of spectacular privilege compared to most Vegas entertainers. The secret to her success, in Betsy's opinion, was the confluence of three things: She was unique, the only Diana there was in Las Vegas. She was channeling a celebrity who, though long dead, was perpetually in the zeitgeist: the world's obsession with the royals never waned. There would always be another movie, another musical, another streaming TV series. Another novel of her life or another biography. And then Crissy or her agent, Terrance, had the brilliant idea to add songs to the show that appealed to a certain demographic—songs that reminded them that, once upon a time, they weren't old. All cover bands and tribute performers mined the emotional gold that was nostalgia, but her sister had found the mother lode in Diana.

And so while Betsy didn't covet Crissy's life—she wasn't even sure she approved of it—she did believe one thing with certainty: her own life in Vermont was much more pathetic than even that of an off-the-strip princess.

* * *

Though Betsy may have been the difficult sister as an adolescent—the one with a seemingly allergic aversion to reasonable behavior—she turned it around in college. Less weed, less alcohol, fewer decisions based on the pleasures derived from immediate gratification. She understood that actions had consequences, and life was a cause-and-effect equation.

And now, while much of her sister's world appalled her, Betsy did like the idea that Crissy lived in a place where it almost always was sunny. She appreciated the fact that her sister was far from the home where their father and stepfather had died, and the ground zero where their mother had passed away. She was jealous that Crissy was three time zones away from their childhood. Betsy craved that, too. She saw the possibilities inherent in putting that much geographic distance between herself and her adolescent muddles and missteps.

One afternoon, long after Frankie had left the investment bank that had made him rich to join Futurium—the very crypto she had heard about in the counseling center's parking lot—he fell back against the couch pillows in her apartment, naked, and told her that he was leaving for Las Vegas to work at Futurium's office there. He added that the word *office* was a misnomer. It was more of a warehouse.

"My sister loves it there," she told him, trying to retain her equanimity in the wake of this bombshell.

"And she's at a second-rate casino. Can you imagine how

much she'd love it if her show was at a nicer place? One of the titans on the strip?" he asked. "The BP makes me cringe. I should take your sister under my wing and set her up at the kind of resort a Dowling girl deserves."

"It's not that bad," she replied, instinctively defending the casino where Crissy worked. "You make it sound like a hot-sheets motel."

"No. Of course not. But it's still run by cretins. Two brothers who don't belong in the business."

"How much do you know about Las Vegas?"

"I know lots. We know lots. Investment banking is all about research and knowledge. I may be in crypto now, but we still do our due diligence. I know who the casino players are, and I know where the politicians stand on every issue that matters to Futurium. It's what I do. And there's a lot to love about Vegas that has nothing to do with the business model we've put together. Futurium's Florida partners and investors saw that when they were deciding where to set up shop. Vegas is warm, just like home, and just like in West Palm, the wealthy can wear their money on their sleeves. So, I totally get what your sister sees in the city. Totally." Then he told her about the Nevada facility where the crypto company had installed its crypto mining rigs—its massive computers—and how it was only a matter of time before crypto and Vegas were synonymous. More casinos were accepting Bitcoin. He described the houses he was looking at online outside the city, and how serene it would be to live near Red Rocks. On Zillow, he showed her the house he was likely to buy. And then he got to the point of his revelation, and it was precisely what she realized she'd been hoping he'd say.

"I want you to come with me, Betsy. There's a place for you, too, with Futurium."

She said yes without hesitation. This was the stars with all their plenary power telling her that a life buoy was being tossed into the water, and it was time to grab it with both hands, and allow herself to be pulled to safety.

Everyone said I was "so verbal." It was like I was a dog that could talk.

But it's always been numbers that interest me. That after-school coding class for "gifted young mathematicians" I got to go to was the coolest thing I ever did in Vermont.

CHAPTER THREE

Crissy

Diana Spencer was an eidolon in both senses of the word: she was idealized and she was spectral. I doubt anyone other than Peter Morgan, the mind behind the TV series *The Crown,* has watched as much video of the woman as I have, but still she never grows stale. Google her. Watch her. Listen to her voice. I always feel her power and her pain, and yet there's also a part of her that remains just out of reach. There's a reason she was beloved that transcended the fact that she married a prince who loved someone else.

Or, let's face it, the fact that she married a man whose idea of phone sex was to fantasize being Camilla Parker Bowles's tampon.

* * *

Once Nigel had finished his avocado toast and left me alone, I took my phone from the cabana side table and stared at the word *Betsy* in my contacts. I had finished my Bloody Mary and eaten the celery stalk, and so I swigged the last of the melted ice. Even in a cabana, ice melts fast in Las Vegas in August.

And then I rang her.

"I'm glad you called back," she said. It was odd to hear her voice. We spoke infrequently since she'd killed our mum. Talking to her was just too much for me. Now she sounded less brusque than she used to, uncomfortable in that short sentence.

I felt an unexpected tug, the magnetism of family and genes, and had to steel my spine so as not to be seduced back in. "Thank you."

"I gather you reached out to Nigel. You needn't fret about me. I'm fine."

"Good. That's . . . good."

"How are you?"

"I'm fine, too. I have some news."

I said nothing and waited.

"I'm coming to Las Vegas," she told me. "For work."

"Oh? There's a convention for social workers at the Aria?" I asked sarcastically.

"When I said I'm coming for work, I didn't mean for, like, three days. For a conference or something. I'm moving there."

For Americans, the expression is *crash and burn*. For Diana, it would have been *all to pot,* as in *Things went all to pot when the cat jumped onto the dining room table and her claws caught in the tablecloth. Then she deposited a hairball onto the queen's salad plate.* I said nothing as the information settled.

"They're taking care of everything," she went on. "I have a moving allowance, they've found me an apartment, they've—"

"Who are *they*? Are you going to work with teens here?"

"No. I'm changing careers. I'm going to work for a fintech company—"

"Fintech?"

"Financial technology. In this case, cryptocurrency. Digital assets."

"What in heaven's name do you know about cryptocurrency and digital assets?"

"This past winter I was working with a wealthy family. Big meadow mansion in Shelburne. Their older son has some learning disabilities and had started self-medicating. He was really out of control. They were on the verge of kicking him out, and that would have been disastrous. Fortunately, they came to us first."

Us was her social services agency. Her shelter.

"And," she went on, "while we got him straightened out, his parents' marriage didn't make it."

"And you started snogging the dad?"

"It wasn't like that."

"It never is," I said, though I recalled with a pang Senator John Aldred and his three children. They were—and I did the math in my mind—now seventeen, fifteen, and nine. I thought of his wife, Sarabeth, who I had met the same night I met her husband, when they were brought backstage to meet me after my second show. *It never is,* I repeated in my mind, but, alas, it always is. "Isn't it a little wonky to be sleeping with a client's father?"

"The optics aren't great. But my *client's* parents had already separated."

I nodded to myself. My sister had a history of dubious paramours and suspect boyfriends. It wasn't only that she was drawn to the proverbial bad boys; often she herself was that magnetic bad girl.

"Anyway," she went on, "his company has a presence in Vegas, and he's relocating there."

"And you're coming with him."

"Yes. But we're not going to live together. At least not right away."

"You've always been a beacon of reticence and restraint."

"I didn't plan any of this," she said.

"What's the name of the company?"

"Futurium."

I'd heard of it. I'd read about the company in the paper and knew they were expanding or consolidating or something in Vegas.

"Doesn't this seem like destiny?" she went on. "I meet a guy and he's moving to the city where my sister lives. Doesn't it seem like fate to you?"

"No. It seems like bad luck."

"We're family."

"A cross we both bear."

"There's someone I want you to meet."

"Your new boyfriend?"

"Your niece."

I sat up straighter. We hadn't spoken in months. A lot can happen in months, but what in holy hell had my sister not shared? My mind went to an infant, since Betsy hadn't had any children the last time I'd seen her. Had she gotten pregnant just after she'd killed our mum? She had a newborn, was that what she was telling me?

"You had a baby?" I asked. It didn't seem possible this Futurium chap could be the father, unless Betsy was lying about the chronology. Still, I asked. "Is the father—"

"Adopted," she said. "Marisa is thirteen. She was in foster care and then I was fostering her. She was twelve when we met. When I heard her story—"

"Her story?"

"A friend of mine in Vermont's Department for Children and Families told me about this amazing tween who, yet again, was about to fall through the cracks and be screwed by the system. Well, we really hit it off. It seemed to me, it was time someone took this child under their wings—for good. I've seen so many kids who became lost because no one cared for them. If I could save one when I got out? I had to try."

"And the Department let you adopt a foster tween?"

"Why wouldn't they?"

"Because you killed—"

"You always say that, but I didn't. I know the facts, I know what happened."

"Let me make sure I have this right," I murmured over her denial. I began to see why this would have been a lot to leave on a voice mail or send in a text. "You've quit your job, taken a new boyfriend, adopted a kid, and now you're starting a new career."

"You make it sound insane. It's a lot, yes, I get it. But I realized in the pandemic I had to blow everything up. I was lonely, I was sad, I hated my life. And then our mother died. It was just too much, Crissy. It was like I was a load-bearing wall, but the load was more than I could bear. I just . . . I just broke."

She had, for years, been the more reckless of the two of us. But when she opened her heart to me, her plan sounded a little less crazy. Her life really had become a heaping plate of haggis. And, as parents had said often to me over the years, there's *never* a good time to have a child. Children, born or adopted, are capable of pantsing the most buttoned-up of adults. "When do you get here?" I asked.

"Next week. We're flying. The apartment is furnished, so we don't have to bring all that much. And Marisa would like to meet her aunt," she continued.

I paused, taking this in. Of course, Betsy had told this adolescent about me. "What's she like?" I asked.

"She's wonderful. I mean, she's different. She's been in foster care since she was five. But she's a great kid. She's kind of a math genius. Even took a coding class for teens when she was eleven. And she's very opinionated—like you. You'll get a charge out of her."

"What does your boyfriend think of her?"

"They get along great. There are literally zero issues between them."

"Was Marisa a factor in your decision not to move in with him?"

"Frankie—"

"That's his name?"

"Yes. Frankie Limback. He doesn't think it sends the right message to his own children to move to Las Vegas and immediately invite a new kid into his home. I agree. His son has been through so much already."

"Is he paying for your and Marisa's apartment?"

"I told you, the company gave us a generous moving allowance."

"But this Frankie person is paying the rent, isn't he?"

"Yes."

A thought came to me. "What color is your hair?"

"Not Diana's, don't worry."

"But blond?"

"Strawberry blond."

That was too close. "Grow it out. Please. Please dye it black." That was our hair's natural color: dark as stovepipe.

"Sis, forgive me, but your kookiness is showing. Get over—"

"People are going to think—"

"I won't embarrass you, I promise."

"I don't want people to mistake you for me."

"We're sisters. We look alike. We look *a lot* alike."

"Which, thank God, is only skin deep."

"That's not true."

"Dye it black!" I said, this time a small rant, and then I said I had to go and hung up. It was dramatic, and I have, for better or worse, a flair for the dramatic. Diana did, too.

But it was apparent that Betsy was about to be back in my world—literally *my* world, Las Vegas—which perhaps justified my pressing the red button on my phone and terminating our call with such extreme prejudice. She was coming here soon, and there was nowhere for me to run, because there was no place in the world other than Vegas weird enough to sustain a Princess Diana tribute show. Besides, this was my town. *My* town.

When I saw Lily, the poolside waitress, I cleared my tab, and asked her to please have room service send an avocado toast to my room. I honestly had no idea whether, to use the blackjack metaphor, it would stick.

* * *

That night, after my second show, I was accosted on the casino floor by Dicky Sherman, onetime child actor superstar, now over-the-hill QAnon crazy, and two of his handlers-slash-bodyguards-slash-entourage-slash–laugh track. Let's face it, you see a lot of famous or quasi-famous people in Las Vegas, even at a casino like the BP. I am ever so slightly renowned in my own niche bubble, but somewhere between less so and not at all in L.A. or Manhattan, and so when some A-listers notice me walking on the strip or out and about on one of my nights off, they suppose I am merely a Diana-obsessed wacko and work hard not to make eye contact.

Of course—and please forgive this humble brag—there are also A-listers who make seeing my show part of their Vegas experience, and they detour from the top-flight casino where they're staying to go slumming at the BP to see me. Having Tom Hanks or Regina King brought backstage and listening to them praise the cabaret was—to quote Larry David, who also liked the show and thought it so odd that he said he might work it into an episode of *Curb Your Enthusiasm*—"pretty, pretty good."

Dicky Sherman was fifty and change, and that number worked for both his age and his waistline. Same with his hangers-on. Between the two of us, we drew a crowd, and people on a casino floor at midnight are often raucous and drunk or maudlin and depressed, and quite possibly holding a plastic booze glass the length of a rolling pin with a milkshake straw so you can really scarf down that piña colada. It was clear from Dicky's inebriated babble that he had been granted an audience that day with our far-right congressional rep, Erika Schweiker, a woman who'd never met a conspiracy theory involving pizza, child abuse, and space lasers she didn't believe. Dicky recognized me from the casino show videos that dotted the shopping concourse and check-in corral, so he—it was inevitable—had to lecture me on what royalty was in America, and why the nation was going to hell. He told me that the Nevada senator with whom I had been sleeping, unbeknownst to him, was a woke pawn and Antifa tool. I nodded and said nothing because I was tired and he was insane and it was midnight, which is late anywhere but Las Vegas.

Just for the record, I don't have a handler or bodyguard who trails me at the casino. I do at the cabaret, but he works for the Buckingham Palace and would be the muscle regardless of who was on the stage. I don't need one, because I know a lot of the women and men in security—the obvious cops and the casino's undercover enforcers—and they always look out for me. Someone comes on to me and it's clear I don't want them there? Casino cops are on them like the Queen's Guard. Or, to use a more American analogy, like Black Friday shoppers on the last TV at Best Buy.

After I had extricated myself from Dicky Sherman's demented discourse, I wandered through the casino with a club soda. A group of twentysomething gamblers were playing what I had come to call Covid Craps: they were blowing on the dice for good luck as if it were still 2019, and then tossing the germ-ridden blocks onto the felt, the high-walled craps table now a giant petri dish. Eventually I went to one of the poker rooms to watch a game unfold there. Most of the croupiers, surveillance observers, and pit bosses knew me, and so they never suspected I was helping a player with covert signals. It was merely a spectator sport for me, and that evening I picked out a table with sharps who knew what they were doing, and played Texas Hold 'Em along with them in my head. In the distance, I could hear the bells and whistles from the slots, but there wasn't anything to see there, despite the spectacular graphics that marked the machines. Every so often, I wondered why some gamblers would gravitate toward machines with violent images from *Lord of the Rings* or *The Walking Dead,* and others would be drawn to childhood staples with less brutal iconography, such as *Willy Wonka* or *The Wizard of Oz.* Regardless, some days it just made me sad, all those people losing money quarters and dollars at a time, and a lot of the slots players couldn't afford to drop twenty-five or fifty or one hundred bucks into the one-armed bandits in the course of an hour.

Roughly two-thirds of a casino's revenue is from the slots and the table games. The rest is largely rooms and food and beverage. Entertainers like me? We exist to fill in the time when the guests aren't on the casino floor. We are but blocks in the void, a line on the revenue sheet that, in some cases, might read only "other."

I had gotten through both performances that night just fine, despite the doubleheader of Betsy's unexpected news and Richie Morley's suicide. Everyone who worked at the BP was shaken by Richie's death. Artie Morley had sent employees an email in which he wrote that he was sad but standing, the business was fine, and he appreciated all of our prayers and good thoughts. He said there would be a memorial service in the coming weeks, and he would keep us posted. It was modestly reassuring. Nigel had offered to keep me company after our second show, but I thanked him and told him I'd rather be alone. I strolled aimlessly for about twenty minutes before settling on that spot of casino carpet in the poker room. I could feel my resolve to build a Berlin Wall between my sister and me here in the desert starting to erode, the imbricated scales shedding one by one, and supposed part of it was a desire to meet my niece. I had no idea whether this child was going to be in my life forever or never. Obviously, Betsy understood kids who'd been through hell: it was what she did for a living, God bless her. As frustrating as I found her, I never lost sight of her efforts on behalf of the sort of prickly outcasts who rarely got happy endings. But to be a mother? I found that unfathomable, and I wouldn't have been surprised if this was her atonement for killing her own mum.

Our own mum.

Yes, I had my demons, but I knew in my heart that whatever succubus lurked inside Betsy made my ghouls look like kittens. I would endure. I heard in my head that old Gloria Gaynor song "I Will Survive," and for a split second thought it was playing somewhere in the casino. It wasn't.

"Do you want a seat? Are you thinking of playing?"

For a moment, I had lost myself. I looked up. The fellow was older than I was, midforties, with a distinguishing swath of gray in his temples, but otherwise dark hair that had not yet begun to recede. He had crow's feet around eyes so dark they were coal colored and cheekbones that were severe. I liked them. He was wearing a black blazer. He was too handsome and too well dressed for the witching hour at the BP. He belonged at a better class of casino.

"No, I'm fine, thanks. Just watching." I motioned at the table. One of the players I had been following was standing. Based on the purple chips he was stacking, I suspected that he was walking away a winner.

"They're good players. Note the guy in the hipster-chic porkpie hat," he said. "Now, I'm not hitting on you, I promise, but you really do look like her."

He was smiling, and I couldn't decide if he was in fact hitting on me or just impressed by how much I resembled Diana. So, I decided to test him. Have some fun. It might take my mind off everything else that was flooding my gray matter like sewer water after a hurricane.

"I know," I admitted. "I look exactly like a British princess. Catherine, Duchess of Cambridge, wife to Prince William, and very likely a future queen consort."

"Clearly, I'm not the first person to tell you the resemblance is uncanny."

"Nope." He'd passed; he'd gotten the joke.

"You even have her eyes."

I lowered my head while raising my gaze, one of my practiced Diana-esque coquette moves. It came straight from my act, which came straight from the hours of film I was always studying. "Are you suggesting it's a mere genetic coincidence that I have a passing resemblance to the late Princess of Wales, not something that I actually cultivate?"

"Oh, you cultivate it, too. Exhibit A? Your hair."

"Wouldn't that be rather kinky?"

"It would be kinky, yes, but this is Las Vegas, so kinky is the new normal." He had a drink in his hands and he took a sip. I guessed it was Scotch. "My younger sister thought Wales was actually whales—you know, big ocean mammals—when she was growing up, and Diana was able to talk to them. Like the *Game of Thrones* lady with her dragons. Like being a whale whisperer. She had this idea that Diana stood on cliffs looking out at the English Channel and all these whales would come and frolic near the coastline. She thought that until she was nine or ten."

"I don't talk to whales," I said, but already the wheels were spinning and I was certain that I was going to work this new material into my show. It was gold, and I knew just how to write it, especially since casino-speak for the most extravagant of gamblers—those high rollers who lost tens of thousands of dollars a night—was "whale."

"My name is Gene."

"Crissy," I said. "But I have a feeling you already know that."

"I do. I came here to see your show, but arrived late. The second show had started. I hear you're an excellent actor."

"I think actors would take issue with that. I used to be an actor. Now I'm a performer."

"Well, I'm going to see your show tomorrow," he told me. "I won't let work delay me two nights in a row."

"What makes you think it isn't sold out and you can get a ticket?" Both shows were in fact sold out, but I also knew there were always ways to get last-minute seats. If he'd asked, I could have gotten him one.

"This is going to sound like male arrogance . . ."

"But . . ."

"I'll get a ticket. Which one would you prefer I came to? First or second? I'd prefer the second, but I'll defer to you."

"Why the second?"

"So we can have a drink afterward."

I thought of my sister and some thirteen-year-old kid packing up their stuff to move to Las Vegas. I saw Betsy buying the child suitcases so she didn't have to use the foster kid backpack: a thirty-gallon black garbage bag. At some point soon, they were going to appear in my life, and there wasn't a bloody thing I could do. I had thought that I wanted to be alone that night. I wasn't so sure anymore.

"Gene, you said?"

"I did."

"Short for Eugene, I suppose."

He smiled grimly. "I wish."

"Then what?"

"You have to promise not to run."

This intrigued me, and so I waited.

"Yevgeny," he answered.

"You're Russian?"

"No. I'm American. My parents and my sister and I emigrated here from Volgograd in 1996. I was a teenager."

"Yevgeny, you said?"

He nodded. "But whatever Russian DNA I have in me is harmless. I don't poison people with radioactive tea, I don't condone attacking sovereign nations, I hate Putin as much as you do. I grew up in Brooklyn, for God's sake. In Brighton Beach. I know more about Coney Island than I do Saint Basil's."

"I insulted you. I'm sorry."

"Not at all. Now, I know you're not British, despite the . . . accent."

"Affectation," I admitted. "It helps me stay in character. And, let's face it, if I were Jasmine or Belle at Disney World, you can bet I would be in character when I was out and about among the guests."

"Where did you grow up?"

"Vermont."

"Well, I can't wait until tomorrow night to witness the full transformation. I'll get to watch you talk to whales and then we'll have that drink?"

I looked him over once more, appraising him. No wedding band. I liked what I saw. "Why wait until tomorrow night? I know every pub—"

"Pub? Really?"

"Really," I said, laying on the British accent like jam on a scone, "and almost every bartender in this casino. Pick your pub and let's have that drink now."

* * *

But first there was Artie Morley.

I rarely saw Artie at the casino, though obviously he was there often. But I had my room and my cabana, and mostly I commuted between those two venues and the theater.

As Gene and I were walking among the protractor-shaped tables where people were playing blackjack—lots of locals tonight, it seemed to me, plenty of T-shirts and sweatpants—I spotted him. He was with two men in dark suits; he himself was in a charcoal suit with gray pinstripes. I was deciding whether to detour over to express my condolences, but he spotted me and beelined across the carpet, leaving the two other men near the corner of the casino where they'd been chatting. I embraced him and told him how sorry I was about Richie, noting for the first time how deep the bags were under his eyes and how his hair had begun to gray. Was all this new? Had his brother's death aged him overnight? I introduced him to Gene and he nodded politely, but he had come to see me and his focus was on me.

"Are you around tomorrow?" he asked.

"I am." I rarely went anywhere.

"I have a window between two fifteen and two forty-five. Would you come by my office?"

"Of course," I said, and I felt a spasm of anxiety. He'd never summoned me to his office. I had a tendency to catastrophize, and ideas began bouncing around in my head like pinballs: The BP wasn't going to renew my contract. Someone from the royal family was suing the casino. Artie didn't want Nigel in the show. I was losing my room or, yes, my cabana. Most of this was the sort of bad news that Eddie Cantone, the entertainment director, would have delivered, but still I began to imagine the worst.

"Is everything okay?" I asked, instantly regretting the way I was making this about me when it was his brother who had just killed himself.

"As far as the Diana show? Absolutely. You know as well as anyone, it's sold out forever. This has nothing to do with the act," he told me, gently squeezing my arm to reassure me that all was well—at least in that regard.

"Okay," I said, but I heard a hitch in my voice.

"So, two fifteen?"

"I'll be there," I agreed, and then Artie shook Gene's hand, thanked me for my condolences, and returned to the men with whom he had been speaking.

"Well, that worries me," I confessed to Gene.

"I don't see why it should."

"No?"

He shook his head. "Maybe he wants you to sing at his brother's memorial."

"Maybe," I agreed, but I didn't think that was it.

"You still up for that drink?"

"Yes," I said. "Absolutely. I could use a nightcap now more than ever. Or, at least, more than ten minutes ago."

"Good. But Crissy?"

I waited.

"I know things. I have an excellent sixth sense. And I don't think you have anything to worry about."

I hoped he was right. But I didn't believe his sixth sense was any better than mine, and mine, it was clear from an awful lot of my life choices, was rubbish.

The coding teacher thought I wanted to design games, because the older kids in the class lived for games.

I like games.

But I was more interested in how things worked. How to solve problems. (I'd say puzzles, but then you'd say games. I only like puzzles if I look at them like problems to be solved.)

CHAPTER FOUR

Betsy

She could have grown into Elizabeth. She could have been Beth. But she'd been Betsy in day care and Betsy in her Vermont village's little cooperative preschool and then the town's bigger (but still small) elementary school, and so Betsy she had remained. She was Betsy when she was a hellion in high school who some days (and nights) made her mother's life an innermost ring of Dante's Inferno, she was Betsy when she was getting her master's in social work, and she was Betsy when she would lose her mother just when she thought the pandemic could cause her no more pain.

Once, she was a mess. She never lost sight of the utter nakedness of her conscious miscalculations and unthinking missteps. There was never anything baleful about her preteen faux pas and teenage flubs—at least the intentions weren't baleful. Sometimes the results were. That was a reality.

By the time that she and Crissy were in their early thirties, however, she believed that she was the sister who was reflective and judicious and made the world better. She was as sure of this as she was that the Earth was round and there was nothing in the firmament but sky and stars and moon.

It was why she went west with Frankie Limback. She believed she was making the right decision—not just for her, but for her daughter. Even for Crissy. She had no premonition that might dissuade her, no augury telling her no. But had there ever been omens warning her away from her worst instincts? And would she have heeded them if there were?

Probably not.
No. Definitely not.

* * *

The first night Marisa was in Betsy's apartment with her, the first night the girl was officially Betsy's foster child, she had a pair of epiphanies. She understood that she was in over her head, because with Marisa, unlike with every other young person she had counseled over the years, there was going to be no respite: no moment when she could say their time was up and send the client back to a parent or older sibling, no moment when the night manager at the shelter would take over, no moment when a psychiatrist would write the young person a scrip that would settle him or her or them down. She thought of her friend at the Vermont DCF who'd introduced her to Marisa and helped convince her that, post-pandemic, these two lost souls would make each other whole. Maybe. But Marisa wasn't a pandemic puppy. She was a twelve-year-old human being with enough emotional baggage to fill the hold of a passenger jet. That sleeping child was her responsibility 24/7, and there was no one to help her, and she was terrified.

But she also felt this was the best thing she had ever done, and in addition to her roaring trepidation, there was euphoria. And on some level that Betsy was still trying to parse—her loneliness, a biological clock, the loss of a father, a stepfather, a mother—she needed Marisa.

She had bought her daughter ivory-colored pajamas with purple lilacs on them, a pattern so prim that even her sister the wannabe royal would have approved. Marisa chose not to sleep in the bottoms, wearing the top like a nightshirt over her underwear, because she said her legs got hot. Betsy had also gotten her a stuffed animal, a dog that looked like a black lab, and Marisa had said, accepting the gift, "Thank you. I once lived in a house where the family had, like, five dogs. They barked at everything: squirrels, other dogs, people on bikes. They were chained to these pegs in the yard, which is the worst thing you can do to a dog. Chain it up. Did you know that? They want to run, but they can't, and they feel super vulnerable because they're tied down. That's why chained dogs bark. When they took me—the social service police—they also took away the dogs. Or someone did. The animal shelter, I guess. The people I lived with didn't pay attention to the dogs, except tell them to shut up. They only kept them to scare people away. But I don't know what they were scared of. Their house kind of sucked. It was pretty run-down."

"Did the dogs scare you?" Betsy asked.

She shook her head. "No. They barked. They didn't bite."

Marisa didn't sleep with the stuffed animal. When Betsy peeked in on her, the plush dog was on top of the dresser.

* * *

Betsy knew from the beginning that Marisa was more than precocious. Good God, a sixth-grade teacher who barely knew the girl had seen her potential and gotten her into some after-school coding class with teens four and five years older than her. She was a tween autodidact and could talk forever. Betsy understood that some foster kids, even adolescents, would still strive mightily for their foster parents' approval. But most didn't. Most knew it was a lost cause by then, and so they grew quiet and withdrawn, a little surly, which was a natural response to the fact that their lives very likely had been a series of betrayals. Not Marisa, however, which was among the reasons why Betsy was drawn to her as soon as they were introduced. Like lots of the kids she saw and lots of the kids in the foster care system, Marisa could be nihilistic and wary. She shared that with her peers. One moment, she didn't give a damn about anything, and the next she was mistrustful and guarded. But then there were those times when she was open and optimistic, as if, despite the odds, she supposed life might not be an endless litany of despicable grown-ups or a world where she had to hoard food in her sneakers or thrift-store snow boots to survive.

And she was about to turn thirteen, one of the hardest ages there is in even the best of circumstances. You're a hormonal dumpster fire.

At breakfast the next day, Betsy asked, "Waffles, pancakes, or French toast?"

It was Saturday. By design, Betsy wanted the two of them to have a weekend together before falling into a routine of school and work. Marisa picked waffles, and Betsy made them for the first time in years, using her late mother's waffle iron. She was unprepared when Marisa said, "Huh. I never saw these made before. I'd never thought about how you get the squares on them."

Betsy did not say, "You've never had homemade waffles?" She kept her incredulity in check and said, "Yup. It's a panini press with squares. That's all."

"Panini?"

"Kind of sandwich."

"The frozen ones have chocolate chips, you know. Not automatically. You have to pick the right kind."

"You prefer your waffles with chocolate chips? I can put some in the next one. I have a bag in the pantry."

Marisa shook her head. "Nope. As one of my foster moms always said, a girl's gotta watch her weight," she explained, and Betsy thought of her sister. She wasn't sure which made her sadder: the idea that a kid who was tall and slender—she had legs like a giraffe—and not quite thirteen was worried about her weight, or the idea that no one had ever made her a homemade waffle.

* * *

What is it like to stand alone in the spotlight, a princess, the people before you in the dark hanging on your every word?

What is it like to be the focus of memory, to know your audience is lingering in a world you have conjured?

She asked Crissy this the first time she saw the show in Las Vegas, years ago now, and years before Crissy had added Nigel. They were in her dressing room and one of the brothers who owned the casino was there. Fellow named Artie Morley.

Before she could respond, Artie said, "It's heady as hell."

As if he knew.

"We're going to put serious money into the rest of the resort," he went on. "Really build this place. You don't have to be 'on the strip' to be a choice property."

Betsy had no idea if the Morleys or their investors ever did put "serious money" into the Buckingham Palace, but when she and her mother had returned a few years later to see the show with Prince Charles now a supporting player and two additional musicians, the rest of the place had felt as sad and bedraggled as ever. The bathroom in her and her mother's hotel room still had disposable plastic cups, and the hangers in the closet were still the sort that were attached to the bar, as if the clientele might actually filch a coat hanger. The pad on the ironing board in that same closet had long streaks of russet-colored mildew. The bedspread on one of the two beds had stains that the paisley couldn't hide, and the mirror over the dresser—pressed wood—was chipped. Their view was a parking lot and a liquor store the size of a small warehouse.

The room her sister lived in was nicer. It was a suite with a kitchenette and something Crissy referred to as the "reading nook." But, still, her refrigerator was little bigger than a plastic milk crate, and the "nook" was a couple of faux-leather chairs and a Naugahyde ottoman.

Before Frankie had announced that he was moving to Vegas, she had wondered when she would bring him west to meet her sister. What would a fintech millionaire think of the downtrodden world where Crissy Dowling cast her spell? She supposed he would see only potential. It was one of the things that made her care for him: he didn't judge. At least not harshly or overtly. After all, he saw how pitiable were her two bedrooms near the UVM campus, and thought no less of her. The truth was, he very likely loved her.

It was absurd in a way.

Because she sure as hell didn't love herself.

* * *

Betsy discovered that Marisa's favorite things included math, fashion, and television. She was fascinated by programs about witches that were set in the present, though she grew intrigued when Betsy told her about New England's real history with witchcraft.

"They hung them?" she asked.

"Hanged," said Betsy, who from the time she was ten had known the correct grammar. "Yes. The past tense of slipping a noose around someone's neck is *hanged*. So, the Puritans *hung* their pictures and *hanged* their witches."

"I don't think the devil is real," she told Betsy.

"Me neither."

"I wouldn't wear black eyeliner if he was."

"Why?"

"Wouldn't want him to think I was a fan. Life can suck plenty even without him. Besides . . ."

"Besides what?"

"People are the real devils."

But Marisa did love her black eyeliner. She also had a series of chokers, one made of leather, and Betsy let her wear them. She wasn't critical, because she recalled what she had been like at that age. And, Betsy noticed, for a girl who sometimes wanted to dress like she was going to a heavy metal concert, her taste in music ran more to Taylor Swift and the latest Taylor Swift wannabe.

* * *

On their first Saturday afternoon together, they used all of that good waffle energy to hike up and down Mount Philo, which took about an hour, and the views of Lake Champlain from the top were picture-postcard perfect. Marisa was miserable. She was not, Betsy discovered, a fan of the great outdoors. So, she took the child to the mall in South Burlington, and there she was in heaven. It was April, and so, among other things, Betsy bought her a windbreaker and blue jeans and a light sweater. Marisa gravitated to attire that was black and designed to make grown-ups uncomfortable. Betsy was able to steer her away from most of it, especially the black T-shirts and hoodies with skulls on them, but she caved when Marisa saw a black sundress she liked, even though it was meant for a young woman. It might have been inappropriate on Marisa, but Betsy took comfort from the idea that at least it didn't suggest she was a roadie for Cannibal Corpse or Black Sabbath.

On Saturday night, the two of them watched television and ate popcorn. Betsy was tired, but she had more confidence than she'd had twelve hours earlier that she could do this. More importantly, she was finding that she liked Marisa's company. The girl monologued through ancient episodes of *Friends,* critiquing Phoebe's fashion choices and Monica's fastidiousness and Chandler's belief that he was very, very funny. Most of the time, her eyes were on the TV set as she spoke, but at one point she turned to Betsy and said, "The six of them would have done okay during the pandemic. They would have been a good bubble."

"I agree," Betsy murmured. She knew the stories of some of the houses where Marisa had lived her short life. Thank God, she'd been in a halfway decent place during quarantine. A lot of foster kids rarely Zoomed in to their classes, and many missed the state-provided free lunch.

"What's so cool is that they made their own family. That's

what the six of them are, you know. I guess that sounds creepy since Rachel and Ross and then Monica and Chandler started hooking up, but they're still like brothers and sisters."

"They are."

"How come you almost never talk about your sister?"

"It's complicated. We're not as close as we once were."

"What does she do?"

"She's sort of an actor."

"Sort of?"

"I mean, she is. But she has a particular specialty."

Betsy felt Marisa staring at her, and the child's eyes grew wide. Betsy was vaguely aware of the sitcom laugh track. "Porn?" Marisa asked, drawing out the single syllable.

"No! Why would you think that?"

"Because she's an actor and you don't talk about her. I mean, I think it would be cool to have a sister. A real sister. And if I had a sister who was an actor? I'd be all blah-blah-blah all the time. Unless she did porn. That would be gross."

Marisa was in her purple lilac pajamas, again minus the bottoms. Betsy was wearing the baggy sweat pants and T-shirt she slept in that time of year.

"What would you like to know about her?" Betsy asked.

Marisa shrugged. "I don't know. Maybe start with why you don't talk about her."

When I knew Las Vegas was where we were going to live, you can bet I googled card counting. (See what I did there? Maybe I am more "verbal" than I think I am.)

I could do it, if I wanted. Memorization on the fly. Super easy. The problem was the law. Thirteen-year-olds can't gamble.

Which makes sense.

Still, I could do it. It's not as easy as cracking a password. But it's very doable.

CHAPTER FIVE

Crissy

He had introduced himself as Gene, but he was Yevgeny in my mind and that was what I began calling him. I liked the phonetics of Yevgeny, the inherent mystery that came with the name. I imagined him a tragic character from a pre–Soviet Union Russia. An associate of Dr. Zhivago, perhaps. An aristocrat from a Chekhov short story.

I brought him to the Tower of London pub, the closest thing the BP had to serious posh. He hadn't planned on ordering a bottle of champagne, but I had asked for a glass and so he jumped in and ordered a bottle of Dom Pérignon that cost three hundred dollars and change. (Even the Tower didn't sell many three-hundred-dollar bottles of bubbly, and so I'm sure the bartender supposed my new friend had just won big. Or, perhaps, that he had no idea what a bottle of Dom Pérignon cost.) Then he ordered himself a Macallan straight up that was going to cost him another thirty.

"Not vodka?" I asked.

"No. I boycotted vodka when Russia attacked Ukraine, like lots of Americans, and haven't gone back."

"Well, I would have been fine with whatever champagne Clifford had popped," I told him.

"Clifford?"

I motioned at the bartender.

"Ah, of course. You really do know every bartender here. You weren't making a joke."

"So, am I a barfly or a drunk?"

He put up his hands, as if pleading his innocence. "Neither! You don't seem like a drunk at all. Or a barfly. You said yourself, you work here—at the casino—so I shouldn't have been surprised that you knew him."

"I wasn't insulted. Just giving you a hard time. You said your last name is Orlov?"

"I did."

"What do you do?"

He stared into the burnt sienna of the drink. God, it was beautiful, I thought. So much prettier than champagne. Then he looked into my eyes and said, "We always ask that question when we meet someone. We ask if they have children or they're married or divorced. We ask what they do. But do you know what we never ask?"

It could have been a straight line, and I had to restrain myself from answering, *Do you do meth? Were you at the Capitol last year on January 6? Do you live in a van?* Instead, I waited.

"If they're content. If they're at peace. If they make other people happy."

I smiled at his sincerity. Then I took a sip of my champagne, almost emptying the flute before responding. "Okay, my answers: Yes. No. And I have no idea. Too caustic?"

"By half."

"But I do entertain people," I went on. "I make them realize that, at the very least, they're not about to die in a cataclysmic car accident in a Paris tunnel. And, you, Mr. Orlov?"

"Yes, yes, and I certainly try."

"Good. Now will you tell me what you do?"

He reached into a front pocket of his blazer and handed me a business card, thick black cardboard with gold lettering. Below his name and vitals were the letters GEI.

"What's GEI?"

"Global Economic Initiatives. We're an investment conglomerate with assets around the globe. Metals. Energy. Telecommunications. Banks. A couple of power plants."

"Oh, my God. Am I drinking with an honest-to-God American oligarch?"

"You are drinking with an investor who works hard and got some lucky breaks. A self-made man. I'm no fan of kleptocracies."

"What do you do for GEI? Do you run metals or banks? Or power plants?"

"Little of this, little of that. Manage how the assets work together, look at our compliance issues around the world."

"Where do you live?"

"Manhattan. Mostly."

"You have a dacha, I suppose."

"A place in Montauk." He shook his head. "You just love the idea that my first name is Yevgeny and I was born in Volgograd."

"If it would make you more comfortable, I will stop making jokes like that."

"I have a thick skin."

"But I will dial it down."

"Thank you."

"And *compliance* might sound like a euphemism for waterboarding, but it must be rather lucrative."

"I make sure our initiatives comply with the regulations in whichever nations we're working. Very legalistic stuff. And, yes, it's ethics, so some people find it boring. I don't."

"Why in God's name are you in Las Vegas? We are the least ethical and least compliant city on the planet."

"Not true. There are Sodoms and Gomorrahs in this world that make Las Vegas seem tame."

The champagne was extraordinary. There was a difference between the house stuff the casino served and this bottle. I emptied my glass and was about to refill it. But, as if he could read my mind, he had the bottle by the neck and was pouring.

"So, why are you here?" I pressed.

"An international conference on management and security. Information security. Network security."

"Here? Usually the only conferences the BP gets are Nevada dentists."

"Yup, here. These conferences have been a lot smaller post-pandemic, and many of the organization's members now join virtually. Not me. I still attend in person. But the organizers went with a . . . a lower-cost casino option. And, to be honest, a lot of us chose to stay at other resorts. I'm at the Venetian."

"Of course you are," I said. The Venetian had a clientele that didn't flinch at seven- and eight-hundred-dollar suites. "Why were you at the BP so late?"

"I told you. I wanted to see your show."

"But . . . why?"

"You sound incredulous."

"I am. You don't seem like my usual crowd."

"The truth?"

"Please."

"I once met Prince Harry."

"Are you serious?"

"I am."

"Were you with him at Eton?" I asked. Perhaps he was younger than he looked. Maybe he was late thirties, not midforties.

"Halo Trust. They clean up land mines in what once were war zones. Harry's a benefactor. We met at a Halo event."

"That was an issue that mattered to his mum."

"Indeed."

I had met people before who knew members of the royal family or their hangers-on, and it always left me feeling a tad ashamed. I was exploiting the mother of a man this fellow had met.

"How well do you and Harry know each other?"

"Not well. We've been in the same room together twice—and both times, it was a very big room."

I was relieved, but didn't say so.

"Anyway, I saw the video billboards for your show, and decided to go. I was just too late tonight."

"So, you travel a lot."

"I do. I spend most of my life on the road. I'm either at conferences or inspecting one of our projects or meeting with investors or government officials somewhere."

"And that's a thing? A network security conference?"

"It is. In this case, the organization hosting it helps corporations be grown-ups and do the right thing—while protecting their assets."

"You're all just making the world a better place." I was pulling his leg, but he nodded as if I had meant every word.

"I hope so," he said.

"My sister used to help troubled"—I corrected myself—"teens in trouble do that. Do the right thing." Bringing up my sister was a reflex since she was on the brain and I seemed to be speaking with a corporate do-gooder, if that wasn't an oxymoron. But I wasn't about to go further: I sure as hell wasn't about to unleash the buzzkill of all buzzkills, by sharing the titbit that my sister was, in fact, often impulsive and irresponsible and now, it seemed, doing what I wanted least in the world, which was parachuting back into my life. At least not yet. Maybe I would in a few hours if Yevgeny and I were still together. Already I was feeling the champagne doing its job.

"What does she do? Social work?"

"Bingo. She used to work with teenage kids who were spiraling, either because of drugs or mental illness or because their families are falling apart."

"Abuse?"

"Often a part of the equation. Learning disabilities, too. It runs the gamut. She can be proper chuffed about what she does. What she did."

"Chuffed?"

I gave him another of my Diana smiles. "Chuffed is pride. But too much so. British expression."

"And now she's stopped?"

"Yes," I said, and I left it at that. "Meanwhile, I sing Petula Clark, a little Dusty Springfield, and I quote Princess Diana. Now that, thank you very much, is how to make the world a better place—especially since some of my audience just lost next month's car payment or rent playing blackjack, or just frittered away their Social Security check at the slots." It may have been the alcohol, and it may have been the idea that he had a job that demanded international travel. But a question came to me. "I wonder: are you a spy? Is all this overseas investment and network security bullshit just a cover?"

He didn't deny it. Instead he took the second flute that the bartender had brought us along with the bottle, and for the first time poured some of the champagne into it. He took a sip and said, "You think I'm with the CIA?"

"Or the KGB."

"The KGB is new and improved. Now it's the FSB."

"Fine. Your cover is GEI: Global Whatever. You travel around the world under the cover of this compliance nonsense—"

"And surveying our assets."

"And surveying your assets, and you go to Las Vegas—"

"Look, I have two homes. Not a boast, because I already told you that when you asked. I could own three, if I wanted. Working for the FBI or the CIA is a terrible way to get rich. Also? It sounds dangerous. I enjoy life too much."

"Where is your apartment in Manhattan? I lived in Queens when I was in New York."

"Murray Hill. It's a nice building and I have nice views to the south and west—"

"So, it's a spectacular corner apartment."

"The east, too. But it's a slender building."

"Sure. That makes your apartment that has views in three directions less impressive. How many bedrooms?"

He paused, clearly unsure about the message he was about to send. "Four."

"Four? And it's just you?"

"Not even a cat."

"Why does a single man have a four-bedroom apartment?"

"Because he's an optimist and hopes someday to have a family."

"You like rattling around in all that space?"

"Right now? I like it best because it's near the tunnel, so it's that much easier to get to JFK. And here's a confession for you: yes, I do travel a lot, but I also eat lots of 'Hello, Fresh' and have bad Indian food delivered to my building when I'm there."

"I notice you haven't categorically denied being a spy. You keep implying you're not, but you haven't come right out and said, 'Crissy, you're mad. I'm not a spy.' "

"If I were a spy and told you, I'd have to kill you. Isn't that the rule?" Then he placed his hand atop mine on my lap, and for a moment I was surprised I did nothing. Was I just being sluggish? But then I realized I liked it—his hand on mine. I enjoyed its carnal proximity to my thigh, and I felt its extra weight through the thin silk of my dress like a hot, steaming towel. He looked into my eyes and said, "I told you: the questions we should ask—the important ones—are about contentment. That, Crissy Dowling, is the meaning of life."

* * *

I awoke with sunlight sluicing through the crack in the curtains, sat up in bed, and watched this Yevgeny Orlov sleep. He was on his side, one arm above the sheet, his face buried in his pillow. I had noticed last night when he was atop me that he had serious biceps, and even now—not tensed—I could see the taut musculature. I looked at his shoulder and clavicle, remarkably hairless, and wondered if it was genetic or he waxed his back. Did spies do that? I didn't care which, but I did like it. I've never felt guilt when I sleep with a fellow I've just met, and I've never, since moving to Vegas, had to sally forth into a walk of shame after a one-night stand the next morning. (Not even with the senator.) After all, we're usually in my suite. I find wantonness rather sporty, and I know well that life is short. We're told that on our deathbeds, no one ever says, "I wish I'd worked more." Well, likewise, I rather doubt anyone says, "I wish I hadn't had so damn much sex."

I glanced at the bedside clock, did the time zone math in my mind, and imagined my sister and her daughter packing up their apartment in Burlington to move here. The thought left me dumbstruck.

It was midmorning and I supposed Yevgeny usually had been up for a while by now. After all, he had a real job with real hours. I decided to wake him by reaching my arm around his chest and nuzzling his ear. I might have reached my arm lower, but I had no idea what text messages or emails were waiting for me on my phone, and what today was going to bring. I knew that I had a two fifteen with Artie Morley, and the fact I had not a clue why he wanted to see me left me anxious. I needed to get moving, and send Yevgeny . . . wherever. Even after a bottle of champagne, I'd refrained from telling him the rather tawdry details of my sister's and my relationship.

I sighed. I wondered what he would do at his conference this morning or afternoon. Speeches? Workshops? Sessions? Did he have meetings of some sort?

As much as I wanted him gone from my bed, I hoped this wasn't going to be just another of my one-nighters. I fancied him. He'd said he was going to come watch my show tonight. I hoped that wasn't mere prattle to get me to the bar and then into the sack, and he really would.

He smiled when he felt my lips on his ear, my mouth inches from his, and he turned his head toward me. He opened his eyes.

"Good morning," he murmured.

"Good morning," I said.

"This is early for you. I can tell."

"You know what time it is?"

"I peeked at the clock." He rolled over and tried to kiss me, but I shook my head. "I don't care about morning breath," he said.

"I don't, either. But I have things to do."

He pecked at my lips anyway. "I'm sure your meeting this afternoon is nothing. No reason to be worried."

"Thank you."

"But this is still your polite way of kicking me out."

"It is."

He climbed from under the sheets and stood there for a moment surveying the room.

"You really do have the ass of an angel," I told him, both because he did and because anyone who either had a rear like that naturally or worked out with such evident diligence deserved the positive reinforcement. Also, I felt bad that I was evicting him.

"So do you," he told me, as he climbed into a pair of black boxers that were draped on one of the two chairs in my little reading nook. (In truth, never once had I read there. Never once had I even sat in either chair. I read in bed and I read in the bath and I read in my cabana, but I would have to have been a genetic royal to sit and read in an armchair. One time, my senator—John—had sat in one when he took a phone call from the Capitol, but that was the only time I could recall someone seated in them. The chairs' sole function was as stands for discarded clothing and my room service trays when I was finished.) "I have a question," he said. "Will I see you before tonight's show?"

There was my answer. I was pleased.

"No."

"Will I see you after it?"

"Second show? Is that the one you're going to see?"

He nodded.

"Then yes."

"Good." He started to button his shirt and went to the window, pulling open the drapes.

"I'm sure you have a much better view from your room at the Venetian," I murmured apologetically.

"Nothing wrong with a view of a swimming pool."

"And a parking lot." I was embarrassed, which was stupid. But I wished I had a room that faced the strip. When I strolled past the A-list casinos on my nights off, I never grew tired of the marquees or the lurid gaudiness of the hotel lights, the great concatenation of color created by millions of bulbs, blinking, neon, scrolling. "What are your plans today at the conference?" I asked him.

"I'm going to a panel at two. And I have a meeting with a staffer for a member of your congressional delegation."

I perked up. "Senator? Representative?"

"Congressperson. Erika Schweiker."

I was both relieved and unnerved. Erika Schweiker was a far-right madwoman. Our senators were both moderate Democrats, including my former paramour, John Aldred. So were three of four congressional representatives. But then there was Erika, our fourth, one of the two who represented Las Vegas. Aldred was defending his Senate seat against her that November, and the polls suggested it was going to be close. So, although I was calmed by the idea that there was no strange coincidence of a new lover meeting with a staffer for an old one, I was unsettled by the notion he was seeing someone who worked with Schweiker.

"Why?"

"Why am I meeting with someone in her office?"

"Uh-huh."

"Banking regulations," he answered.

"Can you tell me more?"

"I could, but you would fall back to sleep. I would, too."

He was being evasive. I could press, but it was none of my business. I didn't know him well enough.

"I'd ask you to wander around the conference with me, but it would be less interesting than anything Princess Diana does."

"And, alas, I am tied up during that panel you're going to attend."

"But not in a good way." I heard a hint of playful lecherousness in his voice. He was gazing out the window and fastening his cufflinks.

"No. Not in a good way," I replied simply.

When he was gone, I went to my phone and scanned the news. I saw that my senator and ex-squeeze had a local campaign rally scheduled that day. I would not be going. I saw there was turmoil in Europe, another dire climate change study, and crypto was expected to bounce back within weeks.

As if on cue, a text arrived from my sister—though it had nothing to do with Futurium. It was a picture of Marisa. There she was, my niece. She looked older than thirteen, but mostly because she was wearing seriously goth black eyeliner and a shade of lipstick that could only be called Harlot Red. She had auburn hair that was considerably lighter than the creosote that was Betsy's and my natural color, and eyes that were brown velvet saucers. She had eyelashes I would have killed for. She was a pretty kid, but she was wearing a studded dog-collar choker and a vintage Sex Pistols T-shirt.

I think you'll like her.

That's what Betsy had texted with the photo.

And so I called room service and ordered a salted caramel sundae sent to the suite—it came with a warm chocolate chip cookie the size of a salad plate—asking them to bring it in thirty minutes so I would have time to shower and get dressed. It wasn't breakfast fare, but I didn't care. I would eat every bite of the dessert, scraping my spoon along the plate for the remnants of the sauce or using that cookie like a sponge, staring out my window at the pool and the corner with my cabana. Then—this morning, anyway—I would adjourn to my bathroom and hover on my knees for a long, anticipatory moment before the suite's black toilet, two of my fingers poised like a small baton before my mouth. When I was finished, I would curl up between the toilet and the bath, feeling both better and worse, focusing on the chessboard-like marble floor, and tell myself that I was mindful. I wasn't, not at all. But it was a running joke inside my head, and it always took me a few minutes after a purge to lower the temperature on my self-hatred and climb to my feet, wash my face and hands—God, those two fingers—and Febreze the room so that by the time I left for my cabana at the pool or wherever I was going that day, I could pretend it had all been just another bad dream.

* * *

I arrived in the waiting room outside the suite where Richie and Artie Morley kept their offices at two. It was in the wing with the count room, so there always were guards, but today I also saw a woman I knew from security standing watch outside Artie's office. She was wearing an earpiece, and her handgun was in a shoulder holster beneath her Buckingham Palace blazer. The doors to both brothers' offices were shut, and I supposed Richie's office was empty. At precisely two fifteen, Mary Gifford, the woman who was the gatekeeper for both Morley brothers and had been at the BP since before either of them or I had graced the casino, escorted me into Artie's office. While I'd waited in reception, she'd told me that Eddie Cantone was behind the door, too. That alarmed me further. Eddie was a throwback to another era. He was easily seventy but had no plans to retire that I was aware of. He knew every act on the strip, and when he spoke, he sometimes ran his fingers through his beautiful hair plugs, now as white as his perfect teeth. He was sitting on the couch against the wall opposite Artie's desk, his rimless eyeglasses in his hands. Both men stood when I entered the office, and Artie motioned for me to sit beside Eddie, and then he pulled up a chair before the couch so we were all seated together. The walls were paneled with fake mahogany, and drapes were drawn across the two wide windows, helping to keep at bay the scorching afternoon—and spare us all a view of the gangly scrub oaks that were the BP's idea of parking-lot landscaping. But the rug was plush, a Persian the colors of ripe blueberries and merlot, and his office had a wrought-iron ceiling fixture: a branding iron that, prior to being repurposed, could have been used to emboss the logo "BP" on whatever the Morleys wanted.

Artie leaned forward, his elbows on his knees and his hands clasped in what could have been mistaken for prayer. I considered remarking on how ominous this all felt to me, but Artie had just lost his brother and whatever fretfulness and disquiet marked his soul likely dwarfed mine. So, I showed uncharacteristic restraint. Instead I asked how he was doing, given Richie's death. And instantly everything changed.

"My brother didn't kill himself," he said, and he let that settle. Eddie was nodding.

"You think he was murdered?" I asked. It sure as hell didn't sound like it could have been an accident.

"I don't think it. I know it."

"Did the police tell you something?"

"The police told me nothing. They don't believe me. They claim they have no evidence it was anything but a suicide."

Eddie was sipping a club soda. Mary had asked if I'd wanted anything when I arrived, but I had passed. Now my mouth was dry. "Are you suggesting they're inept or there's a coverup?"

"First of all, I would have known if he was so depressed he was ready to shoot himself. He wasn't."

One article I'd read that morning, after Yevgeny had left, suggested that the BP's fiscal fortunes were grim, and that was a possible motivation for the suicide. The BP was one of the city's few remaining "family-owned" casinos, so the reporter was alleging more than she was proving. She didn't have annual reports, but she had an unnamed source—a banker—who suggested bankruptcy was a possibility. I thought it would be impolitic to bring that up, so I didn't. Instead, I asked, "Do you have any idea who might have wanted to hurt him?"

Eddie chuckled, but it was morose. "This town will eat its own when it's hungry," he said.

Artie nodded. "Eddie's right."

"So . . . who?"

Instead of answering, he said, "They want to kill me, too. And they'll try. I haven't been home since Richie was executed. Too risky. People are bringing me my clothes and what I need. This casino is now my fortress. It will be here that I make my last stand."

"It won't be your last stand," said Eddie.

Artie stared at him with a thin-lipped smile. "Eddie, I love you. You're the sort of gold-medal bullshitter who keeps this neon cow town from drying up like a turtle without a pond."

"You'll be okay. I promise."

"Honestly: you like my odds?"

"You're the house, Artie. In the end, the house always wins."

"Thank you," he said, though it was clear he wasn't convinced. He turned to me. "So, Crissy."

I waited.

"Two new pals of mine were in the showroom last night to see Diana. They loved it," he told me.

"I'm glad."

"You look relieved."

"I'd say I'm rather in shock. You just told me your brother was murdered, and now you think someone wants to—what's the Vegas colloquialism?—whack you next," I admitted.

"That's not just a Vegas expression," Eddie corrected me.

"I know it's a good show," I went on. "I'm glad your friends enjoyed it, Artie. But I wasn't sure why you summoned me, and this is all a lot to absorb."

"Why did you think I called you in?"

On the spur of the moment, I decided to admit the angst I

had been feeling. "The casino CFO had just died and so I was expecting the worst."

"Which would be what?" Artie asked.

I looked at both men. *Canceling my residency,* I would have said, if I were honest, but Artie was grieving and even I'm not that selfish. "Some sort of bad news about the casino's future," I murmured instead.

"Well, no one's canceling your residency," Eddie said, as if he had read my mind.

"But we need you to do us a favor. To do me a favor," Artie added.

"Of course. Anything," I told him. I was comforted by the news my show was safe, but still reeling from the idea that the man before me feared his brother had been murdered and he was next.

"You're no longer in touch with Senator Aldred, correct?"

"Correct," I said.

"Think he's going to win in November?"

"I hope so. He's a good man."

"I agree. John Aldred has always been on the up and up with us. He's no John Kennedy."

I knew the reference: lots of the gaming world's "pioneers" never forgave the president. Kennedy, when he was a mere senator in the late 1950s, was friends with Frank Sinatra and, thus, Sam Giancana, the Chicago mob boss. Through the Sands Casino, Frank and Sam and their associates poured money into Kennedy's presidential campaign in 1960. Allegedly, Giancana and the president even shared the same mistress, Judith Exner—though not even allegedly on the same nights—and when Kennedy was in the White House, she'd pass messages between the two men. Ah, but eventually Kennedy would place his political future before his friendship with Frank, and put him, and Las Vegas, in the rearview mirror. He'd even allow his kid brother, Bobby, to threaten the power brokers on the strip and the gangsters behind them from his perch as attorney general. (In the end, he stopped his brother from raiding the casinos, but a Vegas grudge runs deep.)

"And, let's face it," I said, "the alternative to John this November brings less to the world than a urinal cake."

Eddie chuckled, but Artie only nodded. "Not a fan of Erika Schweiker?"

"I'm not."

"Well, the good news is that you're a good actor."

I smiled politely, but said nothing.

"Look, I want to keep my casino," Artie continued, "which is in your interests, too, Crissy. They killed my brother because the two of us wouldn't sell the Buckingham Palace—especially not for the bottom-feeder price they wanted to pay. They sent me a message when they killed Richie, but I'm not surrendering. Richie wouldn't want that, and I sure as hell don't."

He stood up and went to his desk, where he retrieved a piece of scrap paper. He handed it to me. It was a phone number.

"We're doing this old school so there's no text between us about this. No sharing a contact that can be traced," he explained. "This is Erika Schweiker's personal cell. That favor? Call her—please—and keep calling until she picks up. Do not leave a message."

"This sounds a little sketchy," I said carefully.

"Politics and gaming have always been a little sketchy."

"Still," I said, "I'm not sure I'm altogether comfortable with—"

"And when you reach her," Artie plowed ahead, ignoring me, "which you will, eventually, tell her who you are and that you have some dirt on the senator. Invite her to the second show one night and tell her she should come backstage afterwards, and you'll give it to her—the dirt."

This was a disloyalty I had not anticipated, and I was aghast and told them. "No. I can't betray John Aldred. I'm sorry, but we parted amicably. Also, his moral compass is quite sound. I can't believe he's done something illegal or debauched."

"You're right."

"Then, what, you've concocted something fake?" I asked, still staggered by this turn.

"Nope. Hear us out. Erika will pressure you. Try to get you to tell her what the dirt is on the phone—without meeting. Pretend you're a woman scorned and you have to give it to her in person. Insist it's something you have to hand over. Something physical." Artie sat down now, twisting the massive gold ring on his pinky. There was a crest on it I couldn't decipher. "But you're not going to give her anything, because there's nothing to give her. You won't even be in your dressing room when she and whatever muscle she brings knock on your door."

"Where will I be?"

"After the show, you'll go back to your suite."

"Who will be in my dressing room?"

"You don't need to know," said Eddie.

"You don't," agreed Artie. "If the point of this was just dirt we had on Aldred, we could turn it over to her ten thousand ways. We wouldn't need you. But that's not the point. The point is to get Erika in a room where we can . . . explain things to her. Tell her to tell her people the casino is not for sale and to back the fuck off."

"Her people."

"Some of her . . . allies. Benefactors."

"Donors?"

"Sure. Call 'em that."

"So, I'm bait?"

"You're not bait," Eddie said, his tone closer to rebuke than reassurance. "Bait gets eaten."

"You're a lure," said Artie.

"Does she even know that John and I had a . . . a fling?"

"Yes."

"I really don't want to do this, Artie. Forgive me, but no."

"That's your answer?"

"What about the police? Why can't you—"

"I told you, the police aren't taking this seriously. Either they honestly don't believe my brother was murdered, or they've been bought."

"Look," said Eddie, and I realized that he was the heavy in their good cop/bad cop dance. "If they get the casino, you're out the door. That's the fact. You're done, you're gone. All we're asking is that you get Schweiker—who is a terrible human being and an idiot—to your dressing room. We'll do the rest."

"Are you planning to hurt her?"

"Of course not! Though it sure would be tempting," said Eddie, and Artie added quickly, stepping on the words of his entertainment director, "They're the ones who are the criminals, Crissy. They're the ones who killed my brother. But, I can assure you, no one is going to hurt her. I got some people who will just make it clear she needs to tell her friends to find a different casino."

I nodded, taking all of this in. "Can you promise me that this won't, in some way, wound or embarrass John?"

"My God, it will help him. You'll be helping to snuff Erika Schweiker as a political threat. You do this and you're doing three things. You're protecting John Aldred. You're saving this casino. And you're covering your ass."

"And if I don't," I murmured, thinking aloud, "John may not get reelected, you lose the casino, and I'm unemployed. Is that your point?"

"Jesus Christ, Crissy, yes," Eddie told me. "That's *our* point."

Outside the windows, I heard the bleating of a delivery truck in reverse. The Morleys' offices were near the back doors to the casino kitchens.

"So?" Artie asked. "Whose side are you on?"

"And how much do you like the idea of unemployment?" Eddie added, his eyes as cool as a lion's appraising a solitary gazelle.

I looked at the paper in my lap. "When should I call?"

"What about now?" Artie suggested. "There's no time like the present."

* * *

When I recall my private moments with the senator, I think often of this: a night when we were alone in my dressing room when he was separated from his wife and we had been seeing each other clandestinely a month. He was seated on the couch, his feet on the coffee table, his impeccably polished wingtips on the floor. He had loosened his tie and was watching me take off my makeup after the second show. He was tired because he had been in the Capitol that day and flown west. I was gobsmacked that he had come to see the show yet again, because he was exhausted. I knew how hard he worked and the committees he was on. The next day he would be seeing his children and the woman from whom he was estranged.

He said, "One of my staffers gave me a Diana quote today: 'I lead from the heart. Not the head.' "

"Why in the name of God were you soliciting Diana quotes? Aren't we a state secret?"

"The U.S. government has many levels of secrecy," he chuckled.

"But why? Does he—"

"No, he doesn't know about us. I asked for Diana quotes because, after seeing your show, I thought she might have something to say about humanitarianism for a speech I'm giving to a bunch of NGOs. Anyway, that quote stuck with me."

"Do you think I should be using it?"

"That's up to you. But it made me realize there are dozens of reasons why I love what you do onstage," he said, his tone growing reflective.

"Thank you."

"Do you know which one is paramount?"

I was blotting my eyelids with a cotton ball. With my one open eye, I saw the intensity of his gaze, tired as he was.

"You reveal more of yourself as Diana onstage than you do as Crissy Dowling offstage. Under the lights out there, in costume, you lead from the heart. In here?"

"In here, I'm an enigma," I said, answering his question before he could. I was being silly, of course, but he didn't smile.

"You are. That's my point. You only let down your guard when you're Diana. That's where you put whatever pain there is in your life."

"My life is pretty painless."

"That's not true. No one's is."

I tossed the cotton ball in the wastebasket. "Is there something you're not telling me?" I asked.

He pressed himself to his feet and came to the vanity. He leaned over and took my face in his hands and kissed me. Then he smiled and said, "Nope. But someday I will pierce that irreverence you wear like armor."

He never did. But when he was gazing at me that night, I saw in that kind and august face—those movie star eyes and that movie star hair—that he understood me as well as anyone who had ever come before him.

Betsy was always worried about what she could give me. She didn't grow up rich, but she didn't really know poor—I mean crazy poor. So poor you eat the dollar store mac 'n cheese that comes in the box, not even the stuff Kraft makes, because the Kraft version costs twenty or thirty cents more.

CHAPTER SIX

Betsy

Betsy hadn't viewed herself as underprivileged or deprived when she and Crissy were growing up, but it was only when she went to college in Massachusetts—on a scholarship and with substantial student loans—that she understood how far from rich they were. In rural Vermont, the monied were discreet. The most expensive car anyone dared to drive in their village without looking ridiculous was a Volvo. Betsy never saw a Mercedes up close until her first year of college, and that was when her roommate's parents picked the two of them up in a silver Benz to take them to dinner.

Their house was a nineteenth-century Victorian in the center of the village, and after their stepfather died, little by little it seemed to wilt like cut flowers in a vase with water grown swampy. It was impossible to keep up with the exterior painting, and the slates on the roof were being chiseled away each winter by ice and snow. The gingerbread trim broke apart and turned into daggers of rotting wood. The screens on the porch were riddled with gashes. The furnace was from the Nixon administration, their mother joked ruefully. (That was not hyperbole. The warranty papers revealed it was from 1973.) The old house was not mute—it creaked and groaned and banged—and amidst its moldering frame could often be heard the skittering of mice and, once in a while, the clawing of squirrels.

Betsy understood that money was tight. Crissy did, too. But they supposed it was tight for everyone. Their mother, a widow, was a high school history teacher.

That changed when they went to college. Their friends had nicer clothes, real jewelry, and second homes in places like Nantucket or an apartment they'd call their family's pied-à-terre in Manhattan or Beacon Hill. Crissy started college a year before Betsy, and she was in New York City at Tisch—again, some scholarship and lots of debt—and Betsy would never forget the things Crissy shared with her when she came home for Thanksgiving during her first year there. When they were alone, Crissy regaled her with the lives of the rich and famous, and the things—physical things—they took for granted. A tiny Marc Jacobs clutch that cost five hundred dollars. Alexander McQueen heels, works of art that would deform your toes for two grand. Gucci cat's-eye sunglasses that cost four digits. The sisters never discussed these things in front of their mother, because they revered her and never wanted her to feel the pain of what she couldn't give them.

Betsy came to understand that her childhood was one of spectacular privilege compared to many of the kids she counseled as an adult. Certainly it was compared to Marisa's—at least financially. But she knew also the secrets and rot that festered in the Dowling house that had nothing to do with the bricks and mortar and horsehair plaster, and wondered if they were as fetid as the things Marisa never shared. She supposed she would learn over time.

Regardless, she wanted Marisa to have a life that transcended a second bedroom in a house at the edge of the UVM campus. Betsy wanted more for her, and she wanted more for herself.

Which, of course, was where the event cascade began. She'd look back and use that expression: event cascade. The chain that leads an overcrowded passenger ferry to capsize in a storm and take hundreds of people to the bottom of the harbor. She grew enamored of the money that seemed there for the taking if she welcomed the embrace of Frankie Limback and his friends from California and West Palm Beach, and opened herself up to a man with a slight dad paunch but a wallet—the digital one as well as the thick leather one—that seemed a bottomless font of coinage and currency. Yes, she was involving herself in things that, even when her judgment was faltering and she was most out of control as a teenager, she would have viewed as suspect. Yes, there were his sphinxlike business interests—whatever his old bank did in the past and his crypto company did now. Of course, she would tell herself, it wasn't *his* bank or *his* crypto company. He was just a money manager and then some sort of crypto manager. Besides, she barely understood the business. Any of it.

But then, not long after the two of them arrived in Las Vegas, they took Marisa.

And by "they," she sure as hell didn't mean the state's social services.

* * *

Just before they moved to Nevada, Betsy asked Frankie why there were no cryptocurrencies named Kryptonite. It seemed like a natural. Or Cryptic, since most of the world didn't understand it. Or, perhaps, Cryptococcus, because there was something unnerving about it all, the way one day a coin might be worth fifty thousand dollars, and the next almost nothing.

They were having lunch outdoors at a sandwich place in downtown Burlington, making plans, months after he and his wife had separated. It was one of those days when, together, they found everything funny, and they were laughing and holding hands across the table. Marisa was still in school, though she only had a week left until summer vacation. Frankie looked at her earnestly across the wrought-iron table and said, "I understand why people find cryptocurrency so mysterious. But I'll teach you and soon you'll see the wizard behind the curtain is just a man. A smart man . . . but not a wizard. You're smarter than anyone I know at Futurium, and that includes yours truly."

"I doubt that."

"I promise you, crypto is no more complicated than derivatives or old-fashioned investment banking."

"Well, I don't understand derivatives, either. I once went on a date with another guy who was in banking—"

"I'm not your first?" he joked. "Your taste in men is kinda troubling."

It was. At least until now, she thought. "No, you're not the first. But he was a lot younger than you," she teased him.

"Okay, now that hurts."

"He tried explaining derivatives to me. I didn't understand any of it—not even something like shorting the market—and I never saw him again."

"You stopped going out with him because you didn't understand derivatives?" Frankie asked.

"There was more to it than that. I was just making a point."

"Futurium's expanding and Vegas will be a part of it," he said. "The money will be insane. It will make that guy's faith in derivatives look like he was planning to retire on the interest from a checking account."

Betsy picked at her salad, unable to look at him. It was a toxic fusion of embarrassment and shame: she actually knew how much interest she had earned on her checking account the previous month. Nine cents. She imagined that her mother had known every month, too.

* * *

"My God, you and Crissy look alike," Frankie said. He was scrolling through her sister's website on an iPad as he sat across from her desk in her office at the counseling service in Vermont. He was slouching like most of her teen clients, sunk into the upright chair as if it were a recliner, his long legs stretched out before him. "Do you look that much like twins in person? How much work has she had done?"

"As in cosmetic surgery?"

He nodded.

"Well, she looks like Diana, right?"

"Exactly like her. It's uncanny."

"So, let me ask you: How much do I look like her? The princess?"

"Definite resemblance. Pretty incredible, actually. If you dyed and styled your hair, you could pass for sure—either as Diana or as your sister."

Over the years, people had observed that she looked like the princess. "Crissy had a nose job. I think that's it."

"You wouldn't need one."

"I don't plan to get one," she chuckled.

He kept burrowing deeper down the rabbit hole that was her sister's life—at least as she and the casino presented it on the website. He'd read aloud a review quote, then follow the link to the review itself, and then watch ten or fifteen seconds of the tribute show's trailer before being seduced by something in the video that would lead him in yet another direction.

"Petula Clark?" he asked. "Who remembers Petula Clark?"

"Crissy's audience does. And we all know the songs, even if we don't recall who sang them."

"Not my kids. Not Marisa."

"Well, my sister's crowd does," Betsy said.

"Touché."

"It's sweet to watch a sea of Q-tips nodding and swaying."

"And Dusty Springfield? And Bonnie Tyler? She does them, too?"

"Uh-huh."

"It's kind of impressive. Most tribute performers in Vegas are one-trick ponies, right? They impersonate one person. Mick Jagger or Frank Sinatra or Diana Ross."

"She's very talented," Betsy agreed. "But she's only Diana. That's the key. She sings songs by other performers because Diana didn't sing. But she sings them as Diana. That's who she sounds like. That's who she is."

"You know, the Sydney Bee Gees don't sound like the real Bee Gees. I heard them when I was in Vegas last month with

Damon and Rory." Damon Ioannidis and Rory O'Hara were other executives at Futurium, but at the time they were still just names to her. Frankie had been to Nevada to meet with a congresswoman on that trip: the crazy woman who still insisted that the 2020 election had been stolen and tweeted photos of her and her children holding assault rifles. She had helped Futurium set up its operations in Nevada, though Betsy still didn't understand why the representative had bothered. Even Betsy knew a crypto company didn't create jobs.

"The real Bee Gees didn't sound like the Bee Gees," she said. "They sounded like the Chi-Lites."

He laughed, a big, hearty guffaw. She liked it when he laughed like that. She liked *making* him laugh like that. Then he looked at her over the tablet, and she could see the approval in his eyes. She couldn't decide whether it was because she knew who the Chi-Lites were or because she had said something snarky, and she knew he liked her more when she had an edge. "I've never heard you sing," he said. "You know, other than along with a song in the car and that one time in the shower. Can you?"

"Yes. But that's my sister's thing. She was always the lead in the high school musicals, and I was always fine with the smaller parts. The way she remembers our childhood, I was this athletic superwoman and she was the actor. And, yes, I was a good athlete. I *am* a good athlete. But my voice is just fine."

"Just fine?"

"Okay. More than just fine."

He pressed Play on the trailer for Crissy's show, and there was her sister's beautiful voice belting out Petula Clark's "Downtown." He paused it. "Now you," he said.

She shook her head. There was no way she was going to play that game.

And yet she did. Not that afternoon and not that night. But she did the next day. It was like a dare.

"You sound a lot like her," he said, when they were ensconced in her bedroom in her apartment and Marisa was in school. She sang as soon as she had climbed back into her underwear, a bit of blissful, postcoital madness. He—her entire audience—was lying on his side in her bed.

"I actually think your voice is better than your sister's. Imagine if you had some training. Imagine if you had a voice coach. If I've learned anything from my time in business, it's this: we all have unbelievable potential. The world is a place you remake in whatever image you damn well want."

She was standing before him. She leaned over and kissed him on the forehead. "I appreciate that sort of faith in oneself," she said. "But I don't think the world is waiting for a thirty-four-year-old ex–social worker from Vermont to make it big on *American Idol.*"

"I understand," he told her, nodding. But she could see that a scheme or a notion was gestating behind his eyes. He viewed himself as an "idea man," using those exact words. *If I don't have an idea by seven in the morning, I'm done for the day and should probably just go play golf.*

"Do you?"

"Sure," he said, but it was half-hearted. Sometimes, it seemed he had limitless faith in her. She'd saved his son, in his eyes. Was there anything she couldn't do?

"I'm really not a singer or an actor."

He pulled her back onto the bed beside him and massaged her shoulders. "For now, anyway," he said, but then added, "besides, you have to learn about Futurium."

She did. She had only the vaguest idea of what it would mean to be an administrative assistant for the company in Las Vegas, but Frankie was confident there would be plenty for her to do. And he was positive they would both love the city and the surreal moonscape that surrounded it.

Positive, he had reassured her. Absolutely—and he used the word as an adjective often when he was excited—fucking positive.

Yeah, I was interested in crypto. I thought it was cool that Betsy's boyfriend was into it. Miners solve problems. It's all computers and math, so I learned all I could.

But I was even more fascinated that Betsy was going to work for Futurium. I mean, I wasn't sure she could balance a paper checkbook.

CHAPTER SEVEN

Crissy

It's easy to look back and say I should have seen this or that coming. All of you reading this are thinking precisely that: *How did Crissy Dowling not know what was happening? I do.* But when you're living in the moment, it's more difficult. When you yourself are in the midst of a hyperobject—the drip-drip-drip death of democracy, your fear of the searing heat from world-destroying mushroom clouds, cryptocurrency—you miss its mass. When you are living in history, you miss the obvious. Think back to February and March of 2020, the start of the pandemic. We had no idea what lay ahead. What was waiting. We were living with a normalcy bias. When we shuttered my show on March 13, 2020—yes, Friday the thirteenth—I thought it would be for two weeks.

Likewise, it's fine to tell me, *Crissy, why in holy hell did you listen to Artie Morley and agree to call Erika Schweiker?* But you weren't there. It was a phone call. I knew it wasn't actually harmless; I'm not daft. I knew there was something slippery going on, I knew that the sinkhole into which I was diving was awash in slime. But I wanted desperately to protect my residency: people do far worse things daily to preserve their power or ensure their jobs are secure. I knew what John Aldred had told me about his peers in the Senate, and their utter hypocrisy when it came to how they voted in the Capitol versus what they honestly believed was the right thing to do. And, I told myself, I was looking out for John—a legitimate good guy—against a fascist bully.

In hindsight, would I have made that call? Those calls?

Yes. Even knowing what I know now, I would do it all—I would do everything—again.

* * *

Diana, Princess of Wales, placed the handheld microphone back into its stand, her rendition of the Petula Clark classic "My Love" complete, and waited for the applause from the packed cabaret to die down. There was a fellow in the front row with a nice face ruined by the toothpick that protruded from his mouth like a fishbone, and a beautiful woman with a silver mane that fell halfway down her back. There was the usual coterie of grandparents from both sides of the pond, because let's not forget: anyone who watched Diana's wedding to Prince Charles was likely well above fifty. Many were well above sixty.

This was my second show, and the crowd was always drunker.

I had called Congresswoman Erika Schweiker twice, not leaving a message either time. She hadn't called back, but even if she hadn't recognized the name "Crissy Dowling" on her missed calls list, by now she or one of her aides had googled me and figured out who I was—and confirmed that I was an ex-lover of her competition for the Senate seat that she craved. And so I had scanned the audience members I could see from the stage to see if she was in the house. She wasn't.

And since I hadn't heard from her, there was no reason not to retreat to my dressing room as usual, especially because I had spotted Yevgeny Orlov seated along the stage-right wall. He was beaming. His presence in the audience—combined with the specter of my sister once more dropping into my life like a bomb, and whatever the hell loomed for the BP and Artie Morley—was making it a wee bit harder than usual to sink into my role. Most nights, it was all muscle memory. Still, I'm a pro (three words I love to say in Las Vegas), and the show was moving along swimmingly.

As even the most enthusiastic people in the audience were

finally dropping their hands back into their laps, I gathered myself and said, my voice a whisper that was amplified by the small mic in my hair, "Yes. My love was softer than a sigh. Was that the problem? There were three of us in the marriage . . . and not in a fun way."

The room laughed, some of it uncomfortable, as usual. I knew the actual Diana quote and always some members of the audience did, too. *Well, there were three of us in this marriage, so it was a bit crowded.*

"And my voice, then, really was softer than a sigh. I say that metaphorically. Because the prince and I had our share of shouting matches. But here is the reality: you cannot win an argument with a prince, even if you are a princess yourself, if the prince is the heir to the throne." I then segued into the story from 1983 when a photographer caught Diana sobbing in front of the Sydney Opera House while Charles—if he noticed her crying, which I considered unlikely—was looking elsewhere. There was a tremendous crowd on that Australian tour, as there was everywhere the prince and princess went in 1983, and I told the audience (transitioning from my winsome Diana voice to my heartbroken one) that I liked to believe that if Ken Lennox, the photographer, had not captured the moment, the nearest onlookers might have supposed she was weeping with joy. "Oh, but other than when I was with one or both of my two boys, there were no moments when I was weeping with joy."

I hadn't seen my robber-baron friend since he had left my suite that morning until I'd spotted him in the audience. When I'd googled him, there were profiles that suggested an almost Jay Gatsby–like ascension: poor little immigrant from the sunken ship that once was the Soviet Union washes ashore in Brighton Beach and, as an adult, becomes an important director at GEI, a company that, good Lord, really did have a portfolio of companies that included banks and power plants.

My second show ended at eleven thirty. I only had to keep it together another half hour. So, as usual, I segued into the story about confronting Camilla Parker Bowles at a dinner party in the late 1980s, and froze as the lights came up stage left, and there was Nigel Ferguson as Charles—old Charles, his hair beneath a flesh-colored skullcap and a thin white-haired wig upon that—saying, "Do you know what my mother's first reaction was when she saw her grandson, William, in the hospital? 'Thank goodness he hasn't got ears like his father.'" As the monologue continued, the audience watched a little breathlessly, wondering whether this would be a moment of devastation or light humor.

I wrote it as light humor, but Nigel always added just the right touch of wistfulness, because, of course, there's nothing about Princess Diana's story that doesn't reek of melancholy, which might be why it is perfect for Las Vegas—a place which, I can tell you firsthand, is secretly the most melancholic place on earth.

* * *

While some tribute shows are designed to have the audience dancing in the aisles, others dig deeper. I hope mine does. They touch a chord of orphic remembrance and remind us who we once were and, sometimes, where we once were: emotionally and literally.

Among the best examples of that might be the show originated by the pair here in Vegas who re-created the Carpenters. I'd seen the show three times, which was two more times than I'd seen any of my other tribute competitors. (I had a reputation among the tribute crowd that I didn't play well in the sandbox—that I wouldn't deign to mingle with the other entertainers. Perhaps. I preferred to view myself as mysterious, not standoffish.) It wasn't merely that the duo's impersonation was impeccable or that "Karen" really could sing or that "Richard" was a spectacular pianist and musician. It wasn't even how much I discovered I loved the Carpenters' music, even though they were recording well before my time.

It was the reaction of the audience. Each time I went, I

watched the crowd, and I listened to what they were whispering to each other between songs or before and after the show. Every Carpenters song was a piercing remembrance for them. When the woman who channeled Karen was singing "We've Only Just Begun," there were people nodding because the ballad was sung by someone at their wedding, and each note catapulted them back to the day they were married. "Goodbye to Love" reminded them of their first heartbreak. "Superstar," a mournful tale of a groupie and the rock star who had clearly used and abused her and now was never coming back, likely resurrected a different recollection for every member of the audience, but every one of those memories was somewhere on the spectrum between outright betrayal and mere unrequited love.

I strove for that with Diana, and the music mattered. I chose my Petula Clark and Dusty Springfield and one key song from Bonnie Tyler with care: it wasn't just the songs, however, or their words; it was what the songs meant to my crowd. The combination of Diana's story and the music I'd added was a time machine. And while everyone's destination was different, they arrived there with, as we like to say, "all the feels."

* * *

Yevgeny looked around my dressing room. I was leaning against my vanity, sipping my postshow herbal tea. He could see himself in the mirror, and he could see the photos that ringed the mirror, most of them hanging on for dear life those days by yellowing strands of Scotch tape. All but one were of Diana alone or the princess with Charles or the queen or her children. The one that was not of Lady Di was an ancient shot of my mother, my stepfather, and Betsy and me sitting on the stone wall in our backyard in Vermont.

"It was fantastic," Yevgeny was saying to me. "Whole show. I loved it. The videos were really moving. And the guy playing Charles? It seemed to me, he was spot-on."

I nodded. The video montages had grown more elaborate every year, and now my choreography occasionally mimicked the real Diana, who would be projected behind me. But the parts that still caused me to shed real tears onstage were when I would turn and watch the videos of William and Harry as boys, no shadow Diana on the wall, and talk about how much joy they brought into my life. I didn't suppose I'd ever have children. Diana was twenty-one years old when she had William. She was, in some ways, still a child herself, and the idea that she was willing to take that on when she did was as laudable as it was pitiable. And yet, from the beginning, she was a lioness of a mum: the nursery was a place of unexpected sanctity for her, which certainly riled some of the royals.

"And you wrote it?"

"Every word."

"It wasn't what I expected," he went on. "I expected it to be sillier."

"There are moments that are pretty damn silly."

"I expected it to be more like a tribute show."

"Sort of like those bands that re-create the Beatles or the Rolling Stones?"

"Exactly," he said. "But it was more like when Bryan Cranston did Lyndon Johnson or Hal Holbrook did Mark Twain."

"You saw them?"

"I saw Cranston as Johnson. Live. I've seen videos of Hal Holbrook as Twain."

"Your life fascinates me. Poor boy from Volgograd makes good. You went to George Mason University, I saw."

"You did your homework. I liked Virginia."

"I'm from Vermont, you're from Volgograd. You went to Virginia, I went to Vegas. That's a lot of *V*'s." I was toying with him because I had learned that George Mason had programs that made it a feeder for the CIA.

"Ah, but there are no *V*'s in Diana Spencer or GEI."

"True," I agreed. "Anyway, I'm not Bryan Cranston or Hal Holbrook."

"Now why would you say that?"

"Fine, I'll be gracious. Thank you."

"So, a drink—once you've changed?"

It was tempting. Head to one of the BP's pubs or take the man straight to my suite. But the idea of Betsy and Marisa, and Artie and Erika—two pairs, unrelated but somehow not—had me agitated. I'd popped my preshow Adderall, which wasn't helping now that the show was over, and I wasn't sure there was enough Valium and cannabis in my goody bag to dial it all the way back.

"I'm thinking about it," I said.

"Okay." A ripple of anxiety crossed his face.

"The problem is, I'm tired," I lied. "I don't know if I have enough juice for my social battery tonight."

"I understand."

"But I want to see you again. There's just a lot going on in my head right now."

"Is that really the truth?"

I nodded. "That's really the truth. Even Diana impersonators in Las Vegas sometimes have—"

"Again, stop demeaning what you do."

"Thank you."

"I return to New York tomorrow."

"Tomorrow," I murmured, repeating the word.

"Your sister still lives in Vermont, right? You must get back east sometimes."

"On occasion," I said, which hadn't been true since Betsy had killed our mother. The funeral had been the last time. I hadn't even returned to see my childhood home one final time before Betsy sold it. And now that my sister was moving here, who knew if I'd ever set foot in the Green Mountains again?

"Add New York City to your next trip. You can stay with me."

"The visits are short," I admitted ruefully. "And I don't get there often."

He folded his arms across his chest. "So, this is it?"

I didn't mean to push him away; I didn't want to push him away. I had pushed away so many people in my life. It's what I did, more times than not. Even John Aldred, when he was ending it, remarked how he wasn't sure he'd ever gotten to know the woman behind the princess. "No. I invited you backstage because I wanted to tell you in person that I hope it isn't. I had fun last night. And whether we had a drink now or not doesn't change the fact that I want to see you again."

"Do you want to talk about whatever that chatter is behind your very pretty eyes?"

Chatter. It was a word used by the royals, but it was also used by intelligence geeks. I had learned that from the senator. One night, he was telling me decidedly nonclassified stories about the history he'd seen in his tenure in Washington, and how often the intel would begin with the word *chatter. There's a lot of chatter right now in Syria.* Or *There was so much chatter before the bombing.* Something about Yevgeny's use of it felt like a sign, and so I went with it. I went to him. Magnate? Spy? I couldn't have cared less. I put my arms around his neck and pulled him into me, kissing him.

When we pulled apart, he asked, "Is that a goodbye kiss? Should I hear Petula Clark in my head?"

"Not at all," I said. "I'm getting a second wind. But, just in case, let's have that drink in my suite. We'll look at our calendars and make a date to see each other again. And—I'm going on the record—I'm going to kick you out and send you back to your hotel before falling asleep. Deal?"

He smiled, and I could see that it was with genuine relief. "Deal," he said, and this time he kissed me.

* * *

In the morning, he was gone. I had stuck to my guns and sent him to his own hotel room before two a.m., which was an uncharacteristically responsible choice on my part, but it made sense for him, too: he had a six a.m. pickup for the drive to the airport and had yet to pack. Still, our two hours together were aces.

I took a long morning bubble bath, which is pretty standard fare for a Las Vegas quasi-diva, but I brought my tablet into the tub—which was black, like my toilet—and learned all I could about cryptocurrency and Futurium, my sister's new employer. The main thing I took away from all that googling was that Futurium was actually the name of the cryptocurrency and the company behind it. The enterprise had offices in Grand Cayman, Phnom Penh, and Las Vegas, though it was unclear whether six or six hundred people worked at each of them. According to one article, a few years ago they'd picked Vegas over Miami, one of the other cities that wanted them, because energy was cheap in Nevada, and the blockchain servers used massive amounts of electricity. The Las Vegas office was west of the strip. I knew the BP didn't yet accept crypto, but I'd heard other casinos were starting down that path.

The whole thing left me baffled, and so my mind wandered to my sister's other big news: the fact she was now a mother.

I didn't speak to many thirteen-year-olds—any, to be precise. When I met my niece, I would be completely out to sea. Not only was she thirteen, she was a thirteen-year-old whose life story would leave most people gutted. *So, Marisa, how many places have you lived? Any idea where the wankers are who first deserted you? How did you wind up adopted by a social worker who was banging the father of one of her clients? How does it feel to have been uprooted like a forest fern and dropped into the stultifying heat of Las Vegas?*

Or I could just ask her about her choice in lipstick. Or go with the obligatory *Cool trainers: where did you get them?* Isn't that what every adult says to every young adult?

I hadn't visited Betsy's Facebook and Instagram pages in months because it made me too sad to have her inside my head, but I went there now, and sure enough, there were photos of her and the girl. There were none of her and the guy she was dating, which made sense since he was in the process of divorcing someone else. But there were Betsy and Marisa eating Ben & Jerry's ice-cream cones in Burlington, mugging for the camera, and there they were at the general store in the village where Betsy and I had grown up. It seemed that Betsy had shown the girl our old house, no doubt regaling her with tales of our childhood and how hard our mother had worked to raise us after her second husband, our stepfather, had died, and all the wonderful things this poor kid had been denied. I think the picture that troubled me the most was one of them from the week before at one of the county fairs that dotted a Vermont August: the child—and she *was* a child—was wearing a crop top that showed more tummy than a tankini, and blue-jean shorts that I feared if she turned around would be cheeky in the worst sense of the word. I'm no royal prude, but this was just plain slatternly. And, of course, the kid had that choker and the black eyeliner and looked every bit a pedophile's wet dream. At every turn, men with dead hearts left girls like that transmogrified—either silenced and benumbed or forever changed into someone else.

Also, she was wearing flip-flops, and the fair was in a field. I shuddered when I thought of how filthy the kid's feet were.

But didn't that mean that my sister was perfect for her? Another disaster in Daisy Dukes? My sister had never been arrested, never charged with a crime, but that was only because she seemed to have a preternatural ability to duck the bullets from the firing ranges she had walked into willingly when we were younger. Our stepfather had died when I was eleven and Betsy was ten, and our mother spent the next seven years trying desperately to prevent Betsy from sabotaging her life. I didn't start purging into toilets until after college, and I had started auditioning in New York, and so I was always the good daughter, the good sister, the good lass. I wasn't the one leaving half-smoked joints in the ashtray of the car, doing mushrooms the night before the SATs, or crashing the car into the back of a manure spreader because I was texting. (Only I knew that Betsy had been texting that moment on a brand-new BlackBerry. And there was no dope in the car that day. And no one was hurt.) And yet she did go to college, and afterwards she did get a master's in social work. There were some dodgy moments, but, in all fairness, she had wound up a largely functional adult.

Until, of course, she killed our mum—though, in truth, she continued to function even after that. How the guilt didn't destroy her was beyond my ken. It would have devastated a normal person.

And still Congresswoman Erika Schweiker hadn't called back. I wondered if I should tell Artie.

By the time I emerged from the tub, it was nearly eleven thirty and Yevgeny had landed at JFK, where it was almost two thirty. He texted me from the car service that was bringing him into the city that he'd slept on the plane and felt great, and reiterated how much he'd enjoyed the show and meeting me. It was rather chivalrous.

I texted him back something far less charming:

> Okay, Mr. Ethics. What do you know about a crypto company called Futurium?

He texted that the town car was approaching the tunnel and he'd call me when he got to his apartment. So, I climbed into a swimsuit and cover-up, and went to my cabana. I couldn't decide which was stranger: my sister being a mother and working for a company whose business I found utterly unfathomable, or two estranged siblings from Vermont winding up in Las Vegas.

When math geeks get number tattoos, they get things like pi—the symbol or the number. And that's cool, because it's like infinity.

When people who aren't math geeks get tattoos with numbers, they get creepy things like 13 or 88 for "Heil Hitler" or 666. (The number 666 isn't as bad as some people think. It's not always the devil. I googled it. There's a whole crowd out there who give it all sorts of angel meanings.)

If I got a tattoo with a number, it would be 5, because I love the commercials for that perfume with 5 in the name. I've never smelled it, but I know it smells awesome. I just know it.

CHAPTER EIGHT

Betsy

She was going to sell her car. (She was going to sell most of her things, which wasn't hard because she hadn't amassed much of value.) And so the last weeks in July and those first weeks in August, now that she had adopted Marisa and made it clear to her that the two of them were in this thing together, they drove all over Vermont. They visited places where Betsy had never been in her life, even though she'd been raised in the Green Mountains. They went to three different county fairs, and eventually, Betsy brought the girl to the village where she had grown up.

The town no longer had an elementary school, and property values had plummeted after it closed. But the older couple who had bought her mother's house were resourceful. (Betsy was her mother's executor, despite her checkered history as an adolescent, because she still lived in Vermont and Crissy had decamped to Las Vegas. Their mother thought it would be simpler to leave her younger child in charge, and it was. Betsy handled it all just fine, though Crissy witnessed her sister's competence mostly through the lawyers.) The new owners had told Betsy at the closing that they were handy, and, clearly, they were. The place looked better to Betsy than it ever had after her stepfather had died, which meant it looked better than it had in a quarter century. (Despite the shadows that lurked in the man's soul, he was house proud.) They had repainted it a beautiful shade of gray: the sky before a thunderstorm. They had had the slate roof repaired and rebricked the top of the chimney. The screens were clean and new on the wraparound the porch, and the flower gardens along the front walkway once more were manicured.

"It was just the four of you in that place?" Marisa asked her, awed by its size.

"Yes. And it was just the three of us after my stepfather died."

"You were ten?"

"Yup. And Crissy was eleven," she said, and she thought (as she did often) about the year and a half that separated them, and how it might have saved her. No, she wouldn't have needed to be saved. Ten was likely old enough to know better. Eleven sure as hell was.

Or should have been.

"How many rooms does it have?"

She counted them in her head. "Twelve," she answered.

"Twelve. For four people. Wow."

Betsy considered knocking on the door and asking the couple who lived there now if the two of them could take a walk through the place. She doubted they would have minded. But it was Saturday. They deserved their privacy. Besides, she wasn't sure she wanted to see the way they had erased her childhood memories or papered over what had been her mother's world. And so she walked Marisa to the general store, which had grown tonier over the years and now sold good wines and high-end craft beers, but still offered homemade brownies and cookies, and she bought snickerdoodles, which they ate by the river across the street. They took photos, which they posted on both of their Facebook pages.

"You said your mom was a history teacher. What did your stepdad do?" Marisa asked.

"He was a reporter. He wrote for a Burlington newspaper."

"What did he write?"

"He covered politics, so he was in Montpelier a lot. At the capitol. But I was pretty young when he"—and here she hesitated—"died."

"Can I read his stories online?"

"I doubt it. Not sure the paper's online catalog goes back that far."

"Do you have any copies?"

She hid her disdain. "No," she said. "If I had found some when I was cleaning out the house after my mom died, I would have kept them. But I didn't," she lied. The falsehood was the idea she would have saved some, because she had discovered folders of clips in a filing cabinet in the attic. She started to read one, but it was a column and there was a headshot beside his byline, and so despite the histrionics of the gesture, she burned it. She burned them all.

"You were in fifth grade when he died. That's not so young."

"I was a lot younger at ten than you were." She considered saying that she had been more innocent, but she wasn't sure that was true. Memory was mist.

"How did he die?" she asked.

"Heart attack." Another lie. She regretted it, because someday Marisa would google the man and learn the truth. She googled everything. Perhaps when Marisa was older and the two of them were settled, she would reveal more of the story. And as the lie settled, her regret dissipated, because today was certainly not the right day to exhume the Dowling corpses.

Meanwhile, Marisa seemed to think about everything Betsy had just told her, chewing a second cookie deliberately. "Do you miss this place?" she asked.

"No."

"Will you miss Vermont when we move?"

"A little. I've only lived here, except for when I was in college in Massachusetts."

"I've *only* lived here."

Betsy turned to her. "Are you worried about Las Vegas?"

The girl stared at the ground. "No. Maybe if Frankie was going to live with us. But he won't be. And—"

"Whoa, you don't need to worry about Frankie. I know you had at least one super creepy foster father, but—"

"Two," she said, holding up a pair of fingers in what most people would have mistaken for a peace sign.

"Two," Betsy agreed, "but Frankie isn't like that. He's a wonderful father to his own children, and—"

"One of them was one of your patients."

She shrugged. "Clients. Not patients. And things happen."

Marisa licked some of the sugar off her fingertips.

"Why do you worry about Frankie?" Betsy pressed. "Has he ever said or done anything that made you feel uncomfortable or unsafe?"

"Nope. And I don't worry about Frankie. Why would I? I just like the idea it's just you and me."

"Good. I like that idea, too." Then she surprised herself by asking, "What do you think of him? Frankie?" She didn't need the girl's approval, but suddenly she was curious.

"He's nice. He's funny. His kids probably aren't wild about him right now. I mean, he's leaving them and moving to Las Vegas. But he takes good care of us."

"You might be right about his own children," she agreed. Of course, she was deserting kids, too. So many teens, she thought, some who were thriving now as young adults and some who weren't going to make it. If anyone had ever asked, she could have named them all, and it was a long list. "Sometimes you have to move for work," she said, acquitting Frankie and, in her mind, convicting herself. "People change jobs. And soon his kids will be going to college. They'd be leaving home anyway. I wouldn't call it desertion."

"Okay," Marisa agreed, though Betsy could tell that she didn't believe that. Then she added, "And I'll say this about him. He must really know how to make money. An investment banker who's now in tight with Futurium? A guy who's going to be there when crypto becomes the coin that people use in Las Vegas? That's cool."

Betsy nodded. Yes, if there was one thing she believed about

Frankie Limback, it was anthropologic: he was an alpha male who was an excellent provider.

* * *

The fairs at the end of August were the ones with the pumpkins that topped two thousand pounds. The ones the size of Volkswagen Beetles. But at a fair in central Vermont earlier in the month, Betsy and Marisa saw one that was fifteen hundred pounds, a massive and gnarly vegetable that had demanded a forklift to be brought into the agriculture barn.

"That would make a lot of pies," Betsy observed.

"It would make zero pies," Marisa corrected her. "That monster is, like, all fertilizer and chemicals."

Betsy looked at the girl, once more surprised by the unexpected things that she knew. "Where did you learn that?"

"Near a place I lived for a while, there was a guy down the road who entered those weird giant vegetable competitions. His pumpkin patch began with lots of pumpkins, but got smaller and smaller as he weeded out the ones that weren't going to win. He told us about all the stuff he fed the ones he was going to keep. The ones that might be giants."

"Kind of like Linus Van Pelt's pumpkin patch and waiting for the Great Pumpkin."

"Who's Linus Whatever?"

It didn't break Betsy's heart that Marisa didn't know who Linus was, but the idea that she'd never seen the Peanuts Halloween special—or, clearly, *A Charlie Brown Christmas*—saddened her.

At all of the fairs, the two of them went on rides that Betsy hadn't gone on in years, some of which left her world spinning, even after they'd exited back onto the grass, and one of which almost had her wanting to fall onto the ground and vomit on her hands and knees. She didn't. But she did wonder, as she had often when she was in her twenties, how her sister—or anyone with bulimia—could do what she did.

They took more pictures for the social networks. Betsy liked the idea that these were photos of a mother and daughter together; she disliked the reality that the child was experiencing all of this with an adult, rather than with a squad of girls on the cusp of adolescence. With friends.

She told herself that Marisa would find her posse in Vegas. She would have friends and they would have money—real or crypto—and neither of them would worry about tomorrow. They were, like Americans for centuries, going west to make their fortune.

And she would be with her sister. Once they had been close; they might be again. Family mattered, even a family as fucked up as hers. Even a family that was down to the siblings.

At one of the county fairs, a deep molten stripe of a sunset between the mountains and the clouds in the distance, they noticed a carny in a black tank top with tattoo sleeves on his arms. He was running a harmless Tilt-a-Whirl, the sort of ride that wouldn't leave Betsy green, and among his tats was a crown and what looked like a family crest or coat of arms with a pair of crossed swords.

"Look, Betsy," Marisa joked. "Maybe that dude is a long-lost member of the British royal family."

"Maybe," Betsy agreed, but she supposed the tattoos were a *Game of Thrones* reference or had a cosplay backstory. He could have been thirty, and he could have been fifty: he was rail thin with a lined face and a ball cap from a Minor League baseball team.

"I met a guy at the Champlain Valley Fair last year who offered to tattoo me," Marisa went on.

"I'm glad you said no."

"How do you know I did?"

"I don't."

"No," the girl said, and she smiled darkly. "You don't."

"So, Marisa . . . do you have a tattoo?"

She shook her head. "No. I'll get one when I'm older and know more what I want."

"That's wise," Betsy told her. She was relieved, but not because she disapproved of ink. She just hated the idea of some criminal pervert at a county fair tattooing an eleven- or twelve-year-old kid.

Marisa approached the carny with the crown on one of his arms, and Betsy trailed after her.

"I like your sleeves," the girl said to him.

"Thanks."

"My aunt is a princess."

The fellow studied her and then Betsy. "Cool," he said. "You two going to ride?"

"Yes," Marisa said. "But there isn't a line, so can I ask you a question?"

"If I say no, you will anyway."

"Yeah. That's true."

"Ask."

"Why do you have a crown on your arm?"

"Because my last name is Crown."

"Seriously?"

"Seriously. I don't make shit up."

"That's all there is to it?"

"Sorry, kid."

"Can I ask you one more?"

Betsy thought that the carny would be exasperated, but he wasn't. He was either very game or very patient. "Sure."

"You didn't believe me when I said my aunt is a princess. Why not?"

"Because you don't look like the type."

"She is, you know. I'm going to meet her in a few days. My aunt is the Princess of Las Vegas."

He looked from Marisa to Betsy, wanting some sort of confirmation. Betsy had never called her sister that before. She'd never thought of her like that before. But Marisa was right. It wasn't merely that Crissy re-created Diana Spencer: it was the way she lived her own life. She kept her distance from the other gig performers in the city as if she were royalty, and retreated during the day to her suite or her poolside cabana at the Buckingham Palace. So, Betsy gave a small shrug, and nodded.

"Well, that's unexpected," he said. "Vegas has a lot of crazy shit, but I didn't know they had an official princess. Maybe she'll knight you."

"I'm a girl, so she can't. Women are dames, not knights."

"How in the world do you know that?" Betsy asked. Once more, she was a little shocked.

"The Internet. When I was googling your sister, I learned about knights and dames. At the Buckingham Palace, the men's bathrooms are for knights and the women's are for dames, which seems pretty stupid in this day and age, since lots of people aren't knights or dames. The hotel either needs nonbinary bathrooms or just bathrooms that anyone can use."

"How much have you been googling her?"

"Not tons. I wanted to get the scoop on the hotel and her act, and why she does what she does."

"Did you figure that out?"

"Nope."

The carny started twirling his finger in a circle and Betsy saw there were people starting to queue up behind them, and so she handed him tickets and they took their seats. Betsy looked at the hills that surrounded them, lush and green, with just a hint of scarlet as some of the first trees started to turn. She kept thinking about how Marisa had distilled what had been for their mother the great question of Crissy's life: why did her older daughter do what she did? Why, of all the things she could have done as an actor, had she chosen to devote her life day after day to raising from the grave a woman who'd died when she herself was in elementary school?

And, of course, Betsy knew. Or suspected she knew. But she was never going to say a thing to their mother.

The closest thing I'd ever seen to the lights of Las Vegas were the county fairs in Vermont. And that's like comparing a baby kitten whose eyes are still closed to a lion that's about to eat you for lunch.

And, here's the thing: I think Betsy felt the same way. She was totally (and I love this word because I'm from Vermont) cowed.

CHAPTER NINE

Crissy

Bud McDonald—Brady McDonald at birth—ran security for the BP and took a special interest in looking out for me at the theater. And so when he came by my cabana that afternoon, I felt a spike of anxiety. He'd been a detective in Boston before deciding he preferred the sun of Las Vegas to the snow and sleet of Massachusetts, and he had a cleft on his chin so deep that he joked to strangers it was a dueling scar. You didn't skim at the BP for all the usual reasons, but the idea that the head of security had helped bust Whitey Bulger certainly kept wayward dealers in line. He sat down in the chaise beside me now, the day after I had met with Artie Morley and Eddie Cantone.

"I have some bad news," he began. "Bad news for you, bad news for me."

I had already sat up and put aside my book. I glanced at my phone, half expecting it to ring, Erika Schweiker choosing this moment to call back. "Okay."

"Artie is dead. I spoke to the police and I expect they'll want to talk to you, too. Mary Gifford says you were one of the last people to see him alive."

The poolside soundtrack and the burble of splashing and conversation—people talking to each other in person, a medley of voices, as well as the monologues that marked cell phone colloquies—went quiet, a susurrus-like immersion beneath a wavelike ringing in my ears.

"Crissy?" My name sounded so very far away.

"How?" I asked him. "What happened?"

"Looks like a suicide, but after Richie, no one believes that."

"Suicide," I repeated softly, the sibilance of the word snake-like in my mind.

He nodded. "Hanged himself in his office."

Hanged. I swallowed hard. It wasn't as if even a co-owner of the BP was likely to have an office with a cathedral ceiling. Artie's ceiling was maybe ten feet. But that was, it seemed, high enough. He hadn't needed a barn or rafters or—

"He used a couple of his neckties and that branding iron. The BP light fixture," Bud was saying.

I recalled it. "I'm sure the police will do an autopsy."

"Oh, you can bet your ass they will," said Bud.

"But maybe not," I said, almost speaking aloud to myself. "Artie told me he didn't believe Richie had killed himself, and the police were involved in some sort of cover-up."

Bud gazed out through my cabana at the pool, the heat rising up like vapors from the concrete. "He told me that, too. But I have faith in the LVPD. I mean, there are cops on the take. Some you can buy. For some people, it's a coin flip: cop or crook? They could go either way. But two brothers killing themselves? That's too suspicious not to open some eyes."

"Is it?" I asked, stunned, but nonetheless playing devil's advocate. "If the casino's money problems really are that bad . . ."

"They're not. The BP may not be doing great. But gambling is pandemic-proof, Putin-proof, and recession-proof." He waved his hand at the crowd in the water. "There's your exhibit A."

"Who found him?"

"Mary," he said, referring to the Morleys' secretary. "She came to work this morning, and there he was."

"God, the poor woman."

"Yup."

"Was there a note?"

"If there was, Mary didn't find it. Maybe the police have one now or Artie left one at home. Maybe he emailed it to someone."

I thought of Nola Hahn, one of the city's gambling pioneers, who divided his time between Los Angeles and Las Vegas, and who killed himself in the Beverly Hilton in 1957. He left behind the pithiest of suicide notes: "No one to blame."

"Who's in charge of the casino?" I asked. "Eddie?"

"Yup."

"And tonight?"

"As far as I know, the show must go on—assuming you feel up to it. All those people in the water right now or standing pat at sixteen at the blackjack tables? Most of them have no idea who Artie or Richie Morley were."

Did I feel up to it? I wasn't grieving. There was a riot of emotions coursing inside me, but the primary current was fear. Someone had, I was quite sure, murdered first Richie and then Artie, and two times yesterday I had rung Erika Schweiker. A U.S. congresswoman. On her private cell. I had called because Artie had asked me. I couldn't help but feel there was a connection here, and while I wondered whether I had some legal exposure—I doubted it, but I knew I had brushed close to something murky—the danger seemed life threatening. There were dead in the water.

"I'm guessing Nigel doesn't know yet."

"I didn't tell him, but he might know. Word is spreading fast through the casino. You've been at your cabana, but there were EMTs and police a couple hundred yards from here."

Which, inevitably, was when I started receiving texts from other employees at the BP and, yes, from Nigel.

* * *

I went to my dressing room behind the showroom to gather myself. I saw that a fan who had been at last night's second show had sent backstage one of the classic Royal Doulton Princess Diana figurines, a porcelain re-creation of the woman that stood about nine inches tall. She's wearing a navy-blue off-the-shoulder gown that falls to her ankles, and striding rather purposefully forward. She's smiling. She has Diana's cobalt eyes. (The first time I had been given this figurine was my second year of the residency, and when I had held it in my hands, it was eerie: this is what I looked like when re-created in porcelain.) I took a selfie with it that I could include with a thank-you note I'd send the fan on my faux Diana royal stationery, and then placed the figurine in my dressing room closet, where I had seven others. After Halloween, once people began thinking of holiday gifts, I would sell them on my Etsy shop, along with all the other memorabilia fans had given me over the year. Each of those statues would bring in at least $250 apiece. When I included all of the commemorative plates, coins, scarves, sweaters, spoons, posters, and framed magazine covers I had been given that year, I'd net about twenty-five grand. I will readily admit, that's not a posh sum for actual royalty. But it is for a teen shelter in Vermont.

My accountant wanted my Diana's Castle shop to fuel an IRA: she had pointed out that very spring when she was preparing my taxes that it would be worth six figures if I'd opened one a couple of years ago. And given that a lot of my salary was my suite and my cabana, given that my half of my mother's estate had been half the sale of a rickety Victorian in a Vermont village that didn't even have an elementary school anymore, it seemed prudent to have a nest egg. But I said no. I would have felt soiled when I made my December trips to the UPS store to ship the memorabilia if I were selling the trinkets to fund my retirement. Besides, how many Royal Doulton figurines that resembled oneself did a girl need? Answer? None. It made much more sense to sell the damn things and give the money to the shelter where Betsy worked.

The only rule I had with the development director was this: my sister could never know that among the anonymous gifts in the annual report each year was one from me. At first, I didn't want her to worry that I was giving more than I could afford.

But, then, after she killed our mother, I didn't want her to know because knowledge, in this case, would encourage contact.

* * *

Between four and five that afternoon I spoke to Nigel, my drummer, and Yevgeny. The first two conversations were about the Morleys, the third was about both the Morleys and Futurium. I did not, however, speak to the police. No one from the LVPD reached out to me. I considered asking Yevgeny why he thought that was, but I was not prepared to tell anyone what Artie had asked me to do—and what I had done. But then it dawned on me: why would the congresswoman call the police and tell them I had called her? Why would she want to link herself in any way with the Buckingham Palace, especially now that the owners were dead and quite possibly executed?

Eddie Cantone had a lot to juggle, but even he rang me. He wanted to make sure I was, in his words, "able to royal up." I assured him I was. Then I told him that I had a question: Did he think the police would want to talk to me about the favor Artie had asked of me yesterday?

"She ever call back?" he asked in response.

"She did not."

"Good to know," he said. "Thank you for trying. But, no, I can't see why they'll want to talk to you."

"Well, they will about Artie."

"Meh. Not so sure about that. But even if they do, all they'll ask you is if he was depressed. You know, in your opinion. They won't ask about the other thing."

"What would you recommend I tell them?"

"For your own sake? Answer he was depressed."

"For my sake?"

"Uh-huh. Say he was in the dumps because his brother had blown his brains out. Say mostly you talked about your show. That's what I told them."

"Okay."

"It won't be a big deal. All pro forma hokum."

"Are you in danger, Eddie?"

"Probably. But I have been my whole life."

Was this bluster? I was concluding it was, when he added, "Trust me, Crissy, I'm a survivor. I've gotten the message loud and clear."

"Are you going to sell?" The question was tinged with self-preservation.

"Won't be up to me. Will be up to the lawyers who manage the Morleys' estate. But they may have alternatives. Options."

"And what if Erika Schweiker calls me back? Do I still—"

"No. At this point, if she calls back, insist it was a wrong number. A butt dial. Whatever. But don't say you have anything on your senator. Got it? Artie is gone—it kills me to say that—and so now we're in the land of the lawyers and bankers."

Then he said he had to go. He told me to hang in there, but immediately retracted the comment, no doubt envisioning how Artie Morley had died, and added simply, "Break a leg."

* * *

Alternatives. Options. I couldn't imagine what he meant. A bank or bankers who would back the estate? Back him, perhaps? Did the Morleys have family who would sell him the BP? Or did he have revenge on his mind, some sort of gang war counter-attack? This was, after all, Las Vegas.

My job security seemed more tenuous than ever. Everyone who worked at the casino was afraid.

After Yevgeny had hung up, he'd emailed me links to articles about Futurium and Bitcoin and crypto technology, and it was all over my head. I told myself I would understand it better when I wasn't distracted by everything else going on, but the idea of digital wallets and transactions recorded in blockchains and money that existed without banks left me knackered.

But it seemed there were Bitcoin ATMs in Las Vegas, despite the fact that most bricks-and-mortar casinos, including mine, did not yet accept crypto on the gambling floor, which was where the real money was made. I read that Erika Schweiker was a big fan of crypto, and the fact she was popping up in my life even here was not lost on me. She boasted in one article that she trusted crypto more than banks, and was thrilled to see Futurium in Vegas.

What left me curious was this: If one of the benefits of crypto was anonymity, why in the world would people who visited a bricks-and-mortar casino see an advantage to it? And weren't the virtual casinos that used crypto already a threat to the real ones? Why, if you were the Bellagio or the BP or the Paris, would you encourage people to gamble in a fashion that meant they didn't have to come to your concrete world? The answers, I supposed, were somewhere in the opacity beneath the deepest waters: the very secrecy that cloaked crypto allowed for money laundering or skimming or losing money with a velocity that might break the sound barrier. Just try drawing down five or ten thousand dollars from a traditional ATM at a casino. But at a Bitcoin ATM? No worries.

Sex workers seemed to love it, too. Cryptocurrency was a great way to get paid. No bank policies or regulations to dial down anyone's libido. It was also useful for corporations that wanted to get their data unlocked after a ransomware cyberattack. Nearly 100 percent of ransomware payments were made in crypto.

But it seemed there was nothing untoward or illegal about anything Futurium did. At least nothing confirmed. One of their three offices was in Grand Cayman, a notorious (or renowned) location for money laundering and offshore shell companies, so the Internet was filled with conspiracy theories about their alleged wrongdoing.

Tomorrow Yevgeny was off to a conference in Dubai. I told

him, when I heard, that I was more confident than ever he was a spy. In response, he urged me to be content.

But that had grown difficult now that the Morleys were dead and, it was clear, I was about to have to reengage with my sister and meet my niece.

* * *

I didn't want my sister near the Buckingham Palace. There was just too much going on.

And yet it was also business as usual. I received one cursory visit from two police officers asking me about the last time I had seen Artie. We spoke in my dressing room. I told the pair what Eddie had recommended: Artie had indeed seemed broken to me, but I thought that was natural since his brother had recently taken his own life. They asked what we talked about, and I said mostly my show: Artie wanted to be sure that I was happy with such details as their marketing, my time slots, and my band. I reported that I told Artie I was. And that was it. I had felt my heart beating faster than usual as I lied, but I knew my performance was solid. My interview with the police lasted fifteen minutes. They were, I gathered, speaking to other BP employees, though they suggested that the only thing suspicious about Artie's suicide was the reality it had occurred only days after his brother's. (I restrained myself from observing how, when it came to things that looked suspicious, that struck me as a pretty damn conspicuous red flag.)

In any case, when Betsy texted the next morning that she and Marisa had arrived in Nevada and spent their first night in their new apartment, I suggested we meet at one of the area's more renowned culinary abominations, an around-the-world buffet outside of the city in Summerlin. Within seconds my phone rang—Petula Clark singing "Downtown"—and I saw it was Betsy.

"I don't have a car," Betsy said. "Can you pick us up? Or we could call an Uber. I don't want to put you out."

Of course, she didn't have a vehicle. She'd flown here. "What did you do with your Subaru?" I asked. "Did you sell it?"

"Uh-huh. I figured I'd buy something more 'Las Vegas' out here. You know, like your convertible."

"I'll pick you up. Give me your address."

I'd heard of the street, though I didn't know precisely where it was. But the fact I recognized the name made me uncomfortable, because I didn't get out much, and the idea that it was familiar to me suggested proximity.

* * *

I retrieved my lime-green Mini from the casino parking garage (I had a free space) and punched Betsy's new address into the dashboard GPS. Sure enough, it was only 2.5 miles away, and I threw a minor wobbly in the car, banging my hands nonsensically against the steering wheel. But then I took a few slow, deep, cleansing breaths and started off, leaving the dim shadows of the parking garage for the blinding klieg lights that illuminate midday in southwest Nevada. I was wearing a scarf and sunglasses that were more Jackie O. than Lady Di, but they were still on point for a diva hiding out at a buffet in Summerlin. I kept the convertible roof closed and set the air-conditioning on deep freeze.

I was at their apartment in minutes, and there was Betsy standing in the two-story complex's parking lot with a man. There was a pool behind a fake wooden fence and some withered palms rising up on the far side. I was happy for Marisa: if you were going to be stuck in the pizza oven that was Las Vegas, a crap pool was better than no pool. I had a hunch the fellow was this mystical Frankie, her new squeeze. He had a robust, salt-and-pepper shag carpet bristling atop his head, and his eyes were hidden by aviator shades. He was tall and thick-waisted, and yet had rather twig-like legs in his khaki pants. I pegged him for early fifties. Most of the cars in the lot were low end, the exception being the black Tesla that I was sure was his.

"I thought I'd pop over and say hello," he said, extending his hand as I climbed from my Mini. "I'm Frankie Limback. I have to tell you: I can't wait to see your show."

"Thank you," I said, surprised by the Bay Shore in his voice. I had assumed an investment banker would annoy me with one of those WASP affectations that turns all *a* sounds into *ah*'s. Nope. "I'm Crissy," I added, "but it seems you've figured that out."

"Hi, Sis," said Betsy. She looked like me, I thought, if I didn't care for my skin and wear makeup and go to a nearby spa and gym. (The BP had a gym, but no spa. Besides, I wanted my privacy when I was making the faces one makes around free weights and treadmills.) She looked tired. She needed a facial and, just maybe, a massage. As she'd told me, her hair was strawberry blond, though there were strands of gray, and it hung long past her shoulders. God, I thought, if my hair were still black, would I be plucking white hairs from it? The idea would have made my legs buckle if I hadn't popped an extra half tab of diazepam. I was the big sister, but she seemed like the older one: the horse that's been ridden hard and put away wet, which was ironic since she'd been living in Vermont, which is among the mellowest places on earth. Apparently, the last year had not been kind to her—which felt right. Kill your mother and you should be cursed with sallow skin and early-onset gray hair.

"You made it," I said. We embraced, and it was awkward, as if we had lost our muscle memory as siblings.

"God," Frankie observed, grinning, "you two look identical. It's uncanny. It's like you're twins."

"Well, we're not," I reminded him, though a part of me was thinking, *Shit. If that's what I look like, my days on stage are numbered.*

He nodded. "Still, it's amazing. Anyway, I wanted to introduce myself."

"Very kind of you. Welcome to Sin City."

"What happens in Vegas—"

"Nope. Don't go there and don't believe it," I told him.

"Got it."

I turned to Betsy. "Where's . . ." and the words trailed away. Usually words don't fail me, but they did then.

"My daughter?" She arched an eyebrow as she finished my sentence for me.

"Sure. Where's Marisa?"

And, as if that were her cue, I saw the girl shutting their apartment door on the second floor, locking it, and then walking briskly down the balcony, tapping a hand on the white metal railing, and down the stairs. She was like a gazelle: all legs and grace, no tween gawkiness. She had that choker and the goth eyeliner, but her lipstick today was closer to Barbie pink, which worked better on a thirteen-year-old than what, it seemed, she usually wore. But she was still dressed for abduction: a skirt the length of a wide belt and a tight black T-shirt.

When she reached us, she stood beside Betsy, and her mother put an arm around her bare shoulder. "I thought we agreed you weren't going to wear that skirt today," Betsy said to her.

"Nope."

"This is Vegas," said Frankie expansively. He was trying to be a peacemaker, but he sounded like a pervert.

"I'm Crissy," I said to her. "It's nice to meet you."

"Yeah," she said, "I googled you plenty back in Vermont and more on the plane. And Betsy has shown me lots of pictures." She gazed at me. "You had a nose job, right?"

"Right. To look more like Diana." I wanted to make it clear that as vain as I am—and I make the bumptious dullards who compete on *The Bachelor* seem rather sporty and carefree when it comes to their eyebrows and boobs—I didn't see one of Vegas's premier plastic surgeons because I thought my nose was too big or too small. I just wanted to replicate Lady Di's as much as possible.

Marisa turned to my sister and, as if she understood intuitively how to get under my skin, said—again calling her mother by her given name—"You should get a nose job, too, Betsy. And dye your hair so you also look like the princess. Just think of all the crazy stuff you could get away with if people couldn't tell you two apart."

Frankie guffawed. "Great minds thinking alike," he said.

Betsy looked back and forth between her boyfriend and her daughter, and I couldn't decide whether she was exasperated or intrigued. But Marisa picked up on the strange, vacillating energy from my sister.

"Or not," the girl said. "Maybe it's like that Billy Joel song. Don't go changing. Whatever. I love you just the way you are."

"You know Billy Joel?" I asked, impressed.

"Not biblically," she said. Then: "My mom says you're bulimic, just like Princess Diana."

"Marisa!" Betsy snapped at her. "I told you—"

"It's fine," I said. The child had no filter. I approved. "I promise, I won't give back whatever we eat at lunch. At least not intentionally. But the buffets out here? Food poisoning is always an option, so you just never know. The best thing about the pandemic—arguably, the only good thing about the pandemic—was that it closed the buffets for a bit, because a sneeze guard was no match for COVID-19. And when they reopened, they had better hygiene in place."

"So, you're off to Summerlin?" said Frankie. I was pleased with the way that Marisa or the heat was making him sweat.

"We are."

"I'll look forward to seeing you again, Crissy," Frankie said. "You show me secret Vegas, and someday I can show you secret Grand Cayman—we have a club there—or secret Phnom Penh."

"You know secret Phnom Penh?"

The bounder winked. "I do. And secret Moscow."

"Frankie's old bank used to do business in Russia, South Korea, and Cambodia," Betsy said.

Her boyfriend said something in Russian, and I understood not a word. He waited a moment and then said in English, "I could show you a restaurant in Moscow with a veal Orloff that would turn a vegetarian into Peter the Great."

"Was he a rather passionate carnivore?"

"He was."

I smiled. The point of his remark wasn't the grilled beef or his knowledge of Moscow restaurants: he was planting the flag that he spoke a little Russian.

"Well, if I ever get to Moscow or Phnom Penh and can't find a cab driver to show me the 'secret' sights, I now know whom to call," I told him.

He stared at me with an intensity that surprised me. My snarky little diss had left him piqued. He had a temper, it seemed. But then he gathered himself and nodded, grinning with his lips shut tight. He kissed my sister on the cheek and said to her and Marisa, "I'll see you tonight. I'll pick you two up and bring you to the house."

"That would be great," said Betsy.

"When do you start bitcoining—or whatever the right verb is?" I asked Frankie.

"We're not Bitcoin."

"I know."

"I've been with Futurium a while now, but I only started out here this month. Betsy starts next week."

"Doing what?" I asked.

"Administrative assistant," she answered. "But Marisa here is my real priority."

"When do you begin school?" I asked her. It was a lame question, right up there with asking a kid about her backpack.

"The anniversary of your death," she said matter-of-factly. "Princess Diana's, that is. Wednesday, August thirty-first."

* * *

Marisa had gone to the Italian section of the buffet and come back with fettuccini Alfredo and garlic bread. Betsy had gone

Chinese, choosing spring rolls and General Tso's chicken. I considered shaming them for their portions and bringing back to our booth a salad, but it takes work to be a bitch, so I dialed it down and grabbed a veggie burger and fries. (Often that was my purge cuisine of choice. But not that day.) At one point when Marisa was deciding on her pasta, I'd had a moment alone with Betsy and said, "That skirt? Really?"

My sister shrugged. "We dressed worse when we were that age."

"Like hell we did."

"Worse for Vermont than that skirt is for Vegas. Look, she wanted to get dressed up because she was meeting her celebrity aunt. You choose your battles with a headstrong thirteen-year-old. Now that we're here, we'll buy some more appropriate clothes."

I let it go both because Marisa was about to rejoin us and because you can't win an argument with a grown woman who mistakes a bandeau for a skirt, and allows her charge to wear it as such.

"So," I asked Marisa after she was settled in against the orange Naugahyde, "where were you living before you and Betsy . . ."

"Hooked up? Not like that," the girl said.

"I wasn't going there."

"Before Betsy adopted me," she said, "I had foster parents in Essex Junction. But I was just a cash cow for them, and when Nancy—that was the mom—finally got pregnant and had the baby they always wanted, they were kind of done with me. I'll admit, I was surprised. I thought they were going to keep me around as the kid's babysitter and live-in nanny. What's that French word, Betsy?"

"Au pair," said my sister.

"Yeah, that. I mean, I was free labor. Wait, I was better than free labor: I was labor the state paid for. But, no, once they had Foster—that's what they named their kid, which felt like a weird dig at the actual foster kid under their roof—I was excess baggage. Still, it was a good year and a half. They were cool. Mostly left me alone."

"How many foster homes have you been in?"

"Seven, I think. Counting when Betsy was just fostering me. The longest was the Shepards and the shortest was the Wilburs."

"Were the Wilburs the family in Essex Junction?"

"Oh, no. A year and half isn't bad. The Wilburs' was, like, a month. I was eight. They had two foster kids older than me—I guess one was my age now—and the dad was having sex with them. Gross, right? So, when the mom got wind, she went to social services and had us all yanked out of there. You can google the story. It was pretty sick, and not in a good way. Sick as in gross." She shared this morsel without drama or affectation. It was as if she were telling me the plot of a TV series she was streaming. "I mean, they had us out of there like lightning. I threw whatever I could in this plastic backpack, and, boom, we were out the door."

"Betsy's and my mum had an old canvas backpack," I said, trying to find a more suitable conversation for lunch. "It had straps and buckles. Serious Army Navy clothing store vibe, but I think it was L.L. Bean. Whatever happened to it?" I asked my sister. I recalled it fondly.

"Not a clue. But, you're right: it was L.L. Bean."

I watched the girl use a piece of bread like a sponge to sop up alfredo sauce.

"Did you never meet your biologic parents?" I asked her. Betsy gave me one of those looks that I suppose Queen Elizabeth was often giving Prince Andrew before we knew what an all-in reprobate he was, and supposed he was merely a randy young royal.

"No. I'll never find my dad. Maybe someday I'll find my mom."

"Marisa's mother tried raising her when she was a baby in the Lund Home in Burlington," Betsy told me.

"Ted Bundy started at the Lund Home," Marisa added. "He's their most famous alumni."

"Alumnus," I corrected her.

"Opioids and addiction," explained Betsy. "It's the downfall of lots of young moms, including Marisa's. I used to see it a lot."

If Marisa hadn't been present, I would have reminded Betsy of her own predilection for THC, and her forays into LSD and—in the end—shrooms. But *shrooms* would have been taking a cleaver to both our souls, so it's probably good that Marisa was there.

"What do you think of Betsy's new job?" I asked my niece.

"Administrative assistant for a cryptocurrency company? Ridiculous. They hardly have any employees. But she's about to make a lot more money than she was ever going to make as a social worker trying to keep a kid like me from becoming my mom—my biologic mom, I mean."

"Do you understand cryptocurrency?"

"Of course. I googled it."

"I don't understand it at all," I said.

"You can buy a small amount via PayPal. I can walk you through it, if you want to invest."

"No," I said. "I'm okay."

"It's a good investment. A few grand becomes a few hundred grand before you know it. Or, a few grand becomes, like, three cents. It's very volatile. But mostly it just goes up."

"Sounds like Las Vegas is the perfect place for Futurium," I said, though I had my doubts.

"It's not gambling," said Marisa. "It's investing. Talk to Frankie."

"In Russian or in English?"

"Hah," Marisa said. I liked it that she got my jokes.

"He is quite the chap, that Frankie Limback," I said to my sister.

"He is. Unbelievably smart."

"Is that what you see in him?"

"It's among the things I see in him. Sometime in the next year or so, he's going to take us to Grand Cayman. Futurium has an office there."

"And a club," I said.

"Yup."

"Grand Cayman and Las Vegas. Awfully strange bedfellows," I observed, though I wasn't sure that was true. Las Vegas was built on tectonic plates of corruption. Las Vegas had people who knew how to bury the bodies so they'd never be found. Did the Cayman Islands? Yes. An ocean is at least as good as the desert when it comes to the sleight of hand one needs to forever conceal a corpse.

"No weirder than Princess Di and Las Vegas," my sister responded.

"Fair point."

"I hear there's been a lot of drama at the Buckingham Palace. Are you okay?"

"You're referring to Artie and Richie Morley?"

"I am. And how . . . how one of them died."

"It's very sad," I said carefully.

"I mean, did it bring back—"

"It brought back nothing. I told you: I'm fine."

"Did you know them?"

"Yes."

"Who are Artie and Richie Morley?" asked Marisa.

"Two brothers. They used to own the Buckingham Palace. They died."

"Car crash?" asked Marisa. "Wait: private plane crash? That sounds like a more Las Vegas casino owner way to die."

"They killed themselves," I said. "But separately. A few days apart."

"Not too suspicious," my niece said, the sarcasm wholly warranted.

"I agree," I told her, wanting to encourage her insight—

reward her intellect—more than I wanted to dismiss her conjecture. But, I went on, "Of course, the police have seen no sign of foul play. If it's a murder investigation, I've seen no indication."

"How will this affect the casino?" my sister asked. "How will it affect you?"

"You sound worried about me."

"Little bit."

"I'm not concerned," I lied.

"If the casino goes out of business, there's always Futurium," Marisa volunteered.

I looked back and forth between the girl and her mother. The irony of the fact that this filly in a miniskirt and my sister were building their future on invisible money while I was assembling mine from the gossamer of memory and nostalgia was not lost on me. I ate another French fry and couldn't help but wonder whether Las Vegas was the best place on the planet for this child—or the worst.

They looked so much alike it was like they were the Olsen twins, when the Olsen twins were kids making a mint in those kiddie movies.

Except they looked like the Princess. I mean, Crissy did more.

But Betsy? She would have made people do double takes if it was 1995 and she was walking around London.

I'd done my homework before meeting Crissy. But, still, it could freak you out to look at Crissy and then at Betsy.

It was so weird. Just so weird.

CHAPTER TEN

Betsy

It was Betsy's first meal with her sister in over a year, and the fact that Crissy drove them far from the strip to some buffet designed for UNLV frat boys with bottomless stomachs hurt her feelings. She was humiliated by the milieu, which might have been her sister's objective. She was also annoyed when Crissy chastised her for the skirt that Marisa was wearing. But her sister listened attentively to Marisa as the girl discussed her foster homes, which must have been illuminating for Crissy, and perked up when the girl gave her an introduction into how crypto worked. Mostly, she was kind to her niece. The only time Betsy could tell that Crissy had disappointed Marisa was when she asked her aunt if they could drive by the Buckingham Palace on the way home, and Crissy said no.

At one point, Betsy inquired if her sister was seeing anyone, and Crissy picked up one of her fries and stared at it like it was an insect—a walking stick or a praying mantis—before putting it back down on her plate. Her lips parted, holding in place as if the mind behind them was rummaging for the right word, and then . . . nothing. "Funny you should ask," she said finally. "But not really."

Crissy had always been circumspect about her relationships when their mother was alive, and Betsy assumed that her social life was a litany of nameless one-nighters and friends with benefits—first in New York and then in Las Vegas. She rarely shared with their mother and her the names of anyone to whom she might be feeling a serious attraction. But Betsy felt a glimmer of hope for her in that oddly evasive and yet possibly hopeful response: *Funny you should ask. But not really.* She sensed there was something more there and pressed, "Not really or not yet?"

"What's the difference?"

"I thought I might have heard something promising in your voice."

"I did, too," said Marisa.

"And," Betsy went on, "it would make me happy if you had someone in your life."

"I have plenty of people in my life."

"A boyfriend."

"I don't need a boyfriend."

Crissy sliced a bite-size piece from her veggie burger with her tinny knife and fork, and pushed it around the plate.

"Mom always thought you and Terrance might become a thing," said Betsy, referring to Crissy's agent. In truth, their mother had *worried* that Crissy and Terrance might become a thing. She didn't distrust the man, but she felt there was something insidious about the way he saw her daughter's eating disorder as an opportunity and not an ailment. "Or you and Nigel, after she met him," Betsy added.

"Wouldn't that be meta?" Crissy said, her tone growing lighter.

"I like Nigel. Mom did, too."

"He's rather like a brother to me."

"He's cute."

"He is."

"But—how would you say it?—he's not your cup of tea?"

"He's my Charles. That's a terrible foundation for any relationship. Also? I shudder to think what would happen to the show if we started a romance and then it all went to hell."

"Fair."

Marisa looked back and forth between the two sisters, her gaze in the end resting on Crissy. "Do you want me to call you Crissy or Aunt Crissy?"

"Crissy will suffice."

"Cool." Then Marisa went on, "When Diana was a teenager, she called Prince Charles 'Pris Chos.' You probably knew that."

"I did. How did you learn that?"

"The Internet."

"Marisa is very good at using the Internet to learn anything," Betsy said, and immediately felt stupid after speaking. It was as if she had managed both to patronize her daughter and say something that suggested she herself was of a generation that was still impressed by computers.

But Marisa hadn't noticed. The child sat up very straight in her chair and said in a British accent that Betsy thought was pretty good but was sure Crissy would view as amateurish, "Yah, we sat inside the hice, before a fire, and the folks were boring as all get-out."

But Crissy smiled at her and replied in her Diana voice, "They were all right Horlicks."

For a split second, Betsy feared that her sister had just said *whore licks,* as if Crissy had suggested to her niece that someone or something was as tedious as lackluster fellatio. Fortunately, the girl was envisioning something very different: "A Horlicks sounds like a creature from Harry Potter," she said. "Is it? Like a troll or a ghoul? Maybe a person who's been hexed into something gross?"

"A brilliant guess. Jolly well done. But incorrect."

"Oh."

"You couldn't possibly have known the answer, so don't beat yourself up. Horlicks is an English drink that's been around forever and some people say helps you sleep. So, a person who's a Horlicks is a right proper bore."

Marisa nodded and repeated the word, and Betsy knew that she would hear it a lot in the coming days—and she did.

* * *

There were moments when Betsy thought she might puddle in the heat of Las Vegas, melt like a Popsicle on the sidewalk. Frankie had warned her, but it was one thing to be told you're about to start living in a desert paved over with blacktop; it was another to be dropped there unceremoniously after a life lived almost entirely amidst the maple trees of Vermont. One of the first things that struck her about Vegas was the utter lack of vegetation. Having grown up in New England, she noticed it. She felt it. She knew she would miss Vermont's autumnal pyrotechnics when the maple, birch, and beech leaves were transformed in their death throes into kaleidoscopes of color.

Marisa did better than her, but that was because she rarely climbed out from the sanctuary of the apartment complex's swimming pool those first days. Betsy had already discovered that, in addition to being a prodigiously gifted mathematician, she was a voracious reader, but now Marisa was reading fewer books and instead devouring articles about Las Vegas, Princess Diana, and cryptocurrency. Betsy had bought her a used tablet soon after she began fostering her (everything worked except FaceTime), and now the girl would stand in the shallow end of the pool and lean her elbows on the concrete side, and devour article after article. Marisa had picked out a bikini that was more revealing than Betsy would have liked when they'd gone shopping, but as Betsy had told her sister, you picked your fights. Marisa allowed Betsy to slather her back and shoulders with sunblock or she'd stand in the water with a T-shirt over the bikini top so she wouldn't get burned, and Betsy viewed that as a win. She discovered that many of their neighbors were retirees who had come to Nevada because it was a great state to stretch your savings: Social Security benefits weren't taxed, nor were withdrawals from IRAs or pensions, and there was no state income tax.

There were lots of people at the apartment building who worked at the casinos. Two doors down was a croupier at the

Venetian and directly below them resided a bartender at the MGM Grand.

The person who Betsy wanted to get to know more was a blackjack dealer at the Luxor, a single woman a decade older than her who had moved here from Detroit after her marriage had collapsed. She had a son who was about to start at Michigan State. Her name was Ayobami, and her mother was from Lagos and her father from London. Prior to becoming a dealer, she'd taught kindergarten, and she had come to Vegas with a job in hand at a school. But then she discovered she could make twice as much helping people lose money at blackjack, and some nights the tips left her—and this was a word Crissy used in her act, but Ayobami used naturally—gobsmacked. Even people who lost big sometimes gave her their last chip. Betsy could see why: she was charming and funny and beautiful. The two of them met at the pool and hit it off. Ayobami had grown up in Michigan and so she had neither a British nor Nigerian accent, but she was capable of replicating both.

"The next time my parents visit," she said one afternoon, soon after they met, "I must bring them to your sister's show. I was born two months before Diana and Charles got hitched. And so even though my mom and dad had been in America a couple of years by then, my mom still watched every moment of the royal wedding while nursing me or changing a diaper."

"I gather it was quite a TV event."

"It was. My parents have a more jaded view of the monarchy now than they did back in the day. Back then, we didn't know that Charles and Diana weren't going to have a storybook marriage or that Andrew was a pig who'd become pals with predators. It would be forty years before the royal family would drive away Meghan Markle and Harry. And, make no mistake, that poor couple was driven away, and it was all because Meghan was biracial. We all know that's the truth. The only one my parents still like is Diana."

"But once upon a time . . ."

"Once upon a time, my parents liked them all. Back then, they viewed even Elizabeth as downright forward thinking when it came to race."

Betsy saw Marisa looking up at them. She was, as usual, standing in the water and reading on her tablet.

"When can we go see the show, Betsy?" she asked.

"I'm not sure," she replied.

"That's been your answer since we got here."

"Scheduling is—"

"You and Crissy have a weird relationship, I get it. But you've still been to see it," Marisa said. The girl knew that Betsy had, in fact, seen it four times. She'd seen it twice pre-Nigel and twice once the Scotsman had been added.

"If you don't want to go again, I could take Marisa," Ayobami volunteered. "There's nothing in it that a thirteen-year-old shouldn't see, right?"

"Not a thing. Of course, Marisa will be the youngest person in the house. You'll be second."

"I've heard such nice things about the show," Betsy's new friend told her. "I can't believe it's not in a bigger casino. Didn't she win a Bolv?"

"I have no idea what that is. But it sounds kind of filthy," Betsy joked. She knew that when Ayobami had said a bigger casino, she'd meant a nicer one. One on the strip.

"Bolv. Best of Las Vegas. I think your sister won Best Impersonator—which is a very high bar out here, since we have nothing but impersonators and cover bands."

Betsy nodded. "Yes, she did win that. Maybe more than once."

"And I know one of our senators loves it. John Aldred. He saw it a couple of times. He was in there at least once with his wife, and one or two times when they were separated."

"When they were separated," she repeated. "Are they divorced now?"

"The opposite. Reconciled," Ayobami answered. "Anyway, your sister *is* the princess, people say. She *is* Diana."

Betsy closed her eyes behind her shades. Inadvertently, with her emphasis on that verb, *is,* Ayobami had touched upon what was for Betsy the most disturbing part of her sister's re-creation. When a person so completely subsumes herself behind the mask of another, what must it be like to stare into the mirror? What must it be like to gaze upon your reflection and see someone else—someone who just isn't you?

* * *

Betsy liked Frankie's Tesla, and not solely because it was electric and had a smaller carbon footprint than a gasoline-powered car. She liked the luxury she felt ensconced in its ventilated, buttery-soft, faux-leather seats. Had she ever been cocooned in a vehicle like that before she met Frankie?

And she liked his new house. His "ranch." It was on a cul-de-sac, one of only three houses at the end of a long road, and one of the other two belonged to a lobbyist who seemed to work with both Futurium and a crazy congresswoman named Erika Schweiker. The third was empty and had been for sale for months.

Frankie called it his slot machine dacha when he closed on it because it was triple fives: five years old, five bedrooms, five acres. It was out toward Red Rocks, and the sunsets were electric. Like a lot of luxury homes outside of Vegas, it felt like a series of modern boxes welded together, and the inside was airy and light: white walls, dark floors, and the most modern kitchen Betsy had ever seen. But it also had touches of new money swag, such as a spiral staircase to the second floor and a flat fountain against one of the living room walls that looked like a modern art painting but made the interior space sound like you were near a waterfall—or, perhaps, like it was always raining, which was ironic in Las Vegas because it almost never was. A marble plinth in need of a bust or, at least, a massive floral arrangement stood in the entryway just inside the front door. The architect had made sure the pool matched the house, three hard-edged squares creating an L, and one block was deep enough for a diving board. The pool, lit blue at night by underwater lights, had a cactarium on the far side that was otherworldly in its beauty. Beside the pool was a pergola constructed of faux teak that looked authentic but, apparently, would outlive Frankie's grandchildren.

The air-conditioning, which was on whenever Betsy was there, was silent.

In Marisa's and her first weeks in Nevada, Betsy wondered sometimes if it would be more in her daughter's best interests to insist that they move in with Frankie now, since she had a sense that eventually they would anyway, and she wouldn't want Marisa to have to change schools in ninth or tenth grade. The house was a twenty-minute drive from their apartment without traffic, but forty when there was. And, of course, he was paying for that apartment, as well as the mortgage on his new home, plus the cash that was heading back east to the woman who was becoming his ex-wife in Vermont.

One afternoon when Marisa was at a day camp Betsy found for teenage computer geeks, she and Frankie were lying in the colossal California king in his master bedroom. It was the only piece of furniture that had arrived for that room, so his clothes were still in boxes or on the elegant hangers he insisted upon in the walk-in closet. Her head on his shoulder, his arm cradling her against him, she asked, "How much of all this house and this new life is from investment banking and how much is from crypto?" She was curious.

"I did fine at the bank. Made a good living. But crypto is insane. Sure, it's a little unpredictable. But it's lucrative, like equities, if you know what you're doing or you invest in the right coin. If you have the right friends. You've heard of the House That Ruth Built? Yankee Stadium? This is the House That Invisible Money Built. My whole fucking life—as you know—has been helping the filthy rich get even richer."

She didn't know that. He'd never been that direct. She ran her two fingers along the hard bone of his sternum.

"Look, you asked," he went on. "Crypto has been very good to me. Guys like Rory O'Hara and Damon Ioannidis. Very generous. Crazy. But generous. And Futurium will be very good to you, too."

"I rather hope so," she murmured.

"Rather," he repeated. "Such a British word. And you said it just now with a slight British accent."

"Now did I?"

"Now did I?" he repeated, imitating her because she had indeed said those three words as if she were her sister onstage.

"One of the weird things Marisa told me is that before Diana met Charles, when she was slumming—so to speak—at menial jobs in London she didn't really need, it was a thing for her and her friends to speak as if they weren't all aristocrats. As if they weren't girls who lived on the cusp of the royal family."

"I have got to see that show."

"Ayobami said there were no seats available on the website until October, but she thought she might be able to get a pair for her and Marisa a little sooner through a scalper she knows."

"That's your new friend who works at the Luxor?"

"Uh-huh."

"I'll get us tickets for the next day or two. You and me and Marisa will go."

"Oh? You already have connections?" She was teasing him, but she wasn't surprised.

"In a few years? Futurium will own this town," he added.

"I don't know. I gather there's an actual mob museum out here."

"And a pinball museum. And you don't suppose pinball machines own this town, do you?"

She smiled at his small joke. "No," she agreed.

"Besides. Damon? Rory? Some of my friends in L.A.? They're Mastabas."

"What does that mean?"

"Okay, I'm about to tell you something, and it's going to sound like more of a big deal than it is. But you were going to figure it out soon enough anyway when you started really working at Futurium."

She waited.

"A mastaba is like a crypt. An Egyptian tomb, but you got the burial chamber and you got a room to store stuff: offerings. And the Mastaba—big *M,* not little *m*—used to be a crime family. A syndicate. Think Mafia, but not just Italians. It began with politics and geography, not ethnicity. Californians and Floridians, mostly. Dudes from L.A. and West Palm Beach. Very sophisticated. Risi e bisi, not spaghetti and meatballs. Money laundering instead of murder. But not so much anymore. Now it's mostly above board. Investments. Political gamesmanship. Anyway, some of our Futurium friends are big deals in the Mastaba crowd."

"Investors?"

"Investors. Owners. Directors. And, yeah, Rory and Damon."

She sat up in bed. "Are you insane?"

"It's not like that. People not in the know think everything the Mastaba does is corrupt. Or if a person has some criminal ties, everything they do is criminal. That's not the case. We all compartmentalize. You know that. You know my old bank's history."

"I don't," she said.

"Then you haven't given it enough thought. Why, a couple years ago, did my investment bank close its Moscow operations, even before Putin went loopy and invaded Ukraine?"

"Because of the sanctions?"

"Exactly. What does that tell you about who we were working with? Who I was working with?"

The obviousness of it had been lost on her, because she didn't think about money or investments the way he did. She thought like a person who used the coupons she got from the supermarket cashier, and recycled her Diet Coke cans for the nickel deposits. "You were working with Russians on the sanctions list," she said, her voice lowered in dismay.

"Yup. When the bank closed the Moscow office, some of our clients there still needed to skirt the sanctions, which only got worse when Putin went full-on Stalin. So, now we help them a little with our crypto. Launder it. And if you're going to provide a safe harbor for Russians, why not the Mastaba?"

"Are you insane?"

"Look, some of our names are controversial, but—"

"Names like Rory O'Hara?"

"Yup. Rory. His . . . type. Dude can be a pussycat one minute, and crazy as hell the next. But he's still a guy with his own jet and a big stake in our place in Grand Cayman. Looks like a five-star hotel, but it's just our playhouse. Our club."

"Crazy as in violent—that being the opposite of pussycat?"

"Little bit."

The words echoed in her mind. *Little bit.*

"Are you in danger? Am I putting my daughter at risk?"

"Absolutely not. I wouldn't endanger you or Marisa or my own kids. Never. That would be fucking crazy. The new Mastaba is not the old Mastaba. It's more like a conglomerate than a crime family."

"Are you sure? I need to know: are you one hundred percent sure?"

"Yes. I am as sure of that as I am of just about anything in business. I mean, no investment is foolproof. Think of the SEC disclaimer: past performance is no guarantee of future results. Of course, I wouldn't say something like that around any of our friends from California or Grand Cayman. Not polite. Not good politics—and we have some very good political clout."

"Who?"

"A congressman. Excuse me, a congresswoman."

"That lunatic, Erika Schweiker?"

"That lunatic, as you call her, is going to be a U.S. senator come November. She will kick John Aldred's ass. And she is firmly in our camp—unlike that puff pastry on the other side of the aisle."

"Is she part of the . . . the Mastaba?"

"Nah. But people in the syndicate give generously to her campaign, and she owns a lot of Futurium. We have each other's backs. If you're gamblers, always take the Mastaba."

"I think I'm going to throw up."

"Isn't that your sister's thing?"

She almost slapped him, but he must have seen the fury in her eyes, and put up his hands and laughed. "It was a joke! Look, I told you, Futurium is more clean than not. It's why the Mastaba wanted in. And as for the Russians? We got a U.S. representative who will soon be a U.S. senator on our side."

"Tell me again: there is no danger."

"None."

"Say it."

"There is no danger."

"And there is no legal jeopardy?"

"Not for you, not for me, not for Futurium."

She nodded, feigning reassurance, though she knew she was whistling past the graveyard. The whole idea they were even having this conversation was a bad sign. She wanted to believe that the era when the strip was run by crime families was long past, but what really did she know? What did she understand about how organized crime divided and conquered a territory? She didn't think she would have brought Marisa into this world—Las Vegas and its casinos—if she had thought she was endangering her. But how often in the past had she looked the other way, submerging her better judgment as if she were holding an inflatable toy underwater until, finally, the pressure got too much, and it breached the surface like a whale? She knew the answer. And she knew the silky allure of crypto (and the jackpot it represented), and the chance to start again.

"Frankie?" she asked.

"Yes?"

"Do you love me?" They'd never used that word: *love.*

He looked so deeply back at her that she thought she could see herself in his eyes. "My God, I do. Yes."

"And Marisa?"

"Like my own kids."

Few men in her life had told her they loved her. She'd said it herself to very few men.

"If I said I wanted out—I wanted to go back to Vermont—what would you say?"

"I'd say you were overreacting, but I'd book us all a flight east."

"Promise?"

"I promise. But Betsy? You have nothing to be scared of. I've been dealing with Russian oligarchs for years. We got this."

"We . . . the Mastaba?"

"We—you and me."

She lay back down and once more nuzzled close to him, bringing her knees to her chest. Suddenly she was in the fetal position. Every reckless and wild thing she had done in the past, she realized, was but a warmup before the workout.

Oh, my God, I never wanted to get out of the swimming pools. I liked the pool at the apartment where we were living, but I loved the one that Frankie had.

I went on Zillow and looked at how much he'd paid for that place.

And I thought of his alimony and child support.

I did the math in my head. Either that dude was raking it in or he had insane debt.

Anyway, Las Vegas was Venus. Humans weren't meant to live there.

So, I lived in the pools.

CHAPTER ELEVEN

Crissy

Late that night, I walked aimlessly through the casino. I saw two beautiful young women with cigarettes, and recalled how, when my bulimia was at its worst, a friend had suggested I start smoking. She was confident that any excess weight—and all weight was excess if you were a twenty-three-year-old woman in New York City trying to succeed as an actress back then—would melt like hoarfrost, but body image and the exigencies of my career weren't really the problem.

Much to my surprise, I was missing Yevgeny. I honestly wasn't sure whether the fellow was in my life, or just represented two nights in the past. We'd texted, but he was still in Dubai, and I had no idea if or when I would see him again. When we'd tried to find a date on our calendars to next get together, we'd failed.

I was still watching the women, feeling wistful for my new Russian American friend, when my phone rang. The number was blocked, but I knew who it was.

I knew.

For whom the bell tolls—and all that rot.

I answered it.

"Is this Crissy Dowling?"

It was indeed Erika Schweiker. I recognized the voice instantly, the angry twang that had launched a thousand memes of mispronounced or misused words. "Yes, this is she," I replied. "To whom do I have the pleasure of speaking?" I asked, hoping to bluff my way out of this.

"You called me. Two times. You must know." Her tone was curt. But this was a woman whose bullying was legendary—she bullied the media, she bullied anyone on the other side of the aisle—and who would probably be curt on her deathbed with whomever the hospice worker was who had the misfortune of shooting her veins full of morphine.

"I'm sorry. I'm rather flighty when it comes to phone numbers and such."

"Look, I know who you are, and I know you had an affair with a U.S. senator."

"He and his wife were separated," I reminded her, and I might have said more, but she cut me off.

"You have fragrantly violated my privacy, so I should fragrantly violate yours."

"Flagrant," I said. It was a reflex.

"What?"

"I believe you meant that I flagrantly violated your privacy. But, regardless, please know that I am deeply sorry if—"

"Before I destroy you, tell me why you called. And by destroy, I don't mean that literally. It's not a threat, so don't run like a crybaby to some reporter with an agenda. It's just a fact. So: why? What do you want? And how did you get this number?"

Nearby was a poker room and I veered inside. It was quieter. Four twentysomething men, locals, were card dead and losing their shirts. They didn't seem to mind. There was an empty chair, and I nodded at the dealer, who recognized me, and pulled it from the table and away from the players. I needed badly to sit down.

"I promise you, you're mistaken when you say that I rang you on purpose," I said. "I confess, I'm a bit of a flake."

"You're full of shit, that's what you are—and a crappy liar for someone who's supposed to be an actor."

I didn't even try to parse her conflation of acting and fabricating.

"People who sleep with John Aldred aren't honored to speak

with me," she went on, "because you don't respect me. I know what you stand for."

And yet she still had not confirmed who she was. I wondered whether this was by design. So, in the event the call was being recorded, I said her name.

"You sound a bit like Erika Schweiker."

"Representative Schweiker to you."

"My apologies. My apologies for that and for phoning your number by accident."

"By accident? Okay, then: Whose number in your contact list is close to mine?"

"I don't know because I don't know your number. Your number—at least this one—is blocked."

"This is your last chance: why did you call me?"

"I had no reason. I promise you it was a mistake."

There was a long pause at her end marked only by her breathing. I was forming another plea in my mind when she spoke. "Okay, Crissy Dowling. I'm going to quote the brilliant Ronald Reagan, who coined the expression 'Trust, but verify.'" (I restrained myself from correcting her a second time and telling her that Reagan was, by design, citing a Russian proverb.) "I am going to trust that you are telling me the truth, but I am also going to verify it."

And, with that, the line went dead. I left the poker room and returned to the raucous tumult of the slot machines, and the incessant burble of conversation, laughter, and applause that is the white noise that marks a casino.

* * *

So, this was the minefield into which Diana had walked. Was I now on the radar of whoever had killed the Morley brothers? I considered going to the police, but I was unprepared to reveal my own moral turpitude. Besides, how would telling the LVPD that I had done a dead casino owner's bidding and was in the rifle site of a demented congresswoman help me to traverse the bombs beneath my feet? Moreover, I might anger Eddie Cantone and put my show—which I had to believe was now on a very shaky stage—further in jeopardy.

The next morning, I called Terrance, my agent in L.A., from my cabana.

"I talked to Eddie," he told me. "Please stop worrying about your career at the Buckingham Palace. Eddie likes what you do; he really does. And if the new owners, whoever they turn out to be, don't want Diana? They'd be insane. We'll find you another residency."

"I hope so. But I can't help but fret."

"This is a lot. I understand."

"Thank you."

"And, of course, there's your sister. I get that, too. How are you two getting along?"

"Fine, I suppose. We haven't seen much of each other," I answered. "But I did a little homework into her new career. Into Futurium. Cryptocurrency isn't much of a thing yet in the casino business."

"Did you think it would be? The gaming laws are pretty strict. I know you have to gamble with American currency."

"There are a couple of really low-end casinos that accept Bitcoin for hospitality charges. Hotel rooms, entertainment, food."

"Man, you cash in some Bitcoin for room service at some dive and you will be living large for a long time. A forty-dollar room at a place like—"

"I know. It's madness."

"But it's coming, Crissy. Even at the Bellagio or the Venetian. The laws will change. Look at Erika 'Guns and Crypto' Schweiker," he said, and instantly my stomach lurched. I hadn't told him that I called the woman and last night she had phoned me back. The coincidence made me feel worse than an hour of airplane turbulence. "Hell, if she ever had her way, the Federal Reserve would be replaced by some sort of crypto clearinghouse. My guess is that it will begin in Vegas with the slots. You'll have your crypto wallet linked to a gaming account, and the new slot machines will accept your coin."

"So, you can dump ten grand into a slot machine?"

"Why not? Soon enough, even your little piece of heaven will be allowing the big spenders to use crypto in the high roller rooms."

"Our high roller rooms are not exactly stratospheric."

"You know what I mean. Crypto just makes too much sense. The people who invest in cryptocurrencies are a perfect fit for the caves with the chip stacks in the thousands."

"But why would you even have a chip stack if you're using crypto?"

"Metaphor. I see people showing their bets on a screen."

"Are the cards real?"

"No idea. Maybe, maybe not."

"God, I just figured Futurium was here because the energy is cheap."

"Soon even that won't matter. The new coins have backends that are less energy intensive. But Crissy?"

I waited.

"Why do you care about any of this? Are you obsessing about cryptocurrency because your sister's in town and has a job in the industry? Look, that's her life, not yours. And when crypto does become common in Vegas? All it will mean is that there will be people in your audience who bought their ticket with a digital wallet."

He raised a valid point. Especially after my talk with Erika, why couldn't I leave a labyrinth that was only going to leave me flummoxed and befogged? I hadn't heard from Betsy since I'd dropped off Marisa and her at their apartment a couple of days ago. And so I thanked him for that reminder and decided to do something wild and crazy when we got off the phone. I would pop a Valium, order a gin and tonic, listen to the Bee Gees, and doze.

* * *

It hit 120 degrees on the strip that day. Off the strip, in the residential neighborhoods and the gated communities in the suburbs, people couldn't walk their dogs on the sidewalks or the pavements without dog booties because it would scorch the animals' paw pads, and if you left your car parked in a supermarket lot and forgot to roll down the windows, you'd best not have bought ice cream: it would melt in the moments before the vehicle's AC kicked in. Good God, you risked heatstroke yourself waiting for the AC to dial down the sauna.

There was no breeze, and the sun's progression skyward gave all of us who lived there dread like a low-level fever. The tourists? They would say, in their desperate delusions of carpe diem, that it was a dry heat and so it was tolerable.

It wasn't. It never was and it never is.

Even my cabana was toasty, and usually it was an oasis in the wasteland. The guests at the pool spent their time in the water, drinking and flirting and hooking up, and hoping the insane heat would bake their hangovers away.

* * *

The second-to-last song I sing is "Kiss Me Goodbye." It wasn't a massive hit for Petula Clark, but it was still a Billboard Top Twenty. It's a poignant song about unrequited love, and the lyrics were perfect for Diana:

So, kiss me goodbye and I'll try not to cry,
All the tears in the world won't change your mind.

I sing it with a handheld mic, alone in a spotlight stage left in the emerald-sequined mermaid dress that Catherine Walker designed for Diana, while the video behind me shows Charles and Camilla growing old together after the princess has died and the two of them have wed.

Then the lights come up, and I return front and center to talk about the things that I—well, Diana—lost after the divorce, such as the title. This meant that Diana, in the last years of her life, was supposed to curtsy to even her two sons.

That night when I finished the song and hit my spot and started to speak, I saw Betsy, Marisa, Frankie, and a fellow I didn't recognize in the second row. For a flicker I lost my focus, because strawberry blond is still blond, and there was my sister—a woman who could have been Diana's sister—in the house. I supposed it was Frankie who had found a scalper with seats or some muckety-muck of great importance at Futurium knew how to get hot tickets for sold-out shows. (Or, yes, lukewarm tickets for off-the-strip eccentricities such as mine.) I hadn't registered precisely what Marisa was wearing before turning to regain the thread, but I saw a lot of skin. The theater could be chilly, and the idea passed through my head, *I hope she's warm enough,* which are five words one almost never puts together in Las Vegas. As I sank back into my role, I did so with foreboding, because I knew they were going to want to come backstage after I finished.

* * *

Bud McDonald told me that my sister wanted to visit my dressing room with three other people. I nodded: I'd seen it coming. Bud had met Betsy when she had come to the show previously. He went to retrieve them, and soon there was another rap on my door and there they were. Bud knew the drill and said he'd be back in five minutes, which most backstage guests understood to mean that five minutes was their window with me. Then he was gone, and Frankie was introducing me to a rather handsome fellow from Newport Beach in a ball cap and boat shoes named Tony Lombardo. I couldn't tell what he thought of the show, but Frankie was babbling about how moved he was and how much he loved it. Meanwhile, Marisa was staring at my vanity like it was Shoplifting Day at Sephora. She was wearing a tight yellow dress with spaghetti straps thinner than the straps for her bra—which I wasn't sure she needed—and heels so high she was almost Betsy's and my height.

"Squidgy," Marisa said. "Is that really a word?"

"It is," I said. I knew where this was going. "It means kind of squishy and gross. Imagine a frog's skin." She had heard the word in that moment in the show when I milk it. I have fun with the word because of its wondrously onomatopoeic qualities.

"Why did that man call Princess Diana that if he liked her?" she continued.

"Don't your close friends have nicknames for you?"

"I don't have close friends," she said, her tone flat. "I don't have any friends. I move around too much."

"Fair enough," I agreed.

"One of my rugby buddies from college still calls me Kegger. You know, as in a beer keg," Frankie volunteered, desirous of being helpful and moving the subject away from a foster child's ineffably horrible life and back to the nicknames of the rich and the royal.

"There you go," I said. "Sometimes we know where a nickname comes from and sometimes we don't. But that man who called Diana 'Squidge' and 'Squidgy' cared for her. As Princess Diana says in that part of the show, she viewed it as a term of endearment." That man was James Gilbey, heir to the gin empire. He and Diana had been recorded surreptitiously on the telephone. In my opinion, the best part of the call—what was called Squidgygate at the time—was the moment when Diana referred to Charles's disagreeably entitled blood kin as his "fucking family."

"Your sister told me how you got into this whole Diana thing," Frankie said. "Man, I had no idea how much I'd love it. You got pipes."

I tried to put aside my sister's lunatic conjectures about why

I did what I did, and recalled Yevgeny Orlov's reaction to the show. Men were always surprised by how much they enjoyed it.

"Men suppose I'm an acquired taste," I said. "I'm not. I'm considerably more potato chips than oysters or asparagus."

"Hey, now, I like oysters," said Frankie. "And, yeah, potato chips. Bring on the trans fat!"

"You will do well in Las Vegas."

Betsy hadn't said anything since they'd come backstage, and I considered asking her how she was settling in, but Marisa picked up a tube of my Clarins eye makeup remover. "Whoa," I said, "that stuff is gold," but she ignored me and squeezed some onto her fingers. Betsy took the tube and the cap from her and handed them back to me. I plucked a tissue for Marisa for her fingers.

"Can I ask you a question?" Tony Lombardo said.

I shrugged.

"Would you ever do your show for Futurium?"

A part of me felt a bit puffed up: he had been circumspect in his opinion about my performance, but, apparently, he liked it. Still, this was an absurd request. "Like what, a pep rally? I'd be the talent at some corporate retreat?"

"More of a party thing. Not really for employees, because we don't have so many. We'd pay you. Obviously. Our pockets are deep. Maybe we'd do it in West Palm Beach. Or Grand Cayman. I have a British friend who's there a lot. Oliver Davies, and he has a crazy thing for Princess Diana."

"Really? How old is he?"

"Not old. Maybe sixty, sixty-two. He met her in 1995 when she went to Moscow. He was a young guy then, working in the British embassy. They went to the children's hospital and the Bolshoi together. They were, you know, hand in glove for two days. You get my drift."

I wasn't sure whether *hand in glove* was meant to be suggestive, but it felt that way. In any case, his idea was a nonstarter. I wasn't the clown at a kid's birthday party.

"That's all very nice. I'm flattered. Thank you. But I'm sorry: I don't do private appearances. I do this show in this theater. That's the only place you will find it. Ever," I told him, adding that *ever* both for my benefit, and out of loyalty to the BP. I was still trying to reassure myself that the death of the Morleys wasn't the death of my show. After I'd spoken, however, I wondered if I had gone too far and I'd angered this Tony Lombardo. Yes, it was a ludicrous ask, but that was still no reason to poke the beast.

But he seemed fine, at least on the surface.

On the other hand, I watched Frankie's countenance transform from one of backstage bonhomie and good cheer to the face of that passenger in the exit row of a jet who's just been told by the flight attendant that they're going to ditch in the Atlantic and be ready to assist in the evacuation.

"But you'll think about it, right—for Tony and his friend? For Oliver Davies?" Frankie said to me.

"I doubt it," I told him, hoping my tone exuded an equanimity I wasn't feeling.

"That's cool," Tony said. "Let it go, Frankie." Then he looked at a text on his phone and added, "Why don't you take the girls home and meet me at the Bellagio? If I'm going to lose some money tonight, I'd like to lose it at a place where I won't be sitting next to a bunch of fist-pumping, GTL locals."

Locals was dismissive enough. But GTL was new to me. So, I asked.

"Gym-tan-laundry," he said. "It seems to me, you have two crowds here at the BP, Crissy. The old folk tourists who come and see you, and the younger locals who come here to gamble, but don't bother to shower after the gym."

Well, so much for his aplomb in the face of my rejection. His condescension didn't merely infuriate or embarrass me: it broke my heart. The Buckingham Palace wasn't the Bellagio, but there were lesser casinos, and I felt a loyalty to the people who came to the BP. I looked at my niece, but I couldn't tell what she was thinking or whether she had read the room and understood what had just happened. Betsy's face, however, was sympathetic, and I could see in her eyes that she felt bad for me. Despite all the dark, sad history between us, she didn't want to see me humiliated.

"So, Frankie: text me when you're there. I'll be playing poker," Tony added. "I feel I got a heater coming tonight."

"You bet, Tony," Frankie said. "On it."

Then Tony gave me a small bow, thanked me for a "solid" show, and left me alone with my niece, my sister, and her bounder of a boyfriend. The silence was awkward but brief, because Frankie needed to get Betsy and Marisa back to their apartment and then reconnect with the man who, it was evident, was a boss who expected absolute fealty. My sister's boyfriend was so obsequious that his reaction gave me a chill that Tony's words hadn't, and the gloaming of my soul only grew worse.

I always knew grown-ups could be dangerous. I told you, I had foster parents go bitchcakes over nothing, and a lot of them had guns. And the Futurium people? Those were some scary freaks.

But they sure spent money. And the first time I was hanging out at a place like the Versailles? I got it. I understood why they made fun of the Buckingham Palace—which, until I saw the Versailles, I thought was pretty nice.

But a casino like the Versailles is way more elegant than the BP. I went online to get the costs of rooms at the BP and the Versailles and compared the restaurants and showrooms, and you could spend a week at the BP for the same price as two nights at the Versailles.

CHAPTER TWELVE

Betsy

Betsy knew that Tony Lombardo had offended her sister when they had gone backstage to her dressing room. What she couldn't decide was whether her sister understood that she was playing with fire when she said she wouldn't perform for Futurium. Crissy had never been especially circumspect: the woman wore some of her emotions on her sleeve (which might have been why she was such a good actor), but she also entombed others in cerebral catacombs so extensive that no shrink would ever exhume them (which also might have explained her prowess channeling the wounded and scarred). When Frankie was driving Marisa and her home after the show, despite the fact her daughter was in the back seat, Betsy asked him, her tone as casual as she could make it, "What was that about? Tony's whole would-you-do-a-show-for-Futurium thing?"

"Just an idea. I guess his pal Oliver Davies met the real Diana. It was spontaneous. He's like that."

"Is he pissed off?"

"At least a little, yeah. I'll find out in a few minutes when I catch up with him at the Bellagio."

"Is Crissy in trouble?"

"Doubt it."

"You're sure?"

"Not really. You don't fuck with Tony Lombardo. People in Vegas are already figuring that out."

"He's not a pussycat like Rory O'Hara?"

"Remember, I said Rory was a pussycat with a vicious streak.

Like Tony, he's Mastaba. Even pussycats have claws. You ever see a cat with a mouse?"

"What did Tony have in mind?"

"I don't think he had anything in mind. He liked your sister's show and thought it might be something fun for Oliver. He's very generous. He was offering to bring her to Grand Cayman, for God's sake."

"For Futurium. For some crypto robber baron."

He shrugged. "He was thinking of his friend."

"How much longer will he be in Vegas?"

"Unsure. Anyway, your sister made it crystal clear that she wants nothing to do with the idea."

Betsy had discovered that she loved the lights on the strip: their flamboyance and ostentation, the way they mocked propriety and reveled in their garishness. She thought of the lyrics from "Downtown" and heard her sister's voice in her head—"the lights are much brighter there"—and felt a pang of sadness when they veered toward the residential neighborhood where she and Marisa lived. That world was drab. If Las Vegas was *Downton Abbey,* she was living with the downstairs help.

"Besides," he said, as they accelerated after a red light turned green, "there are others who could do whatever Tony had in mind. You could do it. It's not like your sister is Meryl Streep. She's a cabaret impersonator of a woman who was known for dying in a tunnel in Paris."

"First of all, my sister is very talented. You saw the way the crowd adores her. There were people there who've seen the show six or seven times. Second, Diana was known for a lot more than that horrible car accident. She was beloved."

"You sound like Crissy—and I like that! Trust me, dye your hair, spend a few weeks with an accent coach, take some singing lessons, and you could be Diana, too." He'd said that to her before. Was he really that confident? Betsy knew that she wasn't, and she couldn't decide whether his faith was founded on how much he thought of her or how little he thought of her sister. Either way, for her to do what he was suggesting was familial treason of the highest order, even if she only resurrected Diana Spencer in Grand Cayman.

"Well, that's never happening."

"I got it. I'm just saying: you and Crissy look crazy alike."

"You were saying more than that."

He took his hands briefly off the steering wheel, raised his arms in surrender, and said, "I promise. I'm letting it go."

She thought again of his Vegas associate Rory O'Hara. Rory, like Frankie, was from Long Island. Rory carried a gun. He was a Futurium lawyer. She'd never met a lawyer who walked around packing heat. Frankie defended him by saying this was Nevada and, yes, Rory was a bit of a gun crazy, but lots of people here were. She recalled their moment in his California king, when he'd told her about Futurium's connections to the Mastaba. He'd reminded her that while the Mafia deserved credit for creating the fantasy island that was Las Vegas, organized crime was now a bit player, bought out years ago by the likes of Howard Hughes or evicted (and sometimes imprisoned) by the RICO Act. "Vegas is very corporate and mostly above board. Not totally, but even Ivory soap isn't one hundred percent pure," he had said to her just that morning, though they both knew that Vegas still had deep veins of venality and vice.

When they reached the apartment, he slid the Tesla into a parking space. They all climbed from the car and he kissed her on the cheek and fist-bumped with Marisa. Betsy thanked him for getting them the tickets, but he merely nodded and said he'd better hightail his ass to the Bellagio.

When she and Marisa were inside, Marisa observed, "Frankie really is Tony Lombardo's bitch."

"Okay: where did you learn to use words like that?"

"I don't know."

"Well, don't use *bitch* that way. It's demeaning to women."

"Sorry," she said. "What word would you use?"

Subservient, she thought, but she didn't say that. *Sycophantic,* maybe. But she didn't say that, either.

Later, while she was getting ready for bed, she stared at herself in the bathroom mirror. She had to admit, despite the absurdity of Frankie's belief that she could do what Crissy did, she didn't have to squint and it didn't take much imagination to see the face of Diana "Squidgy" Spencer gazing back.

* * *

One afternoon when she and Marisa were at Frankie's house and Marisa had parked herself in his pool with her tablet exactly the way she did at the pool at their apartment complex, Frankie leaned forward in his deck chair underneath one of the palms and said to her, his voice hesitant, "This isn't the time or the place, but someday . . ."

"Go on."

"Someday, if you ever wanted, you know that you can tell me about your mother. How she died. And your father and stepfather. I know there's a lot more to the stories. You know I get that, right? Look, you don't like to talk about it, especially your mom, but I read the newspaper stories online again the other day—"

"Why were you bothering? No one got it right. I told you everything," she lied. "You know the truth."

"Shhhhh," he said. "I didn't mean to upset you."

"I'm not upset," she said, though she was.

"I just meant that now that we're here, away from whatever the fuck went down in Vermont, if you ever want to share anything, I'm a better listener than people think. Okay? That's all."

"Thank you," she said, hoping to end it right there. Marisa was too far away to hear them, but for a thousand other reasons she didn't want to discuss the details of how her mother had died or what she knew about her stepfather. *Whatever the fuck went down in Vermont.* Frankie knew the basics. That was all anyone needed to know. She moved her chaise so she was back in the shade from the palm fronds.

But Frankie wasn't prepared to end it right there. Or he was, in fact, a terrible listener and hadn't heard in her tone that she wanted this conversation over. "I mean, you know the traumas in my family. You saved my son's life," he went on. "You did that. But there is so much unsaid between you and me. Your sister—"

"My sister is a mess for ten thousand reasons."

"But when it comes to your mom's death, she blames—"

"Because she knows nothing. She thinks she knows everything. I'm not sure my sister . . ." Had Betsy finished the sentence, she would have said, *I'm not sure my sister can be saved. I thought so before I came out here. But not anymore.* Instead, however, she switched gears and continued, "My sister was in Las Vegas when our mom died. And as for your son: he's a great kid. He was going to pull himself out of that spiral with or without my involvement."

"Lots of great kids don't. I wouldn't have relocated here if he weren't in the place he was in. Emotionally. Psychologically. You got him there—to a good place. You got us as a family to a good place."

To that, Betsy knew, Crissy would have said to him something like *What family? You and your wife are getting divorced and you ran away to Las Vegas.* But their family was in a better place now than it had been two years earlier. Betsy had a perfectly friendly relationship with Carolyn, Frankie's ex-wife. The woman was seeing a new person in Burlington, and it sounded serious.

"Again, thank you. But he did the hardest work. And you and Carolyn did a lot of the heavy lifting."

"We had good coaching."

They were silent, and she was about to close her eyes, though she knew the specters from Vermont would prevent her from drifting off. She thought Frankie was done with this foray into her past. He wasn't. "When you found her—your mom," he said, his voice tentative, "did you know right away? Were you in shock?"

Found her? She didn't find her. She witnessed it. "Let's not discuss this."

"I know the mistakes I made with my parents when they died."

"Enough," she said firmly. She pulled her sunglasses onto the top of her head so he could see her eyes and know she meant business. "Enough." She was not going to be bullied by the best intentions into a conversation she had scrupulously avoided with everyone but the police (and even with them she had withheld so very much) since it happened.

"My regrets dwarf yours. I promise you. I—"

"I have no regrets."

"I ruined the last year of my father's life. I allowed the doctors to give him a colostomy that should never have taken place. What doctor does that to an eighty-two-year-old man whose eyesight is shot and who can't see well enough to change his own goddamn bag, and so he winds up in assisted living? That's fucked up. I'm a guy who had to be called twice—two times—once by the assisted living place and once by the ER after my dad had the stroke that would kill him before I got out of bed and flew to Florida. And don't get me started on my mom. I missed her death by hours because I was playing golf. I—"

"You need to let those demons go. We've been through this," she told him. Frankie's self-loathing would have surprised his Futurium pals, but it was a part of the reason she was drawn to him. He was wounded, too. Yes, he was a very successful businessperson, and he worked with people who, if they weren't criminal, had criminal ties. But two things can be true, she told herself. Multiple, seemingly divergent certainties can coexist. Paul Castellano loved his daughter but allegedly had both her boyfriend and ex-husband killed.

Frankie was ruthless, but he also worked with people who

scared him: people whose blood ran colder than his. He wasn't cruel casually, and that was the difference that mattered.

* * *

Betsy enrolled Marisa in school, and then the two of them took an Uber to the Versailles, a casino based loosely on the opulent French palace, so Betsy could meet more of the Futurium team. Betsy sent Marisa to the arcade room, and she went to the sushi restaurant there with Frankie and some of his Futurium associates, including Tony Lombardo, Damon Ioannidis, and Rory O'Hara, who were already there. There was also a woman named Lara Kozlov, who was a freelance political consultant for Erika Schweiker. Lara was Frankie's next-door neighbor, but she was in Washington as often as she was in Las Vegas. Tony was as close as one got to royalty, it seemed to Betsy, based on the way everyone at the table deferred to him. It wasn't just Frankie. Apparently, it was Tony's grandfather who had started the Mastaba dynasty.

Everyone was closer to Frankie's age than hers: they weren't twentysomething crypto prodigies. Lara, like Frankie, had experience in banking before becoming a political operative, and Damon said he was an engineer, but he was also in charge of Las Vegas operations for the company. He was the chief operating officer in the United States. He'd arrived in Las Vegas after working with Rory in Phnom Penh. Betsy didn't say much as the five of them had a conversation that pinballed between Frankie's former bank, an exclusive, almost top-secret resort they had shares in on Grand Cayman, crypto pioneers they knew who were clean and ones who were—in Damon's words—"dirty as fuck," blockchains, and the Nevada Gaming Commission. The Justice Department had recently seized nearly three billion dollars in stolen Bitcoin and arrested three brothers who were laundering crypto, and they discussed that, too, quite sure that neither a renegade hacker nor the U.S. government could ever infiltrate their systems. Someone had tried to breach the mining farm in Cambodia and failed. They knew that someone would try again there or in Las Vegas, but they were confident their walls would hold.

"How is Erika's war chest?" Damon asked a few minutes later. "What more can we give her?"

"There's always room for more; there always are ways," Lara answered.

Tony picked up a dragon roll with his chopsticks and held it suspended in midair as he answered. "John Aldred has very deep pockets," he observed pensively. "But we're in the hunt. It will help if Aldred does something stupid."

"Like in a debate?" asked Betsy.

"No. Bigger. Dumber," said Tony. He chewed the colorful little ottoman of seaweed and eel. After he'd swallowed, he looked right at her and said, "But we got something in mind. Still thinking it through."

"Why does Senator Aldred dislike cryptocurrency?" she asked.

"Because he's a dinosaur," Lara answered. "Erika and people like her are the future."

Betsy was about to ask Lara what she meant by *people like her*—she viewed Schweiker as an idiot at best, and a lunatic at worst—but then Damon was telling Tony about the pressure they were applying to the secretary of state in the event the November election was close, and then they were on to existing banking regulations and the roles of investment and commercial banks, and it was all over her head. Damon used the word *custody,* and she understood that he meant a crypto investor's storage space. She asked him to tell her more.

"Ownership is ascertained with a seed phrase—sort of like a twelve-word password—and you want to keep it in cold storage," he explained.

"Cold storage?" she asked.

"Offline. On a piece of paper. Weirdly old school for something as new school as crypto. Maybe keep a copy of the seed phrase in a safe. You don't want it online, because it can be hacked."

"And if you forget it?"

"Your crypto is lost forever."

"Gone?"

"All gone. Poof," he said, raising his hands and spreading wide his fingers like a magician.

"Do people ever just memorize their seed phrases?"

"Sure."

Frankie hadn't told her how easily crypto could be lost when she'd gotten her first Futurium coin. She'd written down the randomly generated seed phrase, nine of the twelve words meaningless to her and three that were daggers, as if the computer wanted to taunt her: *juveniles, ghoul,* and *delusion.* The phrase sat in her dresser with her passport. What if she lost it or it was stolen? The very idea of not being able to retrieve that ever-growing pile of money—okay, it wasn't really a pile—caused her stomach to lurch, and she stared down at the avocado and cucumber rolls on her plate, and pawed at one with her chopsticks, but she couldn't bring herself to lift it to her mouth.

"You're alarmed," said Tony.

"No," she lied. "I was just imagining someone misplacing their password. Their seed phrase. Horrible."

"It happened to a guy I know in L.A. He never got any back," he told her.

"Oh, my God. I'm so sorry."

"I'm not. I was the one who found it," he said, and everyone at the table but her laughed. She couldn't decide if this had actually happened or was merely a joke, but she had the sense there was more than a modicum of truth to the story.

After lunch, Frankie's friends were planning on going their separate ways, and Tony left first because he had booked a massage at the Versailles. When the rest of them were finishing their coffee, Rory swiveled in his seat, and Betsy noticed the gun in his waistband. She asked Damon and Lara if they had pistols with them, too. Damon didn't answer, but Lara opened her handbag.

"It's a SIG Sauer P238," she told Betsy, placing a handgun on the table. "Only weighs fifteen ounces. It's cute, right? Don't you love that pink pearl grip? Fits nicely in even my smaller purses."

"Why do you all carry guns?" she asked.

Lara was the one who chose to answer. "Because we can. I can't speak for Damon or Rory or Frankie—"

"You have a gun?" she asked Frankie.

"Not on me. I keep one in the car and another in the house."

"You have two?"

"Uh-huh."

"Did you have them in Vermont?"

"I had one."

She was surprised. She hadn't known.

"To make all this work, you need two *P*'s in your pocket: a pistol and the police," Damon said, smirking. "And we have both."

"And by *this* you mean . . ." Betsy asked.

"What we're building here in Vegas," Damon replied, and then he said in a tone that sounded on the surface as if he were making a joke, but anyone listening would understand was the unvarnished truth, "the Mob Two-Point-Oh. And, someday soon, with a senator in our holster."

Frankie looked at him as if he'd just confessed a crime to a district attorney, his eyes wide and exasperated. Betsy guessed that Damon wasn't supposed to say that sort of thing around her.

"Damon is exaggerating," Frankie told her. "We have friends with the LVPD, but it's not like we have the whole damn force on some gangster-like payroll. I told you: Futurium is mostly above board."

Frankie's damage control was ham-handed, and both Rory and Damon stared at him, toying with the idea of contradicting him. Remind him who was really in charge. But, in the end, the two of them swallowed the last of their coffee and remained silent.

Betsy turned to Lara and said, "I had a boyfriend in high school who went deer hunting. His whole family did. So, I took a safety course and learned how to shoot a rifle."

"What kind of shot are you?" Rory asked.

"Bad. Twice I shot at deer and both times I missed. But I have fired a bolt-action Remington."

"You enjoy it?"

"It was fine," she answered, before turning back to Lara. "You didn't really answer my question. Why do you keep that SIG whatever in your purse?" she pressed.

"Because it keeps me safe."

"Did you carry it when you worked in New York City?"

"I didn't own it when I worked on Wall Street. But there were times when I was overseas when I wished I'd had a gun."

"Is that why you got one when you moved out here? It makes you feel safer?"

"Not feel safer. Be safer. I'm not a paranoid wack job. But I don't worry quite so much now. It's nice to have it."

"The gun."

"Yes. A few months ago, a friend took me to the shooting range and I had the best time. That's how it started. I discovered that I'm much happier as a single woman knowing I have a little pistol."

Betsy turned to Rory. "And you? Why do you carry a gun?"

"It makes me harder to kill," he said simply.

* * *

She texted Marisa that they were finished with lunch, and she and Frankie were on their way through the shopping concourses that surrounded the gambling floor to pick her up at the arcade. Because the Versailles was decked out to resemble the

Sun King's France, it was a high-end version of the BP's homage to the Homes of the Inbred Royals—though, it seemed to Betsy, whoever took over the BP from the Morleys' estate would be wise to capitalize on the reality that Americans were far more likely to devour deeply fried fish and chips than cassoulet and coq au vin. There was opportunity there, even she could see it.

The Versailles always boasted exhibits about Louis XIV, Louis XVI, Marie Antoinette, guillotines, and anything that involved Napoleon, but Betsy doubted that most of the guests were aware of anything other than the idea that the casino feigned extravagance and had lots of chandeliers. The guests were interested in aura, not authenticity, and some of the imagery was gargoyle gothic straight from Notre Dame.

"I have to tell you, Frankie," she said, bringing their conversation back to her own future, "I still have no idea what I'm going to do at Futurium."

"You've got to learn the business."

"I'm not sure I even know what the business is."

They passed the Imperial Hair Salon and Frankie stopped. "I have an idea. Let's double back after we get Marisa."

"To the salon?"

"Yup. Let's surprise her and give her a makeover. For school."

"She's thirteen."

"So? At thirteen, my daughter loved makeovers. We used to take her and her pals to this elegant resort in Stowe—Powder Peak, you probably went there a thousand times—and let them all have makeovers for her birthday. We'd own the joint."

"Does she need one?" Betsy asked. She had never been to Powder Peak. She almost went as a guest with her college roommate's family one winter break, but she canceled at the last minute because she feared she lacked the right clothes and that her secondhand snowboard would reveal how modest her home life truly was.

He pulled her into him and wrapped his arms around the

small of her back. "Nope. She does not. And neither do you and neither do I. But this is Las Vegas. Let's have some fun."

She suspected she knew where this was going, and she wasn't wild about the destination. But she knew also that Marisa would enjoy the experience and that Frankie was about to drop four digits. And so she acquiesced.

How do things fall apart? she asked herself when the stylist began dying her hair the exact shade of blond that had belonged to Diana Spencer, using images pulled from the Internet to match it perfectly. Little by little and then all at once.

Even I could see that Betsy was worried about her sister. Crissy lived in this world of—and Betsy herself used this word with Frankie, and when I googled it, I saw it was perfect—denial.

CHAPTER THIRTEEN

Crissy

The press was ravenous when it came to Diana, from the moment she entered the life of Prince Charles until the night that she died. And though, in the end, they were partly responsible for her death, her relationship with them was more transactional than Diana's most ardent worshippers would like to believe. She had learned that the paparazzi were both the best way to exact revenge on the royals by allowing them to photograph her when she was doing the work that did indeed matter to her—comforting the sick, lobbying against landmines—but also a way to invite them in, so to speak, after the divorce when she was gallivanting about town with new men and A-list celebrities. The press was her power.

So, I created two video montages of headlines and photographs, ending, of course, before the cataclysmic car accident, but including tabloid grabs of her and her lovers, including heart surgeon Hasnat Khan, and the infamous bathing suit pics of her on Dodi Fayed's yacht. (How well did Diana understand the clout of the media? She herself had alerted the *Sunday Mirror* to have cameras at the ready when the yacht was off Corsica.) One montage scrolled behind me when I sang "Don't Sleep in the Subway," and one dotted a he-said/she-said routine I wrote for Nigel and me. Occasionally during the latter montage, when Nigel was presenting Charles's side or the queen's perspective, I would scan the faces of the people in the audience in the first or second row. Without fail, the headlines that would cause them to lean forward, their countenances intense, were not the ones of

Diana consoling the dying and comforting the sick, but the ones of her caught by the paparazzi looking inconsolable or bereft, when her marriage was crumbling and the royal family saw the rift as but a crack in a wall to be spackled.

It will sound rather unsporting of me to say this—a bit of a sly boast, since I look like her—but she was always going to be tabloid fodder because she was winsome and lithe, even when the world around her was an incomprehensible thrum of sadness and despair.

* * *

After Artie died—suicide or murder, it didn't matter—all discussion of a memorial service for Richie evaporated. Conversational dry ice. One moment, it was a date we were waiting for that we would pencil into our calendars, and then it was gone. No one, least of all me, ever broached the idea of a double funeral or double memorial service for both brothers. All of us at the BP and, I imagine, anyone who knew the pair was in a survival mode of sorts.

* * *

Futurium didn't have an office building. It had a half of a bloody warehouse. It was on the outskirts of an executive park west of the strip off Highway 582. I'd passed it when I'd driven Betsy and Marisa to Summerlin and she'd pointed it out to me. It was a massive, unassuming block of concrete beside a bunch of four-story office buildings, clustered in a complex and surrounded by the usual Vegas array of motorcycle dealers, fast-food franchises, and liquor stores.

I looked at it now from the sky on a satellite map on my tablet, a club soda beside me in my cabana. It was August 31, the twenty-fifth anniversary of Diana's death, and my two shows that night would be emotionally fraught. There would be weeping from the diehards. I zoomed in on the building, knowing my sister was inside it. Then I scrolled across the map to the structure where Marisa was starting school. Today was her first day.

And in the offices of the Buckingham Palace, Eddie was doing his best to keep the lights on—"business as usual"—and meeting with lawyers who represented the Morley estate and their real estate appraisers.

It was a big day for everyone, it seemed.

I ordered poolside crudités and hummus, because this make-believe princess who once in a great while purged never bothered to vomit celery and carrots. Then I texted Yevgeny, asking him where he was. I told him I missed him, and regretted the text the moment I sent it. It wasn't because it was untrue, but rather because it was too honest. I feared roping him into the madness of my life and revealing how fragile my career really was or sharing too much of my sordid family history. But I thought if he had the time, I might give him a call and see where the conversation went. Perhaps I would be willing to bare more than I anticipated once I heard his voice.

* * *

I am not so cynical that shows on the anniversary of Diana's death don't leave me moved. The first year I was in the little BP showroom, my eyes filmed up in moments where they weren't supposed to. I'm sure part of the reason I was wrecked was the fact I had a Vegas residency and people were coming to see the show. I understood the BP was not the MGM Grand, but there were tribute performers who would have killed for what I had. But a part of me also felt the pain of the remarkable woman's death.

Because she was remarkable. It's why people loved her then and love her still, and why generations before me were so devastated when she died so suddenly. So tragically.

It's why so many of us—yes, I include myself—exploit her. I am not oblivious to what William or Harry or even Charles would feel if they ever saw my show, and the way I have fabricated a hologram and manipulated memory for my own purposes. What the prince said about love could also be said about truth: "Whatever 'truth' means." *Truth* is open to interpretation. There is a cruelty, conscious or not, to the musicals and the TV series and the documentaries and the novels. There is a cruelty to what I do. After all, those people who knew and loved her are still alive. It's not as if I am resurrecting Anne Boleyn.

But she's irresistible: woman scorned wins big against the patriarchy—excuse me, royal family—and then dies in needless, heartbreaking fashion. It's why I strive to be kind to her memory and always take her seriously as a human being.

It's why I am given so many keepsakes every year on the thirty-first.

And the year that Betsy came west was especially fraught because it was the twenty-fifth anniversary. My dressing room was inundated with flowers and memorabilia. That night I sat alone for a long moment amidst it all, grieving. I thought of her sons and grandchildren, and I thought of the people whose lives she had touched, and tried not to delude myself into believing I was anything more than a conduit to the ethereal magic of the People's Princess.

* * *

My Prince Charles—Nigel—and I went to the BP's Tower of London pub after my second show, because I was knackered by the anniversary. Also, I like the vibe in the Tower, and I'd noticed that one of my favorite bartenders, Cassandra, was among the trio tending bar there that night. Half the time she didn't bother to charge me.

We were both drinking gimlets, which was a tradition we'd shared since the first time he had joined me onstage. The gimlet is one of those classic gin drinks that expat Americans glom on to in London.

A beautiful bar is a beautiful thing, and the Tower was a beautiful bar. It was where I had brought Yevgeny for our first drink. I stared at the bottles of booze behind the bartenders, each row impeccable, each label a study in artistic design. Barware offers wonders in ritualistic and aesthetic artistry: the highball glasses, the martini glasses, all the different kinds of wineglasses and champagne flutes and brandy snifters. I considered whether I was wasting my time on uppers and downers and an occasional eating disorder: perhaps I should just become a full-on, no-holds-barred alcoholic and hang out in taverns and pubs.

"We had some possible buyers in the house tonight," he said. "People interested in buying the BP."

"Well, that is one fuck-all of a damp squib," I said.

"That expression's too arcane even for me, and I grew up in the UK. What in the world is a damp squib?"

"A squib is a bomb. A damp one doesn't explode. Have you never heard that term?"

He shook his head. "Sorry. A little before my time."

"How did you hear about the buyers? Who were they?"

"*Possible* buyers," he answered. "*Possible.* Bud told me," he added, referring to our security chief. "They weren't international—they were all American, I gather—but their names sounded like a gathering of the UN General Assembly. Greek, Italian, Irish. Even Russian. A party of five. Four men and a woman."

"What were their names?"

"The only ones I recall are O'Hara and Kozlov. Kozlov was the woman."

I took this in. There was a slanting beam of light on the bottle of curaçao behind the bar, and the blue grew dreamy and the curvature of the glass erotic. Booze was like that. Had there been Kool-Aid in the flagon, I would have thought no such thing.

"We're doomed, Nigel," I said. "The Morleys are dead. Best case, the BP's fiscal plight was so dire they really did take their own lives. Worst case, they were executed and whoever did that will stop—"

"If they were murdered, it might have had nothing to do with the casino. You're panicking, love."

"I don't think so. There's an awful lot going on."

"There is. But there will always be a place for Diana. My God, this city has a museum devoted to her."

"In a mall. And malls are the giant pandas and snow leopards of commerce. They're going extinct."

"Well, then. You have your plan B," he said, and he raised his eyebrows lecherously.

"Meaning?"

"Well, let's see. You've had a tumble or two with a U.S. senator, and now you have your oligarch friend, Yevgeny—"

"Who *is* American," I reminded him. Usually I didn't think twice about discussing my lovers with Nigel. But now that Betsy had told me how she and our mum had speculated about Nigel's and my relationship, I found myself more aware of my friend's possible feelings.

"Not judging! But didn't you tell me that some rich crypto geek's fantasy is to have sex with Lady Di in Grand Cayman?"

I had told him this. I nodded. "True, true. One of Betsy's bosses, Tony Lombardo, did want me to meet a friend of his. Oliver Davies. But I don't know if he wanted me to actually shag him."

He snapped his fingers. "Lombardo! That was one of the names, too. He was at the show tonight."

I turned to him, now intensely alert. "Tony Lombardo?"

"Yes. That's the name. Bud said it was his second time here."

"Was Frankie Limback with him?"

"Your sister's boyfriend? No."

"Just Tony."

"And four others. They had a tour of the whole property first. We were just the after-dinner mint, you might say."

"They're all Futurium," I said.

"Your sister's crypto company?"

"Yes."

"Interesting."

"It's more than interesting. It's alarming. Tony Lombardo is a Futurium bigwig. When he asked if I'd ever do a special one-off for the company, I told him to, more or less, fuck off. I was polite. Mostly. Still, nothing like pissing off your potential new boss."

He finished his gimlet, absorbing this. He signaled for Cassandra to bring him another drink. "Have you ever visited a crypto casino on your computer?" he asked.

"No."

"You should."

"I don't own any Bitcoin or Futurium or whatever."

"Me neither. But when you told me what Betsy was going to do for a living, I surfed around a bit. They're just like online PayPal casinos, except you're using your digital currency. Roulette, slots, blackjack. You move your money from your digital wallet to your casino wallet and, if you win, back into your digital wallet when you're done. Maybe Futurium is about to open one—or, given the technology, more than one. Maybe that's why they're in Las Vegas."

"Terrance says someday it might be common for casinos to use cryptocurrencies. But why a real casino would want that is beyond me. What's the point of crypto's privacy if you're there in the flesh? What's the point of owning all this actual real estate if you can make the same money virtually? Besides, they wouldn't have to come to Vegas to open a crypto casino if the things are online. They could open it from anywhere. Grand Cayman, if they wanted. Cambodia. Some wonk's basement in Tennessee. Even my sister is going to be working from home a lot of the time, doing whatever it is that she does."

Cassandra brought Nigel his fresh drink. She was nearing sixty and had been bartending in Vegas longer than I'd been alive, and somehow her skin was not cracking parchment. Also, whoever did her Botox and dyed her hair auburn were virtuosos: I only knew her age because she'd told me.

Three older women approached the bar, simultaneously staring at me and keeping their gaze downcast. Submissive, unlike real paparazzi. I knew what was coming and reached into my purse for my Scotch plaid pen with a mini-Beefeater on the clip. Politely they asked me for my autograph, telling me how much they loved the show. I told them how much I loved them. Because I did. I signed two Playbills and a cocktail napkin with Diana's effervescent swoosh, a celebration of the lost art of cursive, and added a pair of X's to each. When they were gone, I told Nigel, "The one in the cardigan. She reminded me of my mum. The cut of her hair. The smile."

"Do you think Betsy would have moved out here if she was still alive? Your mother?"

"No idea."

"May I ask you something, love?"

I knew what was coming, but Nigel was a mate, so I agreed.

"Why won't you forgive her?"

"I've tried, Nigel. I have."

"And you can't?"

"I have as much as I can. Look, we speak. We'll see each other out here. But it's hard. What she did was just so damn stupid."

"It was stupid, I agree. But her self-hatred must make yours seem tame."

"You met my mum," I said, and I could see her face in my glass. A purple scrunchie in her hair, the tiny scar on her chin she'd had since childhood, the eyes the color of moonstones. "I've told you what an extraordinary human being she was. God, the shit she put up with when she was raising us? Getting us both through high school and into college on the salary of a rural Vermont history teacher? In a house that was falling apart faster than Usher?"

"Usher? Is that another British reference I'm missing?"

I looked at him, a little disappointed. "No. American. Poe."

"Ah, I know it now."

"After our stepfather died, I spent my life cleaning up after Betsy, or trying to make our mum's life easier. And how did it all end up? She killed the woman."

"Did it cross your mind that she came here because she wants to be near you? She wants to be in your life? She wants her daughter to know her aunt? Let's face it, you're the only immediate family she has."

"You have to meet that child. I like her. But she's a piece of work."

"Why don't we all have lunch tomorrow? You and me and Betsy and her daughter? Maybe I can suss out what she's thinking and what Futurium is doing."

"Marisa has school."

"Fine. Me and two Dianas."

"That's not funny. She doesn't look that much like me."

"Oh, but she does."

"Do you want to be kicked in the bollocks? Is that something you crave?"

He ignored my threat. "You'll invite her to lunch?"

I looked at those exquisite bottles behind Cassandra. When I'd gotten out my pen for the fans, I'd also retrieved my silver British pillbox with a UK flag on the lid.

"Yes," I said. "I want to know what's going on even more than you do." Then I wrote Betsy a text inviting her to lunch the next day. After it was sent, I reached into the pillbox for a Valium and swallowed the tablet with the last of my gimlet.

* * *

Someone had been in my suite.

At first, I just sensed it, the air electric and alive, as soon as I switched on the lights. Rather like a dog, I thought I smelled someone—something—unfamiliar, and I pulled my pepper spray from my purse, hugging the wall as I walked, the Mace before me like a gun, my eyes soft as if I were atop a horse, scanning the whole of the room. Each time I reached a lamp I turned it on, and soon my suite was brighter than it had ever been at night. My bedroom had a walk-in closet with two louver doors, and the slats were down. For a moment I held my breath, my heart thumping in my ears, as I stared at them. If someone was here, they were behind those doors. I considered backing out of the suite and texting Nigel or Bud. But I told myself I was paranoid because of the deaths of the Morleys, two cadavers that really had nothing to do with me.

Except they did, didn't they? If Futurium was buying the casino and my sister was with Futurium . . .

I hooked two fingers of my left hand through one of the knobs on the door, prepared to mace anyone behind it, and flung it open.

And, of course, no one was there.

Of course.

Just my clothes.

I sat down on my bed, at once relieved and uneasy. I was alone in my suite, and I wanted to believe my fears had been unfounded. But I couldn't.

And then I saw the proof. There it was, propped up against the pillows as if it were a room-service breakfast menu to leave outside my door before bed. It was an envelope-sized color brochure—one page, two folds, three panels—for a resort in Grand Cayman. It was called the Maenads, a reference to the women who followed Dionysus, and the resort's logo was a drawing of a nearly naked woman with a lyre. The Maenads were known for their passion, but the photos suggested a rather stately, conservative, and exclusive ocean resort—or, to be precise, club. It boasted twenty guest cottages behind a tall concrete wall painted peach, rows of royal palms, a spa, an on-site chef for members only, and one of the most gorgeous infinity pools

I'd ever seen. There were no people—guests or models—in the photos.

There was also no number to call for information. There was no website or email address.

When I googled it, I came up with nothing.

I called the front desk and told the night manager that someone had been in my room, and he said he'd look into it. He said to check to see if anything was stolen. I texted Bud the same thing, and he said he was on his way.

I supposed the Maenads was where Tony Lombardo wanted me to resurrect Lady Di for Oliver Davies. While I waited for Bud, I called Nigel to tell him what had been left on my bed. After I hung up, I saw that my hand was shaking.

* * *

When I awoke the next morning, it was instant. Usually the Valium would allow me a few minutes of somnambulant torpor, but not today. I had managed to sleep well, thanks to the amount of diazepam and THC I had mixed.

Me and Elvis. I had no Dr. Nick. But no one could self-medicate the way I could.

In all fairness, I had also managed to drift off because Bud had scoured my room and assured me I was safe. Also, nothing seemed to be missing: no jewelry, no credit cards.

I reached for my phone on the nightstand and saw I had so many texts my first thought was that someone had died. I had chains from Nigel, Betsy, and Yevgeny. Betsy had sent four texts, agreeing to lunch and offering a time and place. Nigel had sent three to ask whether I knew where and when we were dining. And my Russian American friend texted that his schedule had changed and he had checked the cabaret website. He could fly in the night before my upcoming days off and said he might go for a hike out at Red Rocks, while I decompressed in my cabana. And so I suggested, joking, that it would be much more fun for him to take a walk through Futurium's Vegas computer farm. And he texted back:

> Smoke and mirrors. Now you see it, now you don't.
> Futurium will be right at home in Las Vegas.

I stared at the text. If anyone could get involved with a business model that was all smoke and mirrors, it was Betsy.

* * *

The lunch went all to pot the moment Nigel and I pulled into the parking lot of the restaurant. It was five blocks from the Futurium warehouse, part of a chain that specialized in all-you-can-eat pastas and garlic bread. It's perfect if you're a lineman for the Las Vegas Raiders, or you want to carb up to throw up.

We never got inside, however, because when we emerged from my Mini onto the surface of the sun—a newly paved parking lot in Las Vegas at midday, the black deeper than squid ink—Betsy had arrived with backup. She had brought with her Frankie Limback and a fellow I didn't recognize. Both men were wearing khakis and polo shirts, which were untucked as if they were about to promenade on a beachside boardwalk.

Meanwhile, Betsy was wearing a T-shirt that was designed to replicate the iconic Lady Di red sweater with rows of white sheep and a single black one. Her eyes were hidden behind sunglasses with ruby frames that were eerily reminiscent of ones the princess had worn in the late 1980s. I had a pair like them myself. And, strangest of all, her hair was dyed the exact same shade as mine—and the princess's—and she had chopped a lot off.

Frankie greeted us, while my sister and the other fellow held back, standing in the sweltering heat beside her beau's Tesla.

"Before you say one word, Frankie," I began, ignoring his

game-show-host smile, "did you actually drive here from Futurium? It's a quarter mile, max."

"It's also one hundred and two degrees," he said.

"Betsy," I called over to her, "I thought it was just going to be you and Nigel and me?"

"Your sister mentioned you were having lunch, and so I thought I'd tag along," Frankie said, answering for her.

"And the lad over there is your muscle in case I try something funny?"

He rolled his eyes. "That's Rory O'Hara. I think Rory could become your biggest fan, if you let him. He saw the show last night and loved it."

"So, Rory: were you the one who left a Maenads brochure in my room?"

"Guilty as charged," he said, and I was dumbstruck. I had not expected such candor.

"You were in my room? How dare—"

"Whoa! It wasn't like that. How in holy hell could I even get in your room? I liked your show, and I heard you weren't wild about Tony's idea of coming to Grand Cayman. So, I tipped a bellman—excuse me, bellwoman, pretty young thing—to bring the brochure to your room. You should do it, Crissy—go to Grand Cayman."

"That brochure lacked a phone number or website or email. The resort doesn't even exist online."

"The Maenads is pretty exclusive. More of a club," he said. Then he took off his shades, stared at Nigel, and added, "Hey, you brought the prince!"

"So, you're the guy who plays Charles," Frankie observed. "Yup, I can see it."

"Yes, that's me," said Nigel, and he and Frankie shook hands like boxers before a prize fight. "It's a pleasure."

"For me, too," Frankie agreed. Then he focused on me and continued, "Now, we didn't just drive here because it's hotter than hell. Rory tells me there's an Italian restaurant much better than this one about five miles from here. We can all take my car. There's plenty of room for five. Make sense?"

"I hate to be rude, Frankie, but I was hoping that Betsy and I could have lunch alone."

"And yet you brought Nigel."

I was going to ignore him. I was about to call over to Betsy to ask if she minded if Nigel joined us and it was just us three, when the utter absurdity of yelling in the parking lot hit me. And so I started to walk over to her, and Frankie put out an arm like a railroad crossing gate and prevented me.

"Don't touch me," I said reflexively. I was shocked.

"Meant nothing by it, Crissy, nothing at all."

"Betsy, how about you and I eat alone?" I suggested. "Girls only?"

She looked at Rory as if she were six and he were her father. But she didn't say anything and neither did he. He folded his arms across his chest and turned toward the front of the Tesla.

"Frankie," said Nigel, trying to prevent the tension from growing worse, "why don't you all pick an evening to come back to the BP, and we'll talk after the show in an air-conditioned casino bar in the desert in the middle of the night. Let's face it: that's how civilized people do business in Las Vegas, going back to the days of Bugsy Siegel and Kirk Kerkorian."

"You know Kerkorian flew Siegel back to L.A. just before Bugsy was executed?" Rory asked. "You never know what tomorrow's gonna bring in the Wild West."

"You don't," I agreed. I had heard the threat.

"Crissy, I think you and your sister and I can have lunch another time," Nigel was saying to me in his best Clyde Barrow to Bonnie Parker the-woods-are-filled-with-lawmen voice. "Or we all can. But not today."

"Hey, I didn't mean to be a killjoy," said Frankie. "I just don't want to eat here. If we're going for pasta, I want a decent lobster risotto."

"No, this is good," Nigel told him, and then he put his hand on my biceps and steered me back to the convertible.

When we were inside my car, my sister and Frankie and Rory were still standing there in the parking lot, watching us.

"What just happened?" I asked. "What in the world are we doing? Why are we not having lunch? Is it because of what Rory said about Bugsy Siegel? I really want to hear more about this Grand Cayman invitation. It's creepy and—"

"We're leaving," he told me, his tone clipped. "Drive."

So, I did, but as we were exiting the parking lot, I pressed him again. And this time he answered. "That Rory chap had a gun beneath his shirt. In the back, tucked into his belt."

"How do you know?"

"He turned to show me. Wanted to be sure I saw it. Your sister's boyfriend did, too. Also tucked into his belt and beneath his shirt."

I sped through a yellow light just as it darkened red, frightened and confused. "What did you think they were going to do, kidnap us? That's insane."

"They had guns, Crissy. I was not getting in that car, and I was not letting you get in that car. I was not going to let either of us end up like Richie and Artie Morley."

"This is Nevada. You're allowed to carry guns. You have a gun."

"Not with me. Not my style to bring weapons to restaurants."

Already I saw on the car's touchscreen that I had a text from Betsy. I clicked on it, and the automated, female voice read:

> What in the world are you doing? Come back. You wanted to have lunch. So do I. These are my new friends, and if you don't want them to join us, they won't. Just you and me and Nigel, okay? We can eat right here.

"Don't turn around," Nigel said. "Let's see her at the casino."

"I don't want her at the casino. All this pressure from Futurium. And I have no idea what she's doing with this Diana masquerade. You must have noticed the shirt and her new hairdo."

"The casino is safer."

"Because you think we won't get kidnapped there at gunpoint?"

"Hell of a lot harder."

"Let's find a neutral ground. Someplace where my head won't explode because someone thinks my sister is me and asks for an autograph."

"Fine. Saturday. We'll all parley—isn't that the gangster word?—the day after tomorrow."

"What about her daughter? Betsy and I can't hash this out if Marisa is present."

"Isn't the child thirteen?"

"Yes. But I doubt even Betsy would want to leave her alone on the weekend. They just moved here."

He sighed. "Lunchtime. Let's go to that water park off Tropicana. Marisa can hang out at the pool with the bonkers water slides. We'll sit on chaises in the sun, surrounded by lots of people, and your niece can go wild."

I took Nigel's advice, and Betsy and I texted back and forth using voice commands, and she agreed to meet me at the water park two days later at one. She promised it would only be her and Marisa, and I promised it would only be Nigel and me.

"Can I ask you a question?" I murmured, a little distracted, as we arrived at the strip and traffic came almost to a halt.

"Sure."

"Actually, two questions. First, why do you think Betsy was wearing that Diana T-shirt and colored her hair like mine?"

"I suppose to get under your skin. Next?"

"That's it?"

"Maybe there's more to it than that. Damned if I know."

"Well, then: do you think she's in danger?"

"The idea did cross my mind."

"What kind of danger?"

"I have no idea."

"God, now I feel guilty."

"Talk to Betsy about that on Saturday. About her new friends and why they carry guns. Have your heart-to-heart with her about what she's doing. But let's you and I also ask her whether she needs some sort of intervention."

I nodded. That was a good idea.

As we inched along the strip, I tried to dial down both my suspicions and my anger. I failed. She was with Futurium, and Futurium wanted my casino. A month ago, a continent had separated my sister and me; now it was miles. And that was an insufficient buffer to keep at bay all the sadness and hurt that made us who we were.

The new school was fine. The work was easy. But I'd never found schoolwork hard.

And the kids were okay.

But I had no idea if Las Vegas was going to stick, so it's not like I went out of my way to make friends. I was happy enough reading and playing numbers games on my tablet and phone in the pool.

A casino's odds fascinated me. You don't beat the house (unless, like me, you can count cards), and even then you're probably just cutting your losses and getting to hang out at the table a little longer.

For instance, the house edge on a roulette wheel begins at 5.26 percent. And some players are so dim, they look at the wheel and think, "Oh, I bet one number, I have a one in thirty-six chance of winning, because the wheel is numbered one to thirty-six." Hah! Wheels have a zero, and some have double and triple zeros, so the odds might be one in thirty-nine.

And the longer you play, the more you lose. Even I understood why casinos don't have windows or clocks.

CHAPTER FOURTEEN

Betsy

When Tony Lombardo dropped by the Futurium warehouse and gave her the sunglasses and the scarlet T-shirt with the sheep, Betsy had no idea that they were part of Diana's "look." She took the single black sheep as a compliment: She was special. She was unique. That night, Frankie gave her a handbag and a scarf and a floral blouse that had nothing at all to do with Diana. He gave Marisa a retro T-shirt for an eighties punk band and a ball cap and a gift card for a low-end jewelry store in a mall near their apartment. Frequently, the Futurium team was descending upon her with presents, because they said they wanted to make Marisa's and her arrival in Las Vegas as seamless as possible. She thought the gifts were cute and kind, though she did suspect there was more to it than that. After all, these people were either gangsters or were involved with gangsters.

Frankie didn't suggest that she wear the sheep T-shirt the day they were going to have lunch with Crissy. She only grabbed it because it was still in the gift bag on top of her dresser and the morning was getting away from her. (She was finding as a mother that the mornings often got away from her.) She was in a hurry to get to work and get Marisa out the door and onto the school bus. Same with the sunglasses. She grabbed them without thinking twice; they were new and they were there.

Only on Saturday, when she met her sister and Nigel, did she realize that part of their retreat from the parking lot might have had something to do with the T-shirt. At the time, when her sister and Nigel peeled out, she thought it was madness, and she was mystified. Now, however, the question had changed: why was Futurium using her to push her sister's buttons for some reason, preying on sibling rivalries they really knew nothing about?

* * *

After Crissy and Nigel had sped away, Rory went home and Betsy and Frankie climbed into his Tesla, but they didn't head back to the warehouse with the computers. Instead, they drove toward the strip because it was still lunchtime and Frankie knew that she loved looking at the casinos. She was texting with Crissy, and the sisters agreed that they would meet Saturday at some water park with a snack bar for a bite to eat, and Betsy would bring no one but Marisa. Frankie wanted to join them, but she dug in her heels and said no: she didn't want a rerun of what had just occurred in the chain restaurant's parking lot.

A few minutes later, as the two of them were driving past Crissy's casino, they both gazed up at the ever-changing video billboard with, among its other ads, one for her sister's cabaret: "That Rare Woman the World Will Never Forget: Diana, Candle in the Darkness."

"They don't mention your sister's name," Frankie observed, speaking for the first time since she had barred him from joining the sisters at the water park.

"So?"

"I'd want my name up there if I were her. But, I guess, Diana's the draw. Not Crissy."

"Diana is the draw," she agreed.

He pulled off his sunglasses and said, "These are a disaster. I managed to get sunblock all over them. I have another pair in the glove compartment. Would you mind getting them for me, please?"

She took his glasses and opened the door to the compartment and saw his pistol was there. She couldn't recall if he had been carrying it when they had met Crissy and Nigel just now and then he'd tossed it into the glove compartment, or whether it had been there the whole time. She picked it up and made sure the safety was on. The safety was the part of a gun that was stressed most in the firearms course she'd taken as a teen. "If I hadn't met you in Vermont and spent so much time with you and your family," she said, "I'd be creeped out by the idea you drive around with a pistol."

"It's Nevada."

"People keep saying that," she said. "I don't know what that means and I don't care. Why in the world do you need a gun with you? Why do Rory and Lara and Damon?"

"And Tony," he said, chortling.

"Yes, him, too."

"He heads back to Los Angeles on Sunday night."

"You're changing the subject. I want an explanation. Your Futurium folks like guns an awful lot. Why?"

"Too much time around very demanding, very volatile investors. Besides, you had a gun in Vermont."

"No, I didn't."

"Still. You learned how to use a hunting rifle. You know what it's like to fire a gun."

"Here's the deal," she said. "Here are the rules. No guns around Marisa. None. Are we clear?" She handed him his other sunglasses and shut the door of the glove deck.

"Absolutely."

"Thank you."

"Would you do me a favor?" he asked.

"A favor or something for work? As far as I can tell, my whole job is going to be managing travel for all of you, setting up meetings, and making sure your calendars are in sync."

"There will be more to it than that."

"Your club memberships. I forgot. And the expense reports."

"And being our point person on changes to the gaming laws as they affect crypto—especially when Erika Schweiker wins in November. That'll be big. That's where we'll need your smarts."

"You have Rory for that. And Lara. I'll be sending them links to analyze. I'll be a well-paid but highly glorified intern."

"Only as you learn the business."

They were at yet another stoplight. He smiled. He squeezed her knee gently through her jeans and slid his hand a few inches up her thigh. It felt good. It always felt good when Frankie touched her. Their eyes met through their shades.

"So, that favor," he said.

"Go on."

"In the next week or two, we might want you to do a little modeling."

They were now on the strip, moving once again, and he was staring at the road and she was staring at the casinos. She could gaze at them for hours, even during the day. She always saw something new.

"Modeling?"

"We need a pretty girl."

"It's a favor for Futurium?"

"Uh-huh."

"I'm not that pretty."

"You are. You know you are."

Her mind contemplated the worst: arm candy for some creepy friend of Tony Lombardo or Damon Ioannidis. She knew Frankie wouldn't literally whore her out, but she didn't like the sound of this. "What precisely do you need a pretty girl for?"

"A photo shoot for the website. We need an outdoorsy-looking girl as background for a page about why we're in Vegas. We don't want chorus girls or party girls. We want someone who looks like, I don't know, a hiker."

"Really? That's it?"

"Yeah. Get a couple pics of you looking like you just hiked up Mount Philo back in Vermont."

"I did that with Marisa."

"I remember."

She hadn't expected this was the favor.

"And you're eye candy," he went on, "and this way we don't have to fuck around finding a model."

Abruptly he braked and pulled into the long drive that led to Caesar's Palace, and she asked him what they were doing, but he ignored her and gunned the car. He didn't say a word until he reached a spot near the entrance, where a valet raced over to them. There Frankie rolled down his window and told the young man they needed a minute. Then he looked her squarely in the eye and took one of her hands in his and said, "We were just robbed of a nice lunch. Let's you and I have one anyway."

"We don't have things to do?"

He rolled his eyes. "You trust me, right?"

"I do," she said, though, in truth, she didn't. Not completely. A part of their relationship was the way they used each other, though she still believed that she was using him more: he was underwriting her new life and offering her the sort of financial opportunity she had never expected in even her wildest dreams. She was making more in a single week here as an administrative assistant than she made in a month as a social worker in Vermont, and she had little in the way of expenses. She didn't even pay rent. Plus, she was getting Futurium crypto. (Already she'd copied her seed phrase onto the underside of a bathroom drawer. She'd used a black Sharpie, writing meticulously on the particle board. Then she had ripped the piece of paper into shreds.)

"An hour looking like Miss Wholesome Nevada," he said. "That's the ask. That's it."

"That's it?"

"You bet."

"Sure," she agreed. "Why not?"

"That's my girl," he told her, and he kissed her cheek.

The valet was waiting. "Let's go in," he said. "Let's get us some oysters at Gordon Ramsey's for lunch."

Yeah, I learned a lot about Diana. I watched the movies.

I could see why people loved her and why they loved Crissy's show.

One day we were at this water park—me and Betsy and her—and I stood on the steps into this pool with a bunch of runts half my age, and I watched the kids' parents doing double takes when they saw Crissy. It was like they'd seen a ghost.

CHAPTER FIFTEEN

Crissy

Between forty and fifty million people visit Las Vegas every year. That's a big number.

Ah, but would you like to hear a bigger one? Seven hundred and fifty million watched the wedding of Charles and Diana in July 1981. A lot of them are long gone, and many others have grown rather crumbly with age. But a lot are still here, thank goodness.

So, I never had any doubts that my cabaret would succeed.

And, yes, I was doing it before the Netflix series brought Diana into the fold and the Broadway musical opened and Kristen Stewart starred in *Spencer.* I was still doing it years after the series had run its course, the musical had closed, and the movie had come and gone.

I am a survivor. At least, at the time, that was how I viewed myself.

* * *

I didn't loathe the water park, but the moment I arrived, I was reminded of how much I preferred the domiciliary keep of my cabana at the BP. I missed the shade, and I missed the reality that there was considerably less pee in the water at "my" pool than there was at this one. Also, the soundtrack here was designed as ambient noise for splashing and screeching, and while I enjoy a ripping good musical as much as the next person, there was a tad more *Frozen* on this playlist than any grown-up needs, especially when gaggles of tone-deaf preschoolers shriek "Let It Go" without having the pipes.

When Nigel and I arrived, Betsy and Marisa had already planted their flag in a spot with four chaise lounges that, at the moment, offered a sliver of shade. My sister, I was happy to observe, had her hair covered in part by a green ball cap, her eyes hidden by traditional black-rimmed sunglasses. She was wearing blue jeans and flip-flops, and other than the color of her hair, nothing about her screamed iconic dead princess. Marisa said hello to Nigel and me, and then stripped off her cutoff jeans and pulled a replica Raiders football jersey over her head, revealing the slinkiest black bikini a thirteen-year-old ever has worn. My eyes clearly were agog, because she said firmly, "I control my body."

"Of course you do," I agreed.

"Put on sunscreen, Marisa," my sister said, handing her a tube.

The girl rolled her eyes, but rubbed lotion onto her belly and chest, the circles slow and provocative, and Nigel turned away so it was clear he wasn't watching. Then Marisa allowed Betsy to slather sunscreen on her back and said, "So, what is this big meeting about? Betsy wouldn't tell me in the car."

"Because it's none of your business," said Betsy. "I did tell you that."

"I think it is my business, since it affects my Saturday."

"You have before you some of the best water slides in Las Vegas," I said, and I motioned at the pool. "Not a bad way to spend your Saturday."

"Oh, boy: me and a hundred seven-year-olds."

"I see some older kids right over there," my sister said. "By the slide that looks like a dragon's mouth."

"Do you know how creepy that is? When you come out of the tube, you look like something the dragon is puking up." Then she turned to me, a light bulb having exploded behind her eyes. "Wow, Aunt Crissy, now I see why you had us meet here. That slide is right up your alley."

"Marisa!" my sister snapped.

"A human being emerging from the dragon's mouth doesn't resemble vomit," I corrected her. "And, as clearly my sister has told you, I would know."

"Can I see your teeth?"

I smiled for her. I'd recently had my teeth whitened. They looked grand.

"I always thought bulimics had meth teeth."

"I do not have meth teeth. Also, I'm not bulimic. Long ago, I had some issues with bulimia. There's a difference. Finally, I thought we'd agreed that you needn't call me *Aunt*."

"Marisa, do you want us to order you something to eat or drink?" Nigel asked.

"Sure. But none of you answered my question: why are you meeting?"

"Well, since it seems you have to know," I said, "I want to talk to Betsy about whether she needs anything as you two settle in here in Las Vegas."

"God, you must think I still believe in Santa Claus and the tooth fairy."

"You don't?"

She shook her head, exasperated with me. "Fine. I give up. I'll go swim with the toddlers and get upchucked by a dragon. If anyone decides to get food, I'll take a cheeseburger. And a Mountain Dew. Please."

"I could go," said Nigel, a little nonplussed.

"Cool," murmured my niece, and then she sauntered over to the steps that led into the pool, and stood there for a moment surveying the wee ones and their parents in and out of the water.

"She can swim, right?" I asked.

"Yes, of course she can," my sister said, but I noticed her eyes instantly went to the two lifeguards in their high white chairs.

"Will she mind if I don't get the cheeseburger right away?" Nigel wondered.

"You sound scared of her," Betsy said to him.

"I am."

"Don't be. She's thirteen."

"Going on twenty-five."

"Just thirteen," she reiterated. Then she looked me dead in the eye, and said, "So, Sis, let's begin with this: why did you two bolt out of the parking lot the other day?"

"Because your two friends had guns."

"Why do you care? Do you believe they represent any danger to either of you?"

I could tell from her tone that she wasn't being naive or deluding herself. She knew more than she was letting on, and had framed her question to suggest that whatever her new friends were up to, Nigel and I were fish too small to matter.

"We don't get in cars with strange men who carry pistols," I said.

"You're being ridiculous. You both are. When you left, we split up and Frankie took me to Caesar's and we ate oysters. It was heavenly. We had oysters and then lobster risotto."

"You had lobster risotto for lunch?" I asked. It was a knee-jerk question and instantly I regretted it. Both Nigel and Betsy looked at me, their eyes anxious. I put up my hands. "I'm sorry. I only meant it sounded heavy for lunch."

"We split the risotto, Crissy. Not that it matters."

"You're right. I'm sorry."

"My friends think you're kind of paranoid," Betsy went on. Then she looked at Nigel and added, "They think you both are."

"I noted the T-shirt you were wearing yesterday."

"I don't remember what I was wearing yesterday. What about it?"

"Oh, come on: the red one with the sheep?"

She stretched out her legs. "Okay, I'll bite. What is the significance of a T-shirt with sheep on it?"

"You really don't know?" Nigel asked.

"No, I don't. Tony gave it to me. Is it a Las Vegas thing?"

"It's a Diana thing. The design is parroting a classic Diana sweater," I told her.

"I didn't know that. Is that what set you off?"

"It didn't help."

"I think—like everything you're doing right now—you're overreacting."

Again, the bluster. She was hiding behind it.

"Why did Tony give it to you?" I asked.

"I guess he thought it was cute. Maybe when he saw my resemblance to Diana, he thought it was funny."

"Betsy," said Nigel, leaning forward, "what's really going on? Your sister is a brand. Why are you trying to infringe on that?"

"Diana was beautiful."

"So are you," Nigel said.

"I'm not infringing on anything."

"And what in the world are you doing at Futurium?" he went on, his voice so melodious and kind, he sounded more like a therapist than an interrogator. "I mean, surely in this of all cities, there's a need for more social workers who help teens."

"Probably," she agreed. "But I was burned out. I just . . ."

"Just what?" I asked.

"I was just always so sad at the end. The pandemic broke me. It just . . . it just broke me. I still text with some of the kids. Some are doing great. Some aren't. Anyway, it was time for a change. And, eventually, I will be helping people again. Introducing them to crypto, which is the future."

"Helping people get hooked on the weirdness of cryptocurrency isn't the same as helping teens and their families who are losing their shit," I pointed out to her.

"Losing their shit? You of all people should be more careful with your verbiage," she reprimanded me. "Why are you always judging me?"

"Because I'm your big sister."

"Barely."

"And maybe it's because you have a history of making choices that could be called dubious."

"You know how I could respond to that. But I won't."

"Futurium's a pretty secretive company."

"So? Why does that matter?"

"Why does that matter?" I repeated. "Seriously?"

"Look, it's crypto. You don't understand cryptocurrency. I didn't either at first. But there's nothing mysterious about it. It's just another way of doing business. Lots of people use it."

"What, pray tell, do Frankie's friends use it for? To launder money? To hide money?"

"Invest," she said. "Invest. Some are friends who used to use his investment bank before it closed its Moscow office, some are entrepreneurs, some are just sort of, I don't know, visionary. Early adopters. Obviously, it's all above board."

"Obviously," I repeated, but I didn't mean it. "And why do they want to buy the Buckingham Palace?"

"I don't know that they do."

"They were at the show again the other night. A gaggle of them. I believe they're doing their due diligence."

"Well, even if they did, it would have no effect on you."

"Oh, do you know something of their plans?"

"Not when it comes to buying a casino. I just know they love your show. Besides . . ."

Her voice trailed off, and when she didn't resume speaking, I pressed her. "Go on."

"Look, they all have tastes that are kind of highbrow. Like that club they have in Grand Cayman."

"Oh, I've seen pictures. Rory O'Hara had a brochure left in my room. The Maenads. Sounds like a resort for men who want underage girls."

"Oh, for God's sake, it's not. Not every story is Jeffrey Epstein's. But it is very special. I've seen pictures. It's elegant and exclusive, and the Buckingham Palace is . . . it just isn't. It's more down-to-earth," she said, obviously trying to apply lipstick to what she viewed as a sow.

"That's not a reason they wouldn't buy the BP," Nigel observed. "Maybe they want to turn it into a casino that is elegant and exclusive."

"And not down-to-earth," I added, my tone caustic.

"But it's always going to be off the strip," she said. "It's always—"

"May I ask you something?" Nigel pressed.

"Sure. Grill me some more. Why don't we all just go to the pool so you can waterboard me?"

He ignored her frustration and inquired, "Why is Futurium even in Las Vegas? I'm assuming the company plans to get involved in gambling. Be among the crypto pioneers out here, either by buying a property or convincing other places to make Futurium the coin of the realm."

"Futurium now has a coin that's pegged to the dollar. As you know, a lot of cryptocurrencies aren't."

"Actually, I didn't know that," I said.

"So that means they work with more stable assets. As the gaming laws evolve and the casinos start allowing guests to gamble with crypto, they'll begin with the coins that are less volatile. We'll be among the first in. With any luck, we'll have what Tony and Damon call their beachhead before Bitcoin or ETH."

"What does Frankie say?" I asked.

My sister looked annoyed. "Would you please let this go? There is nothing illegal about anything Futurium does."

"Cryptocurrency and gambling are both great ways to launder money," Nigel said. "Put them together, and just think what you could accomplish."

"We're worried about you," I said.

"Don't be. You're the ones who work at a casino where the two owners killed themselves."

"Which," I told her, "should have you alarmed, too, if Futurium is trying to acquire the casino. Look, I don't mean to pretend to be the wise older sister, but you're hanging around with people who carry guns. Are *you* safe? Do you need us to—"

"I need you to have a little faith in me!" she snapped. Then she glared at us both, and I braced for the rancor that she was about to unleash. Instead, however, her eyes pitying me, she shook her head and said, "The way Terrance exploited your . . . your issues . . . is unforgivable."

"I know you feel that way about Terrance," Nigel said, "but look at her. She's fine."

"I'm present," I reminded them both. I almost raised my hand. "I'm here."

"I apologize," Nigel mumbled.

"Betsy," I said carefully, "I'm sorry, but I think Frankie is likely to inflict more harm upon you than Terrance ever inflicted upon me. You believe that I only do what I do because a long time ago, for a brief period, I had a small eating disorder. Yes, that's why I started. But I've grown, and I continue to be Diana because—"

"You do what you do because of what our stepfather did to you, Crissy! You do what you do because he—"

"Stop it," Nigel told her.

"And Terrance took advantage of that and now you encourage it!" she said to him. "If our stepfather hadn't had the grace to fucking kill himself, I promise you, I would have done it for him! I would have killed him. And there was a time when I had the goddamn balls to do it."

"You're overreaching," I said to my sister. "And you're mistaken."

"About which part?"

Nigel was looking at both of us, desirous of stopping the carnage before either of us said anything worse, when Marisa returned, soaking wet, and dripped on top of my sister's back. Betsy glanced up at her when she felt the pool water on her shoulder. When you emerge from a swimming pool in Las Vegas in late summer, you really don't need a towel; the air is warm and you dry quickly. But still Betsy handed her one (hoping for modesty, I suppose), and the girl wiped her face and asked, "When will the cheeseburgers get here?"

"I think that's my cue," Nigel said, standing. Now he was desperate to escape.

"You haven't ordered them?" she asked.

"Sorry," he said awkwardly. I wanted to remind him that he was talking to a thirteen-year-old. I handed him my purse, and he started rooting around inside it until he found my wallet.

"No, he hasn't ordered," Betsy told Marisa. "We were all too busy debating the meaning of life."

The girl looked at her quizzically and then turned to me. "Do you ever swim?"

"I do, yes."

"What kind of bathing suit do you wear?"

"Why?"

"I like your clothes."

"Thank you."

"Have you ever been to this water park before?"

"Once."

"If you ever come back, make sure you wear a one-piece. Some six- or seven-year-old turd who couldn't swim grabbed on to my bikini bottom for dear life like it was a floatie. I had to drag him to his mom so he wouldn't drown or create whatever's the butt version of a nipple slip."

Betsy said to Nigel, "Why don't I go instead? Marisa and I will track down someone at the snack bar who can take our order. What do you two want?" It seemed as if she wanted out now even more than Nigel.

"I'm fine," I said.

"Of course you are," said Marisa.

"A cheeseburger will be great for me, too," said Nigel, and he handed my sister my wallet.

When they were gone, Nigel looked at me. "I'm sorry that conversation went there. I hadn't meant it to."

"Oh, me neither."

"You okay?"

"Peaches."

I grew aware of the relentless thump of the bass from the soundtrack and felt it now in my bones. I closed my eyes behind my sunglasses.

"Crissy?"

"Yes, Nigel?"

"You've googled Futurium."

"I have," I said. I was pleased he had returned to the subject at hand and what really mattered.

"You know what you should have been researching?"

I waited.

"Frankie Limback. He's what all of this—whatever this is—has in common."

"What are you doing?" I asked Betsy.

She told me: she was writing her crypto seed phrase onto the bottom of a bathroom drawer. She said it was in case she ever forgot it.

I nodded like, that's cool, that's the only reason she was doing it. But I was pretty sure she was also hiding it there because she was worried about someone or something, like her new employers. So, later, I put the chain in my tablet in the middle of a meaningless email from the Gap. I also hid there her checking account number.

The next day, we opened a little savings account for me. She gave me an "advance" on my allowance that totaled three hundred dollars, but it wasn't really an advance, because I knew she'd keep paying me an allowance and never ask for it back. She knew it, too.

I have to admit, everything about Futurium began to weird me out after we got to Las Vegas. First of all, I wasn't wild about Frankie's friends out here. I liked him just fine. But the others gave me the creeps. Second, their office was a warehouse. I'm not kidding. It was like one big Costco, but instead of stuff for sale and human beings walking around with shopping carts and screaming toddlers, there were crazy big computers.

But here's the thing: I love computers. So, I did like the idea that the whole point of these ones was to solve math problems to make money.

I remember watching them one day with Betsy and thinking, "That's the future."

And I couldn't believe it was in the hands of—pardon my French—ratfucks like Futurium.

CHAPTER SIXTEEN

Betsy

She didn't see her sister for days after she and Marisa visited Crissy at the water park. Nigel had seemed oblivious to Crissy's willingness to so completely subsume who she was in the guise of another person, which left her wondering: how much did he really know about his "costar"? How much had Crissy told him about her eating disorder and why she had been in rehab? He knew some things. Did he know everything?

The few times that Betsy had seen her sister since she and Marisa had moved to Las Vegas, she'd noticed that Crissy was peppering her offstage conversation with British words and expressions more than ever. Now Betsy could hear that what had once been a slight, occasional British accent—a small affectation—had become dramatically more pronounced. It was as if her sister were a method actor and her life was her role. Her whole life. She was a walking simulacrum.

Not far from where they had grown up in Vermont, across Lake Champlain in Ticonderoga, New York, a retired Elvis impersonator and *Star Trek* superfan had bought the husk of a failed supermarket and in the shell re-created the set of the starship *Enterprise* from the original 1960s *Star Trek* TV series. The whole set. Not just the bridge where William Shatner sat in that chair with Christmas lights posing as functional buttons, but the transporter room and Dr. McCoy's sick bay and Scotty's engineering hub and all the ship's corridors. It was meticulous—and one of those accomplishments that seems futile and strange to the uninitiated, but audacious and valiant to the devout. Apparently, he had items in there pulled from dumpsters and uncovered in deep dives on eBay. But even though that first series had been canceled well before Betsy and Crissy's generation was watching television, their elementary school's fifth-grade class would go there on a field trip the same day they would visit Fort Ticonderoga, the historical site from the Revolutionary War. It was an eclectic—if not eccentric—doubleheader: the rebuilt fort from the 1750s and the rebuilt TV set from the 1960s.

The reason why the starship *Enterprise* was considered "educational" was because it helped the students understand, in theory, a little bit about theater and drama and how TV was made. Forced perspective. Turning a kickball into a dilithium crystal to power the ship's warp drive. The idea that the chairs used in a starship conference room would be the very same ones the Brady Bunch would use in their kitchen. Betsy recalled how they loved the *Star Trek* set at least as much as the fort, though the high point of the day invariably was when some redcoats would fire off a cannon. In any case, on those trips they saw two kinds of reenactors: the paid ones in Revolutionary War garb, and the unpaid ones in cosplay costumes and pointed Spock ears from the old TV series. The latter were obsessed. In Betsy's opinion, if you viewed that sort of behavior on a spectrum, she would have put the eighteenth-century soldiers on one side, the *Star Trek* superfans in their Spock ears in the middle, and Crissy at the other end. Normalcy was on the side of the soldiers, since they were donning those impossibly hot uniforms because it was a job. Maybe they enjoyed it. She hoped so. And while the *Star Trek* zealots weren't getting paid, at least dressing up like Lieutenant Uhura or Captain Kirk gave them camaraderie. A posse. But Crissy? My God, Betsy thought, it was a weird, lonely world, even with the addition of Nigel.

Crissy was three parts Diana and one part diva, and when Betsy and Marisa arrived in town, there were moments when Betsy wasn't sure she saw her sister lurking anywhere behind that accent or those sunglasses or inside that poolside cabana that had become her castle keep.

And the idea that Crissy still blamed her for their mother's death? It made Betsy think of another royal, King George, and his absolute madness.

* * *

It wasn't precisely that Betsy was steering clear of Crissy for the next week. But she was trying to settle into her new job at Futurium and build Marisa's and her new life. She bought a used car, a four-year-old Toyota Corolla that was a robin's-egg blue and had a sun roof. It wasn't as sporty as Crissy's convertible, but she loved how once more she had a vehicle and no longer had to depend on Frankie or Ubers, and everything got so much easier. Once again it was fun to go to the grocery store. And her job demanded more time and focus than she had anticipated, which was good. She wasn't merely coordinating meetings and Zooms for the small cadre of Futurium employees in Vegas, but for people around the world who worked remotely, including some financier who was working from the Maenads in Grand Cayman. She was, much to her surprise, syncing calendars with Futurium's lobbyists in Washington, D.C., and its engineers in two hemispheres, and making travel arrangements for investment analysts in lower Manhattan. She was on the phone with other admins for members of the Gaming Commission or casino execs, and setting up lunches and meetings between them and Rory or Lara or Damon or Frankie. Twice she found herself setting up meetings between Futurium executives and staffers for Representative Erika Schweiker, one of which the congresswoman herself attended. Most of the time, it really did seem that her boyfriend's new associates were on the up-and-up.

But then there were meetings with a team from a commercial real estate firm and members of the Mastaba "family" from West Palm Beach who were far more shadowy than Tony

Lombardo—he of the boat shoes, for God's sake—who had flown in to Vegas because they were going to have something to do with a casino acquisition. Apparently, the BP was one of four they were looking at, all smaller, a little downtrodden, and off the strip. At first, she had been confused, because these properties were nothing like the Maenads. Were they going to demolish one of them and build something new? Bulldoze a second-rate casino into oblivion, because all they wanted was the real estate? But the meetings with architects suggested otherwise, because the conversations and notes from the meetings were about rehabbing and reimagining these relics from another era, not blowing up the buildings and starting from scratch. The Futurium team didn't want to spend a lot of money: they were, it was clear, even to her, going to buy one cheap and spend as little as possible to improve the property. Still, if she didn't know that some (and only some) of these people were members of a crime syndicate, it all would have seemed bureaucratic—and downright boring. And maybe, in that regard, it was above board. She took comfort from the idea that so many Clark County politicians, and even a congressperson, were involved. How corrupt could any of this actually be?

She always carried a heavy sweater or sweatshirt with her to work, because the warehouse temperature was glacial compared to the outside world. It had to be for the computers. She christened her cubicle the Ice Cave. She brought in photos of her mother and Marisa and one of Crissy and her as little girls: they were dressed up for Halloween. Crissy was an angel and Betsy was a devil. Their mother had made them the costumes, and only later would Betsy read meaning into them.

One morning, Frankie stopped by with a bag of miniature doughnuts from a trendy bakery between his home and the warehouse. The little doughnuts were called reels, named after the part of the old-fashioned slot machine that spun, because they were small and came in funky, slot-machine-esque flavors like lemon and cherry and strawberry.

"So," he said, wiping some of the pink sugar from one of the reels off his fingers on a paper napkin, "I'm about to share some news. You can't tell a soul. But I've been dying to tell you. I've been like a kid."

The computers were always whirring. Usually it was white noise that she grew unaware of. But now, as she waited, the sound was everything.

"I am nothing if not discreet," she reminded him.

"I know. And I always want the best for you. You know that, too, right?"

She nodded. She did know this. Or, at the time, she believed it more often than she didn't.

"Okay, this is the smallest part of what I'm about to tell you. I am seriously burying the lede. Got it?"

"Go ahead."

"We're going to make an offer on the Buckingham Palace."

She nodded. "By we, you mean Futurium?"

"That's right. The team thinks that's the one."

Her first thought was her sister. She'd known this was a possibility. "How will this affect Crissy?"

"That's up to her."

"But they love her show, right?"

"They see a lot of potential."

"There's more to this. You're being evasive."

He ran his fingers through his hair. "She pissed off Tony when he asked her to do a special show for Futurium and she said no."

"I figured."

"But it's not a deal breaker."

"Meaning?"

"How much of this is between you and me and how much will you tell your sister?"

"That depends."

"Everything I tell you is a secret. You've signed the NDA.

Tony *would* be pissed if you violated it, and I probably couldn't protect you."

"I'd need protection?"

"If you told Crissy and she did something stupid with the info? I think they might let you go, yeah."

She was relieved that her job was all he meant by retribution.

"If they buy the casino—"

"When," he said, correcting her.

"It could be bad for her?" she asked.

"No. I say that emphatically. It doesn't have to be."

"You have to tell me."

"They think your sister is very, very talented. They love her Diana. But they want something bigger. Flashier. They're envisioning a cabaret about the royals—all of 'em, Diana and Meghan and Harry—with lots of impersonators of English pop stars from a different era. That whole British Invasion thing. Like when the Beatles and the Rolling Stones came to America in the 1960s. I mean, maybe we'll even go as far as the 1980s. You know, not just the 1960s. Imagine a Sex Pistols cover band doing 'God Save the Queen,' while our pretend Elizabeth gets all jiggy," he went on, strumming an air guitar frenetically. "It would be the royals and British cover bands. It's still confidential. And it's far from definite and the show is in the earliest stages. Not even written yet. Obviously. But they do have a couple of writers in mind. And there are other options."

"Such as?"

"Maybe we bring in the Diana musical. A touring production."

"A lot of super tight chorus girls singing that 'Fuckity, Fuckity, Fuckity, Fuck You Dress' number?"

He looked confused.

"That's a song in the musical," she explained. She was feeling unexpectedly protective of her sister.

"You're kidding!"

"I'm not."

"Wow. Crazy."

"I assume you'll keep the casino's name and theme, if that's the plan," she went on. "I mean, the Buckingham Palace is the perfect place for Crissy's show—or that bigger show."

"We'll see. Entertainment doesn't drive a casino. It's always just the icing. Maybe it will be called the Futurium Buckingham Palace."

"That's a mouthful."

"I'm not a writer," he said. "But Futurium will be in the name—it is, after all, the brand—and your sister's casino fits the bill. It has four hundred rooms, and it's a little down-at-the-heels—but not too shabby. It's a place that's definitely seen better days, but it's not like the sheets on the beds are a biohazard. And, of course, it's going cheap since the owners offed themselves."

She nodded. She'd heard in the newspaper that when Richie Morley had put a bullet into his head inside his Jag, the vehicle had fifty-four monthly payments left. "People say they killed themselves because the casino was in financial trouble. That true?"

"It is. So, we're doing your sister a favor."

"A favor," she repeated.

"Anyway," he went on, "we're going to renovate the place and turn it into something pretty interesting: a full-on, no-holds-barred, bricks-and-mortar crypto casino. It will be the mecca for on-site crypto gambling. It may not be the Maenads, which I can't wait to show you. But it's not supposed to be. Still, it will be glorious, baby, glorious," he said, and she couldn't recall if he had ever before called her *baby.* Were his vocabulary and language mutating, too—like Crissy's—but instead of becoming British, they were becoming . . . mobster? Did Vegas cast its spell differently on different people? "We'll have good restaurants, not the usual Vegas mediocrity, and, of course, a lot of talent in the showroom. We're hoping to announce it all in a few days."

"What if my sister doesn't want to be a role player in this bigger production? She's currently the star of her own show."

"I thought there were no small parts? Only small actors?" he asked.

"She's a diva, Frankie. You know that."

"If she balks, you step in. You'd be fine. You look like Diana. Wouldn't have to do much. No reason Diana even has to sing."

"You're making this wild assumption that's something I'd want to do."

"Wouldn't you?"

She shook her head, and she could see that she'd taken a little helium from his balloon. He was disappointed, but something more, too, an eddy in the air she could feel in her small corner of the warehouse. Was he frustrated that she was ungrateful or frightened that her reluctance would get him in trouble? He looked around her cubicle and murmured, his tone incredulous, "But you can't want this. I know you see more to your life than being a . . . a secretary."

"Why are you dismissive of secretaries? There's nothing wrong with being a secretary."

"I bet there could be a crypto bonus in the offing if you did this. Guys like Tony Lombardo and Oliver Davies would be jazzed."

"Oliver? The one who met the real Princess Diana in Russia?"

He nodded. "Practically lives at the Maenads."

"I'm sorry," she told him. She was growing more and more uncomfortable with his desire to have her, rather than her sister, impersonate Diana. "I have zero interest."

He brought his hands together and steepled his fingers. It was clear there was more to this than some innocent but misguided aspiration to *Citizen Kane* her onto the stage. So, she was at once surprised and relieved when he said, finally, "Okay, I hear you."

"Thank you."

"Remember that modeling thing we needed? The pics for the website?"

"Sure. Wholesome pretty girl."

"You doing anything on Sunday?"

"Not really. Maybe taking Marisa to the museum."

"We might do the photo shoot that day."

"Not a big deal. I could do both, right?"

"Pretty much. The weather looks good this weekend. No rain in the forecast."

"Is there ever rain in the forecast?"

"Hah! Nope. That's why I love it here."

"Where are we going to do this?"

"Red Rocks."

"Your house?"

"Oh, no. The actual park. The canyon. The desert with all those gorgeous cliffs."

"I haven't been there yet."

"You'll love it."

"You've been?"

"Yeah. A little scouting with Tony."

She reached for a strawberry doughnut. A strawberry reel. There was just so much that she didn't know.

"So, Sunday?" he asked, confirming.

"Sure. Sunday." She felt bad that her lack of any ambition to be onstage was disappointing him, and so the idea that she could do him a solid by looking outdoorsy and clean-cut gave her comfort. And with that acknowledgment came a thought she was having frequently: morality, at least hers, was more malleable than she had supposed even six months ago.

Yeah, I think I understood crypto better than Frankie. I know I understood it better than Betsy. I was constantly explaining stuff to her, and showing her what she should google.

CHAPTER SEVENTEEN

Crissy

Ask me to do a deep dive into how Diana Frances Spencer smuggled her lovers into and out of palaces and guest cottages, and I'm your PI. Or, at least, your research assistant. And so I was confident I might unearth some interesting skinny on Frankie Limback. I went online and learned that Betsy's new boyfriend had indeed been an investment banker. He had a wife (who would soon be his ex-wife) who was a pediatrician, and two teenage children: a daughter who was a high school soccer star who also took pride in her dance TikToks, and a son who seemed to steer clear of the social networks. I supposed this young man had been Betsy's client and the conduit to the Limbacks. Frankie had gone to Farmingdale and then Hofstra. He and his family had wound up in a suburb of Burlington, Vermont, because his wife had started her practice there and had family in the Green Mountains.

It wasn't a lot, but it was a start, and I was about to close my browser in my hotel suite when I had an idea. I'd been frustrated that the Futurium website hadn't had an employee directory when I had surfed around it, but I'd noticed they had a page full of podcasts they called the PFP, because the host was named Peter: *Peter's Futurium Podcast.* I went back there now and found easily fifty of them. The crypto company seemed to record at least one and sometimes two each month, all between fifteen and thirty minutes long. And there, recorded the previous winter, was one in which Peter was interviewing an investment banker about why he had left traditional finance for cryptocurrency. He discussed how his old bank, Fitzgerald McCoy, had shut down their operations in Moscow years ago—well before Putin invaded Ukraine—because even the prewar sanctions had made business in Russia untenable. That banker was Frankie Limback, who, when he wasn't traveling overseas, divided his time between Burlington and New York City. ("It's an easier commute than you think," he joked, thanking an airline, and then bragging about how frequently he was overseas anyway, for a while in Moscow, and now in Phnom Penh and Grand Cayman.) "It was just too hard for Russian companies to access international capital because of the sanctions—the U.S. and European sanctions," he explained. "And so, after Cleo Dionne and I closed the door on the Moscow bank, I began looking at alternatives to traditional finance. I saw right away that the future—at least my future—was crypto."

Next, I googled this Cleo Dionne. The first thing I found was confirmation that she had been running the Moscow branch of the bank and, along with Frankie, had moved on to Futurium. The second? The woman's obituary. She had died four months earlier in a bathtub in a hotel room at that exclusive resort Futurium executives visited on Grand Cayman (a resort, the obituary writer explained, that was really a small club for the wealthy in the world who wanted to steer clear of the social pages and the limelight). Cause of death? Drowning. She was fully clothed and had a blood alcohol level of point four percent. Not point oh four, a level that's likely to impair your driving. Point four. By accident or on purpose, she had, essentially, drunk herself to death.

She was thirty-five years old. She was blond.

She could have been Betsy's and my sister.

* * *

I didn't hear from Betsy for a few days. I supposed she was working and helping her daughter acclimate to life on the surface of the sun. I did get texts from Marisa, and while they weren't quite innocuous, neither were they incendiary. She wanted to know if I thought she should get a second piercing along the side of her ears (I said to ask her mother) and whether I could procure tickets for Betsy and her to a new Cirque du Soleil show that kids at her school said was "super hot." (I said I could, but the request for tickets had to come from her mother, given the reality that the show was indeed awash in nubile young bodies in provocative contortions.) She asked if I ever went to England to research my own cabaret, which was a clever inquiry. I had, but it had been years earlier. She was curious whether people "ever give you shit" because Diana was an inch shy of six feet tall and I am, by comparison, "a freaking midget." (Her words.) I told her not to use the term *midget* and boasted that I was, like Betsy, five feet, four inches tall—a perfectly good height for a woman, thank you very much—and I wore a lot of heels. Also, I added, most people had no idea that Diana was statuesque. Then she asked if I knew that the princess had once gone to Russia. I did and texted back:

> Yes. And not wanting to encourage non sequiturs, I have to ask: what in the world made you google Diana's two days in Moscow?

All of this Russia talk—including the fact that Frankie had once worked there and the closest thing I had to a suitor was a Russian American who went by Gene but I still enjoyed calling Yevgeny—had me nervous. But my niece's response reassured me. At least a bit.

> I didn't google it. Russia came up when I was looking at all the countries she'd visited and it wasn't in your show. I've never even been to Canada and I've only been to three states. And that counts Vermont.

When I read that text, it made me rather sad.

* * *

I told Nigel about Cleo Dionne's death. His first reaction was that she had the perfect name for a Vegas performer, and if anyone was going to drown in a bathtub, it was going to be a woman with that moniker.

"So, you don't suspect foul play?" I asked him.

"Oh, of course I do. She died in a bathtub on Grand Cayman, for God's sake. That's fishy."

"Was that a joke?"

"Because she drowned? No. Just a coincidence that I chose that word. Who found her?"

"Housekeeping."

"Well, that must have been a treat. Was Frankie Limback with her? I don't mean in the hotel room. Or the bathtub. But was he on the island when she died?"

"That's a great question. Is there a way to find out without asking him?"

"Know any good spies?" he asked in response, kidding.

"No, I don't," I told him. "But I do have a friend who seems quite resourceful." I was thinking, of course, of Yevgeny.

* * *

The queen died that Thursday.

I knew I would have to rewrite parts of the show, because the world was becoming one soggy box of tissues over her demise. I understood that. I was as stunned as everyone.

As anyone.

But the part of me that was Diana was miffed.

The world had been furious with the queen in the days immediately following Diana's death in 1997. People felt she was callous—and especially cruel to her grandsons, expecting them as boys to have stiff upper lips as their mother, estranged from the royal family, was lowered into the ground. Oh, eventually the queen bowed her head—and it was a deep and resonant bow, not a bow that she phoned in—as Diana's funeral cortege passed, but it took her a painful few days to reach the realization that she had to transcend protocol and be . . . human.

You will suppose I watched every bit of the coverage that flooded the news cycle.

I watched some.

But those days? A little went a long way. And I had other things on my mind.

* * *

Yevgeny was arriving on Saturday and planned to go hiking on Sunday, the first of my two days off every week, and then join me at the pool. (The show was dark on Sundays and Mondays.) Saturday, I knew, we'd have a rather scrummy reunion, and I was relieved he hadn't suggested I join him on the hike. Yes, I know that Diana first earned her keep in the eyes of the royal family by donning a pair of well-worn brogues and showing what an agreeable outdoorswoman she could be at Balmoral, but I prefer to exert myself in the hallowed—and air-conditioned—halls of a gym. I was impressed by how well he had already picked up on the things I liked to do, and the things I did not.

How much Yevgeny would know about Frankie Limback was an interesting question in my mind. If he was who he said he was, he might know nothing. If he was, despite what I told Nigel, some sort of spy, he might know something and feign ignorance. Or he might kill me for asking.

No, I was confident he wouldn't do that.

Mostly, anyway.

I didn't want to wait for his arrival to see what he could tell me about where Frankie Limback was when this other Futurium executive had died, and so I called him and asked him what he could find out.

"I'm going to say your sister's Frankie Limback has a type," he began when he rang me back. "You're right: this Cleo person looks a little bit like you and your sister. She also looks like his wife."

"Soon to be ex-wife," I said. "Was he on Grand Cayman with Cleo when she died?"

"I don't know what you mean by with her, but it seems he was at that club. A lot of Futurium was, as well as some Mastaba leaders."

"Mastaba? What in holy hell is the Mastaba?"

"You've never heard of the Mastaba?"

"No."

"It's a crime syndicate. A crime family."

"Futurium's a . . . a front?" This was almost more than I could process.

"No. Not at all. But some of their backers have connections to the Mastaba. Most likely, they put some of their money into Futurium crypto. Some Russian oligarchs have, too."

"And they were on Grand Cayman when Cleo Dionne died?"

"A few. But it doesn't seem like they were up to no good. Nothing I read suggests anyone ever suspected Cleo was murdered."

"So, you really are a spy," I told him.

"I really am not," he insisted. "You need to stop pulling that thread."

I had been joshing, but there was a firmness to his response that was jarring.

"Got it," I said meekly.

"Everything I just told you? You would have found it yourself if you'd known where to dig."

"You said Frankie has a type. Do you think he and Cleo were more than just business associates?"

"It crossed my mind."

"I asked my friend, Nigel, if he thought my sister was in danger. He doesn't know anything about espionage—"

"I don't either."

This was utter tosh, but I wasn't going to call him on it. "Do you think my sister is in danger?"

"I don't see why. She's an administrative assistant for an established cryptocurrency. I don't think you have any reason at all to worry about her or Marisa."

"Okay," I said. "Thank you."

It was only after we hung up that I began to wonder: had I ever told Yevgeny that I had a niece? And, if I had, had I told him her name?

* * *

Red Rocks is a mere fifteen miles from Las Vegas: twenty to forty minutes by car, depending upon the traffic and where in the city you start. But the moonscape—or, given the redness of so much of the natural world there, the Mars-scape—is a primeval diversion from the man-made neon theme park that is the nearby metropolis. There is a casino nearby, of course, but when you are amidst the sandstone obelisks and peaks, some walls touching the clouds at three thousand feet, it's easy to forget that a half hour away people are losing their shirts at the slot machines, ogling strippers, watching the world go by from the ersatz Eiffel Tower, or wondering why in the world they are listening to a lass sing Petula Clark while telling stories about a now long-dead princess. It's a weirdly virtuous activity for the Las Vegas environs, and there are always families, many with small children, because there are plenty of hikes that are not especially challenging.

But then there are also opportunities to scale rock faces, and so the park has its share of climbers and visitors more likely to be packing carabiners than picnics.

Sunday morning, Yevgeny set off for Red Rocks on his own. He asked me if I minded the idea that he preferred his walks to be solitary, and I reassured him that I was relieved. Red Rocks was never going to be my cup of tea. Besides, I had business of my own. There was a woman in the house for my second show Saturday who sent a note backstage that intrigued me. Her name was Britt Collins, and she was writing a biography of Princess Diana (yet another), and hoping to interview me on Sunday before leaving Las Vegas on Monday. She was based in London. I decided it would be worth chatting with this writer and seeing where the conversation went. I might be able to help her, and I did so little for anyone that I might as well offer this homeopathic kindness to a stranger. And—who knows?—I might even learn something I could use in the show. So, I sent a note back that I would be charmed to meet, and asked her to suggest a time and a place.

Yevgeny's and my reconciliation had been energetic the night before and went well into the small hours of the morning. But while he'd slept on the plane west, I'd done two shows. I was exhausted on Sunday, content to loll in bed while he dressed for the desert.

"Enjoy your reporter," he said, and he kissed me on the forehead. And then he was gone, off to a world of scrub brush and red, red rocks in the car he'd rented the day before at the airport.

* * *

The biographer and I met for brunch at a bistro on a side street off the strip, where it was quiet and we could talk. It was about a thirty-minute stroll from the Buckingham Palace. We met at eleven thirty, and the first thing that struck me was that she was a Brit named Britt. I told her I would have to work her first name into my show, and she smiled good-naturedly, clearly supposing I was kidding. I was not. She was my age and a freelance writer, and she had hair that was blonder than mine—it was the color of corn silk—and deep green eyes. She was wearing a skirt and, despite the heat, a cardigan sweater. This was going to be her first book, but she knew her Diana. When she told me stories, they often ended with her laughing in a fashion that was contagious and husky. We talked at length about the queen's passing, and even though I held a bit of a grudge toward Elizabeth for the way she had distanced herself from Diana, I was moved by how much the old girl meant to Britt Collins. I was touched. I learned where I was wrong about the queen and her legacy. It was going to be very difficult for Charles to wedge his yeti feet into his mother's size four go-to-court pumps.

Britt also revealed a few details about how the Windsors felt about the TV series and the musical and the movies I'd never heard before, and I gobbled them up like shortbread—though, I must admit, at one point I had a pang of jealousy that the royal family thought about Emma Corrin and Kristen Stewart but most likely had never even heard of me. That was a bit of a dagger in the back.

At one point over our scones and jam (yes, she ordered that, and so I did, too), she leaned in to me and asked, "Your accent. Is it always this . . . British? Didn't you grow up in Vermont?"

"I did. When I talk about Diana, I tend to fall into the accent. You're not the first person to notice."

"It's good. I grew up in London, and I can assure you it's quite deft."

"Thank you."

"But do you ever—forgive me—worry that you take this all a tad too seriously? This impersonation?"

I sat back in my chair. "No, I don't," I told her. "I want people to have a good time and see a good show."

"Did you ever have a Vermont accent? I suppose there is one."

"There is and, yes, I did. A bit. They got rid of it at Tisch. Pulled it out of me like a bad tooth."

"That's where you went to university?"

"Conservatory. Or, at least, more conservatory than university for me. NYU."

She looked down at a bit of pilling on her sweater and used two fingernails like tweezers to pull some away. "What I mean about taking this Diana impersonation seriously is this: Diana, by the end, was pretty damaged goods. It's none of my business and I'm not writing about you, but I'm curious: what is the greatest tragedy in your life? A heartbreak? A death?"

"I'm not sure what you're getting at," I said, stalling.

She rested her elbows on the table (which surprised me), made a couch for her chin with her linked fingers, and continued, "Why, day after day, do you do . . . this?"

"Not because of a heartbreak or a death," I assured her.

"You're an actor—"

"I was an actor. This is different."

"So, you're not acting?"

"I'm . . . performing."

"You do the heartbreak so well. You do the bulimia so well. It's wrenching."

"Her story is wrenching. It's why it's told and retold."

"And your personal story is not? There's nothing in your family history that makes you shudder with sadness or wince?"

"No," I told her, and here I was acting. "There is nothing there at all."

* * *

At one forty-five, Yevgeny and I texted. I was back at my casino, ensconced in my cabana, deconstructing my brunch with that British writer. I hoped I'd helped her with her book and it hadn't been a waste of her time. I hadn't enjoyed answering her questions about me, but I had reveled in her dish about the Windsors. I'd asked for her business card so we could stay in touch, but she was all out and scribbled her vitals on a piece of paper she tore from her notepad.

Yevgeny cheered me up by texting me a selfie of himself staring at the petroglyphs not far from a picnic area parking lot.

He was wearing a safari hat and shades against the sun. He had done his homework and wanted to see them before he set off on what the tourism rangers considered a moderately strenuous hike. By then I had long convinced myself that at some point I'd told him Betsy had adopted a child and shared with him the girl's name. Just because he had been born in Russia, I needn't be paranoid about everything. Referring to the rock carvings, he texted me:

They're not that old.

I corrected him good-naturedly:

800 years. That seems pretty damn old to me.

And he replied:

The petroglyphs in Chauvet are 30,000 years old.

I googled where in France they were. I texted back asking if he had seen them firsthand. Of course, he had:

We had a project in southern France. The ones there are interesting for ice age paintings. There's a cave lion. There's a rhinoceros.

And that was the very last text I would receive from him. It was the very last text or phone call or technological contact that anyone anywhere in the world would ever receive from him.

I began to worry when my texts at three and four in the afternoon went unanswered, and I was alarmed by five. That gift of fear? It's real. But it was not until almost quarter to eight, as the sky was darkening, that the two detectives came to my hotel suite and told me that three hours earlier, a pair of young climbers had found his corpse.

The climbers, I learned, were college kids, a boy and a girl. Already, one of the detectives hinted, the body had begun to smell in the oppressive, windless Nevada heat.

Part Two

I kept hearing this name, Erika Schweiker, and I had no idea who she was until I looked her up.

My first thought? She was a moron. Even I knew the difference between gazpacho *and* Gestapo. *The Gazpacho Police weren't coming for anyone's guns.*

But she did like crypto. So, that proved that you probably can, in fact, lead a horse to water and make her drink.

CHAPTER EIGHTEEN

Crissy

When my mother died, the waterfall of grief began with phone calls from back east.

When Yevgeny Orlov died, it began with two detectives ringing the doorbell to my hotel suite. My first instinct was that they were hotel security because one of the front desk managers was with them, but then my mind registered *police* even before they showed me their badges—maybe it was the dark blazer on the guy a little younger than me or the dark slacks on the woman a little older—and then it went straight to Betsy. They were a different pair than the two who had come to my dressing room to ask me about Artie Morley, and whether he'd been depressed and what our last conversation had been like. Once we got through the formalities, the manager—a newbie named Harvey with great, slicked-back gangster hair that made him look more boyish than brutish—excused himself. He was clearly unnerved that he was bringing two of Las Vegas's finest to the hotel room of casino talent. Then the detectives joined me in my reading nook. The nook had those two chairs, which I offered them, and I carried in a third from my vanity for me.

"You are among a very small group of people to ever have sat in those," I told them.

"You don't have a lot of guests?" asked the younger of the pair. He'd introduced himself as Detective Patrick O'Connor.

I considered motioning at the bed and telling him that I entertained my guests there, but I couldn't think fast enough of a British expression that would have landed the joke. The one who was in charge, a woman I pegged for midforties who had said her full name was Felicia Johnson (but I could call her "Detective"), got to the point. "A fellow named Yevgeny Orlov had a room key to your hotel suite in his wallet."

"Had?" I asked.

There was a beat. "He's dead. I'm sorry," she told me.

I felt a wave of dizziness, not unlike when my mother had died or when people I knew had passed from Covid.

"Was he staying here? With you?" she went on.

I nodded, stunned. "That's why you had Harvey with you, isn't it?" I asked. I put my forehead in my hands and stared down at the carpet. There was a small stain there the shape of a seahorse that I'd never noticed before. "You needed to find out what door—what room number—the card opened."

"So, he was here with you?" she asked.

"Yes. Last night. How did he die? What happened?" Beside her, Patrick had gotten out a pad and pen and was already jotting notes.

"Some climbers found his body at the bottom of a cliff out at Red Rocks. They summoned the park rangers, who called us."

"He'd been there a few hours," Patrick volunteered, rolling his eyes. Felicia gave him an angry, side-eye glance.

"Do you need some water?" he asked, chastened. I must have looked pale.

"No."

"Food?"

I gazed up at him, disconcerted by his solicitousness. "You have some?"

"No."

"I'm okay. You said he was at the bottom of a cliff. How far did he fall? Did he die . . ."

"He fell about sixty feet," said Felicia. "He may have died instantly, but we won't know much until the coroner has done an autopsy."

"Six floors?" It was one of those questions that's actually a statement.

"Did you consider going with him?"

"To Red Rocks? No, I had breakfast with a writer. At a bistro called Cocoon."

"Was Mr. Orlov meeting someone?"

"No," I said, but then I corrected myself. "At least I don't think so." He hadn't wanted me to go, I remembered. I didn't say that. But I thought it.

"Who was the writer? What's his name?"

"Her name. Britt. Britt Collins."

"Do you have a number?"

"I can probably find it. I have the paper somewhere," I replied, and for the first time I understood that his death wasn't necessarily an accident. I had assumed it was because they'd told me he'd fallen.

"Tell us about your relationship. Tell us how you knew Mr. Orlov."

So, I did. I didn't have anything to hide. I told him what Yevgeny claimed he did for a living (which I suspected they already knew since he had ID in his wallet and perhaps even business cards), how we met, and how he had flown back to Las Vegas for a visit just yesterday. I didn't tell them that I believed it was possible he was a spy. It dawned on me, and I felt seasick when the realization hit me, that if he were a spy—and, dear God, a Russian spy—my naivete in shagging him might be misconstrued as treason.

"The only reason he was here in Las Vegas was to see you?"

"As far as I know."

"What was his state of mind when he left your hotel room this morning?" she asked.

I shrugged. "Chipper. Upbeat. He took great pride in being content. He used that word a lot: *content*."

Now she nodded and Patrick looked at her. I got it. I understood one of the other possibilities they were exploring: suicide. "Was he gambling last night or this morning?" she pressed.

"You don't need me to tell you that. You can just go downstairs and ask. But I can tell you that he wasn't depressed."

"Lots of people take their own lives in Las Vegas," she said.

"Oh, I know."

"And I'm not saying your friend did. But to fall from where he did?"

"It couldn't have been an accident?"

"It could have been, sure. But it would have suggested a certain recklessness."

"Or he liked the view. Maybe he was just content," I said, using one of his favorite words, "and misjudged his proximity to the edge of the cliff."

"Maybe."

I opened my phone and showed them our text chain from the afternoon.

"See?" I said. "He seemed just fine."

They studied the texts, and I could see Felicia scrolling up. Suddenly this felt like an invasion of both Yevgeny's privacy and mine. Moreover, I couldn't recall right away what specifically I might have asked him about Futurium or Erika Schweiker. So, I asked for my phone back, and the detective returned it to me and said, "We may want that again—depending upon where the investigation goes."

"Certainly," I agreed, though I felt the sharp tip of anxiety. "But any of our texts are on his phone, too."

"His phone is gone. Wasn't on him. We're searching for it at the accident scene and the park right now."

"I'm sure it was an accident," I said, though I didn't believe that any longer. Not for a second. "I can see him, enamored, near one of those peaks. And then he slips. I think that's more likely what happened than that"—my voice choked, envisioning his murder—"he threw himself over the side."

Felicia sighed, and for a moment the three of us sat there in silence. Finally, she asked, "Did he ever mention anyone who was angry with him—or anyone he was mad at?"

"In other words, did he have any enemies? Was he meeting someone there or surprised by someone there who was willing to heave him off a cliff?"

"Yes."

"I have no idea."

"Because there are three possibilities: He fell. He jumped. Or he was pushed."

"I understand. But I've spent three nights with him in my life. And zero days. I liked him. I liked him so much. But we hadn't had the chance to get to know each other all that well," I insisted, but my eyes had begun welling up and my voice broke. I didn't sound especially firm. It was unlikely I inspired confidence in my veracity.

"Excuse me," I said. I wiped my nose on the sleeve of my blouse and went to the bathroom for a tissue. I could feel their eyes on me. I tried to gather myself before I returned to them, and I succeeded by breathing in Crissy and breathing out Diana. When I left the bathroom, I sat down once more in the reading nook and said in the voice of an ever-stoic royal, "Well, now. What happens next after this sort of beastly unpleasantness?"

They looked at each other reflexively, before turning back to me.

"He had a suitcase, right?" Felicia said in a tone that was professorial—the Socratic method at work.

"Overnight bag. Leather. Gorgeous. Italian."

"We'll need that. And you'll need to give us anything he unpacked."

"His razor. It's stunning—for a razor. Silver. His toothbrush? It's . . . a toothbrush."

"We'll take that, too."

"And then?"

"We continue to work the scene and talk to people who knew him. He seems to have had a wide circle. We await the autopsy and the toxicology report. By now someone has informed the next of kin."

"And who would that be? He once mentioned to me a younger sister."

"You have a name?"

"No. Sorry."

"Can you give us that number for Britt Collins?"

"Yes, of course," I told them. "I'll go find it."

"One more thing."

I waited.

"Your next show is Tuesday, correct?"

"Yes."

I had this notion from watching too many movies and cop dramas that they were going to ask me to stay in town. Instead, Felicia said, "Any chance there are tickets available? I'll pay for them. I would insist, in fact, so it could never be construed as a bribe. But my parents just loved the show when they saw it a few years ago, and I think it would be a real hoot to surprise them with a pair. I know they'd love to see it again."

"Which show? Early or late?"

"They won't care."

"I'll make it happen," I said.

"No comps."

"Got it," I agreed. I was about to ask for a business card, but already she was handing me one. Then Patrick flipped shut his notebook and handed me his card, too.

* * *

People kill themselves a lot in Las Vegas. They do it all the time. Fun fact: you have a 50 percent greater chance of offing yourself here than in the rest of the country. Not hyperbole. People have studied us, and that's the reality. That's the statistic. Some researchers even suggest we are a suicide terminus: people actually come here to kill themselves.

But that wasn't Yevgeny Orlov.

And now I was more confident than ever that this wasn't the Morleys. Artie was correct about his brother, Richie, and Eddie was right about Artie.

Once I was alone, I drew myself a bubble bath and listened to my "make me sob" playlist—some Elvis, some Karen Carpenter, lots of Marvin Hamlisch, especially three weepers from *Sophie's Choice*—and the tears flowed freely. I had been in there half an hour when, once again, I was adding more hot water, reaching for the faucet with the toes on one of my feet, when a name came to me. Instantly, I grew alert. Cleo Dionne. That person who'd worked with Frankie Limback and died in a bathtub in Grand Cayman. And, just like Yevgeny, it was either a tragic accident or a deeply sad suicide.

Or, as Nigel had suggested about Cleo, a murder carefully crafted to look like one or the other.

When you added them up, there were now four corpses linked to either Futurium or the BP—the casino that Futurium wanted to buy.

I thought of that group Yevgeny had told me about, the Mastaba crime family, and wondered what in the name of God my sister had gotten herself into now.

Or, when I had rung Erika Schweiker, what I had gotten myself into.

Of all the extinction-level meteors roaring toward Planet Crissy, I had a feeling that was the one most likely to crater my world.

* * *

When I emerged from the tub, I got dressed and went for a walk. There was no obvious connection between the deaths: Yevgeny hadn't worked for Futurium, and Cleo hadn't worked for the BP. But there were plenty of reasons why one could intuit links. After all, Yevgeny's calendar had opened rather suddenly, he'd come to Las Vegas, and now he was dead. I wouldn't have been surprised to learn that I wasn't the only reason—or even the main reason—why he was back in town.

I phoned Eddie Cantone, and the call went straight to voice mail. I didn't leave a message. Next I rang my sister.

"Well, this is unexpected," Betsy said. She sounded happy to hear from me.

"You alone?"

"Except for Marisa, yes. Why?"

If I had answered honestly, I would have said because I wanted to talk to her without Frankie Limback nearby. But I didn't have to go there, and so I didn't. "A friend of mine was found dead out at Red Rocks this afternoon," I told her. "His body was discovered at the bottom of a cliff." I was gazing at the strip as I walked, and Las Vegas was well along its nightly transformation into a pinball machine, the last, lingering light from the west giving the thousands upon thousands of casino windows a golden cast. Though it was Sunday, there was traffic, and the asphalt grew congested.

"No! I'm so sorry. What happened?"

There was concern for me in her voice; she supposed I was calling her for comfort, as if our history had gone up in steam and no longer mattered. She also sounded surprised by the news, which I expected. The people around her carried guns, but she didn't. At least not yet. But she was, it seemed to me, bringing her own brand of chaos and disorder into my life in Nevada, just as she had in Vermont.

No, this was worse than chaos and disorder. This was corpse-in-a-canyon shit.

"A fellow I'd seen a couple of times," I answered. "He lived in New York—"

"Let me go into the bedroom," she said, and I heard Marisa asking her what was up and Betsy telling her that it was her aunt on the phone and she needed privacy. I knew when she returned to her daughter that the child was going to interrogate her, and

I considered how much I should reveal. Then I decided that was bollocks; withhold nothing.

"Okay, go on," she said.

"The police don't know for sure what happened. But I just had two detectives here in my suite asking me questions."

"Oh, my God, were you with him? At Red Rocks?"

"No."

"Thank goodness," she said. *Goodness.* It was strange to hear Betsy use that word. It sounded so innocent. So rehearsed. Which was when, for the first time, the idea came to me, inchoate at first, but coalescing fast: if I had gone to Red Rocks with Yevgeny that afternoon, I might very well be dead, too.

I'd seen Betsy nervous. But I also knew she could be a hardass. She seemed way tougher than Crissy.

But when she heard that Crissy's boyfriend—or whatever he was—had died out at Red Rocks? She was scared. That was the first time I ever got that vibe.

And when I did a deep dive into who the Morleys were—I'd heard that name a bunch—and saw they were dead, too?

I knew she was right to be scared. I would have been shitting my pants.

CHAPTER NINETEEN

Betsy

Thank goodness," Betsy said, but she felt as if she were in an elevator that was in freefall, and feared that her voice had cracked. She thought she might be sick right then and there.

"Thank goodness?" her sister repeated, turning the two words into a question, and stretching out the second and third syllables of her response as if she were belittling even the tone of Betsy's brief statement. Had Crissy been closer to this man than she had let on?

"I mean," Betsy continued, trying to gather herself, "I'm glad you didn't witness someone falling off a cliff. That would have been horrifying. Scarring."

"Well, you would know about horrifying and scarring."

Betsy let that go, her mind racing as she struggled to gain purchase on something else—anything else—and sat down on the bed. She told herself this was all a wild coincidence, but she didn't believe that. She'd made a mistake. She'd gone too far. She had let Frankie push her too far. "That's morbid and mean," she replied in a low voice. She was striving to regain control and still hoping to keep this civilized. Survival instinct. And control was critical. "Look, I'm very sorry about your friend."

"Where were you this afternoon? May I ask?"

"I wasn't at Red Rocks," she lied.

"Were you with Frankie?"

"No. I was at the natural history museum with Marisa. I was there with her and one of her classmates, a girl I hope will become her friend. We saw lizards. Sharks. Dinosaur bones. It was all very wholesome." This was, of course, after she had been at Red Rocks. And she had met the two girls at the museum: they were already there with the other child's mother.

"Nothing we do is ever what it seems, is it?"

"I'm not sure what you're getting at. But no one died with me at the museum," she answered. There was silence at the other end, and Betsy knew her sister well enough to know that her eyes were narrowing. She had regained the upper hand, and she needed to retain it if she was going to get through this conversation without succumbing to panic and revealing something stupid. "For a second I thought you might have been calling because you were sad," she continued.

"I am sad."

"You were just accusing me of . . . of I don't know what."

"Where was Frankie?"

"Today? I believe he was playing golf."

"You believe or you know?"

She looked at a photo of their mother on the dresser. It was a little over two years old. The woman was sitting on the coaster swing that Betsy had had installed on the sunniest porch of the old Victorian, a birthday present for her that she couldn't afford. Their mother was sipping a glass of white wine. The porch faced the street, and from there a person could see both the general store and the town clerk's office. When the two sisters had been little girls, they would crouch behind the banister and spy on the activity across the road. The comings and goings at the town clerk were less interesting to them than at the store, but it was watching the town clerk's office where they first heard men speak like pigs—the road crew, for instance, referring to a woman as a cunt because earlier that day she had passed a tractor on Battery Hill—and it was there that they saw one of their elementary school teachers and her husband squabbling as they went in to pay their property taxes. At the store, they witnessed the young mom slapping her toddler when she thought that no one was watching, the child in full-on tantrum mode because he was being denied an ice pop. But they also saw the pride a parent might have when their teenage son or daughter shot their first buck and brought it to the outdoor scale at the store to be weighed, as well as the way teenagers might hold hands when they reconnected after emerging from opposite sides of a car and started into the store for sandwiches or soda or bottles of water and gorp if they were planning to hike the Appalachian Trail.

Betsy never minded watching the dead animals weighed during hunting season. Crissy did. That was another difference between the two of them. Neither their mother nor stepfather had hunted, and so there was never a rifle in their house when they were little girls, but in high school Betsy had dated a boy named Garland, and wound up learning how to shoot.

"I know he was playing golf," Betsy said now. "He was at the country club."

"Frankie ever tell you about his friend, Cleo Dionne?"

"No," she answered. Again, she was lying, and her instinct was to leave it at that. *No.* But it dawned on her that Frankie needed to know what her sister knew—and how. She probably did, too. Because this was bad. Someone was dead right here in Nevada, not in a bathtub on a Caribbean island, and it wasn't that Frankie and his friends weren't telling her everything; they were telling her almost nothing. She was about to say more, but already Crissy was speaking again, and Betsy was relieved to learn that her sister knew even less than she did about Cleo. She'd discovered the usual innuendo about murder or suicide, that was it. "Where did you hear all that?" Betsy asked, hoping she sounded surprised.

"I've been doing my homework."

"Why in the world were you googling her? How did she even come up?"

"Because your friends carry guns. And so I did some digging."

She sat up straight. She wanted to sound firm, not scared. "You know something?" she asked.

Crissy was quiet, no doubt seething.

"You sound a little bit crazy right now," she said. "I know you're upset. I get it. You lost someone you cared about, and I'm sorry. I'm *so* sorry. But there's obviously no connection between his death and this Cleo Dionne person," she went on, which wasn't obvious at all. There very well might be.

"You're deluding yourself, Betsy. You're in so deep in something so criminal—"

"No! No. Sis—"

"Sis?"

"I wish you wouldn't set fire to every olive branch I send your way. But it's not just me. You burn every bridge almost any human being tries to build between you and them. I've lived here weeks, that's all, and I probably have more friends than you. You live alone and you channel a dead woman because she had the same ailment as you, and because of what our stepfather—"

"Are you really going to put on your therapist hat and trot out that nonsense that I only do what I do because Diana had bulimia?"

"Your whole freaking origin story is a coat of crappy paint on a rotting house! Yes, your agent exploited your bulimia. *You* exploited your bulimia! But the truth is that it was our—"

"Stop it! There's a big difference between getting an inspiration for a show because briefly—briefly, Betsy, briefly—Diana and I shared that—"

"That's the opposite of what I'm saying!"

"Briefly—"

"Briefly? You were in rehab! You were institutionalized!"

"I have a residency. Do you know what that means? Do you know what that says about where I am on the Las Vegas ladder?"

She found herself rubbing the front of her forehead with the heel of one hand and closing her eyes. She was relieved, but also feeling a pang of guilt that her attack—instinctive as it was—had succeeded in misdirecting her sister. Sent her spinning out and away from the dead man at Red Rocks. "Jesus Christ," she murmured. "You are impossible to talk to. This conversation began with you calling me because a friend of yours died. And then you implied I was involved. And now you're boasting how successful you are. It's hard to believe there was a time when we could have a conversation without it all going to recriminations and shit."

"You just couldn't stay away. You couldn't leave me be. You had to come here."

That stung more than Betsy expected, but she had asked for it. She had pressed one of her sister's many bruises, and she had pressed it hard. When she said nothing in response, Crissy asked her again, "So, you've never heard of Cleo Dionne? And Frankie Limback was at some country club this afternoon?"

"Yes and yes," she replied.

"I hope you're telling the truth. Because I might just suggest the police talk to you, too. And Frankie. And all your friends at Futurium."

Betsy wasn't sure whether this conversation was more terrifying or exhausting. She knew only that she was in trouble. And so she decided that as soon as she and her sister had finished, she would call Frankie.

* * *

But Marisa came into her bedroom the moment she got off the phone.

"That didn't sound good," the girl said.

"Your aunt and I seem to fight a lot," Betsy confessed.

"Did you always?" She collapsed on the bed and lay on her side. She looked older than thirteen. It fascinated Betsy how chameleon-like the child was: one moment she could seem barely a teen and the next she could look like she was sixteen or seventeen years old. A lot of the kids Betsy had dealt with back in Vermont were like that. It depended upon how hard their shell had become. Marisa was wearing the same T-shirt and shorts she'd been wearing when Betsy had caught up with her at the museum, but what had seemed childlike amidst the natural wonders—some stuffed, some breathing, some replicas—now seemed suggestive, even wanton.

"I need to call Frankie," she said instead of answering her daughter's question.

"So, you're going to kick me out?"

Betsy lay down next to her and stared up at the ceiling. She reminded herself that everything she was doing, she was doing for this child. Or, at least, she was doing it more for Marisa than she was for herself. Frankie could wait a few minutes. He'd regain control of this Red Rocks madness—whatever it was and whatever he'd done.

"No, Crissy and I didn't always fight," she said. "We used to be close."

"What happened?"

Marisa was too young for the whole truth. Besides, how would she even begin to verbalize such things to this thirteen-year-old? Someday, maybe. But maybe not. Probably not. Crissy's past wasn't hers to share. So, instead, Betsy offered up her own demons. Her own history.

"Well, I was a hellion in high school. I've told you that. And she wasn't," she said quietly. Her mind was in two places: she wanted to be present and honest about her adolescence and why she and Crissy had grown apart, but she was also turning over in her head the myriad questions she had for Frankie. She was, more and more, clinging to the idea that the death of Crissy's friend was just a horrific fluke, but she knew in her heart that it wasn't.

After all, the Morleys were dead, and Futurium was buying what had been their casino.

"You said you smoked a lot of marijuana. That seems so not a big deal," said Marisa.

"It's not now. It was then."

"What else?"

"I once stole a neighbor's car. I knew they kept the keys in the mudroom, and they hardly ever locked the front door. Fortunately, I had my driver's license, and the neighbors didn't press charges. They were good people and even went along with my charade that they had loaned me the car."

"Why did you do that? Why did they?"

She took a deep breath. "Who knows why I stole their car. I can't remember. I probably wanted to go somewhere. I was pulled over on the way to Burlington, but I don't recall a particular destination. I mean, I was alone. I think I said something about birthday shopping for my mom. And why didn't they press charges? They liked my mom: schoolteacher and widow. They liked Crissy. Why make all of our lives harder than they already were? I guess that was their logic."

"What else did you do?"

"In the Vehicle Screwups Department, I crashed my mom's car into the back of some crazy big piece of farm equipment. A manure spreader. It was going, like, fifteen miles an hour on some narrow, two-lane road, and I had this new BlackBerry—"

"A BlackBerry?"

"An early sort of smartphone. You could text on it using this little metal toothpick-like thing. And that's what I was doing. Driving with my knees and sending someone a message. Ran right into the back of the manure spreader, set off the airbags, and totaled the car."

"Were you hurt?"

"Kind of. By the airbags, mostly. That really screwed up my mom's and Crissy's life. My crashing the family car."

"But you had insurance, right?"

"Uh-huh."

"So, what was the big deal?"

She recalled their mother's frustration. The borrowed cars. The arguments with the insurance company. Finding rides to work and whatever musical Crissy was in. The canceled dentist appointment that was held up as emblematic of what a train wreck of a human being she was.

"It was one massive inconvenience. And it was embarrassing. Betsy Dowling humiliates the family once again. Schoolteacher's kid fucks up one more time."

Marisa cuddled against her, something she'd never before done in bed. They'd snuggled on the couch watching TV, but this was new. The child was warm like a puppy.

"Tell me the carnival story," she said.

"Again?" Betsy forced a small chuckle for her benefit. She'd told it twice before.

"I like it. It's funny."

And so she did.

"Well, I was seven and Crissy was eight, and our stepfather took us to the Champlain Valley Fair," she began. The annual fair, held the week before and during Labor Day weekend, was the biggest of Vermont's carnivals and agriculture shows. "There was a ring-toss game, and if you won, the prize was one of those antique-looking dolls, where the head is made of glass and the doll has a hoop skirt and glass shoes. They were about two feet tall."

"They would have scared me."

"They were scary. They *are* scary," Betsy agreed. "But we still wanted them. Both Crissy and I did. The ring toss was two bucks for three throws. And so he put two dollars down and, of course, missed the pegs with each one. The rings were pretty small. Not much bigger than the pegs. And the game was rigged so it was almost impossible to win. The pegs weren't on a flat board. It was angled and, if I were to guess, angled in weird ways. Not consistently, like a set thirty degrees, or whatever. I'm sure the board was warped by design. Anyway, after he lost, he smiled at us and shrugged, and we were disappointed because we wanted the dolls and because our stepfather had failed. We thought he was infallible then."

She stopped for a moment, not by narrative design, but because she was seeing the man again. He'd been gone so long, whenever he came back to her, she found herself studying him. Hating him. But what was an actual memory, and what was a memory she was crafting from a photograph? How did Crissy see him? Because even though she lived a life of denial—or minimization, as if his crimes were misdemeanors—she still saw him. All of him. Had Crissy ever been able to grok the idea it wasn't her fault? Probably not.

"So, then the guy running the game said . . ." Marisa prodded her.

"Then the carny said, 'Why don't you keep playing 'til you win?' He was looking at us so sympathetically. He had this Yosemite Sam moustache that was starting to gray, and he seemed like a nice old grandfather. Anyway, our stepfather said, 'Really?' And the carny said, 'Really. Play 'til you win.' So, he did. We were there for a while, as he just kept tossing the rings, and the carny kept handing him more. And, finally, he won a doll. And as the carny gave it to him, he said, 'You have two adorable girls. You have to win two.' And my stepfather said, 'Oh, they can share it,' but the guy said, 'No, no. Keep playing. All good. And it's not like anyone's waiting.' We were the only people there."

"So, your stepdad kept playing," said Marisa. Her eyes were closed, and she sunk deeper into the pillow.

"Yes, he did. Crissy was holding that first doll. Of course. Eventually, he won a second doll, so we could each have one. And as soon as I had mine in my arms, the carny leaned in and said, 'That will be two hundred and seventy-four dollars. I take Visa and Mastercard.' My stepfather said, 'But you told me to keep playing until I won.' And the carny said, all innocent-like, 'I sure did. But I never said for free. I was just suggesting you should play 'til you win. I never said it was a gimme. It was just a . . . a recommendation because you have two lovely little girls and I could see they wanted the dolls.' For a couple of seconds, the two men stared at each other. Then the carny said, 'Look, I can take back the dolls, and we can part friends. It was a misunderstanding.' Then he put out his hands so our stepfather could take the dolls from Crissy and me and return them. But that was never going to happen. The carny knew it. He didn't know my stepfather, but he knew dads generally and he had his scam down. Either a dad was the type who didn't want to be embarrassed or he was the type who didn't want to break his kid's heart. Didn't matter which. And, like a hundred dads before him, our stepfather accepted the fact he had been played and gave the guy a credit card."

"The dolls weren't worth that much, right?"

"They were crap. Carnival crap. They sure weren't worth one hundred and thirty-seven dollars apiece. They fell apart in days."

"But your stepdad really loved you two."

She didn't say anything. She didn't correct the girl, but she didn't deny it, either. But she did recall how neither Crissy nor she cared when the glass feet broke off the dolls or the dresses tore, or one of the heads cracked and they finally threw them both away. The dolls had become soiled for them because they were symbols of the way their stepfather had been hoodwinked. The lesson for Betsy? Life will fuck over even the smartest among us: people like her stepfather, who—despite what later would happen—had brains. She wasn't sure what the lesson was for Crissy that day at the fair. But Betsy knew the memory had torpedoed her, too, and the pain of it could only have grown worse a few years later.

Months, she guessed, after they had tossed the dolls in the kitchen garbage bin.

"Were you ever arrested?" Marisa asked. Her eyes were closed.

"No," she told her. But if she'd finished the thought aloud (which she didn't), she would have added, *At least not yet.*

Sometimes I said things just to make people uncomfortable.

But right away I figured something out about Crissy. I could say any outrageous or "inappropriate" thing to her I wanted, and it might drive Betsy crazy, but Crissy would love it.

It was this inside joke between us that neither of us talked about.

CHAPTER TWENTY

Crissy

I continued walking the strip that Sunday night, blending in with the hordes of tourists. I hid beneath a paisley scarf, feeling brittle and pained.

I'd spoken to Nigel, and he was as shocked as I was by the news that Yevgeny was dead, though he was less sure that my sister was involved. He agreed it was likely that someone had murdered him—this was no accident or suicide—given the Morleys and what we were learning about Futurium.

I got as far as Circus Circus before I turned around. And as sad as I was that Yevgeny was dead, there also were these two facts that left me morose: I hadn't any idea what his younger sister's name was. And Betsy had been spot-on when she'd observed that she'd been in town mere weeks and had more friends than I did.

* * *

The theater was dark on Mondays, and so I was still in bed when the doorbell to my suite rang the next morning. (Oh, who am I kidding? I would have still been in bed, no matter what.) I peered through the peephole and saw the police were back: Felicia Johnson and Patrick O'Connor. This time they didn't have a hotel manager with them. Through the door I told them I'd be right there, and went for a robe. It was nine o'clock, the crack of dawn for me. I'd taken an extra half tab of Valium before turning out the light the night before, and so I'd been in a deep slumber. I looked like hell, and the world felt a bit foggy. I understood this wasn't a great condition in which to speak to a couple of cops, but I wasn't sure how to shoo them away.

"God," I said, seating them once more in the reading nook. My vanity chair was still there from the night before. "Did you two get to go home? Don't you two ever go to bed?"

"Isn't this the city that never sleeps?" asked Patrick.

"That's New York. At least according to Frank Sinatra," I corrected him.

"We're sorry to wake you," Felicia said. "But we have some information."

I put out my hands, palms up, and said, "I can't wait."

"We've reviewed the camera footage from the welcome center at Red Rocks," she told me, and then stopped. Just watched me and waited.

"I didn't even know they had cameras there. It's rather the middle of nowhere, wouldn't you agree?" I said. "Or, perhaps, as middle of nowhere as you can be a half hour from Las Vegas."

"There are cameras at the visitor center and a live cam that chronicles sunrises and sunsets," she informed me.

"And, thus, you can see Red Rocks without ever having to go there. Lovely. Or pathetic. Or typical Vegas," I said.

"You told us you weren't with Yevgeny Orlov at the park yesterday."

"I wasn't."

"But your car was there," she said.

"What? He rented a car at McCarran when he flew in on Saturday. He took that," I told them. It was a reflex to correct the detectives, even though I knew straightaway they were telling the truth. They wouldn't make something like that up or make a mistake that egregious. "I'm sure my car is in its spot at the casino."

"Yes, it is," said Felicia. "But it was in the Red Rocks parking lot yesterday. It's on the camera."

It would be futile to deny it. But I had no idea why Yevgeny would have driven my car without telling me. And, it dawned on me, if he had taken the Mini it would still be at Red Rocks, but Felicia had just confirmed it was back at the Buckingham Palace.

"Was his rent-a-car out there—at the park?"

"It was."

I held up a finger and told them I wanted to check my purse. I went there and rifled through it, and, sure enough, the car key was there. I went to the dresser drawer where I kept my passport and saw the spare key was gone. I poked around inside the drawer with both hands, as if—like a magical totem—it would reappear. It didn't.

"You have both keys?" asked Felicia.

"No. The key in my purse is there. But someone has taken my spare. It's usually in my dresser."

"What other keys would have been on the ring?"

"None. I use a card to get into this suite. I don't have any other keys."

"It's only the key to the Mini that's missing?"

"That's correct."

"How often is housekeeping in here?"

I couldn't help but laugh, despite my anguish that the key had vanished. "Housekeeping? I don't have housekeeping. I had a choice: housekeeping or a cabana. Which would you pick?"

"So, maid service doesn't come here daily?"

"No. I may be a princess, but I do my own sheets. I even have a little vacuum."

"Got it."

"So, what does that mean?" I was still at my dresser. They were watching me intently.

"You're certain that you didn't join him there—in your own car?" Felicia inquired.

"Oh, I'm quite sure."

Patrick looked down at his notepad as if he were disappointed in me. It was as if that had been my chance to come clean and I'd botched it.

"You're on the camera, too," said Felicia, her voice flat.

"At Red Rocks?"

"Yup."

I stood up straight. "Like hell I was. I was at the Cocoon bistro. I told you yesterday, I was with that writer. I was being interviewed. You can ask her."

"We could. But we can't find a Britt Collins who's a writer. At least not yet."

"I gave you her number."

"It didn't work. Maybe she wrote it down wrong. Confused a few digits."

"Well, I wasn't talking to a hologram. I'm sure there are cameras near the Cocoon."

"We'll check. But you are definitely on the Red Rocks cameras. Both at the visitors' center and on the cam that grabs the sunsets. It's a photo shoot of some sort."

I returned to them and sat down.

"I showed you our texts. Why would we have been texting if we were together?"

"Nothing about them said you weren't there together. Maybe you were fifty yards apart. Maybe five hundred."

I considered showing them to the detective once again, but I realized that was how people dig their own graves.

"There's you and a photographer," she continued. "A guy with blond hair who seems to be about your age. You're doing what looks like a Diana publicity shoot."

"That wasn't me."

"Then who was it?"

There it was. The question. It appalled me to think that only recently I had been worried about Betsy's safety. I'd even fretted that she was in trouble.

"That was my sister," I said. "Her name is Betsy Dowling."

"And your car? You lent it to her?"

"No. I did not."

"Then how did she get it?"

"I have no idea."

"I'm sure you're on the casino cameras here retrieving it," said Felicia.

"I assure you, that will be her, too. Dressed to look like me. Or Diana. And using the key that should have been in my purse." I gave them her phone number and address and suggested they talk to her. "I considered calling you about her last night. After you left."

"About Betsy?"

"Yes. I don't know why and I don't know how, but I think the company she works for—Futurium—may be responsible for Yevgeny's death. I think they may even have been responsible for the Morleys' deaths. After all, they're trying to buy this place."

"The Morleys were suicides."

"They weren't."

"How do you know that?"

"Because I saw Artie just before he was killed. He told me Richie was murdered—that Richie didn't kill himself. And Artie wasn't depressed. He . . ." I stopped midsentence. I was telling two detectives who already thought I had something to do with the death of Yevgeny Orlov a different story from what I'd told their associates after Artie Morley had died. I thought of how Eddie Cantone and Artie had asked me to lure a U.S. congresswoman to my dressing room so "friends" of theirs could threaten her. Tell her, as Artie had put it, to order her people to back off the BP.

I needed a lawyer.

I needed to talk to Eddie Cantone.

"Go on," said Felicia.

I sighed, exasperated with myself. "He didn't seem at all of the frame of mind of someone who would kill himself."

"And you know what that frame of mind is?"

"Yes. My stepfather killed himself."

The officers looked at each other.

"I am so sorry," said Patrick.

"I was eleven. Old enough to understand how morose he'd become," I told them. "And Artie wasn't like that."

"We're not working the Morleys. But I will tell the team that is that they should interview you."

"They already have."

"And you told them what you told us?"

"No," I replied. "Not exactly. I was . . . I was in shock."

They believed not a word, I could tell. But Felicia said simply, "I'll tell them to talk to you. Again."

"Okay," I said. But it wasn't okay. I wasn't okay.

"And, you think Futurium may have been responsible for Mr. Orlov's death?" Felicia asked, trying to get us back on track.

"I think it's possible, yes."

"Was he meeting someone from Futurium? If so, why?"

"I don't know," I admitted. "I don't even know if he was." Nevertheless, I told them what I knew about the crypto firm and Frankie Limback and Cleo Dionne's murder or suicide or accidental drowning in a Grand Cayman bathtub, and Patrick was writing it all down, and while a small fragment of me felt horrible for the grief I was raining down upon Betsy and, thus, Marisa, this madness had to stop.

When I was finished, they said to me what I had expected they would tell me the night before, but they hadn't: I shouldn't leave town.

In Betsy's opinion, I still needed a babysitter.

Seriously? One minute I was explaining to her how a blockchain worked or how to crack a password, and the next I was being sent to Ayobami's to do my homework.

Which, just so you know, never took more than, like, eleven minutes.

CHAPTER TWENTY-ONE

Betsy

On Sunday night, the sunset broken into cathedral-like columns of cascading light by clouds that would bestow not a drop of water onto the sand on which this surreal city was built, Betsy asked her friend, Ayobami, the blackjack dealer at the Luxor, to keep an eye on Marisa. Betsy had knocked on the woman's door after getting off the phone with her sister. Then she drove like a madwoman out to Frankie's house. Marisa wasn't pleased that her new mother refused to leave her home alone, but Betsy didn't know how long she'd be gone.

She also wasn't sure what she would say to Frankie, but she decided she had to talk to him face-to-face, not over the phone. She was going to make one thing clear: he'd pushed her too far, and she wasn't going one step further. Someone was dead, and she hadn't signed up for that.

* * *

When she'd texted Frankie that she was on her way over, she'd gotten the impression he was alone.

But when she arrived, she saw two other cars in the driveway, and knew one belonged to Rory O'Hara and was pretty sure the other was Damon Ioannidis's. She looked at the texts she had sent Frankie and they seemed firm, not frantic. But she had written that she was heading out to his place because a friend of her sister's was found dead at Red Rocks, and she could imagine

Frankie calling in the cavalry to support whatever explanation—translation, bullshit—he was going to offer.

Sure enough, when Frankie opened the door, she saw the two other men seated on corner sections of the massive L-shaped leather couch that was backed by the flat fountain waterfall and faced the glass doors that exited out onto the deck and his swimming pool. She felt outnumbered and, yes, outgunned.

"I thought you were alone," she said.

"Nah. When you're building a business, sometimes you have twenty-four/seven work weeks." He kissed her on the cheek, a dry little peck, and wrapped an arm around her waist and escorted her into the living room. She noticed two new paintings, desert wildflowers with tousled effusions of color that were crude imitations of Georgia O'Keeffe. There were no papers on the coffee table, no tablets or laptops—nothing to suggest a meeting. She saw there was a glass of red wine and what looked like a tumbler with Scotch before each of the men, but both had barely been touched. She wondered if, indeed, the pair had just arrived, perhaps pulling into the driveway only moments before her. Neither of them rose when she walked into the room, but they both offered a small wave.

"So, I'm interrupting?" she asked.

"Meh," said Damon. "We needed a break."

She asked Frankie if they could speak alone. In private.

He put his hands together in front of his face, his fingers of each hand aligned perfectly as if praying, and then exhaled with unbelievable histrionics. "If it's to talk about what you texted me . . . no. I think you should hear what everyone has to say."

Was he throwing her under the bus? Or was he just being a coward? She couldn't decide and then she decided that it didn't matter. She was cornered.

"Okay," she began. She and Frankie were standing in front of the pair, and he tried to guide her toward the couch. She resisted. She didn't want to sit down. She was electric with misgivings and distrust. "Today you had me out at Red Rocks doing that photo shoot. When I agreed, I thought it was just to look outdoorsy and wholesome. I expected hiking shorts and—"

"You were in hiking shorts," said Damon Ioannidis.

"And then that photographer insisted I wear that stupid British flag scarf and those ridiculous Wellingtons!"

"Wellingtons?" asked Damon.

"Boots! British boots! You made me look like Diana, which meant I looked like my sister!"

Frankie tried to mollify her: "You looked like a hiker at Red Rocks, baby, that's all."

"No! Look, I did it. I knew I was stepping on Crissy's toes. But I figured it was a harmless wrong, not . . ."

"Not what?" asked Rory.

"Not a someone-was-going-to-get-killed wrong."

Frankie folded his arms across his chest. "You said something about that in your text. I wish you hadn't."

"We all wish you hadn't," added Rory.

"Things like that can be misconstrued," said Damon. "And guys like Tony Lombardo? They're probably reading your texts."

"It's not a big deal," Frankie told them, and then he smiled at her as if he were protecting her. Like she had been chastised, but it was okay now and he had her back. For a long second, she wasn't sure when she had seen that look on his face before, but then she remembered: her office back in Burlington, when he was trying to convince his son that the three grown-ups surrounding the teen—Frankie, his wife, and Betsy Dowling, the social worker—weren't all in league against him and whatever he'd done wasn't cataclysmic.

"Okay?" he said to his partners. They said nothing, and Damon reached for the Scotch. "Who was it who died?" Frankie asked her.

Damon raised his eyebrows inquisitively as he finished a long sip, the implication being that he was genuinely curious.

"You all know," she said. The anger inside her was pounding water against a dam. "You all know."

"Who died?" Frankie pressed.

"Stop it! Stop this playacting now!" she demanded.

"Okay, fine. No more playacting. He had to go," said Rory, and Frankie and Damon's heads both swiveled like bobblehead dolls, and they looked at him like he'd lost his mind. He shrugged at their reaction. "She's a big girl," he added.

"Rory," Frankie began, but it was clear he didn't know what to say.

"Our people in California and West Palm Beach wanted him gone. That's all there is to it. And Frankie? Your girlfriend just admitted that she knew what she was doing was wrong. She made a choice."

"People are going to think my sister was there at Red Rocks," she hissed. "Yeah, I thought I looked a little like Diana, but I didn't know you were framing my sister for murder."

Rory tapped his temple with his index finger. "We all saw the resemblance between you two. It was a natural."

"Crissy's car," she said, her mind trying to latch on to anything that would suggest her sister's innocence.

"Her car was there, too—out at Red Rocks. Your sister is on the BP parking garage camera retrieving her wheels, and then her wheels are on the Red Rocks parking lot cam. We crossed that *t* and dotted that *i*."

Abruptly, her knees were buckling, and she was feeling dizzy and the world was growing dark. Who in the world had retrieved the car from the garage? It wasn't her. Some Vegas model in a wig? She felt Frankie guiding her to a plush corner of the couch and sitting her down, then lowering himself onto the leather beside her.

"Put your head between your knees," he was saying, and she did. It helped, and the men around her sipped their Scotch and their wine, and Frankie massaged her shoulders. The world, in scintillas, began to reform. She heard Rory's voice.

"Orlov was very good at what he did," he was saying. "But he's not the only one who can take out the trash. We need team players, not guys who want to play us."

"I never met him," she mumbled.

"I know. When he was in Dubai on another job—eliminating a guy at a crypto conference who tried to hack our farm in Cambodia—we learned all kinds of shit about him. A woman in Emirates intelligence who's on our payroll clued us in. His background had some holes."

"He's an assassin?" she asked.

"Was an assassin. Very good. Among the best. And even though GEI was just a cover, he was actually an excellent lobbyist. Top drawer! Got to be good friends with Erika Schweiker for us, because of all that GEI nonsense. Anyway, we learned from Dubai that the feds had dirt on him—and turned him. Richie Morley had been their mole, which is kind of ironic, since we had Orlov whack him. I don't think Artie ever knew."

"But Artie . . ." she started to say, the thought embryonic.

"When Artie refused to cave, Orlov took care of him, too."

The dizziness was gone, but she still felt flushed and there was a faint ringing in her ears.

"Look, Orlov was going to wear a wire," Rory was saying. "We couldn't allow that. Hell, he knew too much to live, no matter what. He even wanted the FBI to meet with Crissy, and see if she'd wear a wire—maybe even try and be you. So, we thought, instead of letting them use her to be you, let's use you to be her. Get Orlov out to Red Rocks for a 'meeting,' and point the investigation into his death away from us."

Her mind was reeling as she tried to parse how they had used her to set up her sister, and how they had no compunction with a body count that was now at least four. Hit men. Assassins. She felt soiled, surrounded and scared, her umwelt void of the experience to help her absorb the duplicity and violence that these people saw as unremarkable.

"Tell us everything Crissy told you," Frankie said. "We need to know."

Everything.

What did that mean?

She didn't give a damn about self-preservation now, not after what she had done, except for one thing. Marisa. She had a daughter to care for. For the sake of the girl, she couldn't screw this up. She had to keep that child safe.

Then, when she was out of here, she would determine what she needed to do to protect Crissy.

So, what was *everything*? Or, what was *enough*?

"Betsy?" It was Frankie, his voice concerned.

She gathered herself and told them that two detectives had been to her sister's suite at the Buckingham Palace. She admitted there was a chance that Crissy was going to tell the police about her and Frankie and even Cleo Dionne, whom Crissy had learned about while researching Futurium.

Frankie took one of her hands in both of his and massaged the soft spot where the base of her thumb met the base of her index finger.

"That's what we wanted," Rory said. "The cops heading over to the BP."

"It's okay that Crissy told them about Futurium. And about my friend Cleo," Frankie went on. "Cleo's death was a tragedy."

"Get over it, Frankie. Get over her," Rory told him. "Orlov made sure she felt no pain. None."

"I know . . ."

Was that heartache on Frankie's face? Betsy thought it was. It gutted her.

"We have the right friends at the LVPD," Damon was saying.

"I'm done," she murmured. "No more." She wasn't sure who she was talking to. It was a general appeal into the air.

"Done?'

"No more looking like Crissy, no more Diana."

"Frankie?" It was Rory and he was leaning forward. "Would you tell her that's not possible? Not quite yet? Tomorrow night is the cocktail party at that other dunghill of a casino: Fort Knocks. The meet and greet with the other tribute show performers. We need her for the senator."

"Look—" Frankie began, talking to the other two men in the room, but Rory was shaking his head and Frankie never finished whatever it was he was going to say.

And it dawned on Betsy that her boyfriend, who once she had thought was a master of the universe—and maybe he had been when he'd been a banker—wasn't just scared of people like Tony Lombardo. He was frightened of Damon and Rory.

"Betsy," Frankie said, his voice even weaker than when things had been at their absolute worst with his son and he was scared for the boy, so very, very scared, "you can't be done. As Rory said: not yet. I'm . . . I'm sorry. See, tomorrow night? Monday? That's kind of important."

"No. I want to be an assistant at Futurium and do my job managing all your calendars and meetings and leave it at that."

"It's just that you're . . ."

"I'm what?"

"You're not done yet," Rory said, finishing Frankie's sentence for him in a way her boyfriend hadn't planned when he'd been searching for the right words. He was angry, and he put down his tumbler so hard on the coffee table that she was surprised the glass top didn't break or the tumbler itself didn't shatter.

Which was when she told herself that Rory was wrong and her fear was not going to cripple her. She *was* done. She had to be; she had to be for Marisa and she had to be for Crissy. She was in deep, yes, but she was not underwater. So, she was going to fold her cards, she was going to cash in her chips. They or she could choose any casino metaphor they wanted. The point was, she hadn't killed anyone. She hadn't broken any laws. At least not on purpose. Sure, she'd let that photographer, Tim Whatever, take some pictures of her at Red Rocks. But that was it. No one, she told herself, could argue that she was part of "a conspiracy," because she didn't know what the others were doing.

And so she stood up and stormed past the three men, and only when she reached the front door did she turn back to them. "This is over," she said. "At least my part."

And then she was outside and the sun was setting, and to the east she saw the phantasmagoric halo that was Las Vegas.

* * *

In Vermont, the mushrooms in the woods that day had been as big as human skulls. The two girls thought they had found a mass grave. The sisters were ten and eleven at the time, and it had rained most of September. In addition to their sheer size, the mushrooms had quarter-sized dots the color of pitch that looked like the holes for eye sockets or nostrils. If these were skulls, then this part of the forest had been the site of (worst case) some sort of criminal slaughter or (best case) a centuries-old graveyard that had floated up from beneath layers of dirt and decaying pine boxes.

Crissy took Betsy's arm and let out a small shriek. The sun was setting by six thirty then and it was five thirty in the afternoon, and so the woods already were growing shadowy and dark. They knew the way home. They knew those woods well. But they hadn't been there since the height of the spring, and the forest always was changing. The sisters had ventured there because their mother's backyard trail cam at the edge of the woods had picked up a bobcat, and they were just bored enough after school that day—for whatever the reason, they had no after-school activities—and they were just old enough now that their parents weren't afraid they'd accidentally burn down the house if left alone until their mom returned from the high school. The idea that a bobcat would come so close to the village astonished them, even then. Usually the camera caught only raccoons and squirrels and the occasional deer. And so they had set off, looking for scat or claw marks on trees, not really believing they'd see the animal, but viewing the excursion as something more interesting than homework. The two of them were not long removed from being Brownies, so they still had that Brownie badge work ethic: the relentless drive to cover a sash with pyramidic cloth icons commemorating the ability to splint a finger or think like a scientist or sit with a senior citizen who reeked of urine and feces while she shared a story from her own childhood. Betsy had left the Brownies when her big sister had left, and Crissy had only moved on because she had gotten a part in a community theater production of *Annie* and felt she was too busy or too important to take the next step and become a Girl Scout.

They were off the path when Crissy cried out.

"What? What?" Betsy asked, and Crissy pointed, and there they were. The younger girl started toward them, the older one attached to her as if Betsy's arm were an umbilical cord, and she knew within seconds that they were only mushrooms. But Crissy was behind her, and Betsy found the urge to torment her big sister irresistible. "Oh, my God," she said. "Skulls. People were murdered here. Maybe witchcraft!"

She felt Crissy's fingers grasping her biceps harder, and she thought her brash, confident big sister—the aspiring actor, even then—was going to cry, and so she went on, "I see bones. Lots of them."

Crissy started to pull away, and Betsy let her. The girl turned and ran. She'd gone easily twenty-five yards, racing beneath branches and hopping over mossy rocks when she stopped and yelled back, "Betsy, come on! Let's get out of here!"

Instead, Betsy knelt, as if in supplication, before one of the mushrooms and used two hands to gently lift it from the soft black soil like a chalice in some movie she must have seen that was set in the middle ages. She was careful because it was fragile, but she knew Crissy would perceive her delicacy as respect for the dead. "I think it's from a grown-up," she called back. "But these other ones might be little kids."

"Put it down, put it down!" Crissy screamed. "Let's go!"

And then Betsy stood up with the mushroom and smashed it between her hands, crumbling it into pieces. Crissy screamed with all the drama of a starlet in a slasher pic. The birds in the trees flew away, and if there was a bobcat anywhere near them, it would have fled without hesitation. Betsy smiled demonically, but Crissy never saw the grin. She had turned, sprinting away in full-on drama queen mode. (Later, she'd insist that she also never saw Betsy cave in the mushroom and sprinkle the pieces on the ground.) And because even then the small stupid things Betsy did took on lives of their own and became big stupid things, Crissy got lost in the woods. It's easy, especially when dusk is falling or a person is scared. The disorientation and the confusion spike like a fever, and soon it takes a compass to distinguish north from south. (Once, when Betsy was thirty, she had been housesitting for friends with a dog, and the first time she walked the animal in the woods, she lost all sense of direction and needed the compass on her phone to navigate her way west and back to their property, fighting her way through vines and brambles and decaying birches that had tumbled to the ground, and climbing up and over fallen maples, pine trees, and oaks.)

Crissy got home just as their mother was calling the State Police. She was covered in scrapes, including two on her face that had her more terrified they wouldn't heal in time for the publicity photos they were going to shoot for her next show than the idea that she had seen a pile of human skulls an hour earlier. When Betsy told her they'd only been mushrooms, Crissy shook her head and, for the first time in her life, gave her sister the finger.

The irony to this story, in Betsy's mind?

No, the ironies?

First, a decade later, when the two of them were in college, one of their classmates from elementary school would kill himself not far from where they had seen the elephantine mushrooms. It was during hunting season, and he had wrapped his lips around the muzzle of his Remington 7600 and used his thumb to press down on the trigger. Arguably, the real killer had been opioids. He hadn't told anyone he was going into the woods, and it would be two days before his body was found.

Moreover, Betsy knew intuitively that the skull beneath his hair and the cap he was wearing would have had a hole that looked very much like the black spots on those mushrooms the two girls had found in the woods.

Second, it would be late that night, when their stepfather came home from the newspaper, that under the subterfuge of comforting Crissy, he would do his worst, and she—Betsy—would walk in and catch them.

Catch him.

How much skin had she seen? Her sister's pale, bare legs. Her stepfather's, too, less pale because of the black hair. The room was dark, but the hallway light brightened the room enough. Too much. He was off the bed, she was on it, and then there was the frantic attempt to cover up and reframe the narrative, but you can't cover that up.

Betsy knew intellectually that what happened there wasn't her fault. Years later, when Crissy was in rehab, she'd learn it had been going on periodically since Crissy had been in the fourth grade. But would the man have gone into Crissy's bedroom a little before midnight *that night* if her sister hadn't been lost in the woods and so terribly frightened? If their mother hadn't called the State Police? Would her sister have allowed him to pull her nightgown over head on that particular occasion? Betsy would never know. But she always believed that if she hadn't told Crissy the mushrooms were skulls and demolished one with her hands, that night would not have unfolded the way that it had: their stepfather wouldn't have taken advantage of Crissy's devastation and once more unleashed his own perversions upon her and then, after he was finally caught, taken his own life.

He'd gone to the small carriage barn where they parked the two family cars and hanged himself in the rafters on the second floor. It was why Betsy never, ever confused *hanged* with *hung.*

* * *

Monday morning, Betsy saw Marisa onto the school bus, but wasn't sure whether she still had a job at Futurium. Frankie hadn't called or texted her Sunday night, and that had left her uneasy. She was dressed, but it wasn't as if she dressed for work: it was a warehouse and the dress code, if anyone at Futurium had ever thought of such a thing, was pretty casual. She was wearing jeans and a sleeveless top, planning to bring a sweater or upscale sweatshirt to pull on once she was ensconced in the Ice Cave. She could have gone to work or she could have gone grocery shopping. Hell, this was Las Vegas on a Monday morning. She could have gone to the Bellagio and dropped a hundred dollars into the slot machines.

But then her decision was made for her. Through her living room window, she saw Frankie sliding into the parking lot of her apartment complex in his Tesla and running up the exterior steps to her floor. She opened the door before he could knock and let him in.

"Good morning," he began and he reached for her. He held her for a moment, and she didn't stop him. But neither did she hug him back. She was a rag doll.

"Morning," she said.

"Marisa's at school, right?"

She nodded. "So, do I still have a job? I wasn't sure whether to go to the warehouse or not. I honestly have no idea whether I'm still employed."

"Yes, of course, you are. You still have a job." He rolled his eyes playfully.

"And this look-like-my-sister stuff is done?"

"Almost."

She shook her head because she knew what he meant. "I'm not going tonight."

"It's a cocktail party. A meet and greet. Then a meeting with someone important. Two hours, max. I promise, it will be the last thing you ever have to do as Diana."

"As Crissy!"

"It's harmless."

"You said that the last time."

"It really is. But there are a pair of bigwigs in the Mastaba family flying in from Grand Cayman, and it's complicated. You need to be there."

"Let me guess: one is Oliver Davies."

He nodded and joked, "WAGMI." *We're all gonna make it.*

The meet and greet, as he called it, was a gathering that Futurium had put together for select tribute show performers. It was going to be at Fort Knocks, an over-the-hill casino now so squalid that people had told her you wanted to wear rubber gloves when touching the slots, and the bathrooms were putrescent. (The place was named for the original owner, Benjy Knock, a pal of Bugsy Siegel. Knock thought it clever to pair his name with the vault where the United States stored thousands of metric tons of gold bullion reserves.)

Betsy knew that no big names would be there and it was clear that they hadn't invited her sister: after all, they wanted Betsy to be their Diana. But the biggest of the Michael Jacksons and Janis Joplins wouldn't be caught dead at Fort Knocks, and so it was going to be an array of the also-rans: the Prince who was six and a half feet tall or the Dolly Parton who'd clearly never set foot in Tennessee or the Ella Fitzgerald who, pure and simple, just couldn't sing.

And, in theory, Betsy Dowling as Diana Spencer.

"I told you: I'm out. Someone died Sunday afternoon."

"I hear you. I do. We're both caught in some shit I hadn't expected. I never wanted to involve you."

"Or Cleo Dionne, right?"

"That was different," he said, but she could see the guilt in his eyes. He couldn't save her any more than she could save him.

"I'm not doing this. I'm a mother. I want nothing to do with your crypto friends, other than my job at the warehouse. Shit: I'm not even sure I want that."

"I wish they were friends," he said, and he stepped away

from her and gazed out the window. There was nothing to see. It's not like she had a view. But with his back to her, she could spot his pistol in his waistband. She considered whether that was the point. He had to have slipped it there after getting out of the car.

"See, after the meet and greet, you're going to meet Senator Aldred," he said.

"I told you, I'm not going."

"It won't take long. John Aldred just—"

"No!"

"You're making a mistake," he said, after a moment.

"Whatever you're doing . . . you know it's wrong."

"I don't have the best choices."

"You once said if I ever wanted us to go back to Vermont, we'd leave. You'd book a flight east, and off we'd go. You, me, and Marisa."

"It's not that easy. Not anymore."

"Was it ever?"

"Betsy, c'mon."

"I probably shouldn't go to work today," she told him.

"You really think *that* would be making a good choice?"

"I do."

"So: how will you pay for this apartment?"

He wasn't looking at her, but she could hear the threat in his voice. Instantly she tried to calculate in her head what her expenses were. Should she cash in her crypto? She wasn't sure what the coin was going for today. Did she have enough savings in her old-fashioned checking account at her old-fashioned bank from her short time at Futurium to tide her over until she could find another job here? That would depend, she guessed, on how long it took to become a dealer or whatever—and then on whatever she could make doing what Ayobami did. She knew she couldn't carry this place, modest as it was, as a waitress at some second- or third-rate joint in Summerlin, or give Marisa the life that she wanted for her. Or, yes, the life that she wanted for herself. But it was clear that her sugar daddy was willing to turn off the tap. And while her taste for the illicit might have seemed insatiable before college, she had found her limits and walked away from the worst. Reinvented herself. Futurium? It was backsliding. No, it was worse than backsliding, because people were getting killed. None of her temerity or foolhardiness in the past rose to anywhere near that level of criminality.

"I think you should go," she said quietly. "I think if you stay, we both might say things we'll regret. Things we don't mean but can't take back."

"You're seriously not going to the warehouse today? Is that definite?"

"That's definite. I'm not. I guess I'm calling in sick while we . . . we reassess."

"Reassess what?"

She wasn't precisely sure what she meant. Them? Their relationship? What Futurium was up to and what they were asking of her? "The job description," she said, a half-truth at best.

"You're putting me in a tough spot. You know that, don't you? But you're putting yourself in a worse one."

"I understand," she agreed, ignoring the menace that skulked in that last sentence.

"Your sister doesn't like you, Betsy," he said. "Maybe she loves you. But she sure doesn't like you."

"I know that, too," she agreed. It was as if he were telling her something new.

"And I can't protect you."

"What do I need protection from?" But, of course, the answer was obvious. She could have framed the question with *who* instead of *what*. But she could have named names, if asked. Rory. Damon. Tony. Maybe even Lara.

He put his hands in his front pants pockets. "Okay," he said. "Why not? Take today off. Think about what you want and what's best for you and Marisa."

"I will."

"But Betsy?"

She waited.

"This isn't over. The Mastaba . . ."

"Go on."

"They take whatever the fuck they want. They're used to getting their way."

I know I sound like a smart-ass. Like I think I'm the smartest contestant on Wheel of Fortune. *(Actually, I probably would be. I lived in one place once where we watched that show over dinner, and I swear I saw a lady miss "A dog's life," when the only letters missing were the* d *and the* f. *A cog's lime? Really?)*

But sometimes I miss the most obvious stuff and make the dumbest mistakes.

Like when Frankie picked me up after school. Instead of getting on the school bus, I got right in the car with him. Didn't think twice.

CHAPTER TWENTY-TWO

Crissy

So far, there had been nothing on the news that linked me to Yevgeny Orlov's death—nor had there been an obituary—but I feared it was only a matter of time. Anchors had mentioned him on TV, and I'd seen a brief in the newspaper about the tourist who had died at Red Rocks, but the implication was that it was an accident or, conceivably, a suicide. No one, even the TV reporters or anchors who thought mentioning his homes in Montauk and Manhattan added a layer of tony glamour to the tale, suggested he might be a spy. Still, as soon as the police were gone, I went to see Eddie Cantone, possibly the most senior executive left standing at the BP.

After I'd told him everything I thought the LVPD knew, Eddie sat forward in his chair and picked up two of the gold-plated dice he kept in an ashtray on his desk. He didn't smoke, but the dice looked fabulous in the obsidian dish.

"I'm glad you're here now," he said. "But I was expecting you last night. I kinda wish you'd called as soon as the police came knocking on your door about this Yevgeny Orlov."

"I did call. I didn't leave a message. It seemed like a lot for a message."

"I already knew."

"You did?"

"Hell, yeah. Everyone knows. Harvey Nardozzi brought the two cops to your suite. He called me right away."

Of course. The front desk manager Sunday evening. Harvey.

The whole Buckingham Palace management team—whatever was left of it—was watching this.

"I'm sorry. I shouldn't have waited until this morning."

"A guy flies west to sleep with you and then dies out at Red Rocks? You're on our video getting your car from our garage, and then your car is out there at the park? Damn straight, you shouldn't have waited."

"I told you. That was my sister on the video. Not me."

"Fine. You or your sister." He rolled the dice into the dish and rubbed his eyes. His annoyance was palpable, and he was working hard to keep his exasperation in check. "So, you have an alibi," he said. "You were at that shithouse restaurant off the strip with some writer. That's the proof that it's your sister on the camera, not you. And that's your proof you weren't even out at Red Rocks."

"That's correct. She said her name was Britt Collins."

"Good. But how in holy fuck did your sister get the key to your car and take it from the garage?"

"I don't know. But Eddie?" He waited. "How deeply are you involved in this—whatever *this* is?"

"What do you mean?" His antennae were now raised. I had piqued not his curiosity, but his animal desire for self-preservation. I hadn't meant to, but I had perfumed the air with the aroma of hungry wolves in the woods.

"I mean," I continued, "you were present when Artie asked me to call Erika Schweiker. You know whatever Artie knew. You—"

"And that's over. I told you. Let that go."

"I think I need a lawyer."

"I think you do, too."

"Because I did call Schweiker. Like you asked—"

"No one—"

"She called back and I did what you said, Eddie. I said it was a wrong number."

"She believe you?"

I sighed. "Unsure. But when the police were in my suite a little while ago, they told me not to leave town. So, I don't know whether I should be worried I'm going to be framed for killing Yevgeny Orlov or because Erika Schweiker is going to accuse me of something crazy."

"She is crazy."

"So, does the casino have a lawyer you'd recommend?"

"Like a criminal lawyer? Why would you think any of us would know a criminal lawyer?"

I knew he was being coy. This was Las Vegas.

"I mean, you don't need a real estate lawyer," he continued. "We got those up the wazoo. And now we got estate lawyers hanging around, too: the Morleys' estate lawyers. But criminal lawyers?" He shook his head.

"I only did what you and Artie asked."

He sat forward and clasped his hands in front of him. He looked me squarely in the eye and said, "I don't know what you're talking about. Calling a U.S. representative? Why would you do such a thing, Crissy?"

"Because—"

"Nope."

I understood what was happening intellectually, but in moments of crisis, we can't help but succumb a tad to our inner ostrich. "Eddie," I pleaded, but he shook his head.

"I don't know what you're talking about," he said. He was sufficiently old school that he wore a necktie and kept it in place with a gold clip. It had a diamond on it. Now he pulled his hands apart and fidgeted with the clip with a thumb and a forefinger that belied his age more than his hair, gnarled as they were by arthritis. "But if the death of this Orlov character becomes a serious murder investigation and you become a serious suspect, you do need a lawyer. You're right. But I can't help you. I have no future here."

"At the BP?"

"And Las Vegas. I'm getting out. Leaving town."

"You're . . . you're an institution."

"Institution? I'm a dinosaur. I hired the first magician on the strip."

"You didn't. You weren't even alive when El Rancho brought Gloria Dea into their showroom."

"A woman, eh? Okay, so maybe the second. My point? The people buying the BP got no use for me. I'm not even going to stay in Clark County. I figure I got ten good years left, and I'm going to find a place that's warm and Mastaba-free, and keep my head down. And you? You should do the same. Get the hell out of Dodge, Crissy."

"Because of the Mastaba?"

"And the cops."

"Aren't people innocent until proven guilty—especially in this town?"

"People are innocent, Crissy. People. Not princesses. You of all"—and he emphasized the next word ominously—"*people* should know that as well as anyone."

* * *

When I left Eddie's office, I went first to my suite and called my agent. Terrance and I had been speaking about the death of the Morleys, but it was only that morning that I told him a fellow I'd shagged a couple of times was dead, the police had been at my suite twice in the last eighteen or so hours, and I'd called a congresswoman at the request of Artie Morley—and now Eddie Cantone was prepared, it seemed, to toss me away like sour milk. Terrance said the agency would find me a lawyer in Las Vegas. I shuddered at the cost. But I trembled more at how my life was unraveling.

Then I met Nigel at the castle keep of my cabana, and we

started to drink. (I'd long ago accepted the fact it was always five p.m. somewhere.) I was sitting upright on my chaise, and he was reclining on his side in the one next to me. He had a Guinness, and I a gin and diet tonic. For a while, we scrolled through sites on our phones looking for a defense attorney who might be less costly than whatever firm my Beverly Hills agent found for me, but this wasn't *Better Call Saul,* and I didn't want ambulance chasers who sold their services via billboards. Still, it gave us something to laugh about, even if it was gallows humor at its darkest. We also talked about an appalling gathering of second-rate entertainers scheduled for that night at Fort Knocks, a nightmare of a casino that made the BP look like the Ritz. Nigel had wondered if our feelings should be hurt that we weren't invited, and I said absolutely not. No one of our caliber would be caught dead at a party like that. Then he surprised me by asking, out of the blue, if I might consider buying a gun.

"No, thank you," I said. "I've never even held one."

"Even in Vermont?"

"Even there."

My hair was loose around my shoulders, and he surprised me by reaching over and pushing a strand behind my ears. "I thought I recognized the earrings," he said. They were a pair of moonstones he'd given me for my birthday. We had, by then, the sort of relationship where I thought nothing of his reaching for a lock of my hair like that. It would rather have been like my adjusting the collar on his shirt. His voice, as it was always, was a balm.

"They're beautiful," I said. Then I sipped my drink and told him, "You're not going to convince me to start carrying a pistol because of whatever my sister is up to or whatever happened to Yevgeny. That's a bad idea on a thousand levels."

"You could borrow mine. We could go to a shooting range tomorrow and you could practice," he said.

The fact he owned a pistol had come up soon after we met,

when he was telling me stories about being a waiter and walking home after work in the small hours of the morning, to an apartment that was off the strip and away from the seeming impregnability of the crowds.

"Not happening," I murmured. Near a high top at the BP's Tower of London pub was a pretend suit of armor. It was holding a two-balled flail, though the orbs and spikes were hollow and made of plastic. "I'd sooner swing a toy flail at my assailant," I said.

"Which would be rather ineffective."

"Quite. The thing is, even John Aldred's people didn't carry guns. At least as far as I know," I reminded him, referring to the senator. Nigel was among the circle well aware of John's and my affair. I had presumed a U.S. senator had a security detail, but most didn't. John didn't even have a body man; he had a chief of staff who would be with him on occasion, and sometimes a driver, but they rarely came into the casino, except when he would be in my audience. They were just out there in the ether somewhere, away from us when we'd dine in my suite or find a secluded nook in one of the BP's restaurants.

"You know you're at war, Crissy. I'm not sure that you understand that. But you are and you need to be ready."

"Ready for what? A gunfight in a casino?"

"They killed your friend. They stole your car key and took your Mini, and set you up to take the fall."

"I have an airtight alibi. I was at Cocoon with a writer while Yevgeny was at Red Rocks. And I told the police to go ahead and search my car and dust it for fingerprints and reenact whatever CSI protocols they want."

"I wouldn't be so glib."

"I'm not glib. I'm scared. And I'm cheesed off."

He smiled gently at me. "Save expressions like that for the stage. Even I can't get away with 'cheesed off,' and I'm from the UK."

"You can't use 'cheesed off' because now you're king."

"Oh, you're going to write my promotion into the show? I'm honored."

"Yes, at some point this month I will. One must keep current."

"I hope I will be a king that makes his subjects proud."

"We'll see. You've sure as hell had a boatload of years to grow into the job."

He smiled and raised his glass.

"Look, I don't want a gun, Nigel," I went on. "I barely leave the casino. Between you and Bud McDonald and the rest of hotel security, I feel like I have my own private beefeaters."

"You clearly can't trust the casino. Not anymore."

I nodded. The truth was painful. My home had been violated.

"Have you heard from Betsy today?" he asked. "Since you told the police to talk to her?"

"I have not."

He tilted back his head and finished the last of his Guinness. "They'll be back, you know," he said. "The police."

"I know."

"Tell me something," he said.

"Of course."

"You were here in October 2017."

He knew I was. He knew my history. And bringing up October 2017 to someone who lives in Las Vegas is rather like bringing up September 2001 to someone who lives in New York City. I knew where this was going.

"Yes," I said. "That's right."

"It was October first, right?" Nigel was saying.

"It was," I murmured, and then I recounted for him where I was and what I recalled. Some of it, he knew. But not all of it.

I told him that I was performing the night of the Route 91 Harvest Music Festival massacre. I was new to the scene, but I had my gig at the BP. A shooter opened fire from the thirty-second floor of the Mandalay Bay, murdering fifty-eight people and wounding more than 850. I was still onstage on Sunday nights back then, and I had just the one show each evening. It started at ten p.m. because, at the time, the BP still had a British comedian in the showroom with an eight o'clock gig. So, I had just gone on when people's phones started vibrating. The assassin started shooting at five minutes after ten.

I was singing "A Sign of the Times"—a horrific, oddly ominous coincidence, which is why I pulled the song from the show after that night—when Bud McDonald hopped onto my stage and pulled the mic from my hands and announced, "Everyone, take cover! Now! There is an active shooter on or near the strip!" It was twelve minutes after ten. None of us, including Bud, had an inkling whether the shooter—or shooters—was just outside the BP and about to come inside, and so my audience crouched down between the rows of seats or curled up in balls on the floor. At the time, it was just me and a pianist in the show, and we both crawled under his piano. At first, the people in my audience were calm; I could see some checking their phones, understanding now why the devices had been buzzing in their pockets. But within minutes, we heard screaming outside the theater, lots of screaming, and I began to hear whimpering from behind the rows of seats before me.

The theater entrance and box office opened up onto the lobby above the casino floor, and people were running from the strip into whatever casino was closest. So, although people inside the showroom didn't hear the pops from the AR-15 or the thousand-plus rounds the murderer discharged, they heard the shrieks and the panicked crowd assembling outside the doors. None of us had any idea if this was a lone gunman firing from the Luxor or the Mandalay Bay or some other spot high in the sky, or part of a well-coordinated terrorist attack on multiple casinos. And then dozens of the people who had sought refuge in the BP lobby were escorted into the theater for an added layer of safety, and many of them had blood on their clothing and faces and hands. We could see it vividly on anyone wearing white, and I told Nigel of the two young women in ivory T-shirts, one sleeveless, and how a theater usher was sure they were shot so badly they should be rushed to the ER, but neither had a scratch on her. The pair had no idea of the names of the people whose blood had saturated their clothing and coated their hair like gel. They were in shock, sobbing and scared, and grateful they were alive. Apparently, they had just run and run when the shooting had started, and weren't sure how or why they had been herded into the Buckingham Palace as they'd been part of the crush that had raced north, away from the barrel where the humans were the fish. There was the round girl with the cherubic face—was she even as old as my niece was now?—whose father had one arm around her, while his other flopped at his side or swung wildly like a scarecrow's when he turned to look back at the doors, and it was only then that I noticed the eerily circular, deep claret stain on the shoulder of his rugby shirt.

The BP had us shelter in place, where we stayed until almost one in the morning. Some members of the crowd were distraught that they couldn't reach people they knew who had been at the music festival, and I saw others—in addition to that father—who were wounded and should have been on their way to the ER. I saw folks texting frantically and scouring Facebook and Twitter and news apps for any information that was out there. Even the most stoic in the showroom were beginning to find the claustrophobia as unnerving as the reality that we had no idea how bad this already was or was going to be. The unknown is both a correlative to concrete horror and an aftershock. Dread. Anxiety. The devil you know . . .

I learned later that some of the other casinos had set up metal detectors in their ballrooms or convention centers to make sure that they knew who had guns and who didn't, and because they weren't completely sure there had only been that one shooter. But the BP didn't do that. When the lockdown was lifted, I wandered down to the casino floor. It was surreal. Most of the machines were empty, the swiveling chairs perfectly still. The pit bosses had cleared the tables. But the video slots were continuing to issue their mechanical come-ons, the ones based on movies and TV shows and NASCAR and singers—country and heavy metal—as loud as ever. Louder, in fact, because their cackles and cries were no longer muffled by the ambient noise of human chatter and human bodies in motion.

The next morning, the area gun stores were packed. At least that's what people told me. I had no intention of buying one.

But for days, I was shell-shocked and grieving. We all were. As common as mass shootings are in America, for anyone who experiences one or lives in the shadow of one, there remains a semblance of singularity. *How could this have happened? We must be unique to have shared this cataclysm.* I was mourning people I'd never met, but the utter senselessness of their deaths left me broken. Monday the theater was dark, but we canceled the show scheduled for Tuesday. Even Wednesday seemed too soon, but the casino wanted me to return and I began the show that night with the single lit candle that would become a staple of the act: Diana's face emerging from behind the flame of one long, white taper. But that night, it was for a moment of silence and a light in the darkness.

And, yes, the theater was full. The BP's guests were back at the tables and the slots.

But for weeks all any of us who worked and lived in the city could talk about was the utter horror of what had unfolded that Sunday night. Soon, the "Welcome to Las Vegas" sign became an impromptu memorial. People were leaving photos of the dead and flowers for the dead, and notes that were heartbreaking. It was reminiscent of the memorials that sprung up around lower Manhattan after 9/11: it was smaller, of course, but it still left me weeping whenever I went there.

And I went there often.

I'd see people who were inconsolable because they had known someone who had been killed in the massacre. I'd see people who had been wounded and were paying tribute to those who hadn't escaped.

I never told anyone, but those days I relapsed as badly as I had at any point since I was auditioning in New York City, and there were moments when the purging was almost gratuitous: it was as if I wanted to punish myself for simply surviving. I would eat until I was in pain. I didn't have the suite yet; I had a room, but the toilet was white and the bathroom was small, and I would curl up on the floor, savoring my own debasement in the steady accretion of stink and stain.

"Sometimes, Las Vegas is more small town than big city," Nigel said when I was done. He shook his head ruefully. "Just devastating."

"But people really did live in this emotional space where, even after all that, they were still drawn back to the tables and slots. I heard so many stories of people who survived and thought their living was a testimony to their good luck. So, the next day or the day after that, they expected to win big. Of course, most didn't."

"No. Most never do," he agreed. For a long while we sat in silence. It was morose, but companionable. I squeezed his hand. He knew me far better than people who had been in my life far longer, and I had come to depend on his equanimity. Maybe my sister and my mother had been right, and someday—if I survived whatever unnatural disaster was coming—I should put the bellows to that spark and see what happened. Finally, he said, "Well, if you change your mind about a gun, please don't be shy. I can help. I can teach you."

Guns. The world had too many guns. Las Vegas had too many guns. Those maniacs from Futurium had too many guns.

I swallowed the last of the ice in my drink and popped one of the little yellow pills that would mix well with the gin and tonic. My stomach was empty and I planned to have room service send something to my room, but, in the meantime, I wanted as little food as possible between me and what I supposed would be my afternoon sleep-away.

When Frankie drove me to his house, he was distracted, but he said Betsy was helping Rory and Damon, and Ayobami was working, and so everyone figured I should go to his place and hang out at the pool. He had a bathing suit waiting for me.

The first clue I got that something was wrong was this: the Wi-Fi wasn't working on my tablet. Frankie said, yeah, the router was a mess and someone was coming with a new one. I asked him about resetting it and told him the trick I had learned in coding class: you stick a pen or paperclip into the reset button in the back, and the router will return to the factory settings. Then you just punch back in the password and user name. He said he'd tried that. I said okay.

So, I went up to the guest room where my backpack was to get my phone. And it was gone.

CHAPTER TWENTY-THREE

Betsy

As she and Frankie agreed, she hadn't gone to work that Monday. (Had they agreed? Or had she simply dug in her feet and said no that morning? As the hours passed, she grew unsure precisely how it had all come apart and why she was home.) She would be at the apartment when Marisa hopped off the school bus a half block from the complex. She expected to see her at the front door at three fifteen.

She called Futurium and their young receptionist, Derrick, planning to tell him that he was working for criminals, but hung up when she heard his voice. He might say something to Rory and get himself killed. Maybe her, too. Twice she had gotten as far as punching in all but the last digit of the phone number for the police, but there was the shadow of the dead man out at Red Rocks, and the fact she had been there yesterday.

And so she had spent most of Monday stewing, her mind racing between scenarios with happy endings, and ones that left her shaking with anger and fear, because in those versions she and Marisa were homeless. Frankie stopped paying the rent on her apartment, Futurium fired her, and she and her daughter were living in the car. Or at a shelter.

No, it would never come to that. Ayobami would help her. And she had her crypto.

But then she recalled Tony Lombardo's laughter when he had told her over lunch that he was the one who had "found" a guy in L.A.'s crypto seed phrase.

A little after noon, she envisioned Frankie and Damon and

Rory and Lara having a Bacchanalian feast at one of the casinos on the strip, and she was surprised that she hadn't heard from the man who was or had been her boyfriend. She considered packing two bags, one for Marisa and one for her, and leaving Las Vegas. They could go back to Vermont—*home* to Vermont—without Frankie.

And so, just in case, she left the apartment to fill up the tank of her car and do some grocery shopping. She bought lots of nonperishables so if she and Marisa decided to leave, they'd have road food. She held out hope that any minute she'd hear from Frankie, and he'd tell her they were sorry they had tried to pressure her into going to the meet and greet that night as her sister. They had a Plan B that didn't involve either her or Crissy. And then she and Marisa could ignite whatever ludic youthfulness remained in her soul and do something fun that afternoon. After school. Marisa would be surprised that she was home, rather than at Futurium, but Betsy would put a good face on it. The girl might see through her, but she'd try to shield the child from her anxiety.

No, that wasn't going to happen. She was kidding herself if she thought this was over.

When she returned from the gas station and the supermarket, she sat by the swimming pool, but she was too preoccupied to enjoy the fact that she had access to a pool. It wasn't like she was playing hooky from work. She knew she was playing a far more dangerous game.

How dangerous? Marisa didn't materialize at three fifteen. Or three thirty. Usually, Betsy worked until three thirty, so depending on the traffic, she would get home between three forty-five and four. She told herself now that it was possible Marisa had gotten off the bus with a friend and was getting a Slurpee or some Little Debbie travesty at the nearby 7-Eleven, and was planning to be home five minutes before her. She liked that idea. She wanted her daughter to have friends and settle in. And the kid was thirteen. A very independent thirteen.

Finally, at four, Betsy texted her, trying to sound casual. She wrote to Marisa that she was home and supposed she was on her way home, too, and they should do something fun. She received no response. She texted again at four fifteen, more urgently, asking where she was. Still, nothing. Had it been any other day, the idea that Marisa didn't text her back might have worried her, but it wouldn't have sent her into a spiraling perturbation. Betsy knew what kind of kid she'd been, and she was sure that if she and her mother had had smartphones when she was thirteen, it would not have been uncommon for her to blow off a text (or two) from Mom. But Futurium was fucking with her bigtime, so Betsy could feel her alarm ratcheting up.

She decided that if she had not heard from the girl by four twenty-five, she would call the school. If she waited any longer, the only adults left at the building might be outside coaching football and field hockey and soccer.

But at four twenty, her phone rang, and for a brief second she was overcome with relief, convinced it was Marisa and everything was fine. It wasn't. It was Frankie. And the moment she saw the number and then heard the quiver in his voice—a wobble he tried to hide behind reassurances that whatever was going down was "a hiccup" and all would be well—she understood that he was feckless and spineless and couldn't protect her *or* her child. Marisa wasn't coming home that afternoon.

"She's A-okay," he was saying. "That's the main thing and the first thing you need to know as a parent. I get it."

"What the fuck have you done? Where is she?"

"She's fine. I just told you. I met her when she got off the school bus. And—"

"Frankie, are you insane? You kidnapped my daughter!"

"No," he insisted, "it's not like that. It's—"

"I want her home now. Or I will call the police. I will make it clear—"

"Relax. Just relax and hear me out. Go to that meet-and-greet cocktail party tonight at Fort Knocks, and she will be home right after you. And Marisa doesn't even know anything's wrong. She's happy as can be and perfectly safe."

"That's it. I'm going to the police."

"Bad idea."

"You wouldn't hurt Marisa. Tell me that."

"No, of course *I* wouldn't," he said, and Betsy thought she heard a strange emphasis on the pronoun. *I.* It was as if he wouldn't, but he couldn't speak for the others. "But you can't go to the police. Look, the police already want to talk to you about Red Rocks. I happen to know that. Your sister is accusing you of lots of shit you had nothing to do with. But Vegas is a small town, and the PD isn't all that hard to rein in. They see reason. So, they won't come to see you. Unless they do."

"I don't even know what that means."

"It means we really do have an in with the PD. Damon and Rory made sure of that. There are two detectives who are interested in you, but for the moment they're on the leash. We got a little time."

"Time for what?"

"Betsy, either you or your sister drove your sister's car to Red Rocks. It's on the cameras."

"It wasn't me!"

"But, let's face it, baby—"

"I am not your baby!"

"Let's face it: you were at the park yesterday, and the man Crissy fucked the night before died there. If someone decides this isn't an accident, they'll go right for your sister—which is where they're aiming now, and which is exactly what everyone wants—unless you give them a reason to go right for you. And, your sister, being the unscrupulous mess that she is, is already telling the cops in every way she can that it was you and not her."

"That's not being unscrupulous. That's not wanting to go to jail for a crime you didn't commit!"

"This is all going to end well. I promise. It's just how they do things."

"So, let me get this straight: you've taken my daughter, and now you're willing to tar my sister—or me—with the death of this Yevgeny person? Is that what you're saying?"

"I'm saying you're overreacting. Be Diana tonight at Fort Knocks. Be Crissy tonight. That's all you have to do."

"Put my daughter on the phone right now. I want to hear her voice."

"Your daughter? God, you make it sound like—"

"Put her on the phone with me. Now."

"I'm sorry. I can't do that."

"You can't? Or you won't?" she asked. It didn't matter which. She was a toxic cocktail of ferocity and fear, and the girl was in trouble, no matter what.

"It's not that simple."

"She isn't answering my texts."

"No, I wouldn't suppose she was," he said cryptically.

"We're done, you know. You know that, don't you? This is over. No matter what. There is no coming back from this."

"Betsy—"

Over the thrum of the air-conditioning, she heard a vehicle in the parking lot. Ever hopeful, she went to the window, but it was only a UPS truck. The abduction of her daughter was punitive. They were using the child to punish her.

"Fine," she said. "I'll go tonight—"

"And be on your best behavior."

"Yes. I'll go. But when I get home, Marisa better be at the apartment. Am I clear?"

"She might be a few minutes behind you."

"Am I clear?" she asked again.

"Perfectly. But Betsy? We can get past this."

"No fucking way. You kidnapped—"

"No one kidnapped anyone."

"She will tell me where she was and what you did to her. You realize that, don't you?"

"She's having a great time."

Betsy wanted to believe that. Desperately, she wanted to believe that. It allowed her to justify her own miscalculations and humiliations.

"We'll send someone over to your apartment right now," he went on. "A makeup person—you know, a stylist—and someone with a dress. She should be there in about fifteen minutes."

"Is there anything special I need to say or do at this party?"

"The guy who had that big crush on Diana will be there. Oliver Davies from Grand Cayman. Just use that lovely British accent of yours and pretend you're Crissy doing that Diana play-acting bullshit."

"I don't know Diana the way Crissy does, and I don't have a lovely British accent. It's one thing to pose at Red Rocks. But it's a whole other thing to act like the woman in front of real entertainers who know my sister."

"Most don't know your sister. They know of your sister. But Crissy is not exactly a social butterfly. And she sort of condescends to the city's other tribute performers. That's her reputation, you know. She thinks she's better than they are."

"That's because she is. And what if someone does know her and recognizes that I'm not her?"

Which was when he dropped his last bombshell, disguised, once more, as reassurance. "Oh, you won't have to worry about that. Rory and Damon will be there. One of them will pick you up and bring you home, and keep an eye on you when you're there. If someone seems to know Crissy? They'll whisk you to someone else. Super easy, super clean. The senator—"

"You mentioned him at my apartment this morning. Why the hell does Senator Aldred want to meet my sister?"

"Maybe he's a fan," said Frankie.

She recalled what Ayobami had told her: the man had seen the show a couple of times.

In the parking lot, the UPS guy was leaving. He saw her in the window and waved. She waved back.

"And why does 'keeping an eye on me' sound like a euphemism?" she asked. But she knew the answer. Because it was. She asked herself when Frankie had become such a prick. But she knew the answer to that, too. He probably had been all along.

* * *

The dress was gorgeous. Edwardian, said the stylist. It was dark blue—almost black. The woman was older than Betsy and said she had worked on a dozen Vegas shows. She stressed that she had done her homework meticulously to get Betsy ready for this soiree. The two of them refined how the gown fit in her bedroom, while Rory and Damon were banished to the living room, where they played card games with actual playing cards. It was as if they were trying to channel Vegas gangsters from 1955. In the background, the cable news was continuing to cover the queen's death.

The two men refused to tell Betsy where Marisa was when she asked, and the stylist knew enough not to get involved—or, perhaps, she was involved. But she was very nice and solemnly pointed out to Betsy the dress's copious attributes, such as its fishtail shape—the way it swooshed out like fins at the floor—and subtle ruching.

"Ruching?" asked Betsy.

"Look at the way the velvet is pleated," she explained with a southern accent. "It looks like ripples."

They had a necklace for her with the biggest rock she had ever seen on a piece of jewelry.

"It's not real, right?" she asked, lowering her voice.

"It's costume," the woman reassured her.

In an old-fashioned, cloth-covered three-ring binder, there were photos of Diana from the moment they were endeavoring to replicate: a 1985 White House dinner when, a little before midnight, Nancy Reagan told John Travolta that the princess hoped to dance with him. The actor was awed and agreed, and the floor cleared for the two of them. The photos of the celebrity dyad, the stylist told Betsy, had created a wild fervor in the press, and these were some of her favorite images on the Internet. There was also a page Lara Kozlov had added with details of a trip Princess Diana had made to Moscow in 1995.

"Is there going to be a John Travolta at Fort Knocks tonight?" Betsy wondered.

"There could be, but I doubt it," she said. "He sang a bit, but it's not like he has the catalog for a tribute show. And he isn't dead. The people who take on performers who are still alive tend to be A-listers. It's mostly B-listers who take on the dead." She had been on the floor sewing the hem with inspired dexterity when what she had just implied registered. She stared up at Betsy and said, her voice almost furtive, "I hope I didn't insult your family. Your sister is obviously an A-lister. There are exceptions. You'll meet some tonight."

"I wasn't insulted."

"I hadn't meant anything by that remark."

It dawned on Betsy that this woman dressing her was scared of her. No, that wasn't it: she was scared of the two men in the living room. The stylist stood up and glanced at the door, which was shut, and then touched the wings of Betsy's hair with the fingertips of both hands. "I mean that," she went on. "You know, about the exceptions. There are lots of talented artists who take on the dead and lots of talented artists who take on the living. Just because your sister's residency is at the BP—"

"I understand," Betsy murmured. "May I ask your name? I just realized: I don't know it. I'm sorry." She felt very much like the princess in this gown and felt that the princess would have asked.

"Mitzi," replied the woman, uncomfortable that Betsy had inquired. "But this is just a freelance gig for me. I'm not part of anything."

Twenty minutes later, when Mitzi felt that she had brought the princess back from the dead, she took her by the elbow and led her to the full-length mirror that hung behind the door and showed her how much she resembled Lady Di from her evening with the Reagans and John Travolta. Betsy agreed that Mitzi had worked serious magic. She looked exactly like Diana Spencer when she had enchanted the crowd at the White House.

And that meant that she looked as much like her sister as she ever had in her life.

* * *

It was as if she were at a costume party or masquerade ball. A part of Betsy's mind was focused squarely on Marisa and why she was doing this, and what she and Marisa would do once the Futurium monsters had returned her daughter to her. They were leaving Las Vegas, that was clear. They were getting out. They would return to Vermont, the only world they had ever really known. She would find them another two-bedroom apartment in Burlington surrounded by college kids half her age, and the counseling service would rehire her.

Somehow, she doubted they'd follow Marisa and her back east. She didn't think she was worth the effort, and she didn't believe they wanted this to escalate any further. Marisa was thirteen, and nothing Betsy was involved in was worth upping the ante that way.

No, she was kidding herself. People were dead. Rory, Frankie had told her, was crazy.

The awful truth was that she had no idea what they would do, because they knew how much she knew: the meetings she'd scheduled, the names of the women and men who were there. The involvement of one of Washington's most volatile congressional reps, a woman who, at the very least, wanted to be a U.S. senator.

And once you kidnap a thirteen-year-old girl, you've crossed an immutable line. There's no going back. The fact wasn't lost on her that both Rory and Damon were here with her at Fort Knocks, either trailing her or standing beside her like the president's Secret Service. Damon was going to speak in a few minutes and explain why they had assembled such a remarkable array of also-ran talent, but he still seemed to have time to play the room and keep an eye on her.

For the sake of her daughter, she was doing her very best to be Diana Spencer—aka Crissy Dowling—at the meet and greet. There must have been forty of them in a room that was too small for a ballroom but too big for a meeting room, and while most of the performers were pleasant—they were desperate to please, because approval was currency—they were all hanging on financially by the thinnest of threads. Sonny and Cher, Prince, Mick Jagger. Aretha Franklin. A group someone had to tell her was a Herman's Hermits cover band, because Futurium had wanted British cover bands here. Many of the guests were musicians as well as singers, and they'd take any gig they could get, even if it meant playing the piano in a hotel lobby while the arriving hordes in their flip-flops and cargo pants stood in the check-in lines that snaked in square S's back and forth, back and forth, and the pianist was competing with the mechanical bells and whistles (and growls) of the video slots, and no one was listening to the pianist because everyone was looking at their phones or slurping their first beers or piña coladas. And they were all, it seemed, screwed and abused by their agents—corrupt little worms, according to Buddy Holly—if they even had representation. As the performers were volunteering their tales of woe, Betsy could not get over the endless ways they managed to see their two- and three-hundred-dollar paychecks gnawed to next to nothing by the casinos and their own management.

And then there were the notorious four-wall gigs: a performer would rent space (or a room with "four walls") at the casino. It looked like a residency, but it wasn't. The singers had to do all of their own marketing and get seats in the seats, which was an out-of-pocket expense on top of the rent and paying the crew, and the casino was unlikely to even bother to promote the show on a marquee or inside the concourse. After all, they had their premier shows to sell.

"I lost eighteen thousand dollars in three months at one,"

Aretha Franklin told Betsy, shaking her head, and Sonny and Cher lamented how they'd lost even more with a four-wall gig at Fort Knocks.

She was digesting this when she saw Lara Kozlov approaching. She had a slim leather satchel over her shoulder: it was more of an attaché than a purse.

"Ah, it's Diana. Good to see you."

"Hi," she said. "They didn't tell me you would be here."

The woman shrugged. "Oh, I wasn't going to miss this." Then she ran her eyes over her, inspecting the makeup and the gown. "It's uncanny," she mused. "You look just like her. Someday, Tony will get you to Grand Cayman. That man is very persuasive. You'll love it."

"Thank you," she answered, though she knew that was never going to happen.

"It's nothing. I know your sister wouldn't approve, but that's okay. Our secret."

"Futurium has lots of secrets."

The woman arched an eyebrow. "I'll let that go. I'll attribute that to the stress you're under. Now, come with me into the hallway."

She could see Damon and Rory watching her. "Is that allowed? Won't they be angry if I leave?"

Lara looked at the two men and smiled at them. Rory raised his glass.

"See," said Lara, "you can." Then she placed her hand on Betsy's lower back and pushed her forward from the room and into the corridor, and did not stop guiding her until they were around the corner and in a dead end where the carpet was especially worn and the sad yellow wallpaper had sepia stains from decades of illicit cigarette smoke.

"God, this whole place is a porta-potty," the woman observed, looking around. "So, remember when you first met Tony Lombardo?"

"Yes. It was in my sister's dressing room."

"Good memory. Tony told you about our friend, Oliver Davies. Oliver met the real you in Moscow in 1995."

She nodded.

"Apparently, he was like a schoolboy around the princess. Smitten."

"Lots of people loved Diana," she said evasively.

"He'll be with us tonight. He should be here any minute."

"I was told he was coming."

"Oliver is a character. You'll like him. I know I do. We're going to surprise him with a present. Or, to be exact, you are. We have a replica of a tiara Diana wore when she was still a princess."

"Oh?"

"Yes," she said, pulling it from that attaché. It was entombed in bubble wrap, and she held it by one tip. Even through the plastic, Betsy could see what she supposed were costume diamonds, rubies, and emeralds along spikes that extended from the top like barbs. Or were they costume? These were crypto millionaires. Maybe billionaires. Perhaps every single stone was real.

"I wear it like a headband?" Betsy asked.

"Well, you would, but you're not going to wear it. I had a better idea." Then Lara handed her a pair of white satin gloves that Betsy could see would extend beyond her elbows. "Put these on."

She obeyed. Her arms had been bare because Diana's had been bare that night long ago at the White House. She was grateful for the gloves, because the AC at Fort Knocks was set on freezer and she was cold.

"I'm going to unwrap this bad boy and hand it to you, and you're only to hold it by these two tips. Understand?"

"Yes."

"Good. You're a fast learner. Faster than your sister, that's for damn sure."

Again, she was silent. She wasn't sure what either she or Crissy would gain if she defended her.

"You're going to place it in the hands of the first of the two men that Rory is going to introduce you to. This is Oliver. Really, stick it in his hands."

"There will be two men?"

"The other fellow is Neri Lombardo. He's one of Tony's cousins."

"Okay."

"Don't you want to ask why you're doing this?"

"I'm guessing there's something hidden in the stones or the band. Maybe some crypto keys," she said. "Or maybe this tiara has real diamonds and rubies."

"Or it's poison and you're going to kill him, and that's why I've insisted you wear gloves. Maybe he's not a real friend, after all." Was this the truth? Anything was possible with these people. Lara's grin was enigmatic.

"No," Betsy said. "I'm not going to be an accessory to murder." Or, she thought, recalling Crissy's dead friend out at Red Rocks, *another* murder.

"Even for your daughter?"

She said nothing, but Lara rolled her eyes. "God, you're humorless." She peeled away the bubble wrap and rubbed the tips along the pinnacle of the crown on her own bare forearm. "There. See? No poison. Oliver is a friend—and very supportive of Erika Schweiker. Neri is, too. Satisfied I was only pulling your leg?"

She wasn't sure, but she took the tiara when Lara handed it to her. "Let's get back," Lara said. "And, please, try to have fun. This *is* a party."

* * *

Betsy joined Michael Jackson, Frank Sinatra, and one of the members of Herman's Hermits at the cash bar because the three of them were laughing. Sinatra was paying for their drinks with a handful of quarters and some deeply crinkled dollar bills he had in his jacket pocket. Michael looked less like Michael than Frank looked like Frank, but at least he had the sequined glove and fedora. His jacket had epaulettes. Frank was in a black suit, white shirt, and thin tie straight from the 1950s. The Herman's Hermit bloke—his word for himself, a word that conjured Crissy with all her fastidiousness about accent and attention to detail—said his name was actually Danny. She introduced herself as Crissy Dowling, and the three of them said they had heard incredible things about her show, and expressed their condolences over the recent death of the woman who, for a time, had been Diana's mother-in-law. Michael found two fives in the pocket of his military jacket and bought her a six-dollar glass of Chablis that even Betsy—with absolutely no taste for wine—knew was undrinkable. He wanted to know how she had finagled a residency at the Buckingham Palace, and she answered vaguely, babbling that the show fit the casino's theme, but still it was mostly good luck and timing. Rory was watching her, ready to hop over if he saw or heard something he didn't like.

Soon they were joined by Jim Morrison, Liberace, and a woman who said she was Julia Canter by day and Christina Aguilera by night. They all knew each other, and it was evident from their conversation that the idea that Futurium or Fort Knocks or whoever they thought was hosting this shindig had a cash bar didn't strike them as unusual: they were used to being invited to places to network and then expected to pay for their own booze. So far, none of them had ever met Crissy, who, Betsy was beginning to realize, really was a bit of a legend. Maybe she was considered standoffish, but no one—now that "Crissy" was in the house—was going to jeopardize losing her connections and clout by saying anything snarky. People were full of compliments about the outfit that she was wearing, curious about the tiara she was holding, and generally very kind. The magnitude of her sister's accomplishment, weird as it was, became more real. Even though the BP was a second-rate casino, there wasn't a performer in the room who wouldn't have switched places with Crissy in a heartbeat, and lived their lives in a diazepam haze in her cabana and an Adderall buzz on her stage. They were all struggling, trying desperately to stay afloat in a business where most people drowned. She was digesting this notion, when Sinatra said something about the suicide out at Red Rocks a few weeks back.

"Red Rocks?" she said, the two words triggering a quaver of unease in her voice. "Don't the police think it might have been an accident? And wasn't it yesterday?"

"Sorry, I didn't mean that one," Sinatra clarified, and the entertainers laughed darkly at his words, *that one.* "I meant Richie Morley."

"Oh, of course," she said. Lord, it was only yesterday that Damon and Rory had told her that Yevgeny Orlov was behind the deaths of both brothers. "But I didn't realize Richie had killed himself out at Red Rocks. I knew he did it in his car, but not much else."

"Wow. You really do live in your castle. Yup, Richie and Artie Morley. Richie blew his brains out in a spot with a beautiful view. Artie didn't care what he saw at the end. Pulled the shades before, as they say, turning out the lights." He said it as if he really were the Chairman of the Board—ol' Blue Eyes—in a fifties pic about the mob.

"And the police are sure both brothers were suicides?" Betsy pressed.

Michael Jackson nodded. "I mean, that's what they're saying in the news. It's still being investigated. Supposedly, the BP is bleeding money. You must hear the rumors. It's hard to lose money in a casino, but maybe that pair found a way, and that's why they did it: killed themselves."

"Instead of just declaring bankruptcy? Isn't that what Trump did when he managed to lose money in casinos? Wouldn't that—"

"People tend to lose their minds out here," Sinatra said. "Despite all the lights we have on the strip, things out here get dark fast. And I guess they did for Richie and Artie."

She was nodding, taking this in because already she knew how fast the walls could close in, when she felt Rory taking her by the elbow and telling her there were two men he wanted her to meet. She nodded at the entertainers and allowed him to pull her away from them.

"What have you got there?" Rory asked.

"Lara gave it to me. A tiara."

"God, that woman is smart. Someday, I'd love to poach her from politics," he said. "Now don't forget: you're already on thin ice. You understand that you need to be polite to our two special guests, right? No bullshit: you are Princess Diana at her most charming."

"Okay."

The men were wearing stylish suits, one that was charcoal with white pinstripes and one that was black, white shirts, and no neckties. They both had closely cropped beards. She pegged them for early to midsixties. Hovering a half dozen yards away, his hands behind his back, was a young guy so buffed that his own black suit fit like a superhero's spandex or leather. He was model handsome, with blond hair and ice for eyes. He was watching the two men intently: he was their body man or bodyguard.

"Princess, it is my deepest honor to meet you," said Oliver Davies politely, his accent a very posh British, and bowed. Up close, his nose was spider-webbed with thin red lines. He raised his glass to her: "To the black widow." Neri Lombardo chuckled at this and raised his, too.

She had no idea what Oliver was talking about and looked at Rory, hoping for a cue how to respond. But he gave her nothing, and so she said, "It's a pleasure to meet you as well."

"Thank you for solving our problems in the desert," added Neri.

Now she understood: *black widow* was a reference to the way that she—Crissy Dowling—had helped kill Yevgeny Orlov.

"And what do you two do?" she asked nervously, changing the subject and hoping her own British accent was sufficient.

Rory answered for them. "Oliver here just paid for a lovely church and school in Grand Cayman. And Neri just bankrolled a new business school in Phnom Penh for kids interested in fintech."

"I'm a philanthropist," said Oliver, and she couldn't tell from his tone if he was kidding.

Neri laughed again, and scratched at the skin beneath his tight beard. "Yes, Oliver is a philanthropist. But mostly he's a dilettante who knows far too much about the queen's corgis."

Oliver nodded. "It's true. I am rather an aficionado of all things royal."

"And all things Diana," added Neri.

"You Americans never understand. There are much worse hobbies."

"Not for grown men."

Now it was Oliver's turn to laugh heartily. He seemed to enjoy the roasting. "I could make Diana a full-time job, but my business and charity interests can be demanding. I can't do everything. Neri has just one business. I have many."

She had no idea what to say, but knew she was supposed to say something. "What businesses are you two in?" she asked.

"Fintech," answered Neri. "And resorts."

"You know," Oliver said, "forgive this boast, but I once met Princess Diana. It was Moscow, 1995."

"Yes. You were so kind to the children we met at the hospital. And we delighted in the ballet together."

He was beaming at the idea she knew this. "And we danced."

"And I was charmed."

"Not the way I was. For me, it was what I have come to call a *Nutcracker* moment—a fantasy come to life."

"You're making me blush," she said. "Now, I have something for you. A small gift." She handed him the tiara.

"We should have presents for the princess," said Oliver, raising a single eyebrow lecherously. "But I will never say no to a gift from a beautiful woman," he added, studying the crown. "I think it's a replica of one she wore in 1989."

"It looks a little small for your head," Neri teased him, and he took it from his friend and pressed it onto his own skull. Oliver yanked it from his scalp and held it in his fingers for a moment, gazing at it as if it were the actual one Diana had once worn. He thanked Betsy.

"You're most welcome," she told him. "I hope it finds a lovely place to reside in your home."

"It will," he said. "This gift? It means a great deal to me."

"Well," said Rory, "should we get that photograph?"

And before she knew it, two photographers were in front of them, men with cameras so big they seemed to be from another era, and Rory backed away. But the two guests put their arms around her, Oliver's on her shoulder and Neri's on her waist, and the cameras actually clicked as if it were 1985. When they were done, the photographers showed the images to Rory in the viewfinders, Rory nodded, and then they resumed taking pictures of the various tribute performers, all of whom were grateful for the attention.

"Very nice to meet you, Princess," said Oliver. "Or, I should say, see you again."

"It was a great pleasure," she said.

"Next time I see you, it will be in Grand Cayman, yes? The Maenads? I hear you're coming."

"That's right," she told him. "I can't wait. It will be a treat."

"I know just which cottage you'll be in. We'll have lots of time together."

She smiled, and then Rory was leading her back toward the bar, where he parked her between Sinatra and Liberace. Then he joined Lara Kozlov in a corner a dozen yards away, where she and the men were huddling, while Damon went to the front of the room, stood on a riser before a Futurium banner, and took a mic off the stand.

"Welcome, welcome, welcome," Damon said, and some of the entertainers started clapping politely. "I can't thank you all enough for coming tonight. I can't get over the amount of talent in this room. It's a little overwhelming. Now, my name is Damon Ioannidis. I'm an engineer, but I'm also the chief operating officer of Futurium—your new favorite cryptocurrency."

Liberace leaned over to her and whispered into her ear, "God, who in this room can afford a piece of Futurium?"

She nodded politely.

"And have we got news. Big news," Damon went on. "Are you ready? We are also going to be the owners of your new favorite casino, the Buckingham Palace."

There was a momentary pause as the cover bands and entertainers all looked at one another and then, some unsure what this meant for them but knowing that their enthusiasm was expected, started whooping and clapping as if they'd just won the lottery. The applause dwarfed the clapping from a moment ago.

"Still think Richie and Artie Morley were suicides?" Liberace asked Frank Sinatra.

Sinatra smiled and said, "That's life. Riding high in April, shot down in May."

"Or August, in this case."

"Yup. I'm guessing Richie and Artie's corpses weren't even cold when Futurium made their offer on the BP."

She looked back at Oliver and Neri, and while Neri's face was utterly opaque, Oliver locked eyes with her and winked.

The applause subsided, because Damon started pressing down the air around him with his hands open, the universal signal to simmer down. Then he continued, "We might have our money in the ether, but we have our feet firmly on the ground. On the bricks and mortar of Las Vegas. We won't just house our computers here. No, no, and no. We want to be part of the community. We want to be one with the city. Now, some of you know why you've been invited tonight and some of you have your . . . suspicions. So, let's begin with the basics. Crypto is, before you know it, going to be the go-to currency here in Vegas. We're confident. And not just the Bitcoin ATMs. It's coming to all the casinos. To the slot machines and gaming tables. And Futurium is working with the gaming commission right now, and we're working on our casino licenses right now and we're even working with your representatives in Washington, D.C.—including the always-ahead-of-the-curve Erika Schweiker. Why? Because we are going to be the boldest crypto casino—today it may be the Buckingham Palace, but tomorrow it will become the Futurium BP—in this very, very exciting and very, very brash metropolis. And while the new Futurium casino will be known in part for cryptocurrency, it will also be known for great food and great entertainment. And I mean really special food and really special entertainment. So, without wanting to draw out the drama any longer, I want to invite to the mic Shelley Tutova. Shelley, some of you know, is one of the Vegas burlesque scene's most creative choreographers."

If Ayobami had been with her, Betsy thought, they both would have been smirking. This was going to be a shit show—the whole Futurium casino. The crypto casinos that really wanted to cater to the crypto geeks with serious money? They were boasting that they'd have heliports for flying cars, e-sports arenas, and cryptocurrency trading floors—not second-rate entertainers swaying to the dance moves of a stripper. As even Nigel had observed at the water park, this was something else: combining crypto with a casino to launder for the Mastaba or the Russians or whoever wanted to make illicit money look legit.

Shelley Tutova was in her late forties, Betsy guessed, with raven hair. She was wearing a slinky beige dress that fell to her shins and showed plenty of cleavage. She was pretty in a way that was prurient and just a little bit dirty. In her heels, she was almost Damon's height. When she was beside him, he put an arm around her waist in a fashion that wouldn't have flown in a lot of places—his fingers were on her hip bone and his pinky even a little below it—but seemed just another part of the cultural praxis that was Las Vegas. Shelley pressed her lips against his cheek, and then made a big production of wiping the scarlet from his face, licking her fingers lasciviously and using them like a sponge on his skin.

"So, my next announcement is this. And let's make it official. By Christmas, you will see at the Futurium showroom the biggest all-star tribute show in town. We are going to crush Legends in Concert or the Sydney Bee-Gees or the Rat Pack, and many of you in this room will be the reasons why. Yes, it may have a British vibe, but I promise you, Elvis and Michael and Cher"—and here he smiled at the three singers in the room who brought those iconic American entertainers to life—"there will be plenty of room for you, too. And wait, there's more. Shelley has agreed to be not merely the show's choreographer, but also our artistic director! So, let's give Shelley a hand and hear about her vision."

It was bedlam. Euphoric bedlam. People were applauding as if their gusto or fervor was their audition. Everyone in the room saw the possibility of work, and everyone saw Shelley Tutova, burlesque queen, as their ticket. Betsy clapped, too, but she was looking back and forth at Rory, Oliver, and Neri. She began to outline in her mind all the reasons why it was so important to them that she was here. It wasn't just Oliver Davies. It wasn't just that they hoped to tease the man by dangling before him the confection that someday would await him at the Maenads. It wasn't even that they wanted this crowd to believe that Crissy Dowling was supportive of Futurium's plans to transform the BP into a crypto casino with a different act in the showroom.

It was that they wanted people, including the police, to conclude that Crissy Dowling was at Fort Knocks this Monday night. Right now. That's what that photograph was about: Crissy Dowling with Oliver and Neri.

This party, as bad as it was, was just the tip of the iceberg.

* * *

Damon and Shelley Tutova continued to work the room, thanking the entertainers for coming, while Rory escorted her from the shindig.

"I'm done?" she asked him.

"Nope. But you were very good in there."

"Then what?"

He didn't answer and brought her to the elevator banks, and she realized he was taking her upstairs. Fort Knocks had four floors, and when the door opened, he ushered her inside and pressed the top one, and she felt fear rising in her throat. When they left the lift, the corridor was empty, and the air was stale and she smelled disinfectant. The carpet was ratty and worn. She doubted he was going to attack her, but speculated instead he was pimping her out: there was a creep she was supposed to have sex with. They weren't going to wait until she was in Grand Cayman, they were going to indulge Oliver Davies's fantasies right here and now. Perhaps he was waiting for her behind the hotel room with the double doors at the end of the corridor. She could tell that was their destination.

"You are never going to get me to bed down some pervert with a Diana fixation or—"

He grabbed her elbow so hard she flinched and stopped speaking, and he held her in place. "You will do whatever we ask, because we have that kid you call your own. And, as you've probably noticed, we get what we want. Because if we don't, people die." He looked deep into her eyes and added, his tone softening, "You're not going to bed down anyone. That's already been taken care of."

She nodded, unsure what that meant.

"So, we're good? You understand the stakes?"

"Yes."

He let her go, and they walked down the hallway to the double doors, where he rapped hard above the handle. She could sense someone peering through the peephole, and then the door opened, and there was Mitzi, looking even more uncomfortable here than she'd been at Betsy's apartment. Rory prodded Betsy before him into the room, and there was Senator John Aldred—she recognized him instantly—seated on the couch in the small living room section of the hotel suite. He was wearing suit pants and a robin's-egg blue button-down shirt, but she didn't see his jacket or tie. His hair, though as thick and lustrous as ever, was tousled and unkempt, as if he'd just awoken from a deep sleep. On the table beside him was a wine bottle, empty, the glass the color of claret. She recalled now that Frankie had said she was going to see the senator after the meet and greet—but she'd never expected it would be like this. Weeks earlier, the Futurium execs had complained over lunch at Versailles that he disapproved of cryptocurrency.

When he saw her, his eyes, which had been half closed, perked up. He did a double take and started to stand, but his knees buckled and he fell onto the carpet. He managed to press himself back to a wobbly kneel, but it took Mitzi and a fellow she didn't recognize, a young guy in a suit and an earpiece who was another body man, to get him back in his chair.

"Crissy," he mumbled, and he was so drunk or drugged that his tongue lolled from his mouth on the second syllable. He smiled, but it was lopsided and sad, as if he'd had a stroke. She was struck by the familiarity. Did the senator know her sister personally? It seemed as if he did.

"Why did you do this to him?" she asked Rory, but he ignored her.

"Let's do this," he said to Mitzi and the other man. "I'm sure Crissy wants to return to her suite and her better class of peeps at the Buckingham Palace. Where's Tim?"

"Right here," said Tim, and the photographer who'd taken her picture at Red Rocks appeared from the bedroom with a camera against his chest and a round white reflector twice the size of a manhole cover in one hand. "I think we're better off doing it here than in there," he told Rory, pointing with his thumb over his shoulder at the bedroom. "That chair he was in would—"

"No. I want them in the bedroom," Rory said. He turned to Betsy and studied her for a moment. "Mitzi, can we mess up her hair a little bit? Make her look a little disheveled, too?"

"I'm not doing this," Betsy said, and retreated a step away from the stylist.

"Yes, you are. Your sister and Aldred had a pretty hot thing a while back, and that's how we're going to finish off his reelection campaign."

So, that was it. She was a honey trap. "I told you: no."

"Fine. Walter, break her finger. Left pinky."

Walter, the young guy in the suit, came for her, but she grabbed the empty wine bottle and swung it toward his face. His reflexes were good, however, and he deflected it with his arm, swearing at the pain as the bottle broke into pieces, and he tackled her. She tried to poke at his eyes, but he seized her hand and he was about to snap back her pinky. She managed to knee him in the crotch, but the dress was tight and the blow barely slowed him. Still, he released her finger. Instead, he smacked her under her chin, whipsawing back her head. For a split second she feared that he'd broken her neck. He hadn't, but it hurt like hell, and he picked her up as if she were a giant bag of flour and dumped her into the chair in which Aldred was sitting. The senator's eyes had closed, but they opened now, and once more he murmured, "Crissy. So good to . . ."

"You are one stupid cunt," Rory was saying, as he picked up the largest shard of glass. He aimed it at her and said, "I should fucking maim you."

"Do I break the finger or not?" Walter asked. He had her pinned, her left hand in his, and now he was pulling the digit so far back that the pain was shooting up into her arm.

"Last chance."

Beneath her, the senator said something, a term of endearment, but his pronunciation was so bad that if she hadn't seen her sister's show, she would have had no idea that the word he had murmured was "Squidgy."

* * *

Rory drove her home, and at first neither of them said a word. He turned on the radio and went to a Sirius station that played hits from the 1950s—it was as if he were reaching back to the era when the mob and the Rat Pack ruled the strip and he could call himself a made man, and the stars aligned to give him Tony Bennett crooning "Rags to Riches"—but Betsy switched off the music, and Rory didn't bother to turn it back on.

"What will you do with the photo?" she asked finally.

"Send it to him. Make it clear he needs to drop out of the race. Tell people he wants to focus on his family. Or, suddenly, he believes in term limits. Whatever."

"And if he doesn't drop out?"

"Oh, he won't drop out. We just want to give him that option. But most pols are so in love with the power, they rarely go willingly. And they're fighters by nature. So, he's going to delude himself into believing he can weather this scandal when we release the picture: extramarital dalliance with Crissy Dowling, the Lady Di of Las Vegas, drunker than drunk at a hot-sheets casino like Fort Knocks. His marriage is pretty tenuous, and so I don't know if he'll get his wife to do one of those stand-by-your-man photo ops, but it won't matter, even if she does. He and Erika are neck and neck. You can stick a fork in John Aldred."

They'd posed them on the hotel bed, leaning back against the headboard. Or, to be precise, she'd had her back to the headboard: he was leaning into her. Falling into her. She could barely support him. It took a few shots to get one with his eyes open. They'd unbuttoned his shirt so his bare chest was revealed, but much to her relief, they hadn't forced her to take off her gown.

The photo wasn't explicit, by design, so it would get as much traction as possible and be used wherever they sent it. But they also wanted it clear that the photo had been taken tonight—not when Aldred and his wife had been separated and, apparently, he had been involved with her sister. The dress was the time stamp. That was clearly another reason why they'd wanted her posing with Oliver Davies and Neri Lombardo: journalists could compare that photo with the one of her and Aldred, and confirm it was the same evening.

"Oliver calling me the black widow," she mumbled. "That was creepy. He really thought I was Crissy."

"Of course, he did. As did Aldred."

"Aldred was so drugged, he would have thought you were Crissy."

"Maybe."

"And both Oliver and Neri thought I—well, Crissy—helped kill that dude out at Red Rocks. That's what they meant by black widow. A black widow—"

"I know what a black widow does," he said.

She was unsure whether she was more disgusted with Rory or with herself. She tried to take comfort from the idea this was over and when she got home, Marisa would be waiting.

* * *

When they arrived at her apartment, Damon Ioannidis was sitting on the couch and watching *Monday Night Football.* He must have gone on ahead. But there was no sign of Marisa.

"Where is she?" Betsy snapped at Damon. "I want her home right now."

"What's the score?" Rory asked.

Damon told him. "You have any money down?"

"I do not."

"Me neither."

Betsy looked back and forth at the two men, seething at their duplicity. "Where is she?" she demanded again.

"There's one more wrinkle," said Damon, and he stood. Rory took his seat on the couch.

She glared at them both, then grabbed the remote and turned off the television. "Nope. I don't want to hear it. I want her back this second, I want—"

"I want you to sit down," said Damon. "Look . . ."

"Tell me!" she insisted.

"We can't keep the police at arm's length any longer. Our clout is excellent, but for the sake of appearances, we have to let two detectives talk to you."

"Two who aren't on the payroll," said Rory. "Yet."

"And that's a problem," Damon went on. "This is our business, not theirs. And we made sure Orlov's death was super clean and all the signs point to your sister."

"They're coming by first thing in the morning. Here. To your apartment."

"Well, good," she said. "I can tell them you took my daughter and didn't return her until—"

She stopped speaking because Rory had stood and grabbed back the remote, ripping it from her fingers. He turned on the football game, but he pressed Mute on the volume. "You won't tell them that. Your lawyer is advising you against it," he said.

"I don't have a lawyer, and—"

"You do have a lawyer and it's me. I'm your lawyer."

"Rory will be with you tomorrow when you talk to the police," Damon added. "Be grateful."

"Where's Frankie?"

"With Marisa. Babysitting. All good."

"Not all good! You're all liars and—"

"My fervent hope is the police just want to tie up some loose ends before they arrest your sister," Rory said, cutting her off. "Or, at least, look like they're doing their job before moving on."

"I want my daughter," she pleaded, her voice breaking. When neither man said a word, the unfairness of it all conspired with her fear for the child, and she unleashed the maelstrom inside her. She pounded on Damon's chest with her hands and clawed at his face with her fingernails, howling at him at the top of her lungs to bring back Marisa, bring her back now. She was screaming that she had done everything they wanted and they hadn't held up their end of the bargain, and they had to give her back her daughter, they had to, they had to, they had to that very minute. She was shrieking at them with a fury so formidable, its decibels and violence would have caused a man like Frankie to capitulate, but he wasn't there. This was Damon and Rory, and Rory was saying something about how they would have the cops there that very night—or the neighbors or both—if she didn't shut the fuck up, and then he put his hand on her mouth, and even though she bit hard at the soft flesh where his palm met his fingers, the sweat there disgusting and acrid on her tongue, he wouldn't let go and he pulled her down on to the couch. He had wrapped his other arm around her torso, pinning her biceps against her ribs, and though she was on his lap, there was nothing libidinous in the position: he was a human straitjacket and seemed oblivious to the way she was gnawing through the skin on his palm.

Damon bent over before them, his hands on his knees as if he were a dad umpiring a Little League Baseball game, calling balls and strikes behind the catcher. Still, she squirmed, and just when she thought she was going to extricate herself—Rory was pulling his hand off her mouth, and so she spat at Damon, hitting him squarely in the face—Rory turned that hand into a fist and slugged her. He hit her so hard where her jaw met her earlobe that the wind was knocked from her, her teeth rattled inside her head, and she fell to the floor in a heap. This was even worse than the way the body man had punched her back at Fort Knocks. Then Rory stood and kicked her in the stomach and the ribs until Damon pulled him away, his cheek still wet with her spit, and said, "Rory, stop it, stop it! She gets it!"

She was struggling to breathe, and ran her hand over her jaw and moved it back and forth. She wasn't sure what was worse: the pain or the humiliation. Both, however, were trumped by the despair that Marisa wasn't home, Betsy didn't know where she was, and this nightmare was entirely her fault.

I knew I was in real trouble when Frankie swore he hadn't taken my phone.

I could tell he was lying.

And then he tried to take my mind off it that night by showing me pictures on his phone of Betsy dressed as Diana at Fort Knocks. He said she was "filling in" for Crissy. Doing her sister a solid.

I wasn't going to buy that. There was no way Crissy wanted anyone to be Diana but her—especially not Betsy.

So, actually, I knew this was worse than "in trouble." I was fucked.

He said he was going to drive me to school the next morning because Betsy would be working late.

I pretended like I was all good with this. But I wasn't.

The only furniture he had in that guest room was a bed—just like his own bedroom—so there wasn't anything I could push in front of the door. But you can bet your ass I locked the door. And, just in case, I took one of his crazy expensive carving knives from the kitchen with me upstairs to bed.

CHAPTER TWENTY-FOUR

Crissy

Tuesday morning, on a local news site, I saw the pictures of Betsy—as me—at that appalling meet and greet that had been held the night before at Fort Knocks. I was scrolling on my tablet and there they were. There *she* was. She was in a costume reminiscent of the floor-length midnight-blue gown Diana had worn to the White House when she had danced with John Travolta. Betsy even had a necklace with a similar black rock the size of a baby's fist against her collarbone. She was, I could tell, the belle of the ball at that travesty.

I sent her an oblique but civilized text. My rage was volcanic, but I had to keep my cards masked if I had any chance of learning what in holy hell she and Futurium were doing. Still, I wanted her to know that I was on to her, and I'd seen the photos. When she didn't respond, I figured that the police had grilled her and she was as angry with me as I was with her, and so she was going to ignore me.

Nigel stopped by my cabana a little before noon. He had with him a wicker beach bag, which made him look like a father on holiday. It was the sort of tote in which one expected to find plastic beach toys, such as little shovels and sieves and buckets.

"I saw the pictures from last night," he began. "I'm sorry, Crissy, that's the last straw. You know that, right?"

"I don't know that."

"Has Terrance sent you the name of a lawyer?"

"Not yet."

He sat down in the other chaise. "Well, I'm glad to see you haven't been arrested," he said.

I didn't smile at this feeble attempt at humor, but I did recall the story of how Diana and Sarah Ferguson had been nicked after Sarah's bachelorette party in 1986. The pair had been dressed as police officers and busted for impersonating actual bobbies. Diana had thought it all a scream and eaten bacon-flavored crisps in the van until she was recognized. "I didn't kill anyone, and I wasn't at Red Rocks. So, that's never going to happen," I told him.

"I hope so," he said, but I wanted him to say more. I wouldn't have minded a little extra reassurance or even a redemptive squeeze of my hand. "Do you miss him?" he asked.

He didn't have to say who, and his solicitousness touched me. "Yes. But it's not like Yevgeny was an important part of my life or I'd known him forever. You know that. We spent three nights together, and one of those nights was mere hours because he had a plane to catch the next morning. In some ways, he's rather like a ghost: sometimes, I have to struggle to see his face. I don't even have a picture of him or us on my phone."

"That's sad."

I sighed. "That's my life."

"I know, love. I know."

I was wearing sunglasses, and so I was able to admit, "I've blubbered. In private, yes. But still a right proper cry."

"Ah, but only in private. That's a good royal."

"Thank you," I said. He was, I realized, the stoic one, enduring daily the likes of me.

"I want you to see something," he said. He handed me his phone and showed me another photo from last night, this one from a local gossip blog. There was Betsy dressed as Diana, but this time she wasn't with other tribute entertainers: she was standing with two men in business suits. The caption said it was me, which I expected. What I didn't expect was what followed:

With the Princess are Oliver Davies (l) and Neri Lombardo (r). Although the businessmen are known for their work in banking, cryptocurrency, and resorts—one in Cambodia, one in Grand Cayman, and (fingers crossed!) one here in Las Vegas—they are also philanthropists, building schools and churches around the world. The pair are staying at the Versailles and seemed to be having a wonderful time with some of the strip's most iconic performers at Fort Knocks.

"Those are not the strip's most iconic performers," I said.

"Really? That's your take? Your lover is dead, people think it's you hanging around at Fort Knocks with fintech robber barons, and all you can focus on is the idea that the entertainers who were at that event last night weren't of your stature?"

"Your point?"

"I want to be sure you see the gravity of this."

"How do you know they're fintech robber barons?"

"Code words: banking, cryptocurrency, resorts. Maybe philanthropy. And, I confess, I googled them. There are allegations out there that they're both part of something called the Mastaba: a group of organized crime wankers."

"I think you might be the first person ever to use *organized crime* and *wanker* in the same sentence."

"And not get killed for it? Yes."

"God. I knew Futurium had some connections to the Mastaba. Yevgeny told me."

"You knew?"

"I knew."

"Crissy—"

"Both the real me and the fake me are surrounded by criminals. I think that's why Eddie Cantone is leaving. It's not just that the BP will have new owners. It's that we'll have new owners who killed the old ones."

"Which is precisely why I brought you something."

I waited, and he gave me a dark little smile. "A small gift." He reached into that wicker bag and dropped a handgun onto my chaise by my hip.

"Nigel, no."

"Yes."

"Is this one yours?"

"It's the model I own. A Glock 19. Compact, nine millimeter. I bought it for you this morning. I can take you to a range and give you a tutorial."

I didn't pick it up.

"It's not loaded," he reassured me. "But I have ammunition in here," he went on, gesturing at his tote.

Finally, I lifted it off the canvas. "I don't have a license."

"I know. Tomorrow we'll start the paperwork."

I hated it. But Yevgeny was dead, the Morleys were dead, some woman named Cleo was dead. And I had no idea what my sister and her mobster friends were up to. "You ever read Chekhov?" I asked.

"What about him?"

"This is a paraphrase, but Chekhov said if you reveal a gun in the first act, it best go off by the third."

"I know that quote," he said. "I bought it for you because, your highness, I fear we are in the third act."

I didn't have my phone, so I didn't have an alarm. I guess I could have set the alarm on my tablet, but it didn't cross my mind. I figured Frankie would wake me for school.

He didn't.

I woke up and it was almost ten thirty, and I freaked out. I threw on my clothes, which were the same clothes I had worn the day before, which didn't thrill me, and ran downstairs to ask Frankie what the fuck was going on and to drive me the fuck to school—now I was bitchcakes, and the irony that I was bitchcakes about missing school was not lost on me—but another of his Futurium pals was with him in the living room, and they were tense. They told me the police were talking to my mom and said it was all about Crissy. They said Betsy hadn't done anything wrong, but I needed to stick around at Frankie's that day.

This was bullshit.

But they said I could use Frankie's phone and talk to her as soon as the police had left.

Obviously, that didn't happen.

But it was clear I had to get Frankie's phone—or someone's phone—and call Betsy or Crissy or 911, or I had to hack his Wi-Fi password with my tablet and use that to get help. Because the idea his Wi-Fi was broken was bullshit.

Now, I wasn't sure I could hack a password without an app, but I was going to try. Crypto seed phrases were one thing. Those were insane. (Still, my coding teacher back in Vermont was pretty badass and taught me to never forget what she called her "mantra": NO-SIRS. No Site Is Really Safe. She was pretty ballsy.)

On the other hand, people's Wi-Fi passwords are usually pretty basic.

So, I told the two guys I was going to go to the pool.

And there, with my tablet, I began to work.

CHAPTER TWENTY-FIVE

Betsy

The two detectives had noticed the bruise on her jaw, still fresh and red and the size of a plum. Betsy had told them, hoping her countenance conveyed the right amount of sheepishness, that she had opened a cabinet too fast and done a hell of a job on herself, but she was only aware of it when she spoke—which was a lie. The Advil took the edge off the pain, but it hurt. As did her ribs, where Rory had kicked her. As did her neck. She didn't believe any of her ribs were broken, but she still experienced jagged stitches of pain when she turned the wrong way or when her arm brushed her side. The cops could see the kitchen from the living room in the small apartment, and she pointed out the door above the dishwasher that she claimed had been the culprit.

"A door," the female one, Felicia, had said, nodding, and Betsy thought the woman believed her until she asked if she had a boyfriend or girlfriend. When Betsy said no, she had recently broken up with Frankie Limback, she could see in the detective's eyes that she was filing that bruise away as a cry for help.

If only they could help her . . .

She'd told them that Frankie would never, ever hurt her, and she'd tried to sound adamant because Rory—her "lawyer"—was watching her with eyes cold as a shark's.

Some thug had spent the night, wide awake, in the living room. Damon brought him by. He sat by the front door in cargo pants and an Area 51 hoodie stretched tight by his beer keg of a chest. Half his face was hidden by the sort of beard she associated with Civil War generals and white supremacists, the beard and his greasy mane dyed skater-boy blond. They took her cell phone. She hadn't bothered to have a landline installed yet, but she knew if she had, they would have confiscated that, too.

Rory said little during the interview, but he watched everyone, and he'd looked especially interested when she had revealed to the police that she was now single. She recalled reading somewhere that there was a hand signal that young people who had been abducted and were being trafficked could use to convey to strangers their desperate need for help, but she had no idea what it was. She would have used it when Felicia was studying her—because the woman was studying her, that bruise had been a blinking light—and it frustrated Betsy that she couldn't remember it. At one point, she considered blurting out to the detectives that Rory was among a group of people who had kidnapped her daughter, but Rory had been clear: Marisa might never come home if she deviated from their agreed-upon script. She didn't dare risk any sort of small, subtle flare: after the cops left, Rory would still be here, and she knew he might beat her again. And so she told them that she had not been at Red Rocks on Sunday afternoon; it must have been someone else who had been caught on the cameras. On Sunday, she insisted, she had been cleaning the apartment and then had gone to the museum.

"And last night?" the detective pressed.

"Last night I was right here," she told them. "My daughter did her homework and then the two of us watched some TV. It was a school night."

"Your sister insists you took her car from the BP parking garage on Sunday and drove out there—to Red Rocks."

"I did not," she said. "Never." That felt good: a hard and fast denial. It gave her a small measure of hope she could get through this. She wanted this over and Marisa back, and then she wanted to hit the road. She wanted to be heading east with the girl as soon as tonight. At least that was her hope and her prayer.

"Tell me about your mother's death," Felicia asked, the question out of nowhere.

"Excuse me?" Instantly, the idea of escape vanished from her mind as surely as if it were water sluicing in circles down the drain.

"Your mother."

"What about her?"

"She died the same way as Yevgeny Orlov. Fell off a cliff. And you were with her. You might have been with Orlov."

"What are you suggesting? I'm some sort of serial killer and my modus operandi is to push people from high places?"

"Just asking."

Rory was studying her. They all were.

She'd never told anyone the truth about what happened. It was because she loved her mother and because she loved her sister and because she hated her stepfather. The toxicology report from the autopsy had shown psilocybin in her mother's blood, and Betsy had indeed given her mother shrooms on their hike. It was to help them enjoy the vista from the top of the ridge: enhance the experience. By then Betsy almost never took magic mushrooms, but it was her mother's birthday and she had thought it would be fun. She'd never told Crissy, but she and their mother had done shrooms twice before. It wasn't as big a deal as it would seem. Her mother had enjoyed it, and they really hadn't experienced anything more than what Betsy viewed as a nice dope high. "THC giggles plus," her mother called it. The trees hadn't come to life or the pages in books hadn't magically started turning. The squirrels hadn't become dragons.

"The Vermont State Police concluded it was an accident: your mother was either hallucinating because of the chemicals in her system or simply showed bad judgment—because of those chemicals—and walked off the cliff. That was the conclusion. Accidental death."

Supposedly, the truth will set you free. Wasn't that the expression? Or the myth? There were limits. Telling the truth about Red Rocks would endanger her daughter. But Vermont was different, and she felt an unexpected craving to come clean now about her mother. She was just so tired and so angry and so scared. She had been unable to sleep last night with that guy guarding her door and her daughter kidnapped. "That is how they ruled it, yes," she said.

"Is there more to it than that?"

"That's not what happened. My mother wasn't hallucinating. Neither of us were. Some people believe she thought she could fly or something ridiculous. But it wasn't like that."

"She didn't try to fly?"

"No," she said, shaking her head. She wondered: was it too late to pull this all back? Rory was leaning forward, and the other detective, Patrick, who had said very little as he scribbled his notes, had stopped writing as if entranced by whatever she was about to reveal. Still, however, she didn't have to do this. It wasn't too late.

And yet she wasn't going to stop. She couldn't shoulder it—any of it—anymore. Her reinvention here in Las Vegas hadn't worked because Frankie Limback was cowardly and corrupt, and he had brought her here with a lie. It was over and she was done. Finished.

"My mother didn't try to fly," she continued. "And she didn't accidentally fall over the side, either."

"Then what?"

"She killed herself. She knew exactly what she was doing."

She stopped speaking to let that land.

"Like my stepfather," she went on, "but not like him. He killed himself because of the way he had been abusing Crissy. I walked in on them. You didn't know that, did you? Crissy sure as hell didn't tell you. She doesn't even tell herself. And my mother? She didn't know until the day she died. That very afternoon, Detective. She killed herself because she found out what her dead husband had been doing to her daughter."

"You told her? That day you were hiking?"

"My God, no. Never. I planned to take that to my grave. It wasn't my story to tell. And the man was dead. But you saw what it did to Crissy—what he did to her. The solitude, the body issues, the bulimia—"

"Your sister has bulimia?"

"Uh-huh. Why do you think she became Diana? Why, for that matter, do you think she became someone else? Anyone other than who she was?"

"If you didn't tell your mother, then who did?" Patrick asked. "It was just the two of you on that hike. How did she find out?"

It was the big question. And the answer was the backpack, the very one that Crissy had brought up last month when they had had their reunion lunch at that middling buffet out in Summerlin.

"The day after my stepfather killed himself, my mother was supposed to be one of the high school chaperones on the annual class trip to Washington, D.C. She used to use this ancient L.L. Bean canvas backpack from the 1980s—though it wasn't such a dinosaur back then. And he wrote a suicide note and put it in the backpack. I guess he knew she would find it there. She obviously wouldn't be going on the trip: he knew that, too. But she'd already gotten the backpack down from the attic and had it beside her dresser. I guess he wanted a spot where she would find the note, but Crissy and I wouldn't. So, for instance, the dresser itself was out."

"But she didn't find it?"

"Nope. She just brought the backpack back up to the attic. And she never used it again until that day the two of us went on the hike and did the shrooms. It was bigger than she needed, but—I don't know, once a Girl Scout, always a Girl Scout—she packed it with an actual canteen, chocolate bars for the two of us, gorp, and peanut butter and jelly sandwiches. It was more food than we needed, but she was excited by the adventure. And she recalled how the other times we'd done mushrooms, she'd gotten hungry. The munchies. Again, kind of like THC."

"Do you still have the note?"

"I burned it. Long gone."

"Did he say why he was going to kill himself? Did he say what he'd done?"

"Do you mean what he'd been *doing*?"

The detective nodded. Betsy supposed the woman had heard it all, but her eyes nonetheless went from steely to soft, and her blink lasted a millisecond longer than usual.

"He did," she answered. "More or less. He wasn't explicit. But he was clear enough. He probably assumed my sister would tell our mother. Or I would. But neither of us did. How could we? Our mother's second husband had just died. Try and process that. She was a wreck. And I was ten, Crissy was eleven. What I'd seen, what our stepfather had done. How could we tell our mother and add to that grief?"

"So she only learned years later."

"Decades. Anyway, after my mom read the note, she handed it to me and walked to the edge of the cliff. I thought she was just dazed. Stunned. I thought she was just taking it all in: what sort of person her second husband really was. At that point, I figured she knew her daughters were mostly okay. I was a social worker, and Crissy was out here with a residency. My high school craziness was in the past, and Crissy's bulimia was—as far as Mom knew—also in the past. She always assumed Crissy had an eating disorder because she was an actor. That's what Crissy told people. That's still what she tells herself."

"And you saw your mother . . . what? Jump? Walk off the side?"

"She dove."

No one said anything, and so she repeated herself. "She dove, Detective. She was a very good swimmer and a very good diver. She stood at the edge of the cliff, spread her arms wide, and then dove." She watched as that sunk in.

"You say you weren't at Red Rocks," Felicia said after a moment. "You said it must have been someone else."

She nodded. She hated herself, but she did.

"Do you think it was your sister? Do you think Crissy might have killed Yevgeny Orlov?"

Rory met her eyes. She knew she was supposed to say yes. Or, at least, tell the detectives that her sister was capable of such violence. She had to for Marisa. The girl was their chip, and she had no idea where the child was, even now.

It dawned on her—not with the measured, leisurely light of daybreak but the coruscating, blinding midday sun of Las Vegas—that no matter what she was about to say, whatever words came from her mouth, she was going to screw either her sister or her daughter. There was no answer that could save them both.

The word the coding teacher had used was reaver. *She was in her late twenties and had pink dreadlocks and silver studs up her left ear. She said a* reaver *was like a pirate.*

And she didn't teach all of us how to use "brute force"—again, those were her words—to get a Wi-Fi password. Just me, because she knew I was a foster kid and needed any advantages I could snag, and because she thought I was the only kid in the class smart enough to be a reaver. (That was just her opinion. I'm sure there were kids smarter than me.)

It takes time, and most people don't need to steal their way into a network. You just go to Starbucks or a library or anyplace with free Wi-Fi.

Well, I had nothing but time when I was being held hostage at Frankie's, even if he didn't call it being held hostage because I was waist deep in his swimming pool. So, I took my tablet and put on my pirate's hat. I "reavered up."

And, when I started to work, I realized just how much I knew about Frankie. I hit lots of dead ends. His wife's name and his kids' names and their birthdays: he actually had all these "dad dates" on his calendar on this corkboard in his kitchen, such as their birthdays, Betsy's birthday, even mine. I tried all kinds of Futurium mishmashes and the license plate on his Tesla, and all the crypto lingo he and Betsy used to toss about. WAGMI, for instance.

Nope.

The teacher called this process "brute force" because, basically, you're just punching in combo after combo, adding a hashtag here, an exclamation point there.

It was about one thirty in the afternoon when it dawned on me: I'd heard Frankie make a big deal about the fact that the house was on five acres, had five bedrooms, and was five years old. So, I started punching in combos of fives with random keys.

And none worked.

But I knew I was on to something. This just felt like such a Frankie thing to do. And then it clicked. The triple fives were why he called his house the "slot machine dacha."

And that was it: slotmachinedacha. Not even a hashtag or random key.

Of course, I had no idea how to spell dacha. *It must have taken seven tries before I got it right.*

CHAPTER TWENTY-SIX

Crissy

Nigel was gone, but he'd left the wicker tote with the weapon and the small box of bullets beside the leg of my chaise. When I looked up, I saw Bud McDonald peering into my cabana. Behind him, as if they were gawkers hoping for a glimpse of a real celebrity versus the ersatz version that was me, were Felicia Johnson and Patrick O'Connor. Given that I hadn't a license for the Glock, I sat up and lifted the bag so it was beside me and I could drape my arm over it, if need be. Felicia, Patrick, and I had met because a three-night stand of mine was dead, and I didn't think I should give the two detectives more ammunition to suspect me by parading before them a pistol for which I lacked a license.

"I told them this has to be brief, because you have two shows tonight and need your afternoon rest," Bud said, his voice protective and firm. The idea careened across my diazepam-soaked frontal lobe that they might be here to arrest me because they believed—mistakenly—that last night I was with two crypto crooks, but I was able to swat the notion into some more shadowy corner there. Still, this had to be important if they were back again and insisted that management bring them poolside to see me.

"Well, aren't we becoming the best of chums?" I told them, hoping that a little false bluster would get me through this. "This is three days in a row, isn't it? As Bud said, I'd love for this to be one of our shorter tête-à-têtes."

"It might be," said Felicia, as she sat where Nigel had planted himself a few minutes earlier. Bud and Patrick stood behind her. "We'll see. First of all, thank you for putting two tickets aside for my parents tonight. And thanks for squeezing them into the early show. That was very kind of you."

I gave them my congenial smile, my princess-meets-a-head-of-state face. I had forgotten I'd done that. "It was nothing. I was happy to do it," I said.

"Well, they're excited."

Bud was still present, and almost as if it were choreography, both detectives turned toward him and he got the message. "I'll wait over at the lifeguard station," he said, retreating, but it was a grudging withdrawal.

"So, what can I do for you?" I inquired politely.

"Well," Felicia began, "we have the preliminary toxicology reports on Yevgeny Orlov. Clean as a whistle."

I nodded, but said nothing.

"And the coroner found no injuries on the body that might suggest the death was not accidental—or, perhaps, a suicide."

I planned once more to remain silent, but when she failed to continue, I felt an uncontrollable need to say something. "I suppose I should be relieved because that must mean you no longer believe that I killed him," I remarked.

"We never said we believed that," Felicia said. "We're simply doing our due diligence. You've seen or read the news. We've said all along: this could very well be a suicide or an accident."

"The news," I repeated. "Could that be the police hoping to throw someone off by broadcasting those theories? Make someone believe they've gotten away with murder so they let down their guard?"

Patrick glanced at Felicia, and it struck me as a rather knowing glimpse.

"I'm a right smart bird," I said.

"Well," observed Patrick, "when you fall as far as Orlov did, the sorts of bruises or scrapes you might get in a struggle—you know, fighting for your life at the top of a cliff—might be lost amidst the more cataclysmic injuries. The fatal ones."

"Of course," I agreed politely. There was something sly about where this was going, and I wasn't able to read the room. They couldn't possibly think I was strong enough to win a "struggle" with Yevgeny Orlov at the top of a precipice. Perhaps I was a seductress who enticed him to the edge and gave him one good push from behind. But a cage fight above an abyss? No. "So, what does this mean? It's terrible whatever happened, accident or suicide, and you move on? We all move on?"

"Where were you last night?"

"Ah, that. Your raison d'être for popping by today."

Patrick looked confused.

"The princess wasn't a very good student, but the royal family all speak French," I told him.

"I wasn't—"

"Don't give it a thought," I said. "No, I wasn't at Fort Knocks. I can assure you both that was my sister." When they remained quiet, I continued, "I've already seen the pictures of her on the Vegas entertainment blogs and the photo in the newspaper: the article about Futurium hoping to buy this patch of earth."

"Everyone there thinks it was you," Felicia told me. "Everyone."

"I expected that."

"We spoke to your sister this morning."

"This morning? Why in the world didn't you speak to her yesterday?"

"Investigations move at their own pace," the woman said, not answering my question.

"Well, I suppose you confirmed that she was at Fort Knocks last night and she was out at Red Rocks on Sunday. And she took my car that day."

"We confirmed nothing of the sort. Now, I did point out to her that both your mother and Orlov died in a similar fashion."

"God. Did she dredge up meaningless family history and bore you with her amateur psychology about us? About me?"

Again, Felicia and Patrick looked at each other. Instead of

answering me, Felicia said, "Your sister claims she wasn't at Red Rocks on Sunday. She and her lawyer were firm about that."

"Her lawyer? She already has a bloody lawyer?" I didn't ask, but I was confident that her attorney was someone from Futurium.

"She does. She was clear: she was at the natural history museum on Sunday, and she was in her apartment last night."

"And you believe that?"

Felicia pressed on. "We tried to find video of this writer—Britt Collins—at Cocoon. The one you insist you had brunch with."

"Good. I'm pleased we have that corroboration," I told her.

She shook her head. "They have no video at the restaurant."

I felt a prickle of paranoia. "How convenient," I murmured.

"That means that while we have no reason to doubt your story, we also can't confirm it. We haven't been able to find your Britt Collins."

One of the flaps to my cabana fluttered in the breeze, and there was a cerulean column of sky. "What about our brunch receipt?" I asked. "She picked up the tab."

Patrick shook his head. "Doesn't seem to be the case. Now, there were tables with two women."

"Okay, then. There is a witness I was there."

"The waitress says no woman looked like you. Or, I guess, Lady Di," said Felicia. "We showed her pictures."

"So, they've bought the staff at Cocoon. Futurium has."

"It's possible," Patrick agreed, and Felicia gave him a brief side-eye so sharp it might have decapitated him.

"We have two Futurium executives and two entertainers—two so far—who swear they talked to you at Fort Knocks last night," Felicia informed me.

"You know they're lying in the first case and mistaken in the second."

"Where were you last night if you weren't at Fort Knocks?"

"I was in my suite. I read in bed and fell asleep early. There is rather a lot of stress in my life right now, and I need to conserve my energy for my shows."

"Any proof you were in your room?"

"As in, was I entertaining a gentleman friend? No."

"No witnesses?"

"You really don't believe me?" I asked. God, I would have been better off if I'd had room service send up my libations, rather than just reaching into my own little fridge and small bar. "Forgive me, is there a reason why I even need an alibi? Did something happen last night at Fort Knocks?"

"There are a lot of moving pieces. Whether it was you or your sister out at Red Rocks or at Fort Knocks—"

"It was her—at both places!" I had been trying to remain steadfast and serene, and now sounded barmy. But this was maddening.

"Look," Felicia said, her voice as flat as a still pond. "It doesn't matter what I believe. I'm just telling you what people are saying."

"It doesn't matter what you believe? That's bollocks! I'm a suspect in the investigation of a man who died!"

She shrugged evasively. "We'll be in touch in the next day or two. When we know more."

"Fine," I said. "I have nothing to hide."

"Good."

"May I ask you two something?"

"Of course," Felicia said.

"Yevgeny Orlov. There hasn't been an obituary yet—at least one I've seen. Was he who he said he was? A compliance person for GEI? Or was he some sort of criminal—or even a spy?"

They looked at each other, weighing precisely how much to share. Perhaps they had discussed this earlier, and now one or the other was having second thoughts.

"You must know," I went on. "A spy dies in Las Vegas. I'm sure the FBI would tell you."

"Why would they?"

"Wholehearted involvement behind the scenes? Give you folks a little—and please hear the understatement in my voice—directional guidance?" Looking back, I wasn't pressing them because I was so confident that I wasn't going to be arrested for a crime I didn't commit. Nor was I being cheeky because I wanted to torment Las Vegas detectives for fun. I wanted to know who I had slept with. I wanted to know who this man was who I had liked very much and now was dead.

Which was when Felicia surprised me. "You need to keep your head down," she said firmly.

"Excuse me?"

"You heard me. Accept the reality there are things we can't tell you and things we won't tell you. Focus on these salient facts: three people in your orbit—two Morleys and Yevgeny Orlov—are dead. And Orlov? Either you killed him and there will be repercussions—legal or otherwise—or you didn't kill him and someone wants us to believe that you did. Plus there's that Cleo Dionne you told us about."

"You looked into her?"

"Of course. She may be related to this. She may not," Felicia said. "Either way, you or your sister was at Fort Knocks last night with Oliver Davies and Neri Lombardo. Neri is an officer with the Mastaba crime family. And Oliver has sunk a lot of money into Futurium: paid for the computers on a couple of continents." She raised her eyebrows. "The point of that photo, if it wasn't you, may have been to incriminate you: suggest you're in tight with the Mastaba."

I took this in, and that tiny strand of DNA that linked me to my sister sent me a jolt. "Maybe someone isn't trying to frame me," I said. "Maybe someone is trying to frame Betsy."

"Maybe. Or maybe someone isn't trying to frame either of you. Maybe someone is merely using the two of you to get what they want."

"Which is?"

"Damned if I know."

"Where are they now? Oliver Davies and Neri Lombardo?"

"Long gone. Checked out of their rooms at the Versailles and disappeared."

"Disappeared?"

"Probably on their way back to Grand Cayman right now and a club they have there. But Cambodia is a possibility, too."

"Is someone watching me—other than you?" I asked them.

"Good guys or bad guys?"

"Either."

"I couldn't tell you that even if I knew the answer."

"But you do know the answer."

"Like I said: watch your back. These are people who don't give a damn who they kill."

"Thank you," I murmured, shocked by her candor. I rested my elbow on the canvas tote beside me and felt the hard metal of the gun against bone.

* * *

As soon as the detectives were gone, I asked Bud McDonald if we could chat. He sat down in the cabana, and I told him everything that Felicia and Patrick had shared with me. I asked him if, based on his experience with the Boston PD, Yevgeny Orlov could have been with the CIA.

"I was a cop, so my experience is pretty limited when it comes to spies," he said.

"But you think it's possible?"

"Sure. Want some other options?"

"Yes, please."

"Maybe he was Russian and FSB, and his job was his cover."

"I once teased him that he was FSB."

"And you're still alive? Rule that one out."

Through the cabana flap, a plane came into view as it descended in seemingly slow motion toward the airport.

"You ever wonder why some Americans loved Russia—you know, before Putin invaded Ukraine?" he asked, his tone ruminative. "Yeah, a lot of it was dictator worship. But part of it was just golf course foursomes. A lot of Russian American bromances were born on the links and the nineteenth hole. Either way, if Orlov was FSB or CIA, I suspect the FBI is involved. Which brings me to another option: maybe he was FBI."

"Like undercover?"

"Yup."

"But it's also possible that he was just some businessman with GEI, right?"

"Sure. And maybe no one murdered him out at Red Rocks," Bud said, and he smiled at my naivete. "Look, if he was CIA or FBI, then the cops here know. They just can't tell you."

"Where does that put me?" I asked, and my voice sounded peculiar. A little strangled and breathy. I heard the luffing of a sail. "Did Yevgeny . . ."

"Did Yevgeny sleep with you because he was CIA or FBI or even FSB, and you were an entrée to your sister and Futurium crypto? It's possible. Or maybe he just had a type."

A type. It took me a moment to recall where I had heard that very expression. But then it came to me. It was Yevgeny himself suggesting that Frankie Limback had had a type: Cleo Dionne. Who, apparently, looked like Betsy—who, of course, looked like me.

"My point," Bud continued, "is that there are lots of reasons why people are murdered. But I honestly don't believe the police think you did it because I don't see a motivation. Are you a spy? Are you a mobster?"

I wasn't sure if he was kidding, but I shook my head, just in case.

"Didn't think so," Bud said.

"Crime of passion? Isn't that a thing? I'm a furious lover and I push Yevgeny over a cliff when he isn't expecting it?"

"I guess."

"I didn't, you know. Just so we have clarity."

"I didn't think you did. But steer clear of your sister's new friends at Futurium."

"That's going to be very difficult, now that they're buying this casino."

"I know. Maybe it won't matter in a month."

"Because we'll both be unemployed?"

"Or dead."

"That's a cheery thought."

"Sorry."

"Of course, the detectives would agree with you," I said. "They told me to keep my head down."

"That was good advice."

The reality was that Bud was the third person in my rather petite circle who had suggested that I was in danger: I knew I would be popping one of my little yellow pills the moment he was gone.

Frankie was inside the house, but I knew he was watching me.

I figured he was watching me even when he went to the bathroom.

So, I stared at the browser on the tablet once I'd hacked into his Wi-Fi and thought: do I do this here in the pool or do I go inside and lock myself in the bedroom?

And what would "this" be?

But then I knew. First things first. Get Betsy's nest egg out of Futurium. I had her crypto seed phrase hidden in that Gap email. Her checking account info was there, too. But then I thought, no, not her checking account. If Frankie or someone saw it was gone, that was the first place they'd check. But they probably didn't even know I had a little savings account. So, that was where I'd put it.

Boom. Took a minute and it was gone. I drained it completely. Moved it out of Futurium and into my bank account.

Yup. WAGMI.

CHAPTER TWENTY-SEVEN

Betsy

The moment the detectives had left, she said to Rory, "I want my daughter." They were standing at the window and watching the black car roll from the apartment complex parking lot. She'd followed the script with the police that they'd laid out for her: she told them she had not been at Red Rocks on Sunday. She denied being at Fort Knocks last night. She'd done it for her daughter, and she'd done it because her poor, pathetic, damaged sister was accusing her of the very same crime. The fact that her sister's version of the story had an element of truth—Betsy herself might not have killed the poor guy out at Red Rocks, but her associates at Futurium sure as hell had—and hers had none exacerbated her guilt. She hated herself for what she was doing and doubted she'd ever forgive herself; the list of crimes and misdemeanors on her ledger was long, but this one was bad.

And yet what choice had she?

"The kid's at school," Rory told her.

"Then I will go get her and bring her home."

"Nope." He pulled her phone from his pants pocket—she recognized the pink case instantly—and typed the child a text, reading it aloud to Betsy as he typed with his thumbs:

> Let's do something fun after school today. I missed you last night.

Then he pressed Send.

"Is she the type of girl who checks her phone during class?" he asked.

"I doubt most teachers give their students that opportunity."

"Well, let's see. We'll know soon enough." He put the phone back in his pocket and said, "I had no idea your stepdad was a pervert. That kind of shit? Disgusting."

"So is kicking a woman in the stomach or the ribs," she said. "Or punching her in the face."

"Kicking anyone, man or woman, in the ribs is a pretty shitty thing to do. But it's not perverse."

"Is that an apology?"

"God, no. Anyway, Frankie never told me about your stepfather."

"I never told Frankie."

Abruptly he pointed a finger straight up at the ceiling and said, "I feel a buzzing in my pants. That was fast." Then he reached for the phone and showed her the text he had just received:

Cool. Shopping? Clothes?

"Seems like her teachers don't give a rat's ass if the kids check their phones," he said.

She nodded. But she knew in her heart he was lying. There wasn't a reason in the world to believe that Marisa herself had responded to her text.

* * *

Early afternoon, Damon and the goon who had stood guard at her apartment the night before—still in his Area 51 hoodie—returned to her apartment. He hadn't said much last night and said little now with Damon and Rory present. He made a few innocuous observations about the Monday-night football game and who'd covered their bets and who hadn't. She didn't recognize the names of any of the gamblers.

"So, how long are you going to keep me imprisoned in my apartment?" she asked Damon. She was scared, but she was also hungry and sleep deprived, and her rage that they'd taken Marisa was dwarfing all else. If her ribs and her jaw weren't a constant reminder of the black ice on which she was walking, she might once again have unleashed the hysteria coursing inside her like underground lava.

"No one has kidnapped anyone. Marisa is fine."

"Rory says she's at school. I don't believe him."

"The school would have called you if she weren't there, right?"

"I don't have my phone, Damon!"

Damon looked at Rory. Once more, Rory retrieved the phone with the pink case from his pants pocket and showed her a screen. It was the one that listed the calls that had come in, and there were none that morning. She also saw that there were none from her daughter last night.

"You could have erased the calls from the school," she told him.

"I could have," agreed Rory.

"And I don't believe my daughter even has her phone anymore."

"Ah, but this is interesting," Rory said. "Your sister sent you a text. She says you can't set her up for any nefarious shit you may have been up to with Oliver and Neri last night at Fort Knocks."

"Oh, she's very wrong," said Damon. "There are pictures everywhere of Lady Di in that dress, and people will see them and they'll be the proof positive that she was at Fort Knocks before going upstairs to diddle around with John Aldred."

"Where's Frankie?" she asked.

"Busy."

"Busy where?"

"Sit down!" Rory barked, and she knew from his tone she should obey. She planted herself on the couch. The thug with the beard pulled a can of Monster the size of a bowling pin from his hoodie's kangaroo pocket.

"Here's what's going to happen," he went on. "Pay attention."

"You keep moving the goalposts on me," she said. "I've done everything you asked. And still you don't give me back Marisa. I want my daughter."

"You know as well as anyone that life's not fair," Damon reminded her. "Rory told me what you told the cops about your sister and your stepdad this morning. That's heavy shit. But your life has the potential to get so much better. Or so much worse. It's in your hands."

She couldn't believe that he'd brought that up and almost said so. But when she looked at the faces of the men and read the tea leaves, she knew not to bother.

"Now Orlov? He was always going to be blood in the water," Rory went on. "Accident, suicide. Whatever. But I leave nothing to chance. Think of that old expression, 'three on a match.' "

"I don't—"

"Lighting the third cigarette on one match. That's the one the sniper sees and gets you killed. So, two suicides, the Morleys? Risky, but we'll get away with it. A good bet. But Orlov? He was number three. Eventually, you always roll snake eyes. So, your sister can take the fall for that one. Even if she doesn't, it still makes it all as muddy as Turkish coffee."

"But I didn't . . . I wasn't . . ." she stammered, but, of course, she was there. "How did you even get her car to Red Rocks?"

"Girl we trust drove it. Same one who grabbed the spare key when she dropped off the Maenads brochure in your sister's suite at the BP," said Damon. "Easy peasy."

"I want my daughter and I want out," she pleaded. "I want Marisa and I want to go home."

"Home?" Rory asked, half scoff and half shout. "What in holy fuck does that even mean? Vermont? You have no home.

You have this apartment, and Frankie pays for it. You got nothing. You. Got. Nothing."

Suddenly she was weeping: it was as if she were being sucked down into quicksand and saw no tree limb or vine on which to cling.

"Where's Marisa?" she begged. "Please, please bring me my daughter."

Damon and Rory glanced at each other, and for the briefest of seconds she thought they might relent. But they didn't. "Some of the Las Vegas PD would be happy to call Orlov's death an accident or a suicide and move on. But the FBI isn't letting them," Rory said instead, ignoring her tears. "So, are we feeding your sister to the wolves? Yes. But before she's arrested, and she might be soon, we need you to ask her about Orlov. Are you listening?"

He leaned forward and snapped his fingers in front of her, and she wiped her face with her fingers. She tried to gather herself. She nodded.

"Good," he said. "We need to know if Orlov told Crissy anything about us she could tell the FBI. I want to know who turned him and whether he mentioned anyone. Named names. If so, we'll deal with her differently. We also need to know if he gave her anything. Someone is trying to get the skinny on our political friends here in Clark County and in D.C. I want to know what he said to the princess and how far he—or the FBI—got recruiting her."

"I'm too tangled in this, Rory. I can't do more. I just can't."

They sat in silence, the men occasionally gazing down at their phones. Then Damon and Rory looked up at the same moment, made eye contact, and Rory said, "If you don't want to talk to her, that's fine. We can. And then?"

She waited.

"Then we kill her."

I'd gotten out of the pool and was sitting on a chaise in the shade. I was going to text Crissy a 911 mayday from the tablet. (I'd never given a you-know-what that the tablet's FaceTime didn't work . . . until now.) I decided not to text Betsy. If they had my phone, they might have hers.

But then a big SUV pulled up to Frankie's slot machine dacha, and three people got out. One was a woman I'd learn was Frankie's next-door neighbor, Lara Kozlov, and the other was Erika Schweiker. A congresswoman. I recognized her right away: Barbie Doll blond hair and this black beret that looked like an acorn cap. She sometimes told people she liked it because it kept her hair out of her eyes, and sometimes she said it was paramilitary because patriots had to wear the Second Amendment on their sleeves. (Which, of course, would mean an armband, not a hat, but even I knew most of what Schweiker said made zero sense.) It depended on who she was talking to.

The two of them had a driver, a guy in a black suit, and anyone who was wearing a black suit out here in the middle of the day was a mortician or a limo driver. Or someone with a gun. Security. And Schweiker loved guns, so I guessed it was some combination of the second and third. And given that Frankie had two pistols that I knew of, that meant there were now a lot of guns at Frankie's house.

They were sitting in the living room talking, and they could see me and I could see them. We all waved like it was just another day in Las Vegas (which, I guess, it was).

I dried off pretty instantly when I got out of the pool, and so I grabbed my tablet and walked into the house. I walked to this big island between the living room and the kitchen like I was just getting something to eat. And right there, like I wasn't up to anything at all but playing some dumb game while getting a soda, I texted Crissy that I was being held hostage at Frankie's, I had no idea where her sister was, and there was a congresswoman right now in Frankie's living room. I said I wasn't sure if she should call the police because I was worried about Betsy, and the idea there was a congresswoman here meant Futurium had really powerful people in their pocket. (I loved that expression from the second I heard Frankie use it. Imagine what it would look like to have a tiny human being in your pocket.)

But Crissy was the Princess of Las Vegas.

So maybe she did, too.

I deleted the text chain I had started as soon as it was sent and watched the group until Frankie told me this was business and I should hang out at the pool. I nodded, but put the tablet down in the crevice between the wine fridge and the island counter, and pressed Record on voice memos. I had no idea how much of the conversation I'd get, but it was close enough that I might get some.

When I walked past them on my way back outside, I saw I was right: the guy in the suit had a shoulder holster.

CHAPTER TWENTY-EIGHT

Crissy

I suppose a person can die in a car in a tunnel in Las Vegas, just like Diana. The loop that began beneath the Convention Center is growing.

But it isn't likely. The cars don't race through the tunnels we currently have. They're Teslas that you borrow at one station or another and use like a subway to navigate that small section of the city so you are spared the congestion aboveground: vehicular on the streets and parking lots, pedestrian on the concourses and sidewalks.

You're not driving fast.

And soon, I suppose, you won't even be driving at all. The cars will be automated.

Moreover, I have never been chased by the paparazzi.

And so when thoughts of my death buzz near—and thoughts of our deaths buzz near us all, we never escape the gnawing awareness that we are but suet gnawed to nothing by birds—they don't end with screams and the sound of crashing metal.

But for my sister? I can't say.

In the end, I was grateful she came to Las Vegas.

* * *

Timing, any performer knows, is everything.

I had left the cabana, gone to my suite to get dressed, and was on my way to the theater because I hadn't been there since Saturday night, and every Tuesday afternoon I went there to run through the show on my own. Run my lines, walk the small stage. Even when the world is unraveling, the show must go on, right?

When I was finished, I saw my niece had texted me forty minutes earlier:

> I'm in trouble. I'm at Frankie's house instead of school and he won't let me leave. It's like he's kidnapped me. I don't know where Betsy is, but she's in trouble too. I'm texting you instead of her because they took my phone and I think they took hers. Or they're watching her like they're watching me. I've been in shitty situations before, but not like this. Also, there's this congresswoman with Frankie and a guy with a gun. I don't know if you should call 911. I didn't because of Betsy. But maybe you know what's best because you know this city. No one has hurt me yet. But this is bad AF. Don't text back. I'm deleting this after I send it.

I wandered out to the casino floor, digesting this. I wouldn't call 911. I would call Felicia Johnson. I trusted her. I was fumbling in my purse for her card, pushing aside the gun that Nigel had given me at the cabana, when I saw them: Damon and Betsy. They were passing a craps table and so I detoured toward the slots so I could ring the detective, but when I turned, there was Rory. The British slang would be frit, but I wasn't merely frit—or frightened. I was scared to death. My hands were shaking. He was wearing a blazer, and I supposed it was because he had a gun in his waistband.

"Give me the phone," he said. I hadn't deleted Marisa's text because I wanted to share it with the detective. But I pressed the lock button on the device with my trembling thumb before handing it to him.

"Well," I said, "this is a pleasant surprise. Why in the world do you have need of my phone?"

"Zip it. Cut the accent."

Betsy and Damon caught up to us, and the idea that among the last things I might see before I was executed was a cluster of Hobbit slots, a small throng of video Gandalfs and Gollums, was not lost on me.

"Hi, Sis," said Betsy, her tone inscrutable.

I nodded. I had been told to zip it.

"Before we go," Rory said, "you need to hug me right now. And you need to kiss Damon here on both cheeks." His eyes moved in the direction of the nearest eye in the sky, the camera that was capturing our corner of casino carpet. I did as he said. I even hugged Betsy, though he hadn't asked.

Then he ushered us toward the casino exit. They hadn't taken my purse. Clearly it hadn't crossed their mind I might have a gun.

* * *

"We'll take the Mercedes," Rory said. The steamy afternoon air was a slap after the air-conditioning inside the Buckingham Palace. Diana had died in a Mercedes-Benz—or, to be faithful to her story, had died in a hospital of injuries sustained in a Benz—and so I was not wild about his choice in vehicle.

We drove out toward Red Rocks, and I was unnerved because Red Rocks was where both Richie Morley and Yevgeny Orlov had been executed. This felt ominous. Damon was behind the wheel, and Betsy was beside him in the front. Rory and I were in the back seat, and Rory had a handgun in his hand in his lap.

For one of the few times in my life, I kept my mouth shut.

But my biggest fear was for my niece. If my phone rang or pinged, Rory invariably would look at it and discover, before the screen locked again, that there had been a text from Marisa. That was the real ticking time bomb. I held my purse in my lap, wondering what Rory would do if I unzipped it and reached inside it. Nigel had given me a brief tutorial on the Glock before leaving my cabana, and we'd loaded the pistol there. Would Rory stop me? Would he take my clutch from me? Despite the gun, I felt like I was one of Henry VIII's wives in her dungeon, awaiting her execution.

We drove in silence, and I was struck by how very different these men were from Frankie. Betsy's boyfriend was a charlatan, a weak fellow who pretended to be a player. He wasn't: he was a banker who was in over his head. There was a reason he was told to keep an eye on a thirteen-year-old girl while the big guns had come to the BP to retrieve me. And, clearly, he hadn't even done that right: Marisa had managed to send me a mayday.

It was Betsy who broke the silence when she said, "You're not going to kill us. You can't have another body. You already have four."

I looked at her. I had no idea what she'd been going through, but clearly the furnace had burnished the steel that once had been my reckless badass of a sibling. It had resurrected her. She had a bruise on her face, but otherwise didn't seem injured.

"Only three in the U.S.," Rory said. "And we know the Morleys were suicides. And the third was likely a suicide. Or an accident. Or, sure, maybe a murder. If that's the case, then Crissy here seems the most likely culprit."

You can't pin that on me, I thought. But they could. And they might.

* * *

I had never been to Frankie Limback's home. I was relieved we were here and not in the middle of nowhere. I made a decision as we were sliding to a stop in his driveway: as we all emerged from the vehicle, I would pull the gun from my purse and tell Rory to drop his. I wasn't sure I could pull the trigger, but this had to stop. Unfortunately, as I was unfastening my seat belt, he grabbed my purse. I tried to grab it back, murmuring something incomprehensible about how a lady needs her handbag, but he felt the weight and then his fingers ran like spider legs over the Glock, and he hit me hard on the jaw, my teeth knocking together and the pain shooting up to my ear.

"Fucking Christ, you thought you were going to shoot me? My God, you're a bitch," he said, and he pulled out my gun and stared at it as if he didn't already have one just like it in his hand. Then Damon opened the door and Rory shoved me from the vehicle, and I fell on my side onto the asphalt driveway.

"We're going to go inside, and I am going to aim your very own gun—this one—at a thirteen-year-old girl, and you are going to tell me everything Yevgeny Orlov told you. We are going to go over every minute you two spent together, second by second. And if I sniff the teeniest aroma of bullshit in anything you say, I will shoot her."

"You won't shoot a child," I said.

"How the hell do you know I won't? You know nothing about me."

From the black pavement, which felt like hot sand, I nodded. "You're right," I agreed. "I don't know you."

"Get up," he commanded, and so I did. I saw the sleeve on my blouse had ripped and my elbow was bleeding. I glanced at Betsy. I saw in her face that she believed Rory was capable of anything—but I saw also in those beryl-blue eyes a crescent of absolute, unfettered rage.

I heard the car and the craziness in the driveway, and I went to see what was going on. But already Lara Kozlov was coming outside to get me, and the congresswoman and her guard—or whatever he was—were leaving out the back and heading down the path that led to Lara's house, and they were moving pretty damn fast. Schweiker, despite her acorn "paramilitary" beret, didn't want to be around to see whatever was going to happen next. Lara handed me a shirt and said I should come inside.

CHAPTER TWENTY-NINE

Betsy

She threw her arms around her daughter, and then took a step back, her hands on Marisa's shoulders, and studied her. She was wearing a T-shirt over her bathing suit and was unharmed. Then Betsy pulled the girl to her once again and would have held her like that a long while, but Lara Kozlov herded them to the couch, telling them to sit there beside Crissy. The woman handed Betsy a tissue and she blew her nose, and then used the sleeves of her shirt to dry her face: she hadn't wept—she was too angry to sob—but her eyes had grown filmy with relief that Marisa was alive. She looked up at Frankie, furious, appalled by his woeful, hangdog mien. She counted eight of them in his living room, including herself. There was her sister, Marisa, and the quintet from Futurium—Frankie, Lara, Rory, Damon, and that thug with a beard who'd held her hostage last night. Other than Lara, who sat in a chair opposite the three Dowlings, the Futurium contingent remained on its feet. That meant the four men were standing, and the four women were seated. Betsy was unsure what to make of that. On the coffee table was a glass vase with a replica of Georgia O'Keeffe's stunning green-and-white orchid that hung at MoMA.

"Should I get Tony on the line?" Damon was asking. "He could FaceTime with us."

"No need," Rory said.

"I'm bleeding on the couch. My elbow," Crissy said to no one in particular, sounding a little stunned, and Betsy expected someone to do something—even if it was as simple as Lara standing up and giving her sister a Kleenex, too—but it was as if Crissy had spoken from space.

"So, we have the Princess of Las Vegas," Rory went on. "We have her sister, we have her niece. Whole goddamn royal family. You know, don't you, some people think you were the last person to see Yevgeny Orlov alive—and most of them are with the LVPD?"

"I wasn't," said Crissy. "Whichever one of you killed him was."

"Tell us how you met."

"We met on the casino floor."

"He hit on you?"

"He did."

"Date, time?"

"I don't know the exact date. I'd have to look at a calendar. It was August. It was after my second show."

Rory said, "You have the chance to go home in forty-five minutes. Maybe an hour. But you need to be totally candid about Orlov. No bullshit. Not one word."

Betsy watched her sister rub at the blood on her elbow. "Crissy," she began, unsure how far she was going, but incapable of watching this in silence, "you can't trust them. Anything you tell them they'll use against you."

"Frankie?" Rory said, his voice ice.

Frankie waited.

"Empty her crypto."

"I don't know her seed phrase," he said pathetically.

Rory stood over her. "You memorize it? I bet you did."

She had. But did she give it to him? When you're trying to stay alive, to keep your daughter alive, to inhale one more time . . . you do. You do anything and say anything. She asked him for a pen and wrote down the twelve words, including the three that were a computer's way of tormenting her.

Badminton
Stereo
Ghoul
Collective
Oxygen
Juveniles
Diploid
Marmoset
Supinate
Delusion
Pizza
Recur

She started to hand the paper to Rory, but he said to give it to Damon. Right away, he began typing the phrase into a laptop on the bar.

"Betsy," said Marisa, and her tone was tentative. "There's something I need to—"

"Shhhhhh. This will all be fine, sweetheart," she said, cutting her off and hoping to reassure her. "Don't be scared."

"No. I—"

"Shut the fuck up, both of you," said Rory.

Betsy saw the color was draining from the girl's face. She began to suspect either that Marisa knew something she hadn't shared or these men had done more to the child than anyone had let on.

Damon looked up at Betsy from the laptop. "It's gone. Where did you move it?"

"I didn't," she told them. So, she thought, they've already taken it. Of course. Tony, she supposed. There really was no honor among thieves.

"Come here. We're going to log into your bank account. You moved it there, right?"

She rose from the couch and joined him as he'd asked. She knew there were a lot of guns in the room.

"Which bank do you use? And is it in your savings account or checking account?"

She told Damon the bank, and he went to the website. "Log in," he commanded.

"See?" she asked, after punching in the password. She pointed at the screen. "It isn't there. You can see how little money is in checking or savings."

Damon stared closely at the screen and then took a step back. "Frankie, does she have any other accounts? You involved in this?"

"No! Hell, no!"

"You didn't open up an investment account for her—maybe at your old bank?"

"I did not, I promise you: I did not."

"Crissy, what about you? Did you and Yevgeny hack in and—"

"We did no such thing," her sister said. She sounded less staggered. Almost defiant. And then her pitch rose when she continued, "I don't even understand your bloody crypto. And I am many things, but I am not a hacker."

Rory took his pistol from his waistband. "Well, this is interesting. Betsy? Where did you hide our crypto?"

"Your crypto? It's mine!"

"That much coin for doing the little you did? And then fighting us every step of the way out here? You don't deserve it. No, you don't get to keep it. Not anymore."

"Rory," Frankie pleaded, "c'mon. This has all gone too far."

She felt a noxious fusion of fury and fear. She couldn't take her eyes off the weapon in Rory's hand.

"Don't do something crazy," said Damon.

"Listen to him," Frankie added. "You can't believe—"

"I'm not sure what I believe. I just know that we gave your girlfriend a lot of coin, and now she's hidden it."

"Well, as you said. We gave it to her. So, she can do with it what she wants, right? Right?" Frankie insisted, his voice breaking the second time he asked Right?

Rory aimed the gun squarely at her.

"Rory," whimpered Marisa. "Betsy didn't do anything. It was me, I—"

"Shhhh," Betsy told her, understanding instantly where the coin was. "Don't speak."

"Rory, you can't keep going off script," said Damon. "You need to put the gun away. If she—"

Which was when Rory fired. But he didn't shoot her. From the corner of her eye, Betsy saw Lara Kozlov pulling that SIG Sauer with the pink pearl grip from her purse and aiming it at Rory. "Drop it," she'd said, but those were the last words she ever spoke, because with the speed of a snake Rory pivoted and shot her in the head, the pop and the sudden red splotch where one of her eyes had been happening simultaneously, and the woman's body tilted onto its side on the leather easy chair, a rag doll, and the gun fell from her hand onto that beautiful hardwood floor.

I had seen a lot of crazy shit. But I'd never seen a person killed.

CHAPTER THIRTY

Crissy

Las Vegas was built in a biosphere largely bereft of water, and the classic casinos of the 1950s suggested this brave new world in the American southwest was an homage to the arid landscape of the Middle East: The Sahara. The Sands. The Dunes. The Desert Inn.

It wasn't.

It wasn't a tribute to anything but greed, and the nexus of avarice and chance. The gangsters, hustlers, and self-proclaimed cowboys who invented Las Vegas never had any interest in the natural world. Oh, its creators loved the safe tropes from Egypt or Saudi Arabia. The ones oblivious to religion. So, there was the Aladdin, which was, in some ways, the perfect name for a casino, and then the Luxor.

Remember the very first thing I told you? Las Vegas was built on a bedrock of luck.

But it was bad luck.

For the idea of the city to succeed—what it represented—you had to believe that people always had faith that their luck was about to change. Sure, there would be the whales who could afford to lose hour after hour and day after day, but most of the "guests" who kept feeding the ever-bleating mechanical beasts on the casino floor couldn't. And yet the Las Vegas forefathers were confident that they would stay there and keep losing.

And they did.

And they do.

Have there ever been two more perfect bedfellows than casinos and crypto?

Even long after Elvis had left the building—or Celine or Sammy or Barry or Liberace or Cher or (yes) Diana—the souls at the slots would keep waiting for their luck to change.

Diana had the bad luck to marry a prince, but on her wedding day, everyone alive who watched the wedding on television thought she was the luckiest girl on earth. Years later, the night she died, she left the hotel in Paris with Dodi Al-Fayed after midnight to go to his apartment in the City of Light. Had the two of them spent the night at that hotel, would she be alive today? She had the good fortune—well, Dodi did—to be able to *afford* to stay at the Ritz as long as she liked. But they left.

They took a chance. They thought they could outrun the paparazzi, they could elude both the posse and who they were.

No one escapes who they are.

And yet we live for chance. We love chance.

He was dealt a bad hand.

She dodged a bullet.

I rolled the dice.

So, I *did* roll the dice. Elvis really had left the building—and I had had enough.

* * *

For a moment, there was silence. Frankie and Damon and Marisa and even the thug with the beard couldn't believe that Rory had just shot Lara Kozlov in the head. Not right between the eyes. Through an eye.

But then there was madness. Frankie and Damon were asking him what he had done—why he had done it—Marisa was sobbing, and Betsy had run from the bar to the couch and was shielding her daughter as if the child were a toddler. The men were shouting and still Rory was waving that Glock, and only when he pointed it once more at Betsy did the room grow quiet.

"Lara was FBI," Rory said. "One of our guys in Moscow told me today. She was undercover with the bank in Russia and then as a political consultant to get to Erika. Erika isn't just one of our useful idiots, she's one of their useful idiots. Russia's. Lara was the one who turned Orlov."

"So, you fucking killed her?" Damon asked. "Jesus Christ, you kill an FBI agent, and they will go balls to the wall to get you! Balls to the wall, Rory, balls to the fucking wall! It's one thing to kill an asset like Orlov—and we had this princess here set up perfectly. But now? Lara—"

"She was going to shoot me."

"Maybe threaten you, but she—"

"You don't pull a gun on me. You don't *ever* pull a gun on me. Want to know more? She gave Betsy a tiara with a SIM card hidden behind the big stone. The SIM was supposed to be a copy of the SIM on the phone for Nevada's secretary of state. His passwords, his contacts, his history—just in case Erika needed a little help with vote counting. Instead, the SIM was malware. The moment Oliver or Neri opened it, all of the info and passwords on their phone would go straight to the FBI. You can be damn sure I checked it out before I let either of them do anything with it. So, today I got the word from Russia: Lara was not our friend."

"Rory, it doesn't matter," said Damon. "You can't shoot an FBI—"

"I can! I just did!"

Which was when I rolled the dice. It seemed this madman was willing to kill anyone, including Betsy, Marisa, and me. And so I grabbed the vase on the coffee table with the O'Keeffe orchid and hurled it at him like it was a bowling ball, and reflexively he put up his hands to knock it away, ducking, but still it hit him in the arm. His gun discharged—he didn't consciously fire it—the bullet tearing a hole in the sheetrock, and Betsy, a woman who, as a teen, put the wreck in reckless, grabbed Lara's pistol from amidst the avocado-tinged shards of the vase.

"Put the gun down, Rory," she hissed.

"You won't shoot me," he said.

And so she did. She hit him in the right shoulder, and he cursed at her, but the gun fell from his hand with a thud. His arm was dangling, and the cardinal-colored stain on his shirt was blossoming like a red, red rose. Instantly, she was whirling, commanding Damon and Frankie and the fellow with the beard to raise their hands over their heads where she could see them; she told them to not even try to draw their guns. The only one who hesitated was the muscle with the ZZ Top beard, and so she shot him in the stomach. He bellowed, collapsing to the floor like a wounded moose. Betsy told me to take their weapons, because she knew all of them were, as always, packing. She was right. Suddenly I had deposited three pistols on the coffee table, while holding a fourth—Rory's—in my hand, hoping like hell I wouldn't have to use it.

"Betsy?" This was Marisa, and the voice was uncharacteristically small.

"Yes?" my sister said, but her eyes were moving among the four men.

"When the police get here? My tablet is between the wine fridge and the counter." She pointed at the island.

"Why?"

"I'm recording this. I recorded that meeting with the congressperson."

I turned to her. "You little mole, you."

"Mole?"

"Spy," I said.

I retrieved the tablet, stopped the recording, and called Felicia. I told her where we were and that as wild as was the story I was sharing that moment, we had an audio that—I had a feeling—would knock her blooming socks off.

* * *

The world always is changing. Sometimes we can sense the gravitas of what is occurring, but often it takes an earthquake—and here I am speaking metaphorically, though you can appreciate the literalness of what I am suggesting—for us to feel the tectonic plates shifting beneath our feet. Las Vegas. FBI agents and assets. Cryptocurrency.

Betsy: my sister.

The house was a crime scene, and so we were escorted outside, the cul-de-sac illuminated by the flashing lights from three squad cars. Apparently, there were other members of the Vegas PD, in addition to Felicia and Patrick, who hadn't been bought with Futurium coin.

Felicia was done asking Betsy, Marisa, and me questions. "It's the damnedest thing," I said to Betsy. "I never expected to die in there. They might have planned to kill us. But I never saw it."

"No?"

I shook my head. "I expect, if I die young, it will be in a car crash. Perhaps not a Mercedes in a tunnel. But a Mini with the top down. I flip and . . . well, you know, it's one fuck-all of a mess."

Betsy was rubbing her daughter's back, and she said, "I love you, Sis. I really do. But . . ."

I waited.

"Never mind," she murmured. "This isn't the time or the place."

"No. Go ahead."

"Okay. That poor woman. Princess Diana? Do what you do onstage. I get it. Do what you want. But offstage? Let her ghost go."

"I . . . can't."

"You can. Diana doesn't have to be your Valium. Not anymore."

Everyone from Futurium was gone now. Arrested. But the

Vegas PD, the FBI, and even some FBI task force known as CART—the Computer Analysis and Response Team—were searching Frankie's slot machine dacha. To the east I could see the iridescent Wedgwood of Las Vegas, a chimerical nimbus built on cacti and sand. My sister was spot-on: Diana was my drug of choice, more important to me than the actual pills I popped.

"Betsy?" This was Marisa.

"Yes, sweetheart?"

"Will I get back my tablet?"

The FBI had it. They were thrilled with my niece. She was going to be interviewed a lot in the coming days, more FBI and more police, and by the press. She would be excellent. She'd already talked to a pair of agents, and to Felicia and Patrick from the LVPD. What she had done was not merely brilliant; it was heroic.

"We'll get you a new one in the morning," Betsy replied. "One where everything works. And the cloud will have—"

"I know."

"How are you doing, my little love?" I asked her.

"Okay," she answered. She was quieter than I had ever seen her, and she would be for what remained of the evening.

One of the paramedics who'd checked in on us earlier stopped by. He was about to leave and wanted to say goodbye. "Welcome to Las Vegas," he said to Betsy.

We both looked at the young man.

"Too morbid?" he asked. "Too soon?" We smiled at the gallows humor of it all, mostly out of courtesy, and then he was gone.

Betsy stretched out her legs before her. "I'm sorry, Sis."

There were lots of things for which she might have been apologizing. But I thought I knew. The first I'd heard about the photos of her and John Aldred in the Fort Knocks hotel room had been when she was talking to the FBI.

"The pictures of you and the senator?"

"Oh, those, yes. But I just meant everything. Every fucking thing I've done."

"I doubt those photos will ever see the light of day. And if they do? For all we know, Schweiker will have been indicted by then. I'm sure there's a lot on the audio Marisa recorded."

"Still . . ."

"May I ask you something?"

"Of course."

"You shot one of them in the shoulder and one in the stomach. Were you being merciful?"

"God, no. When I took that hunting safety course, there was a cop's kid in the class. He said if you ever have to shoot a person, aim for the middle: think belly button to sternum."

"That's where you were aiming?"

"Yup, both times. I'm a terrible shot."

"You saved our lives."

"I got lucky."

"So . . . would you like a suite at the BP?" I asked. "You can't possibly want to go back to the place Frankie was paying for."

"God. I really will be homeless."

"You won't," I reassured her. "You're not."

"Besides," Marisa reminded her, "you still have your crypto."

"I do, don't I?" she said, and she sounded incredulous.

"Of course you do," said my niece. "I wasn't stealing it. I was just hiding it."

Betsy seemed to perk up at this realization.

"But I can get you a two-room suite at the BP for a while—if you want," I told her. "I'll take care of it. I suppose the BP is in the same school district that Marisa is in now."

"You'd do that?"

"I have no idea what's gotten into me, but, yes."

She picked up a pebble and stared at it as if it were a rare seashell she'd found at low tide. "Frankie Limback," she murmured. "What was I thinking?"

"We've all shagged punters and reprobates," I reassured her. I pointed at the fluorescent blue waves in the distant sky. "That's my home, you know. Stay here. There are hordes of homeless teens living in the storm drains that could use you."

"You have storms?"

"When it rains—and though it does rarely—it pours. I've seen floods here that were positively biblical."

"I'll think about it," she said. "But that part of my life is probably behind me, even if it is one of the only parts without regrets."

"I understand."

"I mean, I loved the shelter. I loved the kids. And I know what you did to help. Thank you."

"I did—"

"Even after Mom died . . . even when you were so angry with me . . . you still gave us a whopping check. I mean, you hated me. But, still, you were awfully generous."

"I never hated you. I just couldn't cope with having you in my life."

"You gave them five digits year after year."

"The gifts were supposed to be anonymous."

"I knew it was you."

I stood and stretched. We'd take an Uber to the casino, where I would check them in and have room service send to my suite either a very late-night dinner or very early breakfast for three.

Epilogue

Someday, I'm going to write a memoir, and it won't be about being a foster kid, because the world has plenty of those, and it won't be about crypto, even though it would be fun to use DAO or FUD or a word like nonfungible *in a book. It will be about spending my adolescence in a casino. Because, so far, the BP has been my favorite home. (I mean, it didn't have super stiff competition. But you get the point.) I like the new owners. They own other casinos on the strip and are very corporate. They're putting serious "scratch" into the place and into my aunt's show. ("Scratch" is gangster-speak for money.)*

Betsy's and my digs aren't a crib like Crissy's, but I like them. At first, Betsy worried it wasn't wholesome, but I reminded her that nothing about my life has been "wholesome," and, besides, look where that word got her. That photo shoot at Red Rocks and some guy Crissy was snogging winding up dead, that's where. "Wholesome" is overrated, I think.

Not that I'm a fan of "unwholesome," but lots of the people who make a big deal about having the right values are the ones who say the worst things when they're losing a mortgage payment playing video poker at nine in the morning. Look at that nutball, Erika Schweiker. She was always going on and on about "values," and she lost big to Senator Aldred in the election because she was friends with all those Futurium people who were arrested for things like murder. And murder was just the worst of the things that got them busted. I might be a grandmother by the time guys like Frankie, Tony, Damon, and Rory are out of prison. (Rory will be there forever. Frankie sang like a canary—I love mobster lingo—and told everyone that Rory was the one who killed Orlov. So, they have him for two murders, counting Lara Kozlov, and for ordering the hit on the Morleys.)

Even Erika Schweiker might go to jail. The Department of Justice has charged her with campaign finance crimes and political shakedowns. It was all on my tablet.

I'm now in the program for Diana, Candle in the Darkness. *I am officially the Head of Research because I am very good at that. (For my first assignment, I gave Crissy a list of the weirdest ways people learned that the queen had died, including a lot who learned from the account of a pretend American Girl doll on Twitter, and others who heard the news at a bangers and mash competitive-eating championship. The contenders agreed to stop gorging for a moment of silence.) When I'm in college, I'll still be doing plenty of coding and math, but I'll also take lots of history courses, too, because history is everything. I have found seven quotes all about learning from the past or using the past or not repeating the past.*

But, of course, we still do.

Crissy and Nigel are now a "thing," and—my aunt being my aunt—she is rewriting the show. She wants him to have a bigger role. For a crank, she is actually very generous.

My mom deals blackjack, just like Ayobami, who lets me call her "Aunt," which my real aunt does not. I'm like the daughter Ayobami never had. I'm not sure what I am to Crissy, but I think it's somewhere between niece and executive assistant. But she loves me.

And that's the thing about my life now. For the first time ever, I have people who love me. Really love me. Neither Dowling sister had to do what she did that day at Frankie's. But they did. And they did it for me.

Which is why my first tattoo is one word: FAMILY. *It's where you might put a tramp stamp, but it's the opposite.*

I haven't shown it to Betsy or Crissy yet. I'm saving that for when I turn sixteen. In the meantime, I let them both think I wear one-piece bathing suits to Crissy's cabana or the pool now because I've suddenly become weirdly modest.

Or—to quote the Princess of Las Vegas—proper. She told my homeroom teacher when I brought him backstage the other night that I am "a right proper young lady." I'm not sure he agreed, but he didn't contradict her. One of the things Betsy and I have learned when you live at the BP is this: you don't contradict the Princess of Las Vegas. She's about as close to royalty as you get around here.

And we have strippers in the burlesque show named after actual queens.

ACKNOWLEDGMENTS

In *Fear and Loathing in Las Vegas,* Hunter S. Thompson wrote that in the neon city in the desert, "the shark ethic prevails—eat the wounded." And while Vegas can be a merciless place, the people I interviewed there (including the wounded) were generous with their time and candid about the ways the city can make or break a person—or like, most other spots on the planet, simply leave them alone.

The same could be said about the people in fintech I interviewed.

I thank them all, especially:

Sally Olson and Ned Mills, who bring the Carpenters to life and are among the most gifted tribute performers in Las Vegas. When you are next there, be sure and catch their show, Carpenters Legacy. I loved it.

My oldest friend, Adam Turteltaub, who is great fun on the strip, can always find chocolate, and is among the smartest people I know. I've dedicated books to Adam, and will again.

Jerrold H. Bamel, a retired FBI supervisory special agent and now a corporate fraud investigator, who has become my go-to resource whenever the FBI figures in one of my stories. (He also appears in the acknowledgments of *The Flight Attendant* and *The Red Lotus.*) The man is an honest-to-God hero, and I hope someday he writes a memoir.

My great friend Andrew Furtsch, and his son, Matt, who introduced me to the basics of cryptocurrency with the patience of parents. Andrew has also appeared previously in the acknowledgments (and dedications) of my books.

Daniel Roberts, a veteran crypto journalist, who's been writing about cryptocurrency for almost a decade and a half. He helped me understand the complexities of digital currencies and provided enormously helpful notes after reading an early draft of this novel.

Among the books that were especially useful were *The Diana Chronicles* by Tina Brown; *Las Vegas: Then and Now,* by Su Kim Chung; *Diana: Her True Story—In Her Own Words,* by Andrew Morton; *The Gambler,* by William C. Rempel; and *At the Sands: The Casino That Shaped Classic Las Vegas, Brought the Rat Pack Together, and Went Out with a Bang,* by David G. Schwartz.

I took one small liberty with a moment in this novel. The Star Trek Original Series Set Tour museum opened in Ticonderoga, New York, in 2016. It would not have been there when Crissy and Betsy Dowling were in elementary school. But I love the place, and it was too perfect not to use it in Chapter Sixteen.

As always, I want to thank the team at Doubleday, Vintage, and Penguin Random House Audio, all of whom care deeply about books, and some of whom are among my closest friends: Kristen Bearse, Jillian Briglia, Milena Brown, Maria Carella, Todd Doughty, Andy Dudley, Maris Dyer, John Fontana, Kelly Gildea, Elena Hershey, Suzanne Herz, Judy Jacoby, Ann Kingman, Beth Lamb, Nick LaRousse, Lindsay Mandel, James Meader, Lauren Monaco, Nora Reichard, Annie Schatz, Kim

Shannon, Tiara Sharma, Kayla Steinorth, William Thomas, and David Underwood.

I am so grateful to my talented—and imperturbable—agents: Deborah Schneider, Jane Gelfman, Cathy Gleason, and Penelope Burns at Gelfman Schneider; Brian Lipson at IPG; Miriam Feuerle, Andrew Wetzel, and their associates at the Lyceum Agency; and Amy Wagner at A3 Artists. I can't thank you all enough for the countless times you have grounded me and kept me sane, and helped steer my work to screens big and small, and onto the stage. I treasure all of you.

And, of course, there is Jenny Jackson, my genuis editor at Doubleday since 2010, who understands the beating heart of books better than anyone in publishing—and is also one of the funniest human beings I know. Her editorial instincts are (as one of the royals might say) brilliant. She cares about her authors as much as she does their words, and it has surprised no one who knows her that last year her own first novel, *Pineapple Street,* was adored by everyone who read it.

Finally, as always, I bow before the insights, delicacy, and (yes!) candor of my lovely bride, Victoria Blewer, and our daughter, the always amazing Grace Experience. Victoria has been reading my work since we were eighteen years old. (Yes. Eighteen. That means she has read at least 3.5 million words I have written.) Grace has been weighing in since she was in high school—and bringing many of my characters to life as an absolutely fantastic audiobook narrator. I cannot imagine my world without those two remarkable women, and the myriad blessings they bring daily into my life.

I thank you all.

About the Author

Chris Bohjalian is the #1 *New York Times* bestselling author of twenty-four books, including *The Lioness, Hour of the Witch, The Red Lotus, Midwives,* and *The Flight Attendant,* which was an HBO Max series starring Kaley Cuoco. His other books include *The Guest Room; Close Your Eyes, Hold Hands; The Sandcastle Girls; Skeletons at the Feast;* and *The Double Bind.* His novels *Secrets of Eden, Midwives,* and *Past the Bleachers* were made into movies, and his work has been translated into more than thirty-five languages. His novels have been selections of Oprah's Book Club and the Barnes & Noble Book Club. He is also a playwright. He lives in Vermont and can be found at chrisbohjalian.com or on Facebook, Instagram, Threads, TikTok, X, Litsy, and Goodreads, @chrisbohjalian.